PRAISE FOR MEGHAN QUINN

The Wedding Game

"Readers won't have to be reality TV fans to get a kick out of this fun, quirky rom-com."

—Publishers Weekly

That Forever Girl

"A terrific read."

—Once Upon a Book Blog

"A heart-tugging, slow-burning, second-chance romance . . . This is a couple that I couldn't help but root for."

—Red Cheeks Reads

"If you love small-town romances that are rich in scenery, packed with sweetness, heat, and fun, and [are] looking for an easy reading escape, look no further."

—TotallyBookedBlog

"Filled with emotion, laughter, and loads of sexual tension . . . I dare you to not fall in love with Harper and Rogan!"

—Nightbird Novels

"Sweet, sassy, sexy, and sentimental."

—Harlequin Junkie

"Second-chance enemies-to-lovers romance at its finest."

—Bookishly Nerdy

"I'm a sucker for second-chance romances, and add in the small town and I'm hooked. And who better to give me all the feels with a little humor and a mix of sexiness than Meghan Quinn."

—*Embrace the Romance*

That Second Chance

"With each book I read by Meghan Quinn, I become more in awe of her writing talent. She truly has a gift! *That Second Chance* was simply perfect!"

—*Wrapped Up in Reading*

"A sweet, sexy, swoon-worthy, MUST-READ romance from Meghan Quinn, and I would HIGHLY recommend it! I fell head over heels in love with the quaint and charming small town of Port Snow, Maine, and all of its residents."

—*The Romance Bibliophile*

"I'm basking in the HEA goodness of *That Second Chance*, which gets five stars."

—*Dog-Eared Daydreams*

"I adored the small town of Port Snow and the fabulous tight [bond] the Knightly family have not only with each other but their community as a whole."

—*Book Angel Booktopia*

The
Reunion

OTHER TITLES BY MEGHAN QUINN

All her books can be read on Kindle Unlimited

GETTING LUCKY SERIES

BRENTWOOD BASEBALL BOYS

Manhattan Millionaires

The Secret to Dating Your Best Friend's Sister

Diary of a Bad Boy

Boss Man Bridegroom

The Dating by Numbers Series

Three Blind Dates

Two Wedding Crashers

One Baby Daddy

Back in the Game (novella)

The Blue Line Duet

The Upside of Falling

The Downside of Love

The Perfect Duet

The Left Side of Perfect

The Right Side of Forever

The Binghamton Boys Series

Co-Wrecker

My Best Friend's Ex

Twisted Twosome

The Other Brother

Stand-Alone Titles

The Modern Gentleman

See Me After Class

The Romantic Pact

Dear Life

The Virgin Romance Novelist Chronicles

Newly Exposed

The Mother Road

The Highland Fling

The Wedding Game

Box Set Series

The Bourbon series

The Love and Sports series

The Hot-Lanta series

The Reunion

MEGHAN QUINN

 Montlake

Published by Montlake, Seattle

www.apub.com

Amazon, the Amazon logo, and Montlake are trademarks of Amazon.com, Inc., or its affiliates.

ISBN-13: 9781542034982
ISBN-10: 1542034981

Cover design by Caroline Teagle Johnson

Printed in the United States of America

To all the nonperfect families that are actually perfect in their own way.

PROLOGUE

TO: Family and Friends
FROM: Cooper Chance
SUBJECT: 50th Wedding Anniversary

You're invited to celebrate the 50th wedding Anniversary of Peggy and Martin.

- Food and drinks.
- Music.
- Fun.

Party is at the original Watchful Wanderers store. Sunday, June 2nd.

RSVP to Cooper Chance—just reply to this email No presents.

TO: Cooper Chance, Ford Chance
FROM: Palmer Chance
SUBJECT: Re: 50th Wedding Anniversary

Bro,

Please do not tell me you just sent a wedding anniversary invite through an email? Did that just happen?

Palmer—your not-so-happy sister

TO: Palmer Chance, Ford Chance
FROM: Cooper Chance
SUBJECT: I Did

TO: Cooper Chance, Ford Chance
FROM: Palmer Chance
SUBJECT: Re: I Did

You know I hate it when you respond in the subject line. It's more work to delete the subject line and type in your response, than to just reply in the body of the email.

But ignoring that, what happened to the beautiful linen invites I picked out? You can't just send an email for Mom and Dad's 50th WEDDING ANNIVERSARY. We look so . . . uncultured.

TO: Palmer Chance, Ford Chance
FROM: Cooper Chance
SUBJECT: Re: I Did

The invites you wanted to purchase were going to be twelve dollars a pop. TWELVE dollars, Palmer. That's a waste of money, a waste of resources, and just a useless way to kill more trees. Also, while you're out galivanting around the world, who do you think was going to have to address all of those?

Me.

So, I did what was easiest. Sent an email. If you don't like it, too bad.

TO: Cooper Chance, Ford Chance
FROM: Palmer Chance
SUBJECT: Re: I Did

You realize the family owns a multi-billion dollar, franchised, outdoors store, right? Twelve dollars an invite is a blip in the pool of gold Mom and Dad are sitting in. Now we look like cheap asses who send out a wedding anniversary invitation through email.

You're an editor, but you didn't even beef up the text. You made bullet points.

- Food.
- Drinks.
- Music.
- Fun.

^^^ Yup, screams fun, Coop.

TO: Palmer Chance, Ford Chance
FROM: Cooper Chance
SUBJECT: Re: I Did

Once again, if you're not here, you can't have an opinion.

TO: Cooper Chance, Palmer Chance
FROM: Ford Chance
SUBJECT: Re: I did

Just catching up.

The invitation is less than ideal, especially for such a large and monumental event in our parents' lives, parents who have given us every opportunity to succeed in life. I think we need to treat this anniversary with a little more appreciation and a little less

4

complaining about the time and effort we have to put forth in order to make it happen.

I just spoke with Larkin and she is ordering the linen invites, having them shipped overnight, and we will have them sent out ASAP. We will treat the email as a funny save the date. I will reply all and tell everyone to expect a formal invitation in the mail.

Larkin and I will be flying out to Washington on Tuesday. We will be working up until the anniversary party on some very time-consuming tasks. Please be conscious of our time and energy.

I'll be sure to have Larkin schedule in some meetings to go over all party arrangements as well as time with the family, but we won't be staying with Mom and Dad. We booked two rooms at the Marina Island Bed and Breakfast, one being the attic suite so we can conduct business in private.

Please send your itineraries to Larkin and any requests so she can schedule them in.

Thank you.

Ford

CHAPTER ONE
FORD

"Larkin, did you get the invitations sent out?" I call from my desk as I type out a quick email to our head of marketing. I was supposed to receive mock-ups for our rebranding by end of day. It's end of day, and there are no mock-ups.

"I did." Larkin sweeps into my office, tablet in hand and blue light–blocking glasses perched on her nose. "They were sent out at lunchtime. The calligraphist did an impeccable job on the addresses. And as an added touch, I took one of the pictures from your parents' recent photo shoot and made it into a stamp."

I smile. "Did you make sure to send them one?" Larkin nods with a knowing glint in her eye. "They'll get a kick out of that."

"I also got word from your housekeeper that your bags are all packed, your suits are freshly pressed, and the remaining food in your fridge has been taken care of so nothing goes bad while you're gone for the next month."

"Great. And have you heard from marketing about the mock-ups? I drafted an email to ask where they are but thought I would check with you first."

She clutches her tablet to her chest. "Yes, they brought them to me early this afternoon, but they were missing color swatches and a few other things I knew you would ask for, so I asked them for a redo. I told them I'd stay late to grab them so we can bring them with us on the trip tomorrow."

"I can stay late—you don't have to. I'm sure you have to go home and pack."

"I woke up this morning and packed in preparation for late mockups." She smiles, and I can't help but shake my head.

Larkin Novak is one of a kind. I hired her four years ago, and I've given her significant pay raises every year just to keep her. She's efficient, incredibly intelligent, vastly organized, and can anticipate what I'm going to need before I even know it. She's such an integral part of this company and my day-to-day that I don't know what I would do without her.

"Do you ever sleep, Larkin?"

She pushes her ice-blonde hair behind her ear. "Who needs sleep when there's so much to do?"

"You need sleep." I stand from my desk and walk up to her. Carefully, I take her precious tablet from her hands. "Go home. I'll wait for the mock-ups."

She eyes the tablet in my hand and then looks back up at me with those intensely blue eyes. "I get plenty of sleep. A solid eight hours every night."

"Then you need a life. Go home." I chuckle and walk past her to her desk, where I slip her tablet in her work bag, pick the bag up by the strap, and drape it over her shoulder. "Go, Larkin. We have a strenuous month ahead of us with the rebrand and the anniversary party. Have a second to yourself before you're forced to be at your boss's side for precisely every second of every day for twenty-nine days."

The rebrand is the first business-altering project I've taken on since my dad retired, and I'm spending every waking hour working toward perfection—if there's something I never want to do, it's let my dad down, especially after everything he and my mom have done for me, for my siblings.

"You do paint an awful picture of what's to come. If that's the case, I'm going to go grab some dinner, which will be ice cream, and drown my sorrows in my one and only night to myself before I'm inserted into apparent hell on Marina Island."

"Yeah." I grip the back of my neck. "Are you prepared to be around my family? They can be a bit much."

"You act as if I haven't met them before."

"But you haven't been in the same space with all of them together."

"Nervous I'll quit after a week?"

"Yeah." I let out a dry chuckle. "I am." Folding my arms across my chest, I lean against the doorframe of my office and take a second to relax. I'm constantly wearing the CEO hat, and it can be exhausting after a while. Larkin and I have a good enough relationship that she knows when I need to "kick my shoes off" and take a second to breathe.

"It's going to take more than your family to drive me away. You know I can't find a benefits package quite like yours anywhere else."

"Ah, the true reason you stick around," I joke.

"You had me at four weeks' paid vacation and bonus structure." She lets out a familiar chuckle.

"At least I know what will keep you around now." I sigh deeply. "Okay, I should finish up some work before we head out tomorrow." I push off the doorframe and head back into my office.

"Can I order you anything for dinner before I leave?" she asks, tailing after me.

I shake my head. "I have a protein bar in my desk drawer that's been begging to be eaten all day."

"Thrilling." Her sarcasm seeps through, which it seems to do more often after hours. "I have a car coming to pick you up tomorrow, eight in the morning. I'll have a breakfast burrito waiting for you."

"You're perfection. Thank you." I wake up my computer by moving my mouse around. "See you in the morning."

"Bye, Ford." She takes off, and I turn to my computer, focusing on the emails in my in-box. The worst part of the job is sitting in front of me: answering questions from department heads. Oddly, I prefer the mundane tasks like numbers and projections, and I'm good at them.

So good at them that we'll be opening fifty new stores in the coming year, which is the direct reason for the rebranding. We've stuck with the same storefront, color blend, and aesthetic ever since we franchised. Walking into one of our stores, you get a sense it's slightly outdated, with its oak timber logs, forest-green linoleum floors, metal bracket shelving, mustard-yellow accents, and outdoor adventures from a photo shoot nearly fifteen years ago. The stores are successful, but they're not capturing every consumer . . . like the young crowd. In order to keep up with the competition, which dominates the Gen Z market, we need to make sure we're keeping the stores fresh. We have the funds to do so, but we need to make sure we have the right research and development in place to appeal to our customers and make them not just enjoy what they're buying from Watchful Wanderers but to enjoy the experience as well.

Because if anything, the young crowd is always about the experience, something Larkin has been drilling into me since the moment we started the rebranding process.

After I've made a decent dent in my emails, my phone buzzes with a text message. Mom.

When I was seven and Cooper was five, our biological mom overdosed and our grandma became our legal guardian. We lived with her for a few months until she couldn't physically take care of us anymore. At that point, we were placed into foster care. We bounced from house to house for a few more months until we met Peggy and Martin. The minute I met them, I knew—I knew we were going to be a family. I felt it in my soul. And after a year of living with them on Marina Island, a small island off the coast of Seattle, they sat us down and asked if we wanted to be a part of their family permanently.

I'm not one to be sentimental—I'm more logical than anything—but that hug, the one I gave my parents when they asked us to take their last name . . . yeah, I can still feel their arms wrapped around me. I can still smell Mom's lavender perfume and hear Dad's sniffs as he showed his true feelings that day. He gripped me by the cheeks, looked into my eyes, and told me that he would be honored to call me son.

From that day forward, I knew my life would be dedicated to thanking them for giving me a chance in life. And not only me but Cooper as well. Shortly after, Mom and Dad were surprised when they found out they were pregnant with Palmer. They didn't think getting pregnant was an option for them, but life has a tricky way of throwing you for a loop. From a family of four, we became a blended family of five and have been ever since.

I open up Mom's text and read it to myself.

Mom: What's this I hear you're not going to be staying with us? You know the Island's Bed and Breakfast claims to have the best continental breakfast, but nothing beats my homemade pancakes. Are you really going to give up my fluffy, melt-in-your-mouth pancakes for a free continental breakfast of dry muffins and orange juice tainted with pulp?

Smiling to myself, I shake my head at her. Want to talk about a mama bear? Peggy Chance is the definition. She clings to every facet of her children's lives. We were her goals, her aspirations, her fulfillment. While Dad was running the store, she was taking care of the home front, keeping us in line, dishing out responsibilities, and inserting herself into our lives in every possible way.

I type back to her.

Ford: Larkin will be with me. It would be weird for her to stay at the family house.

Mom: We have plenty of room. We can stick her in your room, and you can sleep on the couch.

Ford: My assistant sleeping in my childhood bed isn't exactly what I would call professional.

Mom: Oh stop, Larkin is practically part of the family. I bet she'd love to see where you used to hide away when you were a teenager.

Ford: I'm sure she'd love to obtain any sort of knowledge when it comes to my teenage years to tease me with, but I'd prefer if I keep things professional. Plus, we have a lot of work to do. If we stayed with you, you'd be interrupting our meetings every half hour, on the hour to make sure we're drinking enough water to make our pee clear.

Mom: Hydration is important, especially if you want to stay young looking. Which reminds me, have you started using that eye cream I sent you? You're 36, prime time for having to use an eye cream. I already have Palmer using hers and she's 27. You're behind.

Ford: Good on the eye cream, Mom. Thanks though.

Mom: Well, if you're not going to use it, bring it with you so I can give it to Cooper. He's starting to get some crow's feet.

Ford: Can't wait to tell him that.

Mom: Don't pick on your brother. He's sensitive.

The elevator door dings, and I glance up to the parting doors, expecting someone from marketing to drop off the mock-ups, but instead see a wisp of ice-blonde hair right before Larkin steps off and walks toward my office, a paper bag in hand.

I lean back in my chair and watch her approach me, a smirk crossing her lips.

"What are you doing here?" I ask as she sets the brown bag on my desk. "I told you to go home."

"I couldn't let you not eat dinner." She pulls out two carry-out cups from Gelato Boy, our favorite ice cream place in Denver. She pushes a cup toward me, along with a spoon. "Got your favorite, Gooey Buttercake and Caramel."

"You're trying to make me wake up earlier than I want so I can get in some extra miles on the pavement, aren't you?" I take the gelato and remove the lid. Creamy gelato mixed with caramel glistens up at me, making my mouth water. Didn't realize how much I needed this until now.

"I plan on getting in three miles." She scoops a spoonful. "Which means you have to at least meet me or beat me."

Mouth full of ice cream, I answer, "You know I'm going to beat you."

She smirks. "You always do."

CHAPTER TWO
COOPER

"What's this for?"

I look up to see Dad holding up a bolt. "Dad, don't touch shit. I told you I have everything laid out according to how I need it."

"But this was on the coffee table." He examines the bolt as I struggle to hold up the shelf I'm building for him. A shelf he desperately needed built before Ford arrived so he could color coordinate all his "literature."

Retired Martin is a different man from Shop Owner Martin. Shop Owner Martin was quick on his feet, scrappy, and didn't ever need help. He could look at a stick on the ground and, in a matter of a half hour, whittle a prize-winning flute with an angelic pitch.

Retired Martin is a different species and has apparently lost all faculties in his older years. These days he walks around with one tube sock, one ankle sock, and his shirt inside out and has succumbed to binge-watching reality shows on Netflix while practicing his adult coloring in a book full of swear words.

Get Organized with the Home Edit being his latest binge.

It's the reason I'm hunched over, trying to put together a bookshelf he bought from IKEA, the devil's grotto. What should be an easy-to-assemble shelf has turned into a waste of a night as I try to comprehend the elementary instructions that read more like Satan's playground of insecurities.

"Did you put it on the coffee table?"

He thinks about it and then chuckles. "You know, maybe it was on the floor."

Jesus.

Christ.

"Dad, go back to your coloring book."

"Aww, do you want me to color you a swear word? From the expression on your face, it looks like you have a few building up in your head right now." He taps his chin. "You want a 'Fuck you' page, don't you?"

Sighing heavily while staring down at the directions, I count to five and then say, "Sure, Dad, color me a picture that says 'Fuck you.' I'll hang it on my fridge when I get home."

He wags his finger at me. "Don't tease me, son. I expect a picture of my art on your fridge." He takes a seat in his recliner, a black dress sock pulled high over his calf while a white ankle sock dangles off his other foot.

A total nightmare of fashion, that's what he is. Not that I care about fashion, but for fuck's sake, the man is wearing twenty-year-old cotton shorts with a hole in the crotch.

"How's it going in here?" Mom says, carrying a plate of butterscotch cookies. "Oh, would you look at that, you already have two sides attached. Look at you go." She gives me a jolly fist pump. "Excellent work, Cooper."

Yeah, and it's only taken me half an hour, thanks to Dad's constant jabbering.

"And did I hear you're coloring a 'Fuck you' page for Cooper?"

Dad nods as he carefully lays his colored pencils out on the TV stand he uses when coloring. "Since I've been denied the ability to help our son, I'm going to use my fade technique. Cooper has a work of art coming his way." It's not that I don't want his help—it's just that

15

he's having a stiff day. I can see it in his movements, the bending of his limbs. I'm not about to ask him to join me on the floor. I think he knows it too, or else he wouldn't have asked me to come over.

"Have you seen the fade-in technique?" Mom asks and then thumbs toward Dad. "A modern-day Bob Ross, if you ask me. But instead of happy trees, he dabbles in happy swear words. Did you see the picture I hung in the bathroom?"

Yes.

Unfortunately.

Let's just say when I stood to take a leak, staring at a framed picture of the word "Pussy" wasn't exactly what I expected in my seventy-plus-year-old parents' house.

"Loved the touch of pink," I say, sarcasm heavy in my voice, but neither of my parents appears to read it that way.

"Thank you, I thought it was clever," Dad says.

Mom holds the plate of cookies in front of me. "Cookie?"

The last thing I want to do is prolong this project, but it looks like I'll be here all night anyway. So, I take a cookie and lean back against the coffee table.

"Thanks, Mom."

"The least I can do, since you're making your dad's *Home Edit* project come to fruition. All he's talked about the last week while he waited for that shelf to be shipped is how excited he is to organize his books."

"I already planned on asking Alexa to play some Glenn Miller while I delight myself in color coordination." Dad has a cookie in one hand, a colored pencil in the other, and his head tilted down so I can see the bald spot on the top of his head.

I'm not sure if it's because I'm constantly over here fixing things for them, but man, it seems like my parents have aged drastically over the last year. I try to ignore the pang in my gut at this thought.

"Sounds like a winning night," I say, finishing off my cookies.

"Oh, did I tell you Ellen over at the flower shop received your email invitation?"

"You didn't, but let me guess: she had something to say about it."

"She had no idea it was a joke invite, and when she got the real one in the mail, boy did she stick her foot in her mouth."

"Wow, so embarrassing for Ellen," I say, turning back toward the directions and trying to understand the pictures.

"Oh, you could tell she was thoroughly embarrassed at bunko the other night. I told her some people just don't get your sense of humor."

"Yup, I'm a strange one," I mutter.

"Which reminds me: I ran into Henrietta yesterday, and she asked if you planned on using Cake It Bakery for the anniversary cake. I assumed you already put in the order with Nora, but she informed me Nora said you never came in to see her. Is that true?"

Practicing patience and trying not to grow irritated at the mention of Nora, I say, "Haven't gotten around to it yet."

"Well, you might want to go in soon to talk to her. She's getting booked up with weddings."

"Maybe we don't have a cake; maybe we do something like . . . doughnuts. I can pick some up from Top Pot and make some sort of doughnut wall."

"Don't you even think about an insane thing like that," Dad says. "Those doughnuts belong in mouths, not on walls."

Mom pats Dad's arm. "I think what your father is trying to say is that although we love Top Pot, we would prefer a cake from Nora. She's a family friend, and we've had one of their cakes at every event since I can remember. It would feel wrong to have anything else. Please go see her tomorrow. It would mean so much to us."

I exhale out my frustration. "If that's what you want."

"Thank you." Mom claps her hands. "And maybe when you're there, you can ask her out on a date."

And there it is . . .

CHAPTER THREE
NORA

"Okay, let me read your order back to you. Three tiers, vanilla sponge, strawberry filling, and bubblegum buttercream coat with drips of fudge along the side and two zebras on the top, but the zebras need to be realistic, not cartoon. Did I get that right?"

Mrs. Cano on the phone says, "And don't forget the slogan on the side."

"Ah yes." I read the quote I put down on the order form. "'What a man. You finally made the bed. Yay!!!' And that's with three exclamation points."

"Perfect." Pure joy rings through her voice. "After forty-five years of being married to my husband, he finally figured out how to make the bed. This is cause for celebration."

"With a bubblegum cake, no less. You're a good wife."

"I believe I am to put up for so long with a man who can't make a bed."

"An absolute saint," I say just as the bell at the front rings. "Mrs. Cano, this has been lovely, but a customer just came in. I'll have this for you in two days, ready to pick up."

"Thank you, dear. Have a lovely day."

"You too," I say before hanging up.

I set the phone and pen down, scoop my long black hair up into a bun on top of my head, and then head to the front, where I see a man bent at the waist, taking a look at one of the display wedding cakes I have in the front windows.

"Can I help—"

The man stands tall and spins around, pulling the breath straight from my lungs.

Cooper Chance.

Tall, with black hair and light-silver eyes framed by black-rimmed glasses, he gives off all sorts of PNW vibes with his formfitting straight-leg jeans cuffed at the ankles, showing off his faded brown Thursday Boots. His worn jeans contrast with his pressed slate-blue shirt and olive-green cardigan that just so happens to be pushed up to his elbows. If Clark Kent and L.L.Bean had a baby, it would be Cooper Chance.

A family friend for years.

A faultfinder of a man.

A man who knows how to push my buttons.

And the only guy I've ever had a one-night stand with.

"Cooper," I say, my voice coming out breathless.

He stuffs his hands in his pockets. "Hey, Nora." His eyes scan my body, searing through me with every inch he takes in.

Gathering myself, I adjust the string of my apron. "What brings you in today?"

He looks off to the side. "I, uh . . . I need to order a cake for my parents' wedding anniversary."

"Oh yes, I do recall the email invite I got the other day. It was really poetic. Can't wait to see the kind of fun you so evasively spoke about." When he doesn't crack a smile, I pull out an order pad from under the counter and pick up a pen. Clearing my throat, shaking off the nerves that emerged the minute I spotted him, I ask, "What can I get you?"

"A cake," he answers simply.

When he doesn't continue, I glance up at him. "Yeah, I figured a cake, since, you know, you're at a bakery that exclusively makes cakes. What kind of cake would you like?"

"Hell, I don't know," he huffs out. "A good one."

"Your attention to detail is really stunning."

He drags his hand over his face, and I can't help but notice the way his sleeves cling to his shapely arms. "I don't have time for this. I have two biographies I have to edit today, and both have put me to sleep within the first fifty pages. Can't you just pick flavors and be done with it?"

I set my pen down and fold my hands, making eye contact with those devastatingly silver irises. "Are you trying to tell me you don't have time for your parents?"

"Jesus Christ," he mutters before stepping up to the counter and holding out his large hand. "Where's the menu?"

"That's what I thought." I offer him one of our simple menus. "Here are the sponge flavors, and to the right are all of the fillings. Now, we can also make the outside frosting to be the same as the middle if you want, but honestly, there's no fun in that."

He lifts a brow. "Who the hell picks bubblegum frosting?"

"You'd be surprised," I say, trying to maintain a steady heartbeat at the sight of that one questioning brow.

Carefully examining the list, he sighs. "Knowing Ford and Palmer, they're going to want something classy like a french silk, whatever the hell that is, because that's their personality, but my parents are simple."

"I would agree with that sentiment."

I've known the Chance family for as long as I can remember. I grew up in Seattle, though, which to a kid may as well have been an ocean away from Marina Island, so I didn't get to know them on a deeper level. But because our moms play bunko together, we've been invited to many Chance family events. And we were always those awkward kids who knew each other, saw each other at parties, but never truly mingled. I've known Cooper Chance from afar—well, besides that one night . . .

"They really like butterscotch and chocolate. Do you have anything like that?" Cooper asks, setting the menu down.

"I could do a butterscotch sponge, soaked in butterscotch, with a butterscotch pudding in the middle and a fudge frosting. Do you think they'd like that?"

The corner of Cooper's mouth tilts up, ever so slightly. If I didn't know him better, I would have missed it, but there it is, plain as day—a smirk.

"Yeah, they'd like that," he says as he reaches into his back pocket and pulls out his wallet. "Do I pay for it now?"

Chuckling, I shake my head. "Not the whole thing. I usually take a deposit and then payment at delivery, but no need for a deposit with the Chances. But I do need to know how many people are invited to the party so I can figure out how many tiers to make."

"Tiers?" His nose scrunches. "You're not going to make a sheet cake? I thought maybe you could do a giant rectangle and print a picture of them on the top."

I hold back my smile. "I'm letting you go with the flavors because that's what your parents would like, but I'm saving you from your siblings when I say go with a tiered cake—it will prevent an argument in the future."

He thinks on it. "Yeah, sure, whatever." He stuffs his wallet back in his pocket and takes a step back. "We're good here?" Once again, his eyes roam my body. From my face down to my chest, those intense eyes eat me up, and it feels like a year hasn't passed between us. I almost believe we're back at the bar, his gaze making silent promises of what's to come.

I swallow hard. "We're good."

"So, when your mom asks you if a cake has been ordered for the party, you'll tell her yes so my mom gets off my back?"

I clutch my heart. "I can really feel the love, Cooper."

Rolling his eyes, he turns away and takes off, leaving me to watch his retreating backside. When the door shuts behind him, I audibly exhale as I take a seat at the counter-height stool we keep next to the register.

Cooper Chance.

Can't remember the last time I saw him.

Oh wait, I can . . . when he was slinking out of my bedroom. But that time, as I watched his retreating back, it was naked.

CHAPTER FOUR
PALMER

"Hey, sis, what's up?"

I twirl a roll of tape around my wrist as I stare down at the pile of boxes in the middle of my Meatpacking District apartment. The old parquet floors have seen better days, the walls are caked in paint from years of repainting, making the windows almost impossible to open, and there's a watermark in the right corner of the ceiling where my upstairs neighbor let her bathtub fill too high. And now, the space I called home is practically empty.

"Ford, are you really on your way to Marina Island right now?"

"On the plane as we speak."

"Wait, what do you mean . . . are you flying private?"

"Larkin signed me up for a private rideshare in the air, or something like that. Either way, how are you? Are you in the country? Or back in Europe, soaking up all the local cuisine like usual?"

I stare down at my bank statement, a flood of anxiety filling up my chest as I absorb the numbers, or lack thereof. With my forefinger and thumb, I curl the edge of the paper. "Oh, you know, just taking a break for a second while the next adventure presents itself."

"So, you're in New York, then?"

"Yup. The Big Apple," I say awkwardly just as someone outside screams a profanity that shakes the very walls of my apartment. "Anyway, you're really going to be in Marina Island for a month?"

"Yes. I'll be working on some important things and figured what better place to do it than where the store first originated. Plus, I'll have a chance to help with the anniversary party if time permits. I have the feeling Cooper is overwhelmed with the planning."

"Overwhelmed or lazy?" I ask. "I mean . . . an email, Ford? Really?"

He chuckles. "Cooper doesn't care about the details like we do. I'll have a talk with him when I see him. Larkin tried scheduling a meetup with him, but he has yet to get back to her, so we'll see."

"Maybe try texting him." I chuckle. "You know, since you're his brother and Larkin won't be on Marina Island to be at your beck and call."

"She's not at my beck and call," he says in an annoyed tone. "And she'll actually be there."

"You brought your assistant with you back home?" I ask, surprised. "Are you really . . . wait . . . oh my God, are you staying at Mom and Dad's house?"

"No, despite Mom trying to convince me that it would be normal to have Larkin sleep in my childhood bedroom."

A sharp laugh pops past my lips. "Oooh, I think that would be a brilliant idea, actually. Makes me want to call Mom so she'll cry to you on the phone about needing all her babies under one roof."

"That would require you to actually come home." His tone is light, but I know there's some seriousness to his words.

I can't remember the last time I was home, or with my entire family under the same roof. I've visited Ford in Denver here and there while passing through, but Marina Island . . . yeah, not so much. As a food influencer, I've spent the last five years traveling around the world, blogging about food, and building my Instagram following to over 250,000 followers while getting paid to try food in the most beautiful of places.

But the funny thing about building a platform on social media is that anyone can do it, and even though I'm one of the top influencers, my invitations have started to slow down, leaving me in a tough spot.

The bank account is drying up.

My rent is too expensive.

And I have no real professional experience under my belt to apply for a job.

But, if I'm anything, I'm scrappy like my dad, which means I've come up with a plan.

It might not be my first choice . . . or second, or maybe even third, but it's all I've got at this point.

"Funny you mention coming home." I turn over my bank statement, blocking out the negativity it's emitting. "I was thinking about flying out to Marina Island early. You know . . . to help out with the party." Lies, but I can't possibly tell him the truth. Not super-successful Ford. "And then I was thinking of putting together an epic Instagram journey for the PNW. Something earthy and real, from a girl who actually grew up there." Also, another lie.

"Sounds interesting. Do Mom and Dad know?"

No one knows.

Not a single soul . . . well, besides my best friend.

"No. Thought I'd surprise them. Fly out tomorrow and, you know, stay for a month or two. My lease is up, and I'm putting things in storage. No use looking for another place when I won't be here." He doesn't need to know the truth: that I told my landlord I won't be able to make rent and that I found someone to take over the lease. Thankfully, my landlord was cool about it. But that means I packed up everything that matters and sold the rest of my furniture. Starting tomorrow, I'll be homeless.

All the more reason to "create an Instagram journey" that I have no intention of putting any real effort into, while hopefully making connections as I wait for my next job.

"You mean that? You're really going to fly back home?" Ford asks.

"Yeah," I say while picking up a Sharpie to label my boxes. "I have movers coming early tomorrow morning, my flight has been booked, and now I just have to execute the surprise for Mom and Dad."

"They're going to be thrilled, you know that, right?"

I smile. "I know. It's probably time I came back home, even if it's just for a short period of time."

"Either way, they'll have all their kids together. I don't think we could give them a better anniversary present."

"Do you know what would be an even better present?" I ask.

"What?"

"If you and Larkin stay at the house with me, and we convince Cooper to do the same?"

He chuckles, and the sound is familiar, yet . . . different. Older. Wiser. "Not going to happen, sis."

"Knock knock. I brought tapas," my best friend says as he walks through my front door. When he sees that I'm on the phone, he pretends to zip his lips and then proceeds to tiptoe toward the kitchen.

"I have time to make it happen, but hey, Laramie just got here with food."

"Okay. So, I guess I'll see you tomorrow?"

"Yes, you will," I say, feeling a small ounce of comfort that I'll get to at least hang with my big brother.

"Good. See you tomorrow, kiddo."

We hang up, and I set my phone down on a windowsill.

"Was that the almighty Ford Chance?" Laramie asks, setting out the to-go boxes.

"It was." I join him in the kitchen and lift myself up on the counter, where I take a seat next to the sink.

"Is he thrilled to have his little sister coming home?"

"More excited than I expected."

"And did you tell him the real reason you're going home?" He lifts his knowing, thick brow in my direction.

Laramie is the *only* person who knows about my circumstances, and it will remain that way. We met while attending NYU. He majored in theater, and I majored in business in the hope of being able to help with Watchful Wanderers, but . . . well, we won't get into that. We both reached for the last chocolate milk in the dining hall, we played rock, paper, scissors to see who got to take it, and after a rousing battle, I left with the milk and he left with my phone number. We've been attached at the hip ever since.

"No." I open a box and stare down at the duck confit tapas that would normally make my mouth water but does nothing for my appetite right now. "I told him I was coming home to do some sort of piece on the Pacific Northwest."

"So, he doesn't know you're broke, unemployed, and homeless?"

"Not so much." I pop a tapa in my mouth and chew, even though the flavors fall flat.

"I told you, you could come work with me at the studio and sleep on my couch until the next thing comes along."

I shake my head. "I know nothing about SoulCycling, and I've slept on your couch before—I was one night away from suffering from a serious case of sciatica."

"Just cycling—you don't have to put the 'Soul' in front of it—and you could help with the front desk. We're always in need of more help."

"I think you and I both know you don't need help at the studio and you're going to make up some job for me." I sigh. "No, I think I should go home and figure out what to do."

"Even if that means going back with your tail tucked between your legs?" he asks, handing me another tapa.

"No, they won't know my circumstances, and I'll keep it that way. It's not like my parents are going anywhere, so I'll have a comfortable roof over my head and a full belly thanks to my mom's incessant need to feed people. Who knows, maybe it will be refreshing." I shrug and take a bite of a stuffed mushroom.

Laramie wiggles his eyebrows. "And maybe you'll find a little Lands' End lad to snuggle up to."

I point my finger at him. "Now that's something I can guarantee won't happen. Trust me, I'm in no place to be snuggling up to anyone."

"Not even . . . hunky high school crush Beau . . ." Laramie bats his lashes.

I point my finger at him. "Do not even go there."

"Why not? He was the main reason you didn't want to go back to Marina Island, so wouldn't it just be poetic if you ran into him?"

"Why do I tell you things?" I pop open another box. Lobster wontons. If only these were the comfort I need right now.

"Because I keep you on your toes. Seriously." Laramie pokes me. "What if you run into him? Weren't you totally infatuated with him? I mean . . . I saw your yearbooks—you had hearts circling every picture of him."

"Just drop it, Laramie." My voice grows harsh.

"Oooh, there was some spice on that; not sure I appreciate the sass. Just your best friend trying to get to the bottom of this crush you've been harboring. What's he even doing? Is he married?"

"I have no idea. I don't keep up with his social media. I'm not even sure if he's still living on the island. I don't ask around. So let's just drop it—I don't need the extra anxiety. Going back to Marina Island is all about focusing on me. No distractions. No men."

Laramie offers me a pot sticker from his take-out box, probably as a peace offering. "That would not be the case for me. I'd be hanging around the docks looking for a strong fisherman to whisk me away."

Change of subject, thank God. I squeeze his thick biceps, bringing back our playful humor. "I don't know why you think you're whisking-away material. You're like those Great Danes that think they're lapdogs. I love you, but no one is picking up a six-foot-four man made of muscle unless they have a forklift with them."

He licks some sauce off his finger and smirks. "So you're saying I should fall for a construction worker, then? That can be arranged."

"Oh, Martin, look, there she is, our baby. Yoo-hoo, Palmer, over here. Over here!" Mom yells across the ferry terminal while waving her hands frantically and holding a sign up that reads, PALMER CHANCE. OUR BABY.

Realizing I needed a ride when I got to Marina Island, I called my parents this morning to surprise them with my homecoming. After Mom screeched on the phone for a solid minute, we put a plan into action, and here they are now: my parents, waving their hands wildly while "yoo-hooing" at me.

"Palmer, do you see us? Your parents are right here. Yoo-hoo, Palmer!"

"Yes, I see you," I shout over the herd of people before me. They all turn to give me a look but keep moving.

I adjust my sunglasses over my eyes, tug on the neck pillow I have draped around the back of my neck, and clutch tightly my two rollie suitcases that are half my size. Being broke means you don't get to fly the way you prefer. Instead of sitting up in first class with a glass of champagne and enough space to warrant sitting cross-legged, I sat back by the toilets, where someone must have eaten something foul at the airport because they were occupying the lavatory for an uncomfortable amount of time. Not to mention I purchased a ticket for cheap, which was evident in the lack of cushioning in the seats, the tray table that was the size of my palm, and the surcharge for bags and a drink, and I'm pretty sure they charged me for a seat belt too.

"There she is," Mom says as I finally make my way to them. "Our baby girl."

"Hey, Mo—"

I'm scooped into a hug, my face planted straight into my mom's shoulder.

She strokes my head as she swooshes our bodies back and forth in a bear hug that knocks my suitcases from my hands as I struggle to keep my balance.

"Our baby girl," she repeats over and over as she kisses my cheek. "Look at you and your little bob cut. Martin, do you see her hair? See how short it is. Look at her hair."

"Is it a different color?" Dad asks with a confused grimace. "I thought you had red hair. That's what you were born with."

Holding back the necessary eye roll, I pry myself from my mom's arms. "Laramie put in some highlights last night for me. It's strawberry blonde."

"Is that what the kids are calling it these days? Fruit hair?" Dad chuckles to himself and pulls me into a hug. "You look great." He kisses the top of my head, and then together we roll my bags to their red Subaru Outback that they've had for I believe at least ten years. For people who have millions in their bank account, they sure do live the simple life.

"You packed an awful lot, don't you think?" Dad asks, shoving my bags in the back, and that's when I notice his ill-matched socks. A tube sock with red stripes and an ankle sock with neon letters on the side. What on earth is that about?

"Thought I would stay for a month or two—I plan on doing a showcase on the PNW cuisine."

I prepare myself for my mom's excited squeal, but it doesn't come. I glance at my parents. They're looking at each other, eyes wide.

"Did you hear me?" I ask. "I plan on staying for a couple of months . . . with you guys . . . in your home."

They continue to exchange odd looks.

"Uh . . . I'm going to be living with you." I snap my fingers at them. "Did you hear me. Hello? Mom? Your baby girl will be available to squeeze whenever you want."

When she doesn't say anything, the hairs on the back of my neck start to rise with concern. Why isn't she screaming from the rooftops? Why isn't she doing a mom jig in her mom jeans with her mom moves, mom fingers pointing to the heavens? Why is she standing there, stunned, like a deer caught in the headlights?

Finally, she says, "You know, honey, you've had a long travel day. Why don't we talk about this later?" She places her hand on the small of my back. "Come, come. Get in the car."

"But . . . I said I was staying for a while," I say, confused, my eyes darting between my parents. "Breakfast with your baby for months. Why aren't you thrilled?"

CHAPTER FIVE
COOPER

Car parked, hands on the steering wheel, I stare at the simple crafts-man-style house with cedar-shake exterior that I used to call home. The sun is setting over the large, serene lake that stretches just beyond the house, and the interior lights illuminate the windows with a welcoming glow. I don't see a rental car in the driveway, which means Ford isn't here yet. Not surprising. He's probably still finishing up some work. The man barely pauses long enough during the day for meals.

Sighing, I unclip my seat belt and hop out of my car after making the trip to Marina Island for the fifth time this week. It's gotten to the point where I've started to leave work early, only to finish things up while on the ferry, so I'm not stuck in the commuter traffic.

The phone calls from my parents asking for help have become, I hate to say it, obnoxious. Being the only child who lives near them—half an hour away, to be exact—I'm the one they rely on for pretty much everything—sometimes even the simplest issues, like a clogged sink. They refuse to call a handyman, because even though they have money, they don't dare spend it. Instead, they call on me, and it's impossible to say no, especially when I know they took a chance on two kids in the foster care system. I owe everything to them, even if they drive me insane almost every day.

And I know I can bitch about having to come here all the time, but with my parents getting older, and considering their popularity on the island, I wouldn't want anyone taking advantage of them.

I walk up to the house, but before knocking, I stand on the front porch, my mind drifting back to the time we attempted a family photo shoot before Ford left for college. My straitlaced older brother was hungover from saying goodbye to his friends and kept falling into the bushes. Dad was so flustered and angry that we wound up with a picture of him gripping the back of Ford's shirt to hold him up while Mom had her arms wrapped around Palmer and me. Smiling to myself, I come back to the present, where the bushes are overgrown and the porch's stain is chipping—though I can't bring myself to mind at the moment.

I decide not to bother knocking on the door—I let myself in, and I'm immediately greeted by the sound of my parents laughing, followed by a "Cooper, is that you?"

"Yup," I say, slipping off my boots. I head down the hallway and into the kitchen, where I stumble to a stop. "Palmer?"

My sister waves to me from the kitchen table with a big smile on her face.

"When the hell did you get here?"

She hops up from her seat and comes up to me to give me a big hug. The shorty of the family, she doesn't even reach my chin barefoot. "About an hour ago. Can you smell the plane on me?"

"Gross . . . no." I push her away, and she laughs. "When did you decide to come out here early?"

"A few days ago." She shrugs and pulls her gray knit sweater around her waist. "Thought it would be fun to get in touch with my roots again." She gives me a quick once-over. "Look at you, Mr. Style." Her toe nudges my pants. "When did you start wearing cuffed, formfitting jeans? And look at that hair—very lumber-sexual."

I run my hand over my hair. "It's been like this for a while. You would know if you came home more often." I add a smirk with my comment, so she knows I'm joking . . . well, partially joking. I can't recall the last time she was on the West Coast, let alone here, in our home.

"Well, I'd be more informed if you had a social media account where I could stalk you and the obvious changes you're making in your appearance." She touches my shoulder. "Have you been working out?"

"Your brother has been adamant about obtaining a six-pack," Dad says, barely looking up from the picture he's coloring, most likely for Palmer. He loves coloring swear words for visitors, thinks it's hilarious.

"Really?" Palmer drags out. And, in a ninja-like move, she reaches for my shirt and lifts it, flashing my stomach. Her eyes pop open, followed by a giant grin as I swat her hand away and step to the side. "Cooper Joseph Chance, my oh my, look at you, you little stud." Turning to Mom, she points at me. "Have you seen his stomach?"

Absentmindedly, Mom nods. "Yes, he lent it to me the other night so I could get the laundry done. He was uncooperative at first, sitting shirtless in my laundry tub, but once I started putting some elbow grease against his abs, he giggled the whole time in utter glee."

"Oooh, Mom with the funnies," Palmer says, laughing.

"Do you realize how disturbing that is?" I ask.

"I told him to put 'Mom does laundry on my abs' in his dating profile, but he refused to."

Mouth wide again in humor, Palmer turns toward me. "Oh em gee, you're on dating apps? Which one? Let me see your profile. Do you have sexy pictures on it? Oh God, bathroom selfies? Please tell me you do not have bathroom selfies. I hate when guys take bathroom selfies, especially when they don't remove things from the counter. No one needs to know the intimate details of what toothpaste and deodorant you use when swiping." She reaches for my pockets, searching for my phone. "Where is it? I want to see. Have you seen it, Mom? Is he charming?"

"I helped him put it together." Mom picks up her knitting needles and begins to move them around with fluffy yellow yarn. She's been working on blankets for children at the local children's hospital. She's made fifty-two already and loves receiving pictures from families of her blankets with their kids.

"Oh my God, Cooper, Mom helped you with your profile?" Palmer laughs, gripping the counter.

Yup, this night could not get any worse.

Just then, both our phones beep at the same time. Palmer looks at me, confused. I send her the same glance, and together we pull out our phones. I'm half expecting a text from Ford about being late, but when I see a notification from my dating app, my mouth goes slightly dry.

I swipe open my phone, and the app pops up with a heart above a picture of my sister, declaring I have a match nearby. My balls shrivel up inside me.

"Ewww," Palmer says, looking up at me.

"What?" Mom asks.

"I just matched with Cooper." She dry heaves and covers her mouth.

"I'm not that repulsive, you ass." I push her away just as the front door closes. We all turn to see Ford walking down the hallway in a pair of jeans and a polo shirt.

He glances around the kitchen. "What did I miss?"

Still coloring, Dad doesn't bother to lift his head as he says, "We've established that Cooper has abs, your mom uses said abs to clean laundry, Coop thinks it tickles, and your sister and brother just matched on their dating apps, which has repulsed them, but to me, the romantic match only makes this day that much better."

A smirk spreads across Ford's lips. "Man, I've missed you guys."

"Mom, you have to tell them," I whisper as we decorate her pudding cups in the kitchen while Dad shows off his bookshelf to Palmer and Ford in the living room.

When Mom asked where Larkin was, Ford said she'd hung back at the bed-and-breakfast because she didn't want to step in on any family bonding. Mom and Dad were not too happy about that and immediately forced Ford to call her and tell her that next time she'd better attend any and all family dinners.

When I glanced over at my brother, I relished the embarrassment etched all over his face. The man attempts to maintain professionalism at all times, but it's next to impossible in our family. Especially since Mom and Dad seem to be so attached to Larkin—they see her as one of their own.

Now that dinner is done and the over-the-line phone call with Ford's assistant is out of the way, it's time for Mom and Dad to spill the beans.

Hunched over the black quartz countertops I helped Dad install two years ago—because why hire someone when you can do it yourself, he always says—Mom plops a raspberry in each pudding dish. "We will tell them, we will."

"Tonight?" I ask.

She glances over her shoulder. "I don't think tonight is the best night. You all just got here."

"Which makes it the perfect time. Who knows when we'll be under the same roof again? And once they see the sign outside the house, they're going to have questions."

Mom chops up some fresh mint and hands it to me. I gently set it in the bowls next to the raspberries, the way she likes it. Always the doting son.

"I know, but we're having such a good time, and I'm not sure how they'll take the news."

I lift up the tray of desserts. "Only one way to find out."

I walk into the family room, followed by Mom, just as Ford, Palmer, and Dad take seats on the sofas.

As I hand out the pudding cups, Palmer says, "Some fine craftsmanship on that shelf, Coop. Did you mean for it to be slanted like that?" She takes a sip from her wineglass, one I've seen her refill at least twice already.

I glance over at the dilapidated shelf that's filled with a color-coordinated gaggle of books, set in rainbow order. "Dad suggested it; said he wanted to add character to his display," I say, lying through my teeth.

"I actually told him to use a level to make sure everything was even, but he assured me the shelf was meant to lean. After some intensive searching on IKEA, I found my son was lying to my face." Dad grips his spoon, a slight shake to his hand as he lifts a scoop of pudding to his mouth.

"The audacity," Palmer says with a grin, the little instigator.

I take a seat next to Ford on the cream-colored love seat my parents have had for years. "Lying is the only way I can get out of this house and back to Seattle before midnight."

"He refuses to spend the night here and commute in the morning," Mom says. "Probably hoping for a late-night hookup on that fancy app of his."

"Is that what you use it for? Hookups?" Palmer asks, laughter in her eyes.

"I barely even use it. Haven't had the time with everything Mom and Dad have me doing around the house," I say, the perfect lead-in for Mom.

But, of course, instead of taking it, she says, "Did you know Cooper went to see Nora yesterday?"

"Nora McHale?" Ford asks. "Was it a date?"

"What? No," I say before Mom can interject with her wild fantasies about what could have possibly happened. "I didn't go to see Nora, Mom, I went to order the cake."

"Something he could have done over the phone." Mom conspiratorially nudges Palmer. "But no, he went into the store. I think he's still smitten from their one-night stand."

"Ooooooh," Palmer coos.

"Wait." Ford furrows his brow. "Isn't she friends with—?"

"Can we not?" I ask, growing frustrated. "Jesus, when did my dating life become a point of conversation in this family? To my knowledge, I'm not the only child who is single."

"But you're a divorcé looking for a second shot at love. It's more interesting," Palmer says.

"Larkin always talks about the second-chance romances she likes to read," Ford adds, stealing the attention away from me. Thank God.

Palmer props her chin up on her fist, ignoring her pudding. "Please, tell us more about what Larkin likes."

"Don't even start with that," Ford says. "She's my assistant and that's it."

"Uh-huh." Palmer blinks. "Surrrrre, Ford."

Ford doesn't even bother to respond but instead puts a spoonful of pudding in his mouth.

"You know, your mom was my assistant before we hooked up in the back of the store, in a canoe," Dad says, picking up a raspberry and plopping it in his mouth.

Together, we all groan.

Yes, this is my family.

We might not see each other often, but when we're in the same room, the oversharing and invasion of privacy is boss level.

"On that note, Mom, Dad, don't you have something to tell Palmer and Ford?" I ask.

Mom's eyes narrow at me, but I don't even care. They need to get it over with.

"Are you sick, Mom?" Ford asks, his expression full of concern.

"Are you?" Palmer asks, uncrossing her legs and facing them now.

"No, I'm not sick." Mom sets down her pudding bowl on the coffee table. "I wasn't planning on saying anything to you tonight, since you just got here, but it seems like your brother has another idea."

"What's going on?" Ford asks, setting down his pudding bowl as well.

Mom reaches out and takes Dad's hand in hers. "We've been doing some thinking about our future, and Cooper has been a strong, guiding force behind this decision"—she didn't need to add that part, but fine—"and after some long conversations and tough decisions, we've decided to sell the house."

"What?" Palmer says loudly while sitting up taller. "Sell this house? Our childhood home? The one we're sitting in right now? This house?"

"Do you think they have other houses we're unaware of?" I ask.

"I don't know," Palmer says, panic in her voice. "Maybe they do, and that's where they hide the other halves to Dad's socks."

As a collective whole, we all glance at Dad's socks.

Where *are* the other halves?

"Are you really selling?" Ford asks, his voice strained but not as alarmed as Palmer's.

"We are," Dad confirms with a sturdy nod. "We found a wonderful apartment in the heart of Seattle, right off Western Ave. It's close to Cooper, walking distance to the water, and the apartment building has all the amenities we're looking for, including very socially awkward programmers who are excited to have a mom in the building who's willing and excited to bake cookies for the floor."

"We've made the rounds and introduced ourselves already," Mom adds.

"Wait." Palmer closes her eyes and takes a deep breath. Hands extended, a slight shake to them, she says, "You're going to exchange our childhood memories for a throng of programmers?"

"They're very sweet when you get them to finally open up. Want me to ask if any of them are single?" Mom asks, growing excited.

"No," Palmer practically yells. "I don't get it. What's the appeal? You love it here. You're not city people. You've spent your whole lives on Marina Island—you grew your business here, you raised your children here—why are you all of a sudden going to move to a high-rise apartment in a city you never even liked? Is this what a late-life crisis looks like?"

Ford turns toward me. "Was this your idea?"

"Not really," I answer, feeling the blaze of my siblings' disapproving stares. "They were saying how they couldn't keep up with the house anymore, they kept calling me to fix everything, and I offered a solution."

"You told them to sell?" Palmer asks, standing from her seat. "How could you do that, Coop? You know what this house means to us."

"Hey now, this was our decision ultimately," Dad cuts in. "And ultimately, the house is too big for us. If you visited more often, maybe we'd consider keeping it, but you don't. There's no keeping a large piece of property when we're the only ones who live here. I hate to say it, but we're selling, and you're going to have to clean out your rooms. There are growing families who could benefit from such a wonderful place to make memories."

"What about our memories?" Palmer asks, getting more emotional than I expected.

Yeah, I thought they were going to be caught off guard, but I wasn't planning on this kind of reaction.

"Palmer, you'll still have your memories," Mom says, a worried look on her face.

"No, some other family will." With that, she goes to the kitchen, where I see her grab a bottle of wine and head out to the back deck.

"I'll go talk to her," Ford says, standing. No surprise there—they've always been close.

Which leaves me with Mom and Dad.

Once again.

Unable to look them in the eyes, I stare down at my pudding bowl. "So, that went well."

I glance up to the disapproving expressions in my parents' faces.

"Or maybe not," I mutter.

CHAPTER SIX

PALMER

I tip the bottle of wine back and let the warm liquid flow down my throat.

They're selling the house.

Actually selling it.

To go live in some sort of high-rise where they can bake cookies for strangers who know binary code better than the English language.

Where the hell did that idea even come from?

Dad wears shorts with holes in the crotch—he's not a high-rise kind of guy. Mom takes great care of her garden and grows prize-winning zucchinis. Zucchinis that would make any woman weak in the knees with one girthy glance. Does she think she can have a garden in a high-rise?

And not to be selfish or anything, but . . . where the hell am I going to live?

Yeah, my parents are well off and all, but there's no way in hell I would ever ask them for money, not after everything that happened . . .

And besides, I've spent most of my life hearing my parents tell me over and over again, *We make our own way, we make our own life.*

To prove to them I'm not a screwup, that I didn't need their assistance, that's what I set out to do, make my own path, but boy oh boy did that come back to bite me in the ass.

Now I find myself toeing chipped wood on the deck, thinking about how my life has gotten to this point.

The possibility of being homeless—actually homeless—feels like a punch to the gut. There's nothing left to do but tip back the wine bottle, again and again.

Glug, glug, glug, there go all my plans.

Talk about a kick to the old baby maker.

Childhood house? Gone.

Devious schemes to not end up homeless and broke? Out the window.

Whoosh, just like that, all my worries come flooding back like an endless tidal wave, crashing into me over and over again.

"Hey, slow down there, kiddo," Ford says, popping out onto the deck. He attempts to take my wine bottle away from me, but when it comes to her "grape juice," this mama bear is protective.

"This is my wine; get your own bottle," I hiss.

"I would, but there's none left."

Facts.

Hmm, maybe that's why I'm also more on the emotional side right now . . .

Pffft.

No, wine doesn't make you emotional.

Wine makes you feel . . . it makes you feel . . . like you're galloping on the back of a prancing unicorn.

"Why are you doing that?" Ford asks.

"Doing what?" I pause and take inventory of my limbs.

"You're pretending you're on the back of a horse, galloping in place."

Huh . . . I thought I was just dreaming about that.

"Don't you worry about what I'm doing," I say, straightening up as I motion to the house. "You should be worrying about what *they're* doing." I lean forward and lower my voice to a dramatic whisper. "A high-rise? Ford, come on. They are not a high-rise couple. People who live in high-rise apartments don't know what shopping at a Costco feels like. Can you imagine Mom and Dad not buying in bulk? Honestly, it's too traumatic for me to even think about. Not to mention, they built an enterprise from being down-to-earth nature people. Moving to a high-rise apartment where they have inside jokes with the doorman completely contradicts the foundation they built their family on."

He sticks his hands in his pockets and looks back at the house. "It is rather confusing."

Ugh, Ford. Always the calm one. The sensible one. The responsible older brother who thinks logically, never *ever* thinking with his heart. Not sure the computer in his brain knows how to calculate emotions or play off the drama life hands him.

This is not a calm, pensive moment.

This is an all-out, rear up the rotors, fire up the engines, throw gas on the flames kind of moment.

I'm going to need anger from him.

Outrage.

Drama!

"That's all you're going to say?" I hiccup. "Why aren't you angry?" I sway to the side.

He looks me up and down. "Palm, maybe lay off the wine."

I shake my head and clutch my bottle close to my heart. "This right here, this is my only friend."

"You're using the wrong thing to cope."

"Ugh, get out of here with your big brother sensibility. Can't you see I'm letting myself have a moment?"

"You were having a moment before the announcement." He studies me. "Is there something else going on you're not telling me about?"

43

Sensible and intuitive.

"What? No," I answer quickly. "Why would you think that?"

"Because your eyes are shifty. Because you're acting weird. Because you're having an outlandish reaction to Mom and Dad moving."

"Outlandish?" I say, my voice rising. "Ford"—*hiccup*—"this is our childhood home; this is where you once drove over Mom's garden with a tractor, and then all three of us ran to the market to buy vegetables and restocked the soil with them. Don't you remember the look on Mom's face when she held up her prize-winning eggplant that we bought from the store . . . on sale? You're telling me you're okay with them selling the garden that brought us all together that fateful summer?"

He looks down at the deck and scuffs his shoes across the wood. "No, but I'm willing to talk through things—"

I point to the deck. "This is where we built the biggest Jenga tower, unofficially breaking the *Guinness Book of World Records*."

"Palm—"

"And that window up there? That's the window Cooper broke when he hit the screaming home run off of Dad during the Chance Championship, which in turn bought us our trophy . . . a blow-up slide for the lake."

"I know—"

"And that lake." I fling my arm out to the side. "That is the same lake where you touched your first breast, under the water, like a teenage pervert . . ."

"Why do you know about that?" He sighs and then drags his hand over his face. "Wait, don't answer that."

"And the driveway, that's the place where I first saw—" My mouth slams shut as I realize I've almost said where I saw Beau for the first time, riding his bike, looking like a total dreamboat on a red and black Trek he bought from the Watchful Wanderers.

Seemingly oblivious to my abrupt stop, Ford says, "I know this is where we hold our fondest memories—even the creepy ones, apparently—but Palmer, you have to understand where Mom and Dad are coming from. And I hate to say it, but . . . you're acting out."

"Acting out? You think this is acting out? Oh, I can show you"—*hiccup*—"acting out."

Because I feel the need to prove a point, I search around the deck, looking for something that . . . *oh, that will do*. Wine bottle still clutched to my chest, I step up on the adjoining seat of my parents' picnic table and then stand on top of it, waving my hands—and bottle—above my head. "Now this is acting out," I declare, pelvic thrusting the air and making lewd gestures because, well . . . wine. "Woooo-hoooo, look at me, acting out. Palmer Chance is on a picnic table, waving her hands, acting like a giant . . . whoooaaa—"

Clunk.

Like rain from the sky, my wine bottle slips out of my hand, knocks me in the head, and throws me off balance.

I teeter on the edge of the picnic table, my legs wobbly, and before I know it, I'm crying, "Man overboard!" as I topple to the deck, landing directly on my wrist with a crunch.

"Jesus, Palmer," I hear Ford say right before everything goes black and wine takes me into a pillowy-soft, emotionless dream state.

CHAPTER SEVEN

DR. BEAU

"Wine!" my patient shouts as her eyes fly open and she clutches at her chest.

Palmer Chance.

The brilliantly beautiful, sometimes insufferable, most of the time gregarious woman with a knack for bringing men to their knees. The record holder for most Girl Scout cookies sold on Marina Island, the heiress to the Watchful Wanderers store, and the youngest and only girl of the famous Chance family. Everyone cheered her on when she went off to NYC, rallied when she went viral for posting a video of herself eating snails for the first time, and bragged when she became a famous Instagrammer. Marina Island loves her, and from the blank look on her face . . . she has no idea who I am.

"Where am I?" She pats down her clothes and winces. "Dear God, what is that pain?" Her eyes zero in on me. "And who are you?" She plucks at her shirt while taking in her surroundings. "You're smiling— why are you smiling and hovering over me? Is this . . . is this a secret cannibal, sadist, organ-harvesting cave?"

"Palmer," Ford says, coming up next to her. "You're at the doctor's office."

Her eyes search the exam room, and she shakes her head. "This is not a doctor's office—this is a bedroom converted to look like a doctor's office." She turns to Ford. "Blink twice if they're making you say that."

Yup, she's still drunk.

"Palmer," I say in a soothing tone, "I'm Dr. Beau, and I'm here to help."

Her eyes dart to me, and she gives me a quick once-over, her eyes landing on my chest for longer than I think she would care to admit. "I knew a guy named Beau, but you look nothing like him, and I'm sorry to inform you, but you don't look like a doctor either."

That one perusal from Palmer Chance sets my nerves on fire.

And her comment . . . it makes me inwardly chuckle. *I knew a guy named Beau . . .*

"If I don't look like a doctor, then what do I look like?"

With her good hand, she reaches out and pokes me in the arm. "Just what I thought." She motions for Ford to come to her. "He's an actor," she whispers loudly. "Watch this." Facing me again, she holds her chin high, dried blood crusted along the side of her face. "Okay, *Dr. Beau*, quick, what's this?" She holds up her index finger.

"That is your index phalange."

She nods. "Well, any *Friends* viewer knows what a phalange is, thanks to Phoebe Buffay. What about this?" She opens her mouth and points.

I sigh. "Your uvula."

"Uh-huh. Good guess." She shifts and winces, probably from the break in her wrist I was trying to fix before she woke up. "Okay, I'm suffering from nausea, can't stop eating, and am irritable when people breathe. What's wrong with me?"

"Other than being your normal self?" Ford mutters, pulling a smile from me.

"You're probably pregnant," I say, still taking her questions seriously.

"Are you pregnant?" Ford asks in disbelief.

"What? No." She shakes her head. "I'm quizzing him, Ford," she whispers.

"Palmer, I'm sure Dr. Beau has better things—"

"There's a suspicious mole on my knee—go." Palmer stares me down.

I play along. "I would check it out and then probably refer you to a dermatologist, depending on the size and coloration."

Her eyes narrow. "Diarrhea, pain in my abdomen, gas."

"Irritable bowel syndrome."

She huffs. "Who married McDreamy?"

"Dr. Meredith Grey."

She perks up, gives me another once-over, and then rests her head on the exam table. "He checks out."

"Jesus," Ford grumbles and offers me an apologetic look. "Sorry about that."

"It's fine." I take some wet gauze and bring it to her head, where I wipe away the blood to take a look at her cut. Even though she's drunk and her eyes are slightly bloodshot, I still find myself getting sucked into her green irises. "Looks like you won't need stitches, but I'll do a butterfly bandage to close off the gash, just in case."

"Gash?" Palmer asks, confused. "Who gashed me?"

"Your friend, the wine bottle," Ford says, clearly irritated.

"You know, you think you know someone," Palmer huffs, making me chuckle. "Wait until Laramie hears about this. He will never believe that we could be double-crossed by wine, but the world is always changing, you know, Doc?"

"Oh yeah, always have to be on your toes." I smirk.

She hasn't changed, not one bit.

"Precisely. Because next thing you know, *bam*, your parents are selling your childhood home, ruining all memories and future plans."

Brow pinched, I turn to Ford. "Your parents are moving?"

"We have yet to determine that," Ford says, expressionless.

"Really?" Palmer asks, her eyes full of hope. "Did you speak to them?"

"Let's not worry about that right now. You have a broken wrist and a gash in your head—focus on that," I say.

"A broken wrist? Huh." Palmer examines her wrist carefully. "That would make sense, given the screaming pain that's pulsing up and down my arm."

"Yes, we'll have to cast it so it sets right. While I fix your gash, maybe you can start thinking about what color cast you want."

"Just when you think the world is peeing on your parade, you get to pick out a cast color. Please tell me you have teal—it would complement my hair and eyes."

"Surprisingly, I do."

"You know what that means, Ford." She pokes her brother. "My Instagram is about to be lit."

Palmer has always been the free spirit, and that spirit is shining through right now, as warm and tempting as sunlight as I finish the bandage and clean up, preparing for the cast.

"What happened to Dr. Weazleton?" she asks. "Don't tell me Marina Island is big enough to have two doctors now." Her eyebrows shoot up. "Talk about a spicy competition. How could anyone even choose? *GQ* Dr. Beau or cranky, bald, and snarly Dr. Weazleton?"

"*GQ*, huh?" I ask as I pick up a stockinette, cotton roll, and fiberglass casting tape.

She tilts her head and studies me. "Yes, *GQ*. Stylish hair, gelled just perfectly. Gray, flat-front chinos and a forest-green polo that makes the green in your hazel eyes pop. Square jaw, scruff, clearly works out . . . yes, very *GQ*, if you ask me. Don't you think, Ford?"

Ford is smiling like a fool. "You're so going to regret this in the morning."

"What was that?" she asks, her eyes still on me.

"Nothing," Ford says.

"And look, a little bit of a dimple in your chin. Isn't that cute." Her good arm rises. "Can I touch it?"

"Uh, touch what?" I ask as I lay a pillow across her lap and adjust her exam table so she's sitting up.

"Your chin dimple. I want to press my finger in it, like it's a button." Heat rises in my body as I try to concentrate on casting her arm, but it's proving to be more difficult with every second that goes by. My hands feel slightly unsteady, my mind is confusing the process, and hell . . . she could totally touch my chin dimple. She doesn't even have to ask.

Ford lowers Palmer's arm gently. "Maybe leave Dr. Beau's chin alone for now."

"Right, right, he's focusing. We don't want to disturb a great man at work . . . an attractive man, wouldn't you say, Ford?" Ignoring her praise—praise I wish I'd had many years ago—I slip the stockinette net over her arm carefully and then start rolling the protective cotton around her wrist. The x-rays we took showed a distal radius fracture, the most common type of a fracture, which usually occurs as someone's trying to catch themselves when falling. In this instance, exactly what happened. "So, Dr. Beau, are you single?"

I nearly choke on my own saliva.

"Why don't we just let Dr. Beau do his job, Palmer. Trust me, you'll thank me later." Ford pats his sister's arm.

Yes, please, just let me do my job.

I finish wrapping and straighten up. "Would someone be able to bring her in tomorrow? I'd like to make sure the butterfly bandages are healing the way I want them to."

"Yes," Ford says. "I can arrange for that." He types something into his phone and then sits down in a chair while letting out a pent-up breath. His head rests against the wall, and he looks absolutely exhausted.

Not surprised. The man works himself ragged.

He's the one and only Ford Chance, the reason the Chance family is even on the national map, and the reason my sister has a job.

CHAPTER EIGHT

FORD

"Good morning," Larkin says with a smile as she sits across from me.

The Marina Island Bed and Breakfast has a large dining space with accompanying fireplace, multiple wooden bistro sets with differing floral linens draped over them, and striped green and white wallpaper on the walls, met halfway down the wall by white board and batten. The aesthetic is busy, but also oddly calming, with the soothing natural colors and potted plants scattered throughout the space.

But it does nothing for my mood this morning.

"Good morning," I say, pouring myself a cup of coffee from the carafe that Louise, the owner, brought over to me when she mentioned how tired I looked. Pleasant woman.

Larkin studies me. "You look . . ."

"Tired," I finish for her. "So I've heard." I drag my hand over my face and lean back in my chair. A muffin rests on my plate, along with some fruit, but I have no desire to eat them at the moment, especially since the muffins look dry and incredibly unappetizing. Hate to admit it, but my mom was right about the continental breakfast.

"Does this have anything to do with Palmer and a wine bottle?"

"Talk to your brother, the famous Dr. Beau, this morning?"

"He mentioned a late-night visit. He obviously didn't go into details, but he did want me to check up on you and make sure you were okay. He said you seemed stressed." Larkin props her chin on her hand. "Anything you want to talk about, boss?"

"Not really."

"Does that ever work with me?"

"No." I pick up my fork and stab a piece of pineapple that's seen better days. I examine it and set my fork back down.

"How about this—instead of pretending like we're going to eat these dry bran muffins and semicanned fruit, why don't we head over to Watchful Wanderers? They have food trucks parked out front in the morning. We can grab breakfast and walk through the store, maybe get those creative juices flowing and then go over the schedule for today."

"Yeah, that sounds like a great plan." I tilt my head to the side, taking her in. "Why do you know me so well?"

"Four years of spending way too much time together." She stands and adjusts the rolled-up sleeves of her black-and-blue buffalo plaid shirt. Before we left, I told her to pack casual for the trip. It's just us—no reason to dress up. I'm glad she took me seriously, because she looks comfortable in her leggings, boots, and flannel. "Let's go—I'm not going to take no for an answer."

"When have you ever taken no for an answer from me?"

"It's rare." She smirks as I stand.

I leave a tip on the table, not sure if that's what we're supposed to do, and I follow Larkin out of the bed-and-breakfast. Together we turn right on Marina Ave. "Do you ever miss living here?" Larkin asks as our feet fall in step together.

"Sometimes," I answer. "I don't miss the constant ferry rides and the fear of missing the last boat off the island. But I do miss living near the water. Nothing like a landlocked state to make you realize how much you enjoyed living on the coast."

"I miss the water too," Larkin says with a wistful tone. "A lot. I miss going fishing on Sundays with my dad and Beau. Taking the dinghy out on the channel and sharing a box of doughnuts while we sucked down hot chocolate and whispered so we didn't scare the fish away."

"Every Sunday?" I ask.

"Every Sunday." Her shoulder brushes up against mine. "Beau would skip out on occasion, which led to it being more of a thing I did with my dad when we got older."

"No wonder you were always in Watchful Wanderers," I say, thinking back to the stories she told me of coming to the store with her dad. Even though we grew up on a small island, I don't recall seeing Larkin all too much in the store . . . or at school, for that matter. Maybe because I'm older than her, or maybe because I was always in the back of the store with Dad, learning the ropes on the admin side.

"It was our absolute favorite place ever. I remember when I was twelve, going to the store with Dad and checking out the live snake tank you guys had in the front window for Snake Week."

"Snake Week?" I ask, confused. "I don't remember . . . wait, was it when Dad was trying to bring snake awareness to hikers?" I scratch the side of my jaw as the store comes into view just over the crest of the road. The triangular log cabin–style roof peaks up, followed by the pitched wooden porch and classic carved bear that rests just out front—a pretty famous bear who's been featured in hundreds of thousands of pictures.

"I can't believe you don't remember Snake Week—it was all the town talked about. Your dad brought in a snake specialist, and every day that week, at seven at night, she'd give advice about each dangerous snake we should stay away from while hiking, and then of course countered that with info on the friendly ones. It was enthralling."

"Huh," I say as the food trucks also come into view. "Kind of wish I remembered that."

"I always wondered why you guys never brought it back. It's a great promotion and wonderful for the stores to help sell more product. Free lessons, free food, and products for sale. With social media being so big, you could really make a thing. And you could set up displays in each of the stores. Displays that show off the snakes instead of hiding them."

"What do you mean?" I ask.

"Well, years ago, Dad, Beau, and I were visiting Colorado Springs to hike the famous Incline, but we also went to the Cheyenne Mountain Zoo. Their reptile exhibit was like an art piece. Each tank was designed to highlight the creatures' colors with beautiful marble rocks and inspiring sculptures. I've never seen anything like it. You could do the same here, maybe use products for the snakes to slither over—carabiners and lanterns and the like—really make an exhibit out of it."

Jesus . . . she's so smart.

"That's actually a really good idea."

She smirks at me and nudges my shoulder. "Been sitting on that idea for a while." She points to a red truck. "Gah, the Waffle Machine. Don't mind if I do."

She takes off toward the food truck, and I can't help smiling as she skips right up to the window and waves. I always forget that Larkin grew up here too. She knows the town, she knows the people, she knows the store. She has history here.

"Ford," she calls out. "They have waffles benedict." She waves me over.

Chuckling, I join her, and we both put in our orders. "They have coffee in Watchful Wanderers; want me to grab us some?"

"That would be amazing," she says. "I'll wait for the food and find a spot to sit. You know how I take my coffee, right?" She grins at me.

"With a dash of creamer. And when you're feeling feisty, with a teaspoon of sugar." I raise a brow. "Are you feeling feisty today?"

"Very." She winks.

"All right, then. Be right back."

Leaving the food truck area, I make my way to the original Watchful Wanderers store, the place I spent most of my time growing up. The wood porch creaks under my feet, and the familiar scents of pine and dirt fill me up as I pull the brass door handle.

Since it's early, there aren't many people milling about, which gives me time to take in the store from the entrance. Extremely outdated, the log walls have an orange tint to them, the maple floors have seen better days, and the clothing racks are one windstorm from being blown over. But it still feels like home despite how unpolished it looks.

"Hey, Ford," Kevin says as he walks up to me. "Didn't know you were in town." Kevin is the original store's manager and an avid outdoorsman. His knowledge of products and safety by far exceeds anything I know.

"Hey, Kevin." I give his hand a shake. "Here to celebrate Mom and Dad for the anniversary party."

"I didn't think that was for a few weeks."

"Yeah, decided to come early. We're working on some business things."

"Oh?" Kevin asks. "Hopefully good things."

"Very good things," I answer and then nod to the back. "Think I could grab some coffee?"

"As if you need to ask. Help yourself."

I head toward the back while taking in all the gear we have for sale. I hate to admit it, but even though the store feels like home, I've never felt more out of place. I should know what that stick thing is over there, but I have no idea. And that round object with the pointy things . . . yeah, no clue. And what about that net? Is that for a bear? It's huge!

Shaking my head, I find the coffeepot, pour two to-go cups. Add the right amount of creamer and sugar for Larkin and then head back out to the front, where Larkin is sitting on the curb under an oak tree. The food is in boxes on her lap, and she's wearing an excited smile.

"Do we sell nets to catch bears?" I ask.

"What?" She laughs out loud. "No. Why do you ask?"

I jab a thumb toward the store. "There was a net back there that looked like it could catch a bear."

She chuckles some more. "You are so hopeless, Ford. Didn't your dad ever take you fly-fishing?"

I shake my head. "Weirdly, we didn't do a lot of outdoor stuff because we were always running the store, and when we did get some time away, the last thing Mom wanted to do was anything outdoorsy."

I take a seat next to her and hand her a coffee while she hands me my take-out box.

"I guess that makes sense," she says, taking a sip. "I've taught you well. This coffee's perfect."

Once we're settled, Larkin pushes her hair behind her ear, showing the heart shape of her jaw. "So tell me everything. What happened last night?"

I cut up a piece of waffle and stab my fork through it. "I could feel the tension the minute I walked in the house. Palmer and Cooper were already ragging on each other, while Mom and Dad sat there oblivious. Dinner was pretty good, though. We caught up. Cooper spoke about a nonfiction book he's been working on that's putting him to sleep. Palmer didn't say much about work at all, and when I considered mentioning the store rebrand, Cooper changed the subject to some kangaroo-boxing video he watched that had no purpose whatsoever."

"That's odd, why would he do that?"

I shove a large piece of waffle in my mouth to avoid answering right away. I haven't told anyone about what happened. Partly because I'm ashamed and partly because I don't want Cooper to feel any more embarrassed than he probably does.

I swallow and stare down at my stretched-out legs. "About two months ago, Cooper approached me about possibly helping with the rebranding after Dad clued him in on what we were doing."

"He did?" Larkin asks with a confused expression. "I wasn't aware."

"I didn't tell anyone. Not even our parents."

"I'm assuming the conversation didn't go well."

I scratch the side of my jaw. "I love my brother, you know that, and I'd do anything for him, but he has a track record of showing interest in something and then having zero follow-through. Like the time he wanted to help Dad work on a new layout for the store. He started mapping things out but then just dropped it all when he met Dealia. Or the time I asked him to help me edit an investor booklet. He said of course, but two weeks went by and nothing. Or his attempt at becoming an author . . . he hasn't had the best of luck at achieving things he puts his mind to. He's already sensitive, and I didn't want him to have another failure under his belt. I'm not sure he'd be able to handle it."

Larkin listens intently like she always does. There's no doubt she's the easiest person I've ever talked to and the person I usually go to when I have a problem, business or personal. I shouldn't talk to her about personal things, I know that's crossing the line, but she isn't just an assistant to me—she's a friend. And that's information I keep close to my chest. Despite crossing the line, because she's naturally a good friend, I need to try to keep things as professional as possible, even though I lean on her hard when it comes to personal things . . . I can't help it.

"And I know that makes me look like an ass," I say, moving my fork around my food, a nervous habit I tend to do when I'm uncomfortable. "You know, the fact is that I'm betting on my brother to fail before he even has a chance to, but I have to at least try to protect him from himself."

"Does this feeling you have, the need to protect him, circle back to his divorce and what happened with Dealia?"

"Yes," I answer honestly. "From the beginning I knew they weren't going to last, but I never said anything. I just . . . I saw how they differed, how she wanted more, and I knew he wasn't going to be brave enough to leave his circle and make it happen. He's always been cautious despite the grand plans he has in his head. I was afraid the same thing was going to happen with the rebranding. That it would be another instance where he has these ambitions but never does anything with them. I couldn't take the chance." I take a sip of my coffee, letting the hot liquid burn down my throat. "It was obvious Cooper wanted nothing to do with talking about the store last night."

"Which is understandable—it must be a raw topic for him."

"I'm assuming it is, but we haven't talked about it since. And then when we were having dessert, Mom and Dad broke the news to us that they plan on selling the house and we have a month to say goodbye to our childhood home. And"—I let out a sigh—"we'll have to clean out our rooms."

"What?" Larkin sits taller. "They're selling? Why?"

"They said the house is too big for just them, which I can understand. It's large, but I have a cleaning service come by every week. The yard is taken care of every week too. I'm not sure if it's an issue with the house being too big or if the house is too lonely." I can understand what lonely feels like. Being in Denver, I can understand having a space that feels so empty, and not wanting to be there all the time. But at least that's something I put on myself. My parents didn't ask for this loneliness, and that breaks my heart.

Larkin nods. "I was going to suggest the same thing. If you think about it, they really just have Cooper. You visit as much as you can, but I know you rely on FaceTime, and when was the last time Palmer visited?"

"I'm not even sure."

"Maybe the house holds memories for you, but maybe it's too painful for your parents to stay there when their children are never home anymore." Larkin shrugs. "But that's just me guessing."

"It's a pretty good guess." I take another sip of my coffee, trying to ignore a twinge of guilt. "And then of course Palmer flew off the deep end about our parents moving, took it harder than I expected. I think there's something going on that she's not telling me."

"Like what?" Larkin asks, her blue eyes so intent that I can't help but feel completely comfortable sitting here, talking about my family.

"I don't know. There was panic in her eyes when Mom and Dad said they were selling the house, but it wasn't the kind of panic I was expecting . . . it's almost like them selling is going to hurt her more than just losing the memories. When I asked her about it, she of course denied everything. Then proceeded to fall off the picnic table, put a gash in her forehead, and break her wrist."

"Oooh, ouch. Is she okay?"

"She's fine." A small smile pulls at my lips as I peek up at Larkin. "She sure did enjoy hitting on your brother, though."

Larkin's eyes widen. "Stop! She did not, did she?"

"Yup." I nod. "Said he belonged in *GQ*. Wanted to press his chin dimple."

A roar of laughter falls past her perfectly pink lips. "Wow, Beau did not tell me that. Ugh, I'm so mad at him now."

"At least we can count on him for doctor-patient confidentiality."

"I need to know everything that happened. Was he blushing? Did he let her touch his chin dimple? Did he tell her he thought she was pretty? Because he says that to me every time he sees her. Even when I was texting him this morning, he mentioned how nice she looked, even with a cut on her forehead."

It's no secret between Larkin and me that Beau has always thought Palmer was pretty. Two years older than her, he's a medical phenom, having accelerated through his program to the point that he was able to have a practice of his own at just twenty-nine. But for all his accomplishments, you'd think he was still a shy teenager. He's always been smitten with Palmer but has never made a move.

Ever.

"There was no blushing, but he was smiling a lot. And I stopped the chin-dimple pushing before it could materialize—you know, trying to save my sister some dignity. But do you know what the best part of it all was?"

"What?" Larkin asks, leaning forward, her eyes sparkling with humor.

"Palmer didn't even recognize him."

"Seriously?" Larkin claps her hands together as her head falls back. "She was that oblivious? I mean, I know he looks completely different from the boy he was in high school, but she didn't recognize him at all?"

I shake my head. "Not a clue. Then again, she was also inebriated off bottles of wine. I have a feeling when she goes in for her checkup this morning, she's going to have a rude awakening."

"Oh man," Larkin laughs. "To be a fly on the wall . . ."

Chapter Nine

PALMER

"Mom!" I scream from my bed, barely able to lift my arm from the weight of the horrendous teal cast encasing it. "Mom! Something's going on. Mom!"

My head pounds, my forehead stings, and my mouth feels like cotton. Something terrible has happened and I need answers, now.

The hallway creaks, announcing my mom's approach, and before I can take my next breath, she's busting through the door, hairbrush in hand, ready to swat at any predator that might have sneaked into my room.

"What's happening?" she asks, out of breath.

I lift my arm. "What the hell is this?"

"Oh." Mom lets out a sigh of relief and presses her hairbrush to her chest. "Sweetie, you took a tumble last night. Don't you remember?"

"Uh, no."

"Oh dear, really?"

"Really." I press my hand to my forehead. "Ugh, and the headache I—what's this?" My fingers graze over something gauzy.

"You fell off the picnic table last night, got a cut on your head, and broke your wrist."

"I broke my wrist?" I ask in complete shock as I inspect my arm. What the actual hell? Was I really so drunk that I don't remember breaking my wrist? I examine the cast again. I guess I was. "Well, at least I had the presence of mind to choose an appealing color."

"You don't remember going to the doctor's at all?"

"No."

"Well, that is concerning. Good thing we have a follow-up appointment in thirty minutes."

"Thirty minutes?" I ask, swinging my legs over the edge of my bed. "Were you going to wake me up and tell me?"

"I thought the extra sleep would help you."

I sniff myself and wince. "Mom, I smell like a dumpster that's been sitting out in the sun for too long." My feet land on the cold hardwood floor, and I head to my dresser with attached vanity, where I get a look at myself for the first time.

"Satan," I gasp loudly, catching my reflection. "Dear Jesus, I look like Satan." My hair is sticking up on all ends, a small amount of blood is dried around my hairline, and yesterday's makeup is smeared across my face.

Who the hell was in charge of putting me to bed last night? "Oh my God, Mom, you let me go to bed with makeup on? Don't you know what that will do to my complexion?"

"Before you start snapping at me about your skin-care routine, I will have you know I attempted to wash your face, but you kept—and I quote—'cannon blasting' me with your cast arm. You know it's very unsettling when your daughter treats her broken wrist like a bazooka and points it at you."

I chuckle. "Sorry, but that's kind of funny."

"Oh yes, your father got a real kick out of it." Mom sniffs the air. "You know, you might be right: I think we need to hose you down before you go for your checkup."

"Ew." I clutch my shirt to my chest. "Don't smell my sleeping air."

"It's hard not to. I've been in here long enough that you've wafted it toward me, and dear, it's unpleasant."

"Oh my God." I stride past her into my en suite bathroom and turn on the shower.

"What do you think you're doing?" Mom asks from the doorway.

"Uh, taking a shower."

"You can't get your cast wet. I'll have to help you."

I look my mom straight in the eyes. "Over my dead body will you wash me naked."

"Was it when you were in Prague?"

"Mom, drop it," I say from the side of my mouth.

Leaning in, she whispers, "I think it's a mother's right to know exactly when her daughter got her nipples pierced."

This is my worst nightmare. This, right here. Sitting next to my mom, freshly showered and scrubbed—thanks to her assistance—getting questioned about my pierced nipples. I knew coming back to Marina Island would be difficult, but I didn't think it was going to start like this.

"It wasn't in Prague."

"Greece?"

"No."

"Australia? Those Aussies have a way of convincing people."

"What? Where did you get that idea from?"

"Their accents. They're so alluring."

"You need help." Desperate for a distraction, I glance around the old converted Victorian home. "When did the doctor's office switch to this? Who feels comfortable getting checked out in an old mansion? Kind of freaky, don't you think?" The living room is filled with seats and couches that are far from modern or stylish. And, according to the sign, the "exam room" looks to be in the dining room, shut off by a pocket door. Call me skeptical, but this doesn't read "doctor's office." And yet, no one seems to care.

"Do you seriously not remember anything from last night?" Mom asks.

"No. Why? Did I ask the same question then?"

Before she can respond, the door opens to another room, and a nurse comes out, holding a tablet.

"Palmer Chance, we can bring you back now."

"Bring me back"? That's a term nurses use when they're weaving with a patient through a hallway, not through a doorway.

As I stand, Mom joins me, and I shoot her a look. "What do you think you're doing?"

"Going back with you."

"Mom, I'm twenty-seven. Pretty sure I can handle a follow-up appointment."

"Is that so?" she asks with a raise of her brow. "What exactly happened to you, again?"

"You know . . . the whole wrist thing and then, uh . . ." I pause and think about it, but nothing comes to mind. "Ugh, fine. Come on."

With a smirk, she places her hand on my back, and we walk into the exam room together. I take a seat on the table while Mom takes a seat in a chair. The room is a light-teal color with dark-stained wood, a combination I don't care for too much. But the curtains are a nice soft touch to the sterile space.

"How are you feeling this morning?" the nurse asks.

Other than trying to scrub the thought of my mom bathing me out of my memory, completely fine.

"Little confused about how this all happened, slightly in pain, partially embarrassed—do you have any medications for that?" I joke.

The nurse smiles. "I'll ask Dr. Beau."

Dr. Beau . . . Beau . . . my stomach drops for a brief second before I shake off that feeling. No, it's just a coincidence. Dr. Beau—he must be new.

The nurse takes my vitals and asks me a few questions, and then she enters some notes into her tablet. "Dr. Beau will be right with you." She closes the pocket door, and I can hear her still tapping away on her tablet on the other side.

Not wanting to talk about my health, or the bomb that was dropped last night, I revert to an easy topic—the party. "So, Cooper ordered a cake?"

"He did. I believe it's some sort of butterscotch thing." Mom folds her hands on her lap as she takes in the exam room. "Those curtains are quite lovely."

"Butterscotch?" I grimace. "Why would he choose that? God, first an email for invites, now a butterscotch cake? What is going on with him?"

"I think he's stressed. We've been asking a lot of him lately. I believe he's overwhelmed. And butterscotch is a nice flavor."

"Well, then he needs to speak up." I brush a piece of lint off my leggings. "If he's overwhelmed, then I can take over. Butterscotch cake . . . honestly. You two are old, but you're not unsophisticated."

Just then the door slides open, and in walks a tall man in a pair of navy-blue chinos, a white polo shirt, and a matching white lab coat. His short brown hair is styled to the side, typical brown boots finish off his casual outfit, and when he looks up with a smile, his hazel eyes meet mine.

Well, *hello*, Dr. Beau.

"Palmer, how are you feeling?"

Oh, look at him coming in with a deep, masculine voice—a voice that oddly feels familiar . . .

Do I know this guy?

Mentally taps chin

"Uh, Palmer, Dr. Beau asked you a question." When I don't answer, as I'm too busy trying to place him, Mom adds, "You'll have to excuse her; she's failing to act normal this morning."

Dr. Beau laughs, and I am not kidding you: the sound of his laugh actually hardens my nipples. Just like that.

Laugh.

Nipples hard.

I'm pretty sure that's the first time this has ever happened to me. I need to text Laramie. Hell, at this point, I need to call him, because I've been on Marina Island for less than twenty-four hours and I've already broken my wrist, cut my head open, and experienced hard nipples from a man's laugh. This is easily best friend material that needs to be dissected and discussed.

Dr. Beau sets down his tablet and approaches. My eyes land on his chest, and I know my eyes aren't deceiving me when I notice the outline of his pecs under his white lab coat.

Oh, Dr. Beau . . . you naughty man, getting your workout on and then wearing shirts that show off the time you spend clanking metal around in the gym. Bravo.

As I'm mentally applauding the man for his obvious workout routine—I bet his abs are better than Cooper's—Dr. Beau reaches up and grips my head, sending a waft of his cologne in my direction.

"Tom Ford," I say, taking a deep sniff. "Oh yeah, that's Tom Ford."

"Oh dear. No, honey, this is Dr. Beau," Mom says, stepping up to me and pressing her hand to my shoulder. "I truly think she has lost her senses. Could she have suffered a concussion last night?"

"Possibly, but she checked out fine last night," Dr. Beau says, his aura doing all kinds of different things for me.

"No, he's wearing Tom Ford, Noir Extreme," I say and, for some reason, take Dr. Beau's arm and sniff the length like it's a line of coke—something I've only seen done in movies but imagine this is what it feels like nonetheless.

Also . . . maybe I have lost it a little. I don't sniff strange men's arms. *Where's the class, Palmer?*

Dr. Beau chuckles. "She's correct on my cologne, so maybe she hasn't lost all of her senses."

"See?" I look at my mom and tap my nose. "Schnoz is still working."

"And your memory?" Mom asks, hand to her hip.

"My memory is fine—I was just drunk. Sometimes when you drink, you forget things." And sometimes the next morning, it takes longer to process things.

"Uh-huh." Mom's eyes light up. "Is that why you've failed to acknowledge Dr. Beau?"

"Failed to what?" I glance over at the doctor. "I said hi."

"Technically you didn't, but that's okay," Dr. Beau says, now leaning against the cabinets in the exam room, arms crossed over his chest.

"Okay . . . fine . . . hi, Dr. Beau. You're wearing Tom Ford Noir Extreme, and it smells nice. Thank you for wrapping up my arm last night, which forced my mom to bathe me this morning. That was not at all humiliating or scarring."

"Scarring for the both of us," Mom whispers and then adds, "I found out her nipples are pierced."

"Jesus Christ, Mom! Things the doctor doesn't need to know."

"It's not like it's a secret—they're practically pressed against your shirt now." As a group, we all look down at my chest, and yup, would you look at that. That's what happens when you can barely dress yourself—the bra is skipped.

Dr. Beau clears his throat. "Well, we should probably get on with the—"

"Can you please check her head, Dr. Beau?" Mom cuts in. "It's very concerning she woke up this morning with no idea why she had a cast on her wrist and couldn't recall her fall. And the fact that she hasn't acknowledged—"

"I said hi," I practically yell. "I said he smells nice—what more do you want?"

Mom gently places her hand on my shoulder. "Sweetie, this is *Dr. Beau.*"

"We established that. And I'm Palmer, and because of you, this stranger knows I have pierced nipples."

Mom shakes her head. "No, Palmer, this is Dr. Beau Novak. Larkin's brother, and the boy who saved your life in the store fire."

My eyes snap to him, and just like that, I instantly recognize that hazel gaze.

But . . . no, is it really him?

He's taller.

Bigger.

His voice is deeper.

His . . . his clothes are sharper.

He's all man. Not the same boy from high school. Not the same boy I hoped and prayed would look my way, and surely not the same boy who almost kissed me the night of the fire.

This can't be him.

Can it?

Dr. Beau clears his throat and offers a shy smile. "It's, uh . . . it's been a while, Palmer."

Oh.

My.

God.

It has . . .

CHAPTER TEN
COOPER

"I'm going to kill her," I mutter as I plow through the rain, dodging the spray from the cars as they drive by. I love living in Seattle, except when I have to walk in the rain.

You would think by now I'd come prepared for the too-frequent rainfall here, but nope. Not prepared at all. Instead, I'm power walking for cover, hands tucked in the pockets of my jeans, my T-shirt clinging to my chest and my boots getting their fair share of water sloshed around them.

As my destination comes in sight, I jog the rest of the way and then whip the pink door open, only to be assaulted by the fresh, buttery smell of cake.

A bell sounds off in the small cake shop, announcing my arrival. From the back, Nora calls out, "Be right with you."

Not wanting to get her shop soaking wet, I wait by the door and let myself drip on her rug. While attempting to do some editing this morning, I got a text from Palmer saying she'd changed the cake order to something more refined. When I pressed to find out what "more refined" meant, she didn't reply, which meant I needed to take matters into my own hands.

Nora steps out of the back of the bakery, wearing a bubblegum-pink apron and wiping her hands on a matching towel. When she spots me, she stops, and her hand slowly goes up to her mouth. Humor flashes through her eyes.

"Don't say a goddamn word," I mutter as I push my hand through my soaked hair.

"I wasn't going to." She holds back a smirk that's tempting the corner of her lips.

"You're lying. I can see it in your eyes."

"It's just . . . you've lived here your whole life. You'd think you could at least carry around a folded-up poncho or something."

Her long black hair swishes back and forth as she moves forward, and I feel an awkward ache in my stomach as I remember the way that hair swished against my bare chest. Does she ever think about that night? From her cool composure whenever she sees me, I'm going to guess no, but hell, I think about it. It's why I always feel like my body is itching when I'm around her—because I want to talk about it, but I have no clue how.

Especially since I was the one who left.

"I wasn't intending on walking in the rain, but my sister didn't give me a choice," I say, burying thoughts of the past beneath my present annoyance.

Nora smiles softly, her deep-brown eyes soothing the tension in my chest just enough to keep me from flying off the deep end.

"Let me guess: this is about the cake and how she switched the flavor order."

"You guessed right."

She stands from her stool and brings it around the counter and sets it down. She pats the top. "Take a seat, Cooper."

"I don't want to get your floors wet."

"That's why mops were created." She taps the stool again. "Take a seat, let's talk."

Sighing, I walk across the black-tiled floor, my boots squeaking with every step, and when I see her start to laugh, I point at her. "Not a goddamn word."

She throws her hands up in the air. "I wouldn't dare comment on your soggy boots or soaking wet jeans—or your flooded hair that keeps sending droplets of water down your face and almost makes it look like you're crying."

Yeah, she's not affected at all, but that little laugh, that chuckle . . . hell, it ignites a burning need inside me.

"Great, glad we're not talking about it," I say, using sarcasm to avoid the real, unspoken reason I'm here. I take a seat and let out a deep breath. "She changed the cake."

"She did."

"To what?" I ask.

"You know, this could have been done over the phone," Nora says, leaning over the counter. Calling me out, just like that. How long will it take before she calls me out about our one-night stand?

And yeah, this conversation could have been done over the phone, but ever since I saw her the other day, I've felt this burning need to see her again. It's been a year, a whole year since I even thought about her, and yet, just like that, seeing that perfect smattering of freckles along her cheeks, those innocent yet daring eyes question me . . . well, before I knew it, I was traipsing through the rain for one more look.

One more interaction.

I shake my head, water dripping on my arms. "No, this needed to be done in person because I need you to know how serious I am."

"Oh, okay, so this is a serious conversation. Glad we established that."

Smart mouthed, quick witted—I've always liked that about her.

"Do you want me to take notes or anything?" she adds. "Is there going to be a quiz at the end of this?"

I push my hand through my hair again, and I catch her gaze landing on my biceps for a few brief seconds before they snap back to my eyes. Ignoring her perusal, I say, "Don't be a smart-ass."

"Are you fragile right now?"

"No," I answer, brow creased.

She smirks. "Then I can be a smart-ass."

Groaning, I cut to the chase. "What cake did she order?"

All too happy with herself, Nora flips through a stack of orders and pulls a single sheet out. Holding it up, she clears her throat. "Your sister ordered, and I quote, a 'rosemary and lavender infused sponge with a blackberry compote generously spread in the middle and covered in a barely iced lavender buttercream. Five tiers, stacked one on top of the other, and decorated simply with a sprig of rosemary on the top.'" She sets the paper down and smiles at me.

"Fuck that. Why do you even have a rosemary lavender cake on the menu?"

"I don't. It was a special request."

"You should have told her no."

Nora gasps. "Tell Palmer Chance no? I would never."

"You did this on purpose." My eyes narrow on her.

"Did what?" she chuckles.

"You enjoy this, don't you? Seeing my life in disarray and taking advantage of it?"

"I hardly see how a cake order could put your life in disarray."

"You clearly don't know my family well enough."

"You fail to realize just how well I *do* know your family, which is why I'm getting so much joy out of these cake orders." The knowing smirk not only irritates me, but it also makes me want to lunge across the counter and wipe it off with my own mouth.

Hell, I can still remember just how soft her lips are. I can feel them imprinted on the side of my neck, on my collarbone, and the way they traveled down my stomach.

Clearing my throat—and the thoughts out of my head—I say, "I'm the cake orderer—"

"Is that an official title? Does the cake orderer get to wear a crown of any sort . . . ?"

"Remember what happened the last time you were a smart-ass to me?" I ask, snapping and addressing the elephant in the room.

She doesn't even blink. "Yes, you gave me a spanking."

Jesus.

"Is that what's going to happen here?" she continues. "If so, I do need to point out there's a row of windows behind you for possible voyeurs, and the kind of spanking you enjoy does go against health-code regulations."

"I didn't spank you," I say, my face heating up.

"Oh, you did. I felt it. I heard the snap."

I might have spanked her.

"We're getting off topic."

"You were the one who brought it up. I was fine not talking about the fact that we've seen each other naked, touched each other's private parts, and then you ignored me for over a year until you needed a cake for your parents' anniversary party."

Why are all the women I know mouthy?

Do I give off some kind of vibe that begs snarky females to bring me to my knees?

Because . . . fuck.

"Am I making you uncomfortable?" Nora asks, laughter in her voice.

"Is it that obvious?" I drag my hand down my face.

"Only a little, but I'm having fun."

"Glad someone is," I mutter and then take a deep breath. "Listen, no lavender rosemary cake. That shit sounds gross. Stick with the butterscotch—I know my parents will like it."

"Hmm, funny, Palmer said the same exact thing, but about her cake."

"Palmer thinks she knows everything about food, but she doesn't. Trust me, the butterscotch is what they'll like. And if she tries to switch it, let me know immediately."

"Okay, and how would I need to inform you? Should I send out a smoke signal? A bird with a note? A barbershop quartet to your office?"

"Text me," I deadpan.

"Oh, so you do have a phone." She taps her chin. "See, I thought since I never heard from you—"

"You're such a fucking smart-ass."

Smiling, she leans on the counter, and for a brief second, because I'm a man, my eyes float down to her cleavage and then back up. Her eyes fire up, and hell, the air grows thick as we both stare each other down. I've done some pretty idiotic things in my lifetime, but not calling Nora after the night we spent together, that's at the top of the list. Which only means one thing—I should ask her out. Make up for past mistakes. I take a deep breath, gathering my courage . . .

The door opens behind me, breaking the palpable attraction between us. Slowly, I tear my eyes off Nora and glance over my shoulder toward the new customer. My spine goes rigid.

"Dealia," I say breathlessly while putting some distance between Nora and me. "What, uh . . . what are you doing here?"

My equally confused ex-wife takes in the scene and nervously grips her take-out bag. "I thought I would bring my best friend lunch." Her bewildered eyes scan me up and down. "What are you doing here, Cooper?"

Ah hell.

Not calling Nora back was a huge mistake, but even bigger than that? Sleeping with my ex-wife's best friend.

Chapter Eleven

FORD

Knock. Knock. Knock.

I ignore the beating my door is taking as I try to differentiate between two fonts. One has a thicker *W*, the other is more streamlined, modern, devoid of any sort of whimsical feeling. Why the hell is this so hard? Fonts shouldn't take up this much headspace, and yet here I am, spending an hour agonizing between the two.

Bang. Bang. Bang.

And that incessant racket isn't helping.

BANG. BANG. BANG.

"Jesus," I mutter before getting up from the two-person table in my room and heading over to the door, where the relentless pounding continues.

Muscles tense, irritation at an all-time high, I fling the door open to see my sister on the other side, a crazed look in her eyes and her clothes in disarray. "Palmer, what the hell are you doing?"

She pushes past me and invites herself into the sitting area, invading my space without a single word. She huffs, she paces, she looks around. "Where's Larkin?"

"Out for a run." I close the door behind me. "Why?"

"We need to talk."

"Can this wait? I'm kind of busy."

She scans the room again. "Busy doing what?" She looks me over, her eyes skimming me from head to toe, taking in what I know is my disheveled hair and rumpled appearance. Her hand clamps over her mouth, some sort of realization taking over the stern look she was wearing when she stormed in here. "Oh my God, did I . . . you know . . . disturb your private time?"

"What? No," I nearly shout. "No. I'm working."

"Are you sure?" She glances over at my bed, the disorderly sheets and rumpled floral comforter. "Because I know you, and I know you like your bed made every day. Which leads me to believe . . ."

"Jesus, Palmer, no. I was not doing . . . *that*. I didn't have time this morning to make my bed. I barely got any sleep last night thanks to you."

She lightens up. "Aw, were you worried about me, Ford?"

"Yes," I answer honestly while heading back to the table to take a seat. I'm worried because I don't think I've ever seen Palmer like that. Like . . . something more than just losing her childhood home sent her into a tailspin. "Do you normally drink like that?"

"No. Yesterday was a special occasion. It's not every day your parents decide to kick you in the crotch with their abhorrent news."

"Is that why you're here? To talk about them selling the house?" I ask, trying to read through the tough facade she seems to wear whenever she's around the family. From the way her eyes don't connect with mine, I just know there's something deeper, something she's not telling me.

She shakes her head. "I'm currently riding the denial train on the whole house thing until it's absolutely necessary to accept what's happening. They don't even have a sign on the front lawn. I'll believe it once I see it—until then, I'm not going to bother letting it take up space in my mind."

"Probably a smart move, given your inability to compartmentalize," I say, my gaze drifting back to the damned fonts.

"I'm not going to lash out at you for that comment." She takes a seat across from me and lifts my chin up, forcing me to look at her. "I need you to focus on me." She snaps her finger in front of my face. "Focus, Ford. Right here, you and me."

I set my paper down and lean back in my chair. "What do you need, Palmer?" I fold my arms over my chest.

She rests her cast on the table and leans forward. "Dr. Beau . . . he's . . . *the* Beau."

Ah, she figured out who Beau was at her appointment this morning.

"Yes, that's correct," I answer casually, even though everybody on the island knows how much Palmer crushed on the guy back in high school. Not sure she knows that I know, but her feelings were evident just from one look through her yearbook.

"Did you know this last night? That he was a doctor here on Marina Island?"

"I did. You know, since his sister is my assistant and all. We do occasionally talk about our siblings."

"How is he a doctor? I didn't even know he wanted to be a doctor. I thought it took forever to get a medical degree. Doesn't he have, like, eleven more years in medical school?" She throws her arms up in the air.

"Fast-tracked. Top of his class. Took him nine years to complete everything, including residency. He studied with Dr. Weazleton as well and then took over the practice and moved the office to where it is now. I'm surprised Mom and Dad never told you."

"No one said anything. And, uh, can we talk about how different he looks? I mean, he's all beefy and handsome with his manly man features." I raise a brow at her. "And his hands were soft and large and . . . God, Ford, you have no idea the kind of embarrassment I put myself through this morning."

"This morning?" I ask, surprised. "Can't be any worse than last night."

Her eyes widen. "What the hell did I do last night? Oh, dear God, I didn't try to lick him, did I?"

I wince. "Is that something you normally do? Lick men?"

She rolls her eyes. "Just once, when I was in Italy. The chef who made me the most amazing pizza of my life smelled like the pepperoni he used, and for some reason I got caught up in the scent and ended up licking his arm. It was not my finest moment, I will admit that, but I found something out about myself. I tend to lick people that I think smell good, and Dr. Beau smelled heavenly. Oh God, did I lick him?"

"There was no licking—"

"Thank God for that—"

"But you did attempt to put your finger in his chin dimple." Her mouth falls open. "Don't worry, I spared you from doing such a thing. From the look on your face, the chin dimple was not mentioned."

"It was not." She groans. "Why, why did this happen to me?"

"I think it was a lethal combination of the denial train you're on and your choice to indulge in a copious amount of wine." When she slouches in her chair, I say, "I think I should also tell you that you told him he looks like he belongs in *GQ*."

She rubs her hand carefully over her forehead, avoiding her butterfly bandage. "Please tell me you're kidding."

"Nope. It happened."

She shakes her head. "This is exactly why I never come back here—the past haunts me."

"How is the past haunting you?" I ask. "If anything, it's more the present that's ruining things."

"You don't get it." Palmer stands from her chair. "There's history with Beau."

"Because he saved you from the fire at Watchful Wanderers?"

"That's not even a blip on my radar when it comes to Beau. Also, when did he become so . . . so . . ."

"*GQ*?" I tease.

"Yes." She flings her good arm to the ceiling. "God, he was all kinds of handsome in that lab coat. I just wanted to tear at it and bury my—"

"Hey, slow down. I don't need the details about exactly what you want to do to Dr. Beau, but I do want to know what you're keeping from me."

She straightens. "What do you mean? I'm not keeping anything from you. Why would you say that?"

"The panic in your voice isn't telling at all." When she doesn't say anything, I sigh. "You said the fire is barely a blip, that there's history with Beau. What history, exactly?"

"Oh, that." She swallows hard and walks over to the window. "Just some other history." She spins on her heel. "Did you know Cooper ordered a butterscotch cake for the party? I rectified that decision."

"You're sidestepping. What are you not telling me?"

She shakes her head. "Nothing. Don't worry about it." She walks toward my door but then pauses and points at the mock-ups near the fireplace. "What are those?"

I glance at them and then back at Palmer. "Nothing you need to worry about."

Her eyes narrow. "I'm worried."

"Don't be. Worry about yourself. Seems like you have a lot going on."

"Are you rebranding the store?"

I stand and walk to my sister. I spin her toward the door and lead her out of my room. "Worry about what you're going to do about Dr. Beau, since it seems like there's *history* there."

She whips her head back to me. "Was there anything else I did? You know, just so I can be aware?"

"I think we pretty much covered it."

"Perfect," she mutters as she leaves. I shut the door behind her and stare at the mock-ups near the fireplace.

I need to clear my mind, and I only know one way to do that.

Chapter Twelve
LARKIN

In the distance, the Marina Island ferry approaches for its two o'clock shuttle. There normally aren't many people coming to Marina Island at this time, nor are they leaving, which makes me wonder why they've always kept the time spot.

I dangle my legs off the old rock wall that lines my favorite running route and overlooks the bay while I let the afternoon sun heat up my already heated and sweating body. The water crashes into the cliff below, sending ocean spray up against my legs but not soaking me.

I miss this. The ocean, the sun glaring off it, the smell of salty air. I love living in Denver, but something about being on Marina Island puts a smile on my face. When Ford asked if I'd be opposed to coming back here for a month, I jumped right on the opportunity.

It's home, and even if my parents are no longer with us, I still feel like they're here. I know that's one of the main reasons Beau came back to Marina Island—to be reminded of our parents, to feel their presence. And the fact that he realized his dream of being the town's general practitioner and converting the old Victorian house on Marina Ave into his practice . . . I know Mom and Dad would be more than proud of him.

The pounding of approaching footsteps pulls me from my thoughts. I turn just in time to see Ford running in my direction. His white Under

Armour shirt is drenched in sweat and clinging to every surface of his chest, revealing his thick pecs, his defined shoulders, and the deep divots of his abs. His strong legs propel him forward, and I have to look away to gain my bearings before he arrives.

He's your boss, Larkin.

Your BOSS.

It doesn't matter that he looks like the modern-day version of Prince Eric but with silver eyes that pierce right through your soul every time you look at him.

It doesn't matter that he's incredibly smart, ambitious, and driven, unlike anyone you have ever met.

And it certainly doesn't matter that he is one of the nicest, most considerate men you have ever met.

He is your boss and that's it. The man who signs your paychecks. The man who gave you a chance at working for him when you had no experience, just a story about how Watchful Wanderers was the last remaining connection you had to your deceased father.

"Hey," Ford says, slowing his jog until he's only a few feet away. "I was wondering if I'd find you out here, since you never returned to the inn."

"Sorry. I'll make up some work later tonight. I was just enjoying a little bit of time with the waves."

He nods, and his understanding shines through. "No need to make up any time. I asked you to come to Marina Island, so take all the time you need. I know what it means to you to be here."

See . . . considerate.

Good looking.

Sweet.

Charming.

It's honestly quite devastating.

And he gets me.

We lost Mom when I was in middle school. Dad was our rock. He made sure we were going to be okay. Beau and I both clung to him for support. And even with Dad's busy schedule as a plumber on the island, he always made time for us. Every weekend we were doing something outdoors, and even if the weather was bad, Dad would make the most of it. Watchful Wanderers was one of his favorite places to go, even if we didn't even buy anything but just looked. We would look together. And when he passed, I felt lost. I was jumping around from job to job, never really doing anything too important or interesting. And that's when Beau heard Ford was looking for an assistant. I'd never applied for something—in person—so fast. I walked into Ford's office, claiming we had an appointment, and laid it all on the line. I told him he needed me, and I needed him. I left convinced he thought I was crazy, but the next day he called me and told me I got the job, on a trial basis, given my lack of experience.

Thankfully, that trial basis turned into the best thing that's ever happened to me.

A job that keeps me close to my dad, keeps me intrigued, and keeps me close to . . . well, Ford.

"Thank you. I was just going to get up and jog back to the bed-and-breakfast."

"You're going to ditch me like that, just as I arrive? Brutal, Larkin." He takes a seat on the wall with me. "Can't you hang out with your boss a little bit more?"

I chuckle. "It will be a hardship, but I guess so."

He dangles his feet over the edge like me, but his scrape the ground. "So, Palmer stopped by," he says in a conspiratorial tone.

"Oh, I like where this is heading."

Ford turns toward me and props one of his legs up on the wall. He's always been one to make eye contact—it's one of the things that I think makes him a great boss, not just with me, but with everyone who works for him. He doesn't try to listen to you while he works on his computer. Instead, he gives you his undivided attention.

"You will. She came barreling into my room, realization and humiliation written all over her face. She asked me if I knew that Dr. Beau was *the* Beau."

I chuckle. "That's too funny. I mean, he does look older, but I don't think he looks that different."

"You see him often—it's been a while for Palmer."

"True."

"But she said something that made me want to talk with you."

"Oh? Are you here to gossip, Ford Chance?"

He chuckles and nods. "I am. Not very boss-like of me, but when it comes to my siblings, they're so closed off that I'm always prying for information."

"I'm not judging, just delighting in you loosening the tie every once in a while."

He holds his arms out, and I keep my eyes straight ahead, refusing to take in his rock-hard biceps or the way his shirt pulls across his sculpted chest. "No tie in sight—I'm completely loose."

I laugh. "Okay, let's not get crazy. I don't think I've ever seen you truly let loose."

"Not sure I know how to." He shrugs. "So, she said there was history between her and Beau."

"You mean the whole fire thing?"

"That's what I asked, but she said that was barely a blip in their history. I know Palmer had a crush on him back in high school, and she never admitted it, but I wasn't sure if . . . you know, anything happened between them. Has Beau said anything to you?"

"No!" I grab my phone. "He's never mentioned anything."

"What are you doing?"

"Texting him. I want to know what kind of history she's talking about." I reach out and touch Ford's hand as a thought comes to mind.

"Oh my God, what if they were intimate? Urgh, I would be so mad if he never told me."

Ford's eyes land on my hand, and I realize I'm touching my boss in a way I probably shouldn't be touching my boss. I quickly snatch my hand away and pull up my text thread with Beau, ignoring the obvious loss of my mind.

"What are you asking him?" Ford says, completely ignoring my slip as well.

"When he's at the office, I have to be straight to the point because he usually texts me back in between patients." I type out the message and hit send. "I just asked if he ever got intimate with Palmer."

"Wow." He chuckles. "You're right, you do get straight to the point."

My phone beeps in my hand, and I read the text out loud. "'Where is this coming from . . . is Ford asking you to ask me?'" I laugh as Ford frowns. "Caught red handed."

"Hey, you want to know too."

"I do, desperately. Don't worry, I'll play it cool." As I type back, I read my text out loud. "'No, he would never do that. But he did say that Palmer mentioned there was history. I was just curious.'"

"Perfect," Ford says with a smile. "Do you think he'd tell you?"

"Not sure." My phone dings, and we both look at each other with giddy expressions before I open the text and read it out loud. "'Palmer mentioned history, huh? Interesting.'"

"He's being coy." Ford leans in closer, and the feel of him entering my personal space sends a wave of goose bumps down my leg.

"He is, but not for long." I type, trying not to show how shaky my hands feel from his proximity. "'Sooo . . . is that a yes? Were you intimate?'"

"Man, you are brutal," Ford says as he stretches his arms behind him. I keep my eyes on my phone.

"Being the older sister, it's my responsibility to make sure I keep my brother in line. You are aware of the older sibling responsibilities?"

"Far too familiar. But I think your relationship with your brother is better than what I have with my siblings."

"You really think your relationship with your siblings is that bad?" I ask.

He looks out toward the ocean. "We used to be close. Really close. There are times I remember laughing so hard with them that we'd all be on the floor, clutching our stomachs. And we'd get away with mischief around the house, like taking Dad's stash of gummy bears and trying to toss them in each other's mouths. The one who missed the most had to replace the gummies we ate. Just . . . small things, you know? And now, well, it could be better. I know it could be way better, but I'm not sure what to do. We all seem to be stuck in our own lives. Beau and you make the time to hang out."

"We also only have each other," I answer as my phone dings.

Ford nods toward my phone. "What does he say?"

Opening the text, I read it out loud. "'The history between me and Palmer is going to stay that way—between us. Sorry, sis. Not dishing any info on this topic.'" I glance up at Ford. "Damn it. It's got to be good if they're both not saying anything to us."

"Think it would be wrong to get Palmer drunk again?"

I laugh. "I mean, I think that needs to be our last resort."

Ford stands from the wall. "Want to jog back with me?"

"Jog back . . . or race back?"

His eyes sparkle. "You know you can't handle this speed."

"I think you might be surprised. Last one to the bed-and-breakfast has to buy dinner."

"You know I'm buying dinner on the business, right?"

"Yeah, because you're going to lose."

And then I take off, pushing up the hill, letting my legs propel me forward. When I glance over my shoulder to see where Ford is, I catch him closely behind, his eyes attached to my ass in my short spandex shorts. I quickly look forward, a blush staining my cheeks.

TO: Ford Chance, Cooper Chance
FROM: Palmer Chance
SUBJECT: The Party

What has been done for the party? Obviously the cake and invitations have been fixed, but what other things can we check off the list? We have less than a month and we really need to make this party amazing. Mom was telling me how excited she is about it . . . and grateful. It needs to be good.

TO: Ford Chance, Palmer Chance
FROM: Cooper Chance
SUBJECT: Everything is taken care of

TO: Ford Chance, Cooper Chance
FROM: Palmer Chance
SUBJECT: Re: Everything is taken care of

Cooper!! Stop doing that. Seriously, you're just being a pain in the ass.

And when you say everything is taken care of, what exactly is everything? Because I had to go change the cake. Your choice of butterscotch and fudge?

Might as well hire a clown and balloon artist for entertainment.

Also . . . what did you book for entertainment? In your invitation, you said there would be "fun." So, what's your version of fun?

TO: Ford Chance, Palmer Chance
FROM: Cooper Chance
SUBJECT: Re: Everything is taken care of

Funny you mentioned it, I did hire a balloon artist.

And don't worry, your buckets of wine will be there. I have a crane dropping in a bathtub of fermented grapes just for you.

Oh and P.S. I went back to Cake It Bakery and changed the cake again.

TO: Ford Chance, Cooper Chance
FROM: Palmer Chance
SUBJECT: Re: Everything is taken care of

I don't see how you find this so funny. Don't you care about Mom and Dad at all?

We need to make this spectacular. We need to blow their socks off. We need to show them how much we love them.

TO: Ford Chance, Palmer Chance
FROM: Cooper Chance
SUBJECT: Re: Everything is taken care of

I think you're failing to realize something, Palmer. I show them how much I love them every goddamn day by showing up at their house for dinner because they want to see one of their kids. I take care of them and the house. I help them with their projects even if they seem simple and mundane. I show them I love them through being present, not through some party. Check yourself before you start shooting off what needs to be done.

TO: Cooper Chance, Palmer Chance
FROM: Ford Chance
SUBJECT: Re: Everything is taken care of

I think what Palmer is trying to not so eloquently say is that we should go over the party plans and make sure everything is locked in. We appreciate all the work you've put into the party, Cooper, but now that we are here, present, ready to help, we want to make sure we've got everything covered.

The Reunion

I propose we meet up at Mom and Dad's this weekend, surprise them with some brunch and then when they go on their Sunday hike, we finalize all the details of the party.

Does that work for everyone?

And remember, we are in this together. We might have different opinions, but we have one thing in common, our love for Mom and Dad. Let's remember that moving forward into this meeting.

CHAPTER THIRTEEN
PALMER

"What are you doing?" Laramie asks over the phone. "Do I hear . . . nature?"

"I'm walking."

"Walking where? To get coffee?"

"No, just walking."

"For the hell of it? Girl, I know you bonked your head a couple days ago, but are you sure nothing more serious happened? You know I'm all about fitness, but when have you ever just gone for a walk?"

"When I came back to Marina Island." I let out a harsh breath as I stroll along the stone wall that lines the harbor. "I had to get out of the house. Mom keeps wanting to teach me to knit, and Dad is blaring a podcast about how things are made. And then there's the constant nagging about cleaning out my room and sifting through what I want to keep and what I want to get rid of. I needed a second to breathe, so I told them I was going to go around and take some pictures of the island."

"Have you?"

"No, I called you instead."

"A commendable choice, but since you're already there, why don't you follow through on your farce? You know, really create a checklist of must-see places in the Pacific Northwest? Might not hurt."

"You mean actually come up with some sort of PNW extravaganza?"

"Why not? Who knows, maybe it'll lead you to something more. What else are you going to do while you wait around for the next best thing?"

Up ahead, I spot the bed-and-breakfast. Its quaint white picket fence bordering the sidewalk is filled with colorful flower beds, so it's hard to miss. Ford was smart staying there. I wonder what he's up to. Since I have nothing better to do, might as well go bother my older brother.

"Maybe you're right," I say. "I think I'm going to need some sort of outlet. My family is already starting to drive me nuts, and unless I figure out a way to get a paycheck in the bank, I'm here for a while."

"You still haven't told them?"

"Oh hell no. And I won't be telling them about my lack of job, money, or roof over my head."

"The trifecta of accomplishment. But seriously, your family is loaded—don't you have some sort of trust fund you can lean on?"

"No," I say as my mind immediately goes to the night of the fire and how that changed everything.

"Then why not just ask them for help?"

"Because I can't."

"Because of your pride?" Laramie asks, sounding annoyed.

"No, because . . . because I don't deserve their help," I say, just as my eyes connect with the Victorian house up ahead, reminding me of the man who works there.

So much happened.

So much I don't talk about . . . with anyone.

"How do you not deserve your family's help? That's what family is for, Palmer."

"Yeah, I know, but this is different." A figure moves past one of the Victorian house's windows, and just from the silhouette, I know it's Beau. "I didn't tell you . . . I, uh . . . I ran into Beau."

91

"Beau? Who's Beau—oh wait . . . *the* Beau."

I nod, even though he can't see me. "Yup, but he's Dr. Beau now."

"Oh, now that has a nice ring to it. Let me guess, given your luck, he has a 'call me daddy' vibe, doesn't he?"

"I'm pretty sure I almost called him that when he was examining my head and I got lost in the dignified smell of his cologne. Tom Ford."

"Ohhh, devastating to one's burning loins."

"Yeah, and those loins were ignited and roaring." I take a deep breath. "He's all grown up, Laramie, even more handsome than before. And because I'm completely obtuse, I didn't recognize him. Granted, I was hungover and still trying to comprehend what was happening, but he looks different. Incredibly masculine, filled out in all the right spots. But thanks to my love of wine, I'm pretty sure he still thinks I'm an idiot."

"Well, I mean, it's not every day he bandages someone up for cracking their head open with a wine bottle. You never know, maybe he found it charming."

"Trust me, he didn't. And it didn't help that my mom told him my nipples are pierced."

"How did your mom find *that* out?"

I sigh. "She bathed me the morning after the incident."

"Jesus . . . Mary . . . and Madonna, why on earth would you let your mother do such a thing?" Laramie's voice is full of disgust.

"Still trying to figure that out." I catch Larkin approaching with a take-out bag, and she gives me a wave when she spots me. "Hey, I need to go."

"You're going to leave me with the information that your mom bathed you?"

"Yes. Enjoy."

I hang up and catch up to Larkin.

"Hey," she says cheerfully with a smile that could make anyone's day brighter. How Ford hasn't fallen in love with this girl, I will never know.

She's the total package. Stunning beauty, incredible smarts, and a heart of gold. Whenever I've hung out with her, I've always wondered why she's not doing more, why she's sticking around as Ford's assistant when she has so much more potential.

"How are you feeling?" Larkin asks.

"Better," I answer, leaving out the part where I'm completely humiliated from outwardly lusting after her brother. "Are you guys having lunch?" Larkin nods. "Think I can crash and hang out for a bit? I won't eat anything."

"Don't be silly, we have plenty of food to go around."

I hold my stomach. "Really not that hungry—just looking for some company that isn't an old married couple fighting over the temperature of the house."

She chuckles. "Can't make any promises about temperature arguments. Your brother likes to freeze me out, but we can offer you some company."

"That's all I'm looking for."

Together, we head into the bed-and-breakfast and straight up the stairs to the top floor, where Ford has set up shop. "I'm going to apologize about the mess in advance. The rebranding has forced us to lay everything out across the bedroom."

Huh, so Ford *is* rebranding. Just like I suspected. Dad mentioned something offhand the other day, and I clocked those mock-ups the last time I was here, but I didn't think he'd rebrand without consulting the whole family. After all, when it comes to big decisions about the business, Ford always asks us, even though we don't work for the company.

"I'm sure it's not half as bad as Cooper's bedroom growing up," I say, hiding my surprise. "You basically needed a boat to enter his room so you didn't drown in the crap on his floor."

"And let me guess, Ford was the tidy one? Despite the mess we have upstairs."

"You guessed right. He had a spot for every single thing in his room, and if it was out of place, he would know about it."

"Did he use a ruler?"

I chuckle. "I think maybe a few times, but it was more to be obnoxious than anything."

When we reach the room, Larkin walks right in without knocking. I love her comfort level with my brother.

I remember the first time I met Larkin, back when I was fresh from graduating college and visiting Ford in Denver. I thought she looked familiar, but I couldn't place her. Then Ford told me about her story, and it all clicked. I'd seen her plenty of times around the island . . . with Beau. Yeah, we were never close with their family, though I do remember seeing her in the store with her dad—but my eyes were more focused on Beau whenever they were around. Ford told me how she'd come to him, practically begging for a chance to work for Watchful Wanderers, even if it was to clean the toilets. Anything to keep that connection with her father. I thought it was endearing, and then I spent some time with her and realized what a ball of sunshine she is. Seeing her interact with my brother, how she cares for him, pushes him, makes him consider a new way of approaching the business—it's obvious how in sync they are. I just wish for his sake that he'd realize their partnership could be so much more.

"Look who I found," Larkin announces while setting the bag of food on a small bistro table.

Sitting at an old mahogany writing desk, Ford looks up. When he sees the guest is me, he gives me a strange look before standing and shuffling some papers together, which he rests facedown on the desk.

"Palmer, what, uh . . . what are you doing here?"

I take in the poster boards scattered over the sitting area of Ford's suite. I think they've multiplied since I was last here. Logos in different colors are printed across them—Watchful Wanderers logos, but modernized. Instead of the brown and green logo I'm so used to seeing, these logos are orange and blue and neon green. Instead of a homey, family feel that gives you comfort, they look like a bunch of corporate logos that don't read expensive—just impersonal.

"I thought I'd stop by." I scan the room again, my eyes falling on one logo in particular, bright orange with a fox as the mascot. What on earth is that? Reminds me of some sort of wannabe tractor company. "What's going on in here? Looks like rebranding to me, Ford."

Larkin looks between us. "Oh, I'm sorry, was I not supposed to—?"

"You said something to her?" Ford asks Larkin.

"I thought . . . I'm sorry. I didn't realize." Larkin stumbles over her words, and I feel a pang of sympathy for her.

Ford looks off to the side. "Could you go get us some drinks so I can talk to my sister?" His tone is clipped.

"Oh yeah, sure thing," Larkin says, her head down. I don't think I've ever seen Ford talk to her like that, and it shows from her reaction that he hasn't. Larkin scurries out of the room, shutting the door behind her without another word.

"You didn't have to send her out like that!"

"She's fine." But then his eyes soften as they travel toward the door, almost as if he's trying to keep this angry exterior, but there seems to be some longing there. Guilt.

"Is she?" I ask. "Because it looks like you just embarrassed her."

His eyes pull away from the door, and he clears his throat. "Listen, Palmer, don't tell me how to handle my employees. I have enough going on—I don't need that from you too."

"'Too'? What do you mean 'too'? What else have I done?"

He lets out an irritated sigh. "The bickering with Cooper over emails. Do you really think that's something I want to read, given how busy I am during the day? I don't want to be the peacemaker between you two all the time."

"You're not the peacemaker all the time."

He lets out a dry laugh. "Okay."

"Uh, excuse me, but what's with the attitude? I thought I would come here and talk to my loving older brother . . . could you perhaps direct me to where he is?" I glance around the room.

"Palmer, I don't have time for this. I'm under a lot of stress—"

"With rebranding the store?"

He grips the back of his chair and stares down at the wooden seat. "Yes, with rebranding the store."

"Why didn't you say anything? This is a huge deal, Ford, the kind of thing you include everyone on. Does Dad know?"

"Yes, of course Dad knows."

"So why didn't you say anything to me or Cooper?"

"Cooper knows as well."

"What?" I say. Once again, I've been left out of the family business. It's like high school all over again.

When I was in high school, I told my parents I wanted to help with the store in any way possible. Contrary to what my brothers probably think—thanks to my teenage groaning—I actually loved everything about the store. It always felt like home to me. But at that point Ford was already in charge and starting the franchising process. Mom and Dad told me to talk with him. They were sure he would give me something good to do, at least an internship.

He gave me nothing.

He told me that the store wasn't my passion and to not rely on something safe, to reach for something I actually wanted.

But that's what I thought I wanted. Despite not loving nature as much as Cooper always did, I still loved everything about the store—the memories, the smell, unpacking new products. Spending weekends in the back office with my dad, listening to him teach Ford everything he needed to know about business and management. I listened, I learned, and out of spite, I took that information and ran with it. I ran away to other countries, searching for that happy.

And the sad thing is I never found it.

"What do you mean Cooper knows?" I repeat, heart pounding.

"He hangs with Mom and Dad—Dad told him."

"That's great," I say. "So, everyone knew but me? Were you going to tell me?"

"Frankly, no," Ford says. "This is a big decision, and I don't need too many cooks in the kitchen."

I glance around at the mock-ups, taking them in once more as a fresh wave of hurt washes over me. "Well, looks like you need at least one cook in the kitchen, because these are all trash."

Ford blinks, stunned. "They're not trash."

"Really, Ford?" I motion to the fox one. "How does that represent our family, or the company Mom and Dad built from scratch? These are impersonal and totally miss the mark. You might not value my opinion, but you should consult with someone close to the company, because you're going to spend a hell of a lot of money on something that honestly . . . is going to fail and make the family look like a bunch of fools for trying to be something we're not."

Anger searing through me, I spin on my heel and head out the door, leaving him in shocked silence. On the stairs, I bypass Larkin without saying a word. I hear her say something, but I completely ignore her and walk right out of the inn and onto the sidewalk. I stand there, still fuming and unsure where to go.

Everyone knew about the rebranding but me. If that doesn't speak volumes about what happened in the past, I don't know what does.

Tears well up in my eyes as I try to catch my breath.

God, I've never felt so . . . so . . . lost.

What the hell am I even doing here?

I thought this place would help save me, but all it's done is tear me down, one day at a time.

With my good hand, I grip my forehead and take a deep breath. That did not go as planned. I thought seeing Ford was going to put me in a better mood, but all I've managed to accomplish is to get into another fight with one of my brothers. Am I really so unhappy that I try to make everyone around me miserable too?

That would be a depressing realization.

I contemplate going back up there and apologizing, but for what, exactly? I have the right to be upset. Ford has been cutting me out of the family business for as long as I can remember. And this is just another example.

I never fought him on it because . . . well, because of everything that happened, but then I came to him last year about the company's social media presence, the lackluster Instagram account and how to beef it up, make it more appealing and useful to attract customers. He pushed me aside.

Today was no different.

Holding back my tears, I turn to the right and run smack into a strong, tall statue.

"Hey there, you okay?"

Oh God, I know that voice all too well now.

Slowly my eyes travel up until they meet a pair of hazel ones.

Dr. Beau. Why, oh why does he have to be here, right now, while I tear up on the sidewalk?

"Fine," I say, tilting my head down. "I, uh, was just heading to, uh, lunch."

He tucks his index finger under my chin and lifts my eyes so I'm looking at him. "Going to lunch with tears in your eyes. Doesn't seem like everything is fine." He nods toward Pickles and Cheese, the local sandwich shop that serves the best roast beef sandwich I've ever eaten. "Join me."

CHAPTER FOURTEEN

DR. BEAU

Her eyes skirt over to the shop, and I can practically see her mind whirling, silently debating what to do. I have a feeling she's going to say no, and I wouldn't blame her if she did. I'm probably the last person she wants to have lunch with, given our few previous interactions, but seeing her upset on the sidewalk, looking distraught and then catching the tears in her eyes . . . yeah, I couldn't just leave her by herself.

"I'm looking for someone to split a roast beef sandwich with me," I say, knowing she probably needs the encouragement. "Come on, we can sit outside, and you don't even have to talk."

"Your expectations for a lunch partner are low," her shaky voice jokes.

"Better than eating with the skeleton in the office I normally eat with."

"Barely a step up if you compare the two." With a deep breath, she nods. "Okay, I'll join you for lunch."

"Perfect." Together, we walk across the street and step up to the outdoor counter. I order a large roast beef sandwich to split, extra horse-radish sauce, a fruit cup, and two waters. I pay despite Palmer putting up a fight, and then we both take a seat outside under a red and white umbrella. We're off in the corner to grant us some privacy, which seems like what Palmer needs right now.

Instead of talking, I fold my hands together, lean back in my chair, and wait for our sandwich to be delivered—despite all the questions I'd like to ask her, starting with, *How long are you here for?* Followed up by, *Would you like to go on a date with me?*

But as promised, I don't talk. We sit in silence. Awkward, uncomfortable, agonizing silence. What I wouldn't give to be in her brain right now, to hear her thoughts.

Does she regret all the things she said to me?

Did she really not remember who I was?

Does she ever think about me?

Yeah, that last one is wishful thinking.

But hell, I've never stopped thinking about her.

Our sandwich is dropped off, along with another basket. I take one half of the sandwich and place it in the basket with some fruit and a fork and hand it over to her.

She shoots me a shy glance. "Thank you."

"My pleasure," I say before picking up my sandwich and taking a massive bite. I feel her eyes on me, so when I make eye contact with her, I say, "What?" my mouth full of roast beef.

She chuckles quietly. "Take a big enough bite?"

I chew. Swallow. "It's better that I take big bites to silence myself."

"Oh." She smirks, and I'm relieved to see the tears that were present on the sidewalk are gone, which means my work here is done. "Well, you don't have to be quiet if you don't want to."

"Just respecting your privacy. Seemed like you were upset back there. I won't pry."

With her good hand, she picks up the sandwich and struggles to keep it together. Roast beef falls out the side, the bread starts to slide up, and there's no chance she's getting that in her mouth in one piece.

She sets it down with a frustrated groan. "How long do I have to keep this cast on?"

"Up to eight weeks."

"Eight weeks?" she says, her voice rising. "Seriously?"

"Which is why you need to come up with a better story than falling off a picnic table, because after eight weeks of having a cast on your arm, you're going to want to impress people."

She spears a piece of fruit with her fork. "You don't think falling off a picnic table while clutching a bottle of wine is going to impress people?"

I shake my head in humor. "I'm not sure it would speak to your brand of jet-setting around the world and eating the finer things."

"Especially since it was the seven-dollar wine from the Liquor General," she whispers.

A hearty laugh pops out of me. "Yeah, that might set you back a few followers."

"You're probably right." She attempts to pick up her sandwich, but all the meat falls out again and she grows even more frustrated. Not sure she wants my help, I step in anyway and pick up the sandwich for her, nodding for her to take a bite. "Oh God, you don't have to feed me," she says in horror.

"Just take a bite. Once it's smaller, you can probably grip it yourself."

"This is humiliating," she mutters as she leans in and takes a bite.

"More humiliating than asking to press my chin dimple?" I raise a challenging brow.

She groans. "I forgot about that."

"I didn't." I wiggle my eyebrows, and she chuckles. I jut my chin out in her direction. "It's yours to poke if you want to."

"I would rather fall off the picnic table again than follow through on that drunken request."

I gasp in feigned shock. "Why, Palmer Chance, is my chin dimple not appealing to you anymore? Does this mean you're going to revoke my *GQ* card?"

She tries to uncap her water but struggles, so I reach out and do it for her. "Thank you," she says quietly before she adds, "You just love addressing the elephant in the room, don't you?"

"Might as well, right?" I nudge her foot under the table. "It's not that big of a deal, you know."

"Easy to say when you're not the one embarrassing yourself."

"Isn't that what being a human is all about, though?" I ask. "Moments of embarrassment mixed in with joy and sorrow? We have emotions for a reason, and what's life without experiencing them all, even if it means hitting on your doctor?"

I lift her sandwich, and she takes another bite.

"Plus, you're never going to have any good stories to tell in your old age if you go through life like a stone wall, feeling nothing. Some of my best stories were born from embarrassing moments, and those stories brighten people's days."

She swallows. "Okay, so brighten my day with one."

"I thought me personally feeding you was brightening your day already, but I see you're demanding." She smiles, and I love that I can turn her day around. I love that we can have this interaction without the past drowning us. "Something to brighten your day? Hmm . . ." Just the thing comes to mind. "Well, as you know, I went to medical school."

"What?" She gasps. "No, I had no idea."

"Sarcasm—you're speaking my love language." I offer her another bite, and she takes it. "But yes, I went to medical school, and because I'm so amazing, I was in an accelerated program. But because the work-load was not only ambitious but exhausting, I found myself worn down most of the time. I survived on a healthy diet of Red Bull and Snickers."

"Seriously?"

I nod. "Oh yeah, gained a solid twenty-five pounds while going through school. You wouldn't have recognized me."

"Kind of like I didn't recognize you now?"

"Worse. But that's beside the point. I was going through my clinicals after a long night of studying, and I'd had barely any nutrients, because—"

"Snickers and Red Bull."

I point at her. "Precisely. And before I know it, I have to administer a steroid shot to a lady who has fifth disease."

"What's that?"

"A children's disease. Kids just get a rash on their cheeks and arms, sometimes body, but adults have much worse side effects. This lady, for instance, just looked like she got off the surface of the sun. Her body was bright red, and she could barely use her hands. Well, I had to give her a steroid shot in the glute . . . which happened to be the first time I ever stuck someone in the butt."

Her lips turn up. "Please tell me you fainted."

"Oh, I fainted, and I fainted hard. I was so scared about breaking the skin that I got myself worked up to the point that the room started to spin, and instead of asking for assistance, I powered through. I wound up sticking her, but before I could actually administer the drug, I face-planted right into her crack and bounced off and onto the floor."

Palmer lets out a roar of laughter as she clutches her chest. "No, you did not face-plant into her butt."

"Afraid so. We went cheek to cheek, if you know what I mean."

"Stop." She laughs some more. "Oh my God. Was the needle just hanging out of her?"

"Oh yeah. From what I heard, she had to waddle to the door and call for help. It took over a year to recover my dignity among my peers."

Her face practically glows with joy as she spears a grape. "You're right, other people's embarrassment does brighten one's day. Thank you."

"Anytime, Palmer." I wink, savoring the moment, basking in the fact that I made Palmer Chance smile.

CHAPTER FIFTEEN

COOPER

"You're quiet tonight," Dad says from his camping chair.

"Not much to say," I answer, adjusting our telescope.

Once a month, Dad and I drive up to Marina Point with our telescope and spend the evening finding planets and taking pictures of them. The tradition started a few years ago, when Dad heard a couple in the store talk about how they were buying some camping gear for their trip up to Canada, where they were spending four nights looking at all the planets with a group of friends. Dad called me up that night and told me he needed me at the house ASAP.

I rushed over, nervous there was something wrong, only to find Dad hovering over the computer asking me what kind of telescope I thought would give us the best view of Saturn. After deciphering where the hell this new endeavor had come from, I sort of took up the new hobby with Dad.

Now Mom packs us a dinner and sends us on our way.

"When someone doesn't have much to say, that usually means they have a lot to say. Does it have to do with those classes you've been taking?"

I finish adjusting the telescope and then take a seat in my camping chair next to Dad. I open up our cooler and hand him a beer. I crack open our favorite microbrew, from a place in Seattle, and take a sip.

"No, the classes have been fine—better than fine, actually. But it's not like they've helped."

"What do you mean?" Dad struggles to open his can, so I gently take it out of his hand, open it, and hand it back. He mutters a soft "Thank you" before I answer him.

"Ford didn't even let me tell him about my ideas."

Dad waves his hand as if it's nothing. "You have to give him a second to think. You know he's not friendly to anything new. I'm sure he'll come through." Dad pokes me. "But that doesn't seem to be it. What else is bothering you?"

"A bunch of shit is bothering me."

"Okay, let's start with one and go from there."

Looks like the planets are going to be put on hold for now.

"I know we were all raised the same and were given the same opportunities in life, but whenever I'm around Palmer and Ford, I just feel like I don't belong."

"What do you mean?" he asks. "You're part of this family—of course you belong."

"I know. I know, but I feel like we're cut from a different cloth. And I don't mean to drag you through this, because you don't need to know the fine details, but a prime example is the party. They take my choices as if I don't care about you and Mom, where that's not the case at all. I obviously care, and I'm grateful for the both of you, more than you'll probably ever know, but I'm just not into the fancy shit like they are. And it makes me look like an ass."

"They are particular to the fancy, aren't they?"

"They are." I take a sip of my beer. Dad nurses his—he's only allowed one. "We're meeting tomorrow to go over the party, and I know my opinion won't be valued, even though I'm the one who's with you two the most."

"Then say that."

I shake my head. "It won't matter."

Dad studies me from the side. "Is that what's really bothering you? Some simple fighting with your siblings?"

I roll my teeth over my bottom lip. "No."

"Didn't think so." Dad reaches for the cookies Mom packed, sticking with our tradition of eating dessert first. He hands me one. "Go on, speak up. What's going on?"

I take a bite of the butterscotch cookie and then slouch in my chair. "So, I saw Nora this week."

"Ahhh, for the cake, right?"

I nod. "Yeah, and seeing her, I don't know . . . it made me think."

A goofy grin spreads across Dad's face as he nudges me in the shoulder. "Made you think what it would be like to ask her out, huh?"

"Yeah. I mean, the last time we hung out—"

"'Hung out,' okay. Is that what the kids are calling it?" Dad lets out a hearty laugh.

Ignoring him, I continue. "We had a really good time, but then I remembered who she is, whose friend she is. So, I never called her for a second date. Seeing her again, talking to her . . . hell, Dad, it was easy. It was fun. The conversation between us felt flawless. I don't think I've ever had that kind of banter with anyone else. And she's funny, doesn't take shit."

"Your mom and I always thought she'd be perfect for you."

"Yeah . . . I know," I say, thinking back to that night, how they're the ones who forced me to go talk to her at the bar . . . when they were my "wingmen." I shake my head at the memory. "And when I was there the other day, I couldn't stop myself from indulging in being around her. I was seriously thinking about asking her out on a date when Dealia walked into the bakery."

Dad cringes. "Hell, did she really?"

"Yeah, and she looked horrified to catch me talking to Nora. Before she could say anything other than 'What are you doing here,' I fucking bolted."

"Smooth." Dad chuckles. "So, basically, you're sour about the fact that you like a girl, but you don't think you can ask her out because she happened to be the maid of honor at your wedding?"

I take a long pull from my beer. "That about sums it up."

"I see." Dad is silent for a few seconds. "I think you should still ask her out."

"What?" I ask, shocked. "Dad, she's—"

"I know who she is, and guess what? Life is short. You don't have much time on this earth, so why waste it pushing away the things you want? Why do you think I started Watchful Wanderers? Because it was a dream of mine. Almost every single person in my life told me it was a stupid idea because of the competition already in Seattle. But I didn't listen to them. I had a dream, and I wanted to make it happen."

"Not to be a dick, but asking a girl out isn't my dream. It's nothing like starting a store."

He sips his beer. "Asking Nora out might not be your dream, but she's a stepping-stone to finding what you want in life. Start with Nora and work your way toward more." He glances in my direction. "You and I both know you're not happy. It's about time you stop dreaming and start creating. Don't wait for things to happen for you—make them happen, Cooper, because I guarantee before you know it, you're going to be an old fart like myself, not giving a damn about his socks and wondering how life slipped by so quickly."

I take a bite of my cookie and give it some thought. "Do you think I'm wasting my life away?"

Without skipping a beat, Dad nods. "Yes."

◆ ◆ ◆

I lie across my sofa, telling myself to relax.

Everything is going to be okay.

Hell, I went through an intense session today with my therapist, who I've been seeing for about a year now. We spoke about the conversation I had with my dad while stargazing and how his advice was solid. I need to take it. I also need to stop worrying about what others might think and take charge of my life.

Step up and make things happen.

If I fail, then keep moving forward; don't let it be a roadblock.

That's why I find myself taking a deep breath and staring down at a text. I spent a good half hour typing it out in my notes before I even considered copying and pasting it over to my text messages.

It's never easy hearing your dad tell you he thinks you're wasting your life, but maybe it was the kick in the ass I needed. My therapist certainly thought so.

Ever since my divorce, I've felt like I've been in a constant standstill. My job, which I actually hate, is stagnant. My love life is nonexistent. And my relationship with my siblings . . . treading a thin line of disastrous. But I've done nothing to improve my life.

Well, that's not entirely true. A few months ago, I attempted to do something about my job. I mustered up the courage to present an idea to my brother, but Ford shot that down right away, killing the little bit of confidence I'd gathered to ask.

But Dad is right: maybe taking baby steps toward things I want is exactly what I need. If someone asked me if I'm happy, right here, right now, the answer would be an easy no. So, it's time to make things happen. It's time to take that step forward and put myself out there.

I stare down at the text one more time, and without looking back, I send it.

And then it hits me.

Like a tidal wave, regret washes over me as soon as it's delivered.

"Jesus Christ," I say, frantically clicking on the text, praying that Apple came up with some sort of "take back" or erase button that will help their consumers retract idiotic text messages that should never be seen or read.

But in the midst of pounding on my phone, wishing for an erase button, I accidentally "heart" my own text.

"Goddamn it," I say while heat prickles at the back of my neck. "Shit. Shit. Shit."

I liked my own goddamn text.

Not just liked it, *hearted* it.

I don't even know how I did that, but it happened. Why is that a thing? Why can you heart your own texts? And who in their right mind hearts their own texts?

I drag my hand over my mouth, wondering what to do now. Do I text her and tell her I didn't mean to heart my own text? Or do I just ignore the blatant heart emoji over my blue box?

Bringing attention to it seems like a bad idea.

But ignoring it also makes me feel like an even bigger idiot than I am.

Is the text even heart worthy?

I read over the text again.

Cooper: Hey, Nora. It's Cooper Chance. Not sure if you kept my number. Thought I would say hi . . . so, hi.

"Oh, fucking hell," I mutter, leaning back on my couch and tossing my phone to my side.

That's what I came up with? After half an hour?

Why did I even think that was good to send?

Dude, where is your game?

Nonexistent.

I pick up my phone and read it again.

Slowly nodding, acknowledging that this is pretty much the worst text a man could send a woman he's interested in, I also come to terms with the fact that no, that text is not heart worthy. Not even close.

Beer. I need more beer.

I'm about to stand from my couch when my phone dings with an incoming text, sending my nerves into a tailspin.

She texted back.

Oh hell . . . she texted back.

Jesus, do I even look?

Or do I go crawl in a hole, never to be seen again?

I need to look at the text, if anything, to at least make sure she didn't cut me off as a client. If I need to order a new cake, I need to get on it sooner rather than later.

Wincing, I pick up my phone and open up the screen to her text.

Nora: Why did you heart your text?

"Christ," I mutter. Of course she would point it out. That's the kind of person she is. That's why I find myself gravitating toward her—because she's bold, she doesn't care what other people think, and she says what's on her mind.

There's no use backing out now. I sent her the text—I hearted the text—and now I need to reply.

Cooper: I really thought it was a great opening statement. Deserved some love.

Making lemonade out of lemons. That's the only thing I can do at this point. Luckily, she texts back right away, not making me sweat out a response.

Nora: How long did it take you to write said opening statement?

Cooper: Cool guy answer—off the top of my head. Real answer—half an hour.

Nora: LOL that took you half an hour? Was hearting it part of the plan?

Cooper: The hearting it was a mistake. I was hoping there was a delete option but instead I hearted it.

Nora: So, you spent half an hour working on a text message and then sent it, realized it wasn't great, then tried to delete it—even though that's not a thing—and hearted it instead.

Cooper: That would be the gist of this loathsome and shameful interaction.

Nora: Loathsome and shameful . . . labeling it already?

Cooper: How would you label it?

Nora: Intriguing.

The tension and nerves that have built in my chest ease as the smallest of smirks tugs at my lips. Maybe this isn't as bad as I thought it was going to be. Sure, she's busting my balls, but I wouldn't expect anything less.

Cooper: Intrigued, huh? Was it the hearting my own text?

Nora: It was, makes me think that even though you look like the modern-day man, you have the tendencies of an old curmudgeon which, oddly, fascinates me.

Cooper: Or a divorcé who is extremely nervous.

Nora: Oooh, interesting take. But I think I'm going to stick with the curmudgeon.

I laugh, immediately grateful for how easygoing Nora is. Not sure this would have gone as well with someone else.

Cooper: I think you just like saying that word in your head.

Nora: I've actually been saying it out loud and it feels nice coming off my tongue. Very pleasing to say. Try it.

"Curmudgeon," I say, just for the hell of it.

Cooper: Hmm, it is pleasing to say out loud, but it isn't as aesthetically pleasing as some other words I've come across.

Nora: Oooh, educate me, please, Mr. Editor. Dazzle me with your words.

That's me—Mr. Editor. Not even sure how I got into the job, to be honest. I always enjoyed reading fiction, and when my plans for traveling around the world with Dealia didn't pan out right away, I started freelance editing, something I'd done on and off in college for extra cash. Before I knew it, a nonfiction publisher picked me up, and I've been stuck ever since.

I only wish the material was more interesting.

But, on the positive side, I do know a lot of words.

Cooper: Splendiferous.

Nora: Sounds made up. Like someone doesn't quite know if they're trying to say an adverb, verb, or adjective and kind of threw them all together. Next.

I smirk and hunker down into my couch while propping my socked feet up on the coffee table.

Cooper: Cataclysmic.

Nora: Okay, Debbie Downer. I'm saying no not just because you went to the opposite extreme to splendiferous, but also because the C's and T's are harsh coming off my tongue. Next.

I glance up at the ceiling, trying to think of a word that would beat "curmudgeon"—which, honestly, feels jumbled on my tongue at times. Oh, I've got one.

Cooper: Ephemeral.

Nora: Use it in a sentence, please.

Cooper: Palmer's choice in cake flavors was ephemeral.

Nora: Ehhh, I know you can do better. You've got one more shot at this. Hit me with a good one or I'm afraid this texting conversation must come to an end, despite its brilliant and satisfying start.

I lean forward, a huge grin on my face as I stare down at my phone. One more shot, huh? Given where my head was at when I started this conversation, I have the perfect word.

Cooper: Incipient.

Nora: Please use it in a sentence.

My smirk grows even wider as I type out my response.

Cooper: Even though this energy between us is incipient, I would love to see where it goes.

Nora: I see what you did there.

Cooper: Did you like it?

Nora: You'll have to text me tomorrow to find out. Good night, Cooper.

Hope blooms inside me as I text her back.

Cooper: Am I going to be required to dazzle you with my words again?

Nora: Possibly. We will see what I'm interested in tomorrow. It changes from day to day, after all. Until tomorrow . . .

Cooper: Good night, Nora.

I set my phone down on the coffee table and stand from my couch. Hands behind my neck, I let out a long breath of air and pace the length of my living room.

Holy shit, I can't believe I just did that.

Looks like someone is back in the game.

CHAPTER SIXTEEN

FORD

I knock lightly on Larkin's door and then step back, hands in my jeans pockets. I slept horribly last night, probably the worst night's sleep I've had in a really long time. And I know it had everything to do with how I treated Larkin yesterday.

After having to cool down the email battle between my siblings, I was pushed into the reality—not by Palmer but by self-realization—that the mock-ups we had done are all shit. And what sucks is that they were all my idea. The colors, the logos, the fonts. I spent hours and hours meticulously going over every last detail, and it's all led to one terrible conclusion: not only am I not good at my job, but I apparently know nothing about the store.

But those mock-ups—although bothering me—are not what kept me up all night. It was what Palmer pointed out to me. How I spoke to Larkin, how her shoulders slumped as she walked out the door to "retrieve" our drinks. It was callous of me, and I've never spoken to her like that before.

It made my gut churn with guilt, and I couldn't wake up quickly enough to apologize.

It's early, only eight, but I wanted to clear things up with Larkin before I head to my parents' for what I know is going to be an immeasurable amount of stress added to the stress I'm already carrying on my shoulders.

And to handle that stress, I need Larkin at my side. I need her . . . helping me.

I need her smile. Her jovial attitude. Her compassionate heart.

I need her as a friend. My, uh . . . my best friend.

After a few seconds, Larkin opens the door wearing her spandex running shorts and matching sports bra. She's in the midst of tying up her hair as her gaze meets mine, her face completely devoid of makeup. I keep my eyes trained on hers, even though they want to wander down and observe her from head to toe. I can't deny that my assistant is gorgeous—just like I can't deny the times I've found myself looking up from my desk, just to catch a glimpse of her through the glass walls of my office.

"Ford," she says, her voice coming out a little breathless. "Is everything okay?"

"Uh, yeah. Do you have a second, or are you heading out for a run?"

"I was, but I have a second."

I nod toward her bedroom. "Would I be able to come in?"

She props the door open. "Of course."

I walk into her bedroom, which is significantly smaller than mine but has the same aesthetic, covered in wall-to-wall flowers. Flower wallpaper, flower curtains, flower bedding, even flowers in vases. No matching patterns or coordinating colors—it's just all thrown together to make you feel acutely crazy.

When she shuts the door behind me, I clear my throat. "I wanted to apologize about yesterday."

She bends down and ties one of her shoes. "Apologize for what?"

"For the way I spoke to you while Palmer was there. It was uncalled for."

"You asked me to get drinks; that's what assistants do. It's not anything to worry about, Ford."

But I am worried about it because I can sense tension between us. I can feel it, and Larkin is the one person I can rely on to boost my mood; the last thing I want is for there to be tension between us.

She stands but avoids eye contact with me, something she rarely does. Her mouth is saying one thing, but her body language is saying another, so I reach out and press my fingers against her soft cheek and gently guide her to look at me. When she does, those brilliantly blue eyes cut right through me, almost catching me off guard, as if I've never truly looked into them before. "You know you're more than just my assistant, Larkin."

You're my best friend.

My emotional support.

The fun in my arduous day.

And that realization hit me hard last night as I was staring up at the canopy of my flower-covered bed.

She clears her throat. "Well, either way, it's not a big deal and doesn't warrant an apology." She picks up her phone and earbuds and heads to the door again, but I step in front of it. Her eyes widen as she looks up at me.

Hell, I don't think I've ever been this up front with her, this forthright. It's always been simple business, with an added layer of friendship, but now there's something different in the way she's looking at me, as if she's trying to mask how upset she is.

And that's what I don't like. It makes me feel . . . like an ass. I don't ever want to hurt her feelings or make her feel less than special. Because that's what she is: special.

Really fucking special.

I know I'm veering into unprofessional territory—my mind is foggy with where to draw the line—but I need to clear things up with Larkin, even if it means casually trapping her in the world's tackiest room.

"Things are weird between us. I can feel it. You're avoiding me, you barely looked at me yesterday after Palmer left, and you skipped out on dinner. You can't tell me—"

"I was embarrassed." She shrugs, as if her admission didn't nearly knock my feet from under me. "But last night I realized you shouldn't have elicited such a reaction from me. At the end of the day, I'm your assistant, you're my boss, and it was just a simple request."

"Not for you," I say, resisting the instinct to reach out and pull her into my chest, offer her a hug, to reassure her that she's so much more than just my assistant. "You're more than that, and we both know it. Now stop letting me off the hook. I'm sorry for being an ass."

The smallest of smirks passes over her lips. "You weren't an ass, Ford."

"But . . ."

She chuckles. "There is no but."

"You're avoiding me, though."

"I'm giving you space."

That's the last thing I need from her. Space. No, I am desperate to make sure there is no space between us, especially because of the space that's pulling my family apart.

I don't need space.

I need . . . *hell, don't go there, man.*

I shake my head and curl my fists in my pockets so I'll keep my hands to myself.

Don't fucking touch her. She's untouchable. And you shouldn't want to touch her. Jesus. But then, I can't help but blurt out, "I don't want space from you. Last night was a shit night. I barely slept, eating alone was miserable, and I woke up this morning with one thing on my mind: making sure you were okay. That *we* were okay."

"I'm fine, Ford. Asking me to get drinks isn't going to break me. If anything, it was a good reminder as to where I stand in the company. Sometimes I get so caught up in working closely with you that I forget what I was hired for . . . getting drinks being a huge part of that."

And that's where the problem lies, because last night, as I played what I'd said to Larkin over and over in my head, I realized that she is so much more than an assistant.

"Maybe the first year that was your job, when you were getting your feet wet, but not now." I take a step toward her, but I don't know for what reason as I keep my hands firmly stuck in my pockets. I just have an urge to be close to her. "I value you more than I think you know. I've come to realize you're one of the reasons I keep working my ass off. You push me, you challenge me, and after how weird things were last night, I realized that I can't lose you. You could pretty much ask me for anything at this point, Larkin, and I would give it to you."

And that's the truth. I would give her *anything*.

Her eyes slowly flash up to mine, and for a brief second, it feels like she wants to say more, that she wants to reach out as well, close the distance between us. As we stand here, in this god-awful floral-printed room, something deep within me surfaces, something I haven't felt in a really long time. Something that shakes me to my damn core.

Yearning.

Yearning for something more.

I wasn't lying when I said she was different, that I would give her anything she wanted, because I would. And maybe it's being here, on Marina Island, seeing her in her happy place, or maybe it's being around my family and their incessant comments about how perfect Larkin is for me, but all last night I kept thinking about her in a very nonassistant way. I was considering our friendship and how close we've become, how she knows me better than anyone, how she's the one person I go to for everything—and not just for work but for personal things as well.

I look forward to seeing her in the morning. Catching that smirk of hers.

I love running with her, pushing her harder, challenging her on the roads.

I love the way she can think three steps ahead of me and know what I need emotionally before I even do.

And I love spending time with her.

Yesterday's tension and distance made for a rude awakening that I need her in my life, and as more than just an assistant.

"You would give me anything, huh?" she says, her voice cracking ever so slightly.

"Anything," I say, holding my breath.

"If that's the case . . ." She closes the distance between us, and my mouth goes dry as she pats my chest. "Come have a juice with me downstairs."

"What?" I ask, in a daze.

"A juice . . . come sit down with me for a second."

"Oh . . . yeah . . . sure," I say, stumbling over my words. I wasn't expecting her to say that. Hell, what was I expecting her to say?

Kiss me?

I've lost my ever-loving mind.

I blame the lack of sleep.

Together we walk down to the dining area, where there are some juice pitchers sitting out next to the dry muffins.

"Let me get the drinks this time," I say, making Larkin smirk as I internally shake off any residual awkwardness. "What do you want?"

"Surprise me. I'll grab us a table."

Feeling better already, I take two glasses and fill them halfway up with apple juice and then top the rest off with cranberry. I bring the glasses over to Larkin and set hers down in front of her. "Cranberry-apple, mixed by yours truly."

"Now that's first-class service." She takes a drink, and I sit down across from her. "So, you have your brunch with your family today—are you apprehensive?"

"A little apprehensive. I'm hoping Palmer and Cooper will show up with open minds, but after what happened with Palmer yesterday, I'm going to guess that won't be the case."

"Maybe you start off with an apology, set the expectations so they know you want to cooperate, not dictate, which we know is something you tend to do when it comes to your siblings."

"You think I dictate?"

She grins while taking a sip of her drink. "You've copied me on every email you've sent them. I've seen your responses. Although they're well thought out and even-keeled, they do come across as dictating. You let them know exactly what's going to happen, end of story."

"That's only because they can't seem to agree on anything, so I cut off the bickering before it can go any further."

Larkin reaches out and places her hand on mine. "Just go in with an open heart, okay?"

I stare down at her hand and then back up into her eyes. "Okay," I answer, feeling a bout of nerves hit me all at once. "What . . . uh, what do you have planned for today besides a run?"

"Changing the subject—how Ford of you."

I laugh while she removes her hand and finishes off her juice. "I'm going to spend a little time with Beau. I believe we're going into Seattle for dinner. There's this pierogi place he was telling me about that I really want to try."

"Sounds like fun."

"Also catching up on some work that I pushed aside yesterday. I plan on going to the coffee shop to do it. You know"—she leans in—"to get away from all the flowers for a second."

"Do you get dizzy in your room?"

"No." She chuckles.

I lean back, feeling better. "You mean you're not playing the soundtrack to *My Fair Lady*, clutching flowers to your chest, and spinning around your room?"

"Do you know how much money I'd give to see you do that?"

"Let me guess, your fourth-quarter bonus?"

"And so much more." She stands from her chair, and I do as well. We take our empty glasses to the small tray next to the trash and then we walk out of the bed-and-breakfast together. "Thanks for stopping by to check on me." She nudges my shoulder. "That's what makes you a good boss."

"Thanks for being understanding, and I'm sorry again."

"You don't need to apologize, Ford." She squeezes my arm. "We're cool." She winks and then takes off. Looking over her shoulder, she calls out, "Have a good day."

I wave and watch as she jogs down the street, her ponytail swishing back and forth across her shoulders.

Hell.

Hands in my pockets, I turn my back and, with a deep breath, head to my parents' house.

◆ ◆ ◆

"Mom, these pancakes are amazing," I say, taking another helping of two.

"That's right, you eat up." Mom's expression is far too satisfied as she watches me scarf down the breakfast she insisted upon making everyone. "Much better than that bed-and-breakfast, right?"

"Hell of a lot better."

"So, does that mean you're going to change your mind and come stay at the house with Larkin?"

"No. Nice try, though."

Palmer stumbles into the kitchen, her hair a wreck, an oversize T-shirt hanging over her torso, and baggy flannel pants topping off the look. "Coffee," she mutters, searching for a mug.

She looks rough. Not that I'm a prince in the morning, but her appearance . . . I wonder if it has anything to do with our tiresome email chain. I know I'm exhausted and overdrawn from dealing with them. I wonder if she's feeling the same way.

Go in with an open heart.

Larkin is right: I dictate to my siblings, even though I don't intend to do so. I just want the bickering to end, so that's what happens. I step in and shut it down. But today, I'm going to strive to address my siblings differently. Who knows, maybe it will help.

"Good morning," Mom says. "Only took you half an hour to get down here after I told you breakfast was served."

Mom wasn't supposed to make breakfast. I was surprised when I walked into the house and smelled my mom's heavenly pancakes. We were supposed to make them brunch, but I'm not going to complain either, because I'll never pass up breakfast made by my mom.

"Sorry," Palmer says while pouring herself a coffee. When her cup is to the brim, she makes her way to the table where Dad and I are sitting, Dad intently working on a coloring page that he's spent the last two days—from what he's told me—coloring. When she looks up, she spots me, and immediately she frowns. "What are you . . . ugh, we have that thing, don't we?"

Cool, calm, and collected.

"You're on top of it this morning, sis." I give her a winning smile.

Her eyes narrow. Oooh, don't poke the bear. Apologize, like Larkin suggested.

"Watch yourself, Ford." She takes a sip of her coffee, and Dad looks up from his coloring book.

"That had a threatening tone to it," he says and then motions his colored pencil between us. "What's going on here?"

Palmer straightens up. "Dad, were you aware that Ford is rebranding without any help from the family?"

She's going to make it hard on me to apologize; I can tell already.

"I am," he says, going back to coloring.

"And you're okay with this?" Palmer asks.

"If he didn't include you, there must be some sort of reasoning behind it."

"Here, honey," Mom says, placing a plate of pancakes in front of Palmer. "Eat up."

"You know, Palmer, about that," I say, gearing up for my apology. "I wanted to—"

Slam.

The front door closes and Cooper calls out, "Sorry. The ferry was behind." He makes his way into the kitchen and takes in Palmer's scowl and my annoyance at being interrupted. "Breakfast is already served? What did I miss?"

Clearing my throat, I say, "I was actually trying to—"

"Cooper, my beautiful boy, sit down, I'll get some pancakes," Mom says while patting Cooper's cheek.

"Breakfast? I thought we were making you brunch."

Apparently no one wants me to apologize; that's fine, I can take Palmer off to the side later. Instead, I focus on keeping the conversation on course today. No fighting, even though the air is feeling thick with sibling tension. We are here for a reason: to plan a party for Mom and Dad. We need to keep it that way. "Mom didn't give us a chance to make breakfast—beat us to it."

"As if I wouldn't feed my babies," Mom says.

"We appreciate it," I say. "But do you think you guys could take off for your hike now?"

"Are you kicking us out of our own home?" Dad asks.

"Yes." I nudge Dad. "Go on, we have things to talk about."

Dad grumbles something under his breath while packing up his colored pencils. His movements are slower than normal. His hands shakier than what I remember, and as he lifts from his chair, I notice the hitch in his stance, the clutching of the back of his chair. He's gotten worse.

From the kitchen island, Mom clears her throat, giving us pointed looks. "Before we leave, your dad and I want to remind you that you three still need to go through your rooms and clean them out."

Palmer drops her fork and turns in her chair. "You were serious about that?"

"Very serious, so it would be really helpful if you please emptied out your rooms. Take what you want to keep and get rid of what you don't want. But if you can do it in the next week, we would appreciate it." Mom tacks on her motherly smile. "Thank you, sweet children." Then, hand in hand, Mom and Dad both leave, Dad leaning on Mom for support.

Well, that did not set the tone I was looking for.

When the front door shuts behind them, Palmer whips around to me. "They can't be serious. They really want us to clean out our rooms? Like . . . pack them up?"

"That's exactly what they asked," Cooper says, joining us at the table with a plate of food.

"Was this your idea too?" Palmer asks Cooper, already bringing the wrong energy to the meeting.

Cooper opens his mouth to answer, but I cut him off before things can get too heated. "Hey, we're here to talk about the party. Are you both ready to discuss? Anyone want to lead the discussion?" There, not dictating, keeping it open to them.

"Oh, so you don't want to talk about the rebranding?" Palmer asks.

Jesus Christ.

I move my hand over my mouth and take a deep breath. "Palmer, I told you—"

"He told you about that?" Cooper asks. "That's shocking."

Hell . . .

Deep breaths, man. Open ears. Let them talk. Let them work through things.

"I still can't believe you knew and I didn't," Palmer says. "And why is it shocking that Ford would tell me?"

"Maybe because you don't care about the store." Cooper pops a blueberry in his mouth. "And Dad told me about the rebranding. Since I believed my opinion was valued in this family, I asked to have a hand in it, maybe bring some of my own ideas, but Ford said no." Cooper bites down on a piece of bacon, and both my siblings stare at me, fury in their eyes.

This is not how I envisioned this breakfast going.

CHAPTER SEVENTEEN
COOPER

From the look in Ford's eyes, he was not expecting me to call him out like that.

But what I've learned from my therapy sessions is that staying quiet is only causing me unnecessary stress that I don't need to carry around.

Granted, Dr. Jefferson probably wouldn't say my passive-aggressive comment was the way to go, but hey, baby steps, right?

"Wait . . . what?" Palmer asks, trying to wrap her head around what I said. "You wanted to be a part of the company decisions? Since when?"

"Since I thought I would try something new. Since I fucking hate my job. Since I fall asleep at my desk every day, wondering if I should be doing something better with my life. And when I finally nutted up and decided to do something about it, Ford rejected me."

Ford takes a deep breath. Is he . . . is he counting to ten?

What the hell is that about?

"I didn't reject you," Ford says, his voice calm. "I . . ." He pauses and takes a deep breath again. Dude is trying to find his zen. I shouldn't laugh about it, but it's semicomical seeing him try to keep his cool. "We are getting off topic. I would love to discuss your thoughts on the party and where we stand." He picks up a pen and paper from the table. With a smile, he asks, "Cooper, what have you done so far?"

"Why did you reject Cooper, Ford?" Palmer asks, arms folded across her chest.

Ford lets out another pent-up breath as his palms fall flat on the table.

"Isn't it obvious?" I snap. "He needs control over everything."

"That's not true," Ford says, his restraint slipping as his neck veins start to show. "I don't need control over everything, *but* I do need us to stay on topic, which is the party. So, Cooper, what have you done?"

Did he not just hear himself take control? Is he that obtuse?

"Just like you don't need control over this meeting?" I ask.

"Oooh, good one," Palmer says, giving me a fist bump. Ford starts to rub his temples just as Palmer asks, "Seriously, Ford, why are you trying to cut us out?"

"I'm not trying to cut you out." He draws mindless circles on the piece of paper, but the grip on his pen belies his calm as his knuckles whiten out.

"We might not be invested in the company like you, but we still own shares. We should have some say."

"You do get a say," he says, eyes flashing with annoyance.

"And when would we get a say?" Palmer asks. "Because as far as I'm concerned, we grew up in this store as well; we spent hours upon hours helping it grow. We were part of the family photo shoots showing off the gear, we helped with social media, we went to investor meetings with Dad, promoting the family aspect of the store. You might be the CEO, but we are very much invested too."

"I know," Ford says through gritted teeth.

"Do you? Because it seems like you've forgotten that," Palmer continues. "You told me not to worry about the mock-ups."

"Because they're not finished," Ford says, raising his voice. There he goes: he's met his tipping point. "They're not even close to being finished. Why would I bother you if they're not in the final stages?"

"They were on poster board," Palmer points out.

I sit back and chew on my bacon while I watch Ford turn into a ball of irritation. I know I shouldn't enjoy it, but I kind of do.

"They were on poster board so we could see them better." He grips his pen with both hands and stares down at the table. "Can we get back to the party, please?"

"They looked pretty final to me."

"They were not final," Ford shoots back.

"If they weren't final, then why didn't you source Cooper's help?"

"Jesus Christ, because I didn't want to see him fail, okay?" Ford says, tossing his pen and sitting back in his chair.

Excuse me?

"What the fuck?" I ask. Talk about a shitty thing to say about your brother. "Fail. Why the fuck would I fail?"

"I don't know," Ford says, gripping the back of his neck. "Maybe because you have these grand ideas but zero follow-through. Maybe because whenever it comes to the store, I've never been able to rely on you. Maybe because I'm trying to protect you from yourself."

"Protect me from myself?" I push my plate away. "Why the fuck would I need protecting from myself?" He's way off base. This is exactly why I can't talk to my family—because when I do mention things like the improvements I've made in my life, they don't believe me. Granted, I've fucked up in the past. I've flaked before when Ford has asked for help, especially when I was trying to save my marriage, but that doesn't mean that's the person I am now. All they see is the old Cooper. They don't notice the strides I've made in my life, thanks to therapy, or even listen to me when I try to tell them I'm taking classes to help better myself. They don't see that.

Not sure they ever will.

"Because you're toxic when it comes to your own ambitions," Ford yells. "Need an example? This goddamn party. Months ago, you said you'd take care of it, and look where we are now—still no idea what the fuck is happening with it, and we're two weeks out. You couldn't even order a proper cake."

"Hold the fuck on." I sit up as well, rage burning through me. "I did not sign up to be the party planner of this family; it fell on me because you two are never around. And that cake is what Mom and Dad would like, not what you two fancy shits want."

"Butterscotch and chocolate?" Palmer says. "Cooper, no one likes that but you."

"You know, Palmer, if you actually spent time with Mom and Dad instead of gallivanting around the world, you might actually know they like butterscotch and chocolate. It's why I went back and changed it . . . again."

"I'm not gallivanting around the world, Cooper. I'm working. I'm living, something you should try doing rather than holing up in your apartment, afraid to step outside."

I want to scream. I want to shout.

That's not me!

That's not the man I am.

It's the man you think I am.

"I'm not afraid to step outside of my apartment—I have responsibilities. I have to be the one to stay close to Mom and Dad, who need help more and more every day. You guys don't see it because they put on a show when you're here. Do you really think they're going on a hike right now?" I shake my head. "They go to the park and sit on a bench, where they rest and hold hands while they talk. They've slowed down. And you're both too wrapped up in your own lives to see that. It's why they're moving closer to me in Seattle, for their health."

"If that's the case, they haven't been like that your entire life," Palmer says, knowing how to press the right buttons. "You were scared even when you were married to Dealia. She wanted to—"

"Do not fucking bring her up, do you hear me?" I say with such anger that I can actually feel my pulse pick up. "My marriage is off limits, unless you want to talk about skeletons in your own closet . . ."

"I don't have any skeletons," Palmer says.

"No? What about the fire at the store?"

Her head whips toward me. "Cooper," she says, and I can actually see the panic in her eyes. I'd feel bad, but she's pushed too hard, leaving me with very few fucks to give.

Palmer quickly stands from her chair, abandoning her coffee. "This is exactly why I never come home: because we don't get along. We've never gotten along. We attempt to act like we have some sort of sibling comradery, but let's just face it: we haven't been friends in years. So, what's the point of coming here, withstanding this torture, only to be brutally reminded of exactly why I chose to leave?"

"Then why the hell are you here if you hate it so much? Why didn't you just stay in New York until the party?" I ask.

She starts to answer but then closes her mouth, her expression uneasy. There's something more. Something she wants to say but is holding back.

"Why *are* you here?" Ford asks, pressing her for answers. "You said you're working on a PNW piece, but I haven't seen you do anything for it."

"You haven't even been out of your hotel room long enough to notice me going anywhere, Ford. Plus, my plans changed once I broke my wrist. Hard to be cute with a cast." Palmer expertly puts on a mask of indifference, but I know by now that whenever she slips on that mask, she's just hiding from something she's not ready to face just yet.

"Nah, there's something you're not telling us," I say. "Which means you can't sit up there on your high horse and judge me when clearly not everything is going well in your life."

"Everything's fine." She inspects the nails on her good hand.

"Then why are you so defensive?" I ask her.

"Because I don't need you prying into my life. I'm fine—drop it."

"Palmer," Ford says in a more soothing tone, "it's clearly not fine if you're getting upset. What's going on?"

"Oh, now you're going to care?" Palmer asks. "Or are you just going to slap a Band-Aid on my problems and move along? Because that's what you're good at when it comes to me and Cooper. You think you know what's best, you attempt a short-term fix even though we didn't ask for it, and then you turn a blind eye and move on, never actually scratching the surface of what we need. And what we need is not for you to anticipate what is missing in our lives, but for you to actually listen to what we're saying."

"I do listen—"

"Then you would have known that I want something more than what I'm doing with my life," I say. He would have heard me when I told him a year ago that I was making changes in my life after my one-night stand. He was calling to check up on Mom and Dad, asked how I was, and I told him I was making some strides. But he didn't listen—he brushed it off, didn't ask me what kind of strides but instead told me he had a meeting and had to go. "You would have seen I wanted to give the rebrand a shot. But you assumed you knew what I needed instead. Which was to apparently not embarrass myself—your words, not mine."

"I never said 'embarrass.'" He looks between us, studying us. "So, what . . . I'm a shitty brother, is that what you two are trying to say?" Ford pushes away from the table and gets out of his seat. He grips the back of his chair, his knuckles turning white as he looks down at the table. "Clearly this was a bad idea. We can't seem to pull our shit together whenever we're around each other lately." His weary eyes connect with mine. "Remember how close we used to be? The long talks we would have on the phone?" He glances at Palmer. "And what about all the times you used to visit me in Denver? Maybe I haven't talked to you about the rebrand because you barely talk to me now. And here I thought I was attempting to bring us together."

"How can you do that when you have no idea what's going on in our lives?" Palmer asks.

"I'm not a goddamn mind reader. If shit is hitting the fan for you, you need to talk about it."

"Why would I talk to someone who doesn't listen? You don't ever listen, Ford. You choose what you want to hear."

He slowly nods. "Okay, so this is all my fault, then?" He spreads his arms wide. "I'm the shit person in the family? Fine. I'll take responsibility for that on top of everything else." He slams his chair into the table and walks past me. "Don't worry about the planning. Larkin and I will take care of it. Rest assured, you two don't have to lift a finger."

I slam my chair into the table as well, knocking over an empty glass of what was once orange juice. "I was doing a fine job with the plans. No one needs you to be a hero, Ford."

He turns to look at the both of us and plants his hands on his hips. "I don't know why Mom and Dad enjoy having us around each other, because this is what it always turns into: a pissing match. Who is better? Who is doing the most with their life? Who is the loser of the bunch? Well, I'm fucking sick of it. I'm . . . hell, I'm sick of you two. I've busted my ass to make a name for this family, and all you two can do is complain about it, be ungrateful—"

"We're not ungrateful," Palmer yells. "We just want to be a part of it. You won't let us."

"You don't want to be a part of this," Ford yells back. "It would actually mean that the both of you would have to show an ounce of responsibility and follow through on your plans, something you know nothing about."

"Really? Because I'm pretty sure I've created a job for myself out of sheer grit and follow-through," Palmer says. "But you wouldn't know that because you don't actually know me."

"And we don't know you because you don't fucking talk and you're never home," I say to Palmer.

Standing in a triangle, we all stare each other down.

Shots have been fired.

Words have been said.

And our hatred is all out in the open, like a bleeding heart, lifeless on the table.

An outsider looking in might see this fight unfold and be confused. What are they actually fighting about? Is it about the rebranding? The party? Not being open to listening to each other? The fire? It's a culmination of it all.

Our pent-up frustrations were unfolded. Instead of communicating over the years, we've held it in, we've protected our truths, keeping them close to our hearts. And with one speed bump, all our grievances came tumbling out.

Slowly, Ford nods. "Glad we had this meeting. Incredibly productive. Glad we had no problem pointing out each other's flaws and all the reasons we never hang out, but we couldn't say one goddamn word about the party." He glances between me and Palmer. "I'm out. Done. I'm not participating in your sparring matches, I'm not indulging your fights, and I'm not bothering to figure out ways to help you. You're on your goddamn own. As for the party, Palmer, you handle the food since that's what you're good at. I'll take the venue since it's at the store, and Cooper, you take the rest since you apparently know Mom and Dad so well. If you want to talk to me, you know my email."

With that, Ford takes off and slams the front door behind him.

I glance at Palmer and then head off too, but not before saying, "Clean out your room. Deny it all you want, but Mom and Dad are moving."

And then I'm gone too.

CHAPTER EIGHTEEN

LARKIN

Ford: Are you back?

Larkin: Headed to the Bed and Breakfast right now. Everything okay?

Ford: Can you come to my room when you get here?

Larkin: Of course. Be there shortly.

"Everything okay?" Beau asks.

"I'm not sure." I place my phone in my lap and chew on the side of my cheek. "Ford needs me to come to his room when I get back."

"Oh yeah, he wants you to come to his room, huh?" Beau teases as he stops at a stop sign.

"It's not like that, and you know it."

"It's not?" Beau asks as we close in on the bed-and-breakfast. "Because you spent the entire night talking about Ford."

"I did not," I insist. "I talked about my job."

"I would say twenty percent of it was your job, eighty percent was him."

My cheeks heat up. "That's an inaccurate percentage split."

"Really? Because tonight I learned about Ford's workout routine, what he likes to eat on certain days, and how he pulls on his hair when he's frustrated and can't figure something out, so you've resorted to using a squirt bottle in the office to keep him from losing all his hair."

"That's just a funny anecdote. I get to spray my boss with water; how is that not entertaining?" I keep my eyes trained on the road in front of us as Beau drives slowly down Marina Ave.

"Level with me, Larkin. You like him."

"I don't like him," I say as he parks in front of the bed-and-breakfast. *Avoid eye contact—your brother can see right through you.*

"Larkin . . ."

"Beau . . ."

Sighing, he shakes his head. "Fine, don't tell me, but when you wind up in love with your boss, don't come crying to me about how you can't handle your feelings."

"Hey, you're all I have—no matter what happens, you always have to listen."

He chuckles. "Yeah, I know. Don't worry, when you do figure out that you love him, I'll be here with an open ear."

I poke his side. "Damn right, and you know it goes both ways. The listening ear, especially when it comes to looooove," I draw out, making him roll his eyes.

"Don't start with me."

"What? You can harass me about my *boss*, but I can't say anything about Palmer?"

"There is nothing to say." He grips the steering wheel, as if he's ready to drive off as quickly as he can to avoid the topic of Palmer Chance.

"You are such a liar, but that's fine, that's fine. It will all come out at some point."

"Yes, it will all come out," Beau says suggestively.

"You've lost it. Too many pierogis for you." I open the door of his car. "Thank you for dinner, by the way. You didn't have to pay—I am the older sibling, after all."

"That doesn't mean anything. And I'm trying to butter you up."

"I told you: my job is in Denver. I'm not moving here."

He sighs. "It's because you're in looooove."

"I'm leaving now." I get out of the car and then dip my head back in before shutting the door. "Text me, would love another dinner date with you."

"I will, and good luck with whatever Ford needs. Hopefully it's not anything to do with your obvious attraction to him."

"You're a family practice doctor, not a love doctor—now get out of here."

He laughs as I shut the door. We both give each other a wave, and then I'm walking into the bed-and-breakfast with a little bit of pep in my step as I take the stairs and head straight for Ford's room.

I'm concerned that the brunch didn't go as well as he had hoped. His cryptic text message leads me to believe that I need to be prepared for an irritated Ford. Closed off, short, clipped—he doesn't show that side of him very often, but when he does, it takes a while to calm him down. I might be in for a long night.

When I reach his door, I give it a few knocks.

"It's open," he calls.

I turn the knob and cautiously step inside. I scan the dimly lit room and find him over by the fireplace, sitting in a floral wingback chair, back curved, arms resting on his legs as he pokes at some burnt wood with a fire poker.

The room has an eerie feel to it—not what I was expecting. Honestly, I thought I was going to come in here and find him pacing the length of the space, hand in his hair, ready to fire off, but that's not the vibe.

His shoulders are hunched over, he's wearing a plain T-shirt and sweatpants, an outfit I've never seen him in before, and he doesn't look fidgety or mad, more . . . sullen.

I quietly shut the door behind me and make my way toward the fireplace. "Hey, how are you doing?" I ask, taking a seat across from him in a matching wingback chair.

Eyes cast down toward the fire, he doesn't bother to look at me. "Do you think I'm an asshole?"

"What?" I ask, confused, brows pulling together. "No, why would you think that?"

"Controlling?"

"Controlling in what way?" I ask, trying to be as cautious as possible while assessing the kind of mental state he's in. "I think you're controlling on the business front, but not in a bad way—in a way that holds your employees to a certain standard, and that's the reason you're so successful, why the company is so successful."

"Do you like me? As a human, do you think I'm a decent guy?"

"Of course," I answer, completely confused as he glances at my lips and then back up to my eyes.

"You like me as a friend?"

Uh, what's happening?

"Ford, I—"

"Do you think I understand you?"

"Ford, where is this all coming from?"

He tilts his head to the side, the light from the flames of the fire bouncing off his hardened jaw. "Answer the question, Larkin."

"Do I think you understand me?" I venture, uneasy. "I mean . . . yes. I think we've spent enough time together to know each other well."

"No, do I *get* you? Or do you think I've only chosen what I want to hear about you, only scratched the surface."

Something happened at brunch today, and it has shaken Ford to his core. I can see it in his distraught eyes, in the slight tremor in his hand, and the worried tone of his voice. But what exactly? What has made him question himself so much?

"I think you get me," I answer honestly. "I think you are one of the few people who gets me, and do you know how I know that?"

"How?" he asks, staring down at the fire again.

"Because when I came to you for a job, all you had to hear was my story. You didn't need to hear about my qualifications, or lack thereof; you heard my story and you understood. You knew I needed to feel close to my dad after his death, and working for the store would do that. You gave me a shot, and ever since then, not only have you given me the chance to stay connected to my dad, but you continue to challenge me, to grow my skills, and motivate me to grow professionally. You know exactly what I need and when I need it. You can anticipate my needs, and no one else does that like you do."

Still not looking at me, he slowly nods.

In all the years I've worked for Ford Chance, not once have I ever seen him like this, so . . . dejected. There isn't an ounce of his usual charismatic confidence, and it's incredibly concerning. He's a rock, someone I can lean on, and right now, he seems to be missing the strength that makes him the amazing man he is.

"Where is this coming from?"

His jaw tics with tension as he studies the fire in front of us. I'm afraid he's not going to answer and I'm going to have to pressure him, but finally, "My siblings hate me."

"What? No, why would you—"

"They practically told me they hate me." He sets the poker down. "They told me I'm a shitty brother, that I don't understand them, I don't listen. That I'm a workaholic, that I only scratch the surface when it comes to them, that I really don't care about them . . ."

"They said all of that?" I ask, completely shocked.

"Yes." He leans back in his chair. "I've only wanted to protect them." He smooths his hand over his eyes, and my heart lurches in my chest. I could not imagine what that kind of confessional blame would feel like. If Beau said those things to me, the hurt would bring me to my knees.

"Ford, you *do* protect them."

He shakes his head. "I isolate them. I suppress them."

"You don't suppress them. Their accomplishments and successes aren't on you; that is not your responsibility."

"And they're right, I don't think I even know them, but even worse . . ." He looks at me. "I don't think I know myself or this company."

Oh man, they really did a number on him. Sure, he might have issues with his siblings, and yes, he seems quite lost at the moment, not just with his brother and sister but with the company, with himself. For the past month I've felt that he's been withdrawn, confused at times, second-guessing himself, and I'm not sure if it's from the impending reunion with his family or if he's been stressed with the party, but I can't stand by and listen to him talk about himself in such a negative way, not when he's one of the best men I've ever known.

He's thoughtful, intense, driven, but so caring, especially with me. He watches out for me, helps me, guides me, makes me feel like I'm important.

I need to do the same for him.

"Ford, if anyone knows this company, it's you. You live and breathe it."

He shakes his head. "I know the business side of it. I know the accounting, the numbers, the logistics. But when it comes to the heart of the company, the heart of myself, the heart of my family, I'm disconnected. Hell, I can't even come up with a new logo for a company I've known my entire life."

I sit back and try to understand where he's coming from.

He's clearly had a rough day. Having the truth, even if it's a semi-truth, thrown at you, is tough to swallow. And I have a feeling this is going to haunt him. It's going to throw him off, and he's not going to accomplish everything he wants to accomplish while we're here, especially the store branding.

But the fact that he doesn't think he knows himself or the store—or his siblings, for that matter—makes me feel sad for him. That sense of disconnect can't possibly settle well, especially not with Ford.

That needs to change. Right now, Ford needs to be reminded of the kind of person he is, and I very well might be the one to do that.

"Then let's find out who you are," I say.

He glances up from the fire. "What?"

I put on a smile. "Let's find out who you are. If you think you don't know yourself, you don't know the company, what better place to look for yourself than the very place you grew up, where Watchful Wanderers originated? And while we do that, we can connect on another level with the company. Who knows, maybe it will spark an idea for the rebrand."

"And how do you propose we do that?" he asks, his voice flat.

"I think it's time we get earthy, Ford."

"Earthy?" He raises a brow, and I hold my breath, hoping he might be coming back to me.

"Yeah, earthy. When was the last time you went into one of the stores and just . . . bought things to play with?"

He scratches the side of his cheek. "Probably never."

"Never?" I ask, shocked.

"Yeah, never."

"Well, that needs to change." I glance around his hotel room and spot a pad of paper and pen. I quickly grab it and then sit back down. Pen poised, I say, "Okay, what should we do?"

He sits up. "Uh, what do you mean?"

"We need to make a bucket list."

"A bucket list? How is that going to help?" He shifts up and turns toward me.

It's working: he's starting to come out of his funk—slowly, but he's coming out of it.

"Well, if we make a bucket list of things to do, maybe along the way you'll not only start to find yourself, but you'll also start to understand the company on another level, the ground level, the customer level. And from there . . . maybe the perfect rebranding will come to you."

He scratches the side of his jaw as he contemplates my idea. "What would this list entail?"

"Why, all the things you haven't done, of course." I smile. "And don't worry, I'll be right by your side to capture it all in my permanent memory bank, so whenever you need to be brought down a level, I can remind you of the time you went fly-fishing and ended up catching your own crotch."

That grants me a smile.

He lifts his chin. "I have more finesse than that."

"How would I know? I only know you in a suit and tie behind a desk. It's time to get down with nature, Ford Chance."

"Earthy."

I nod. "Yes, earthy."

He stands from his seat and starts to pace. Yup, this is exactly what he needed. Pleased with myself, I watch his wonderful mind start to churn with ideas. "Maybe we go to the store and walk down each aisle to assess what we think I should do."

"That could work. We could also make a short list right now and add things to it when we're at the store. But at least you would have a starting point, so you're not overwhelmed."

"That's a good idea." He continues to pace. "But we do need to make time for me to clean out my room at my parents' house."

"Clean it out?" I ask, an idea coming to mind. "That's perfect."

"What's perfect?" he asks, his brow pinched.

"That's exactly where we'll start: in your childhood room. What better way to find yourself than to revisit your childhood. We can create the bucket list and then move forward from there."

"Yeah, I guess that might be a good place to start." He looks at me. "But there's no way you're helping with that."

I stand from my chair. "Oh, I'm helping you clean out your childhood room. That would be an absolute dream come true." I rub my hands together. "I can only imagine the little golden nuggets of blackmail I'll find. Maybe old letters to childhood girlfriends. Maybe an embarrassing photo or two. Maybe a collection of stamps or coins, or something you never told anyone about but you cherish. I need to see all of these things."

"That's exactly why you can't help me."

"And that's exactly why I will be helping you." He grips his hair, and I point at him. "You're going to go bald."

He drops his hand and shakes his head. "Hell, what would I do without you, Larkin?" The adorable, needy look in his eyes makes my stomach flip, and Beau's taunting comes to the forefront of my mind.

I don't like my boss.

Because he's just that, my boss.

But am I maybe slightly infatuated? And when I say "slightly"? I mean . . . very slightly. Like a sliver. A whisper.

Yes.

But it's hard not to be when he's so . . . so . . . perfect.

"You would survive without me, but life wouldn't be as interesting." I smirk.

"You got that right."

I take a step toward him, closing the distance between us. Even though he's had a rough day, I love seeing this side of him, this human side. I love seeing him relaxed and in a pair of sweatpants. I love seeing his vulnerability, and I love even more how he has no problem being vulnerable in front of me.

"Are you feeling better?" I ask.

"I am." His eyes meet mine. "Thank you, Larkin. I know this isn't part of your job responsibility, but I appreciate you coming here tonight and talking with me, talking this out."

I reach out and squeeze his arm. Lately it seems like I can't stop touching him. "You realize you're more than my boss, right? You're my friend too, and I'm always here for you, whenever you need it. Today was tough. I'm glad that you texted me. I would have been upset knowing you went to bed angry, frustrated, or dejected."

"All things I was feeling . . . until you showed up." His grateful eyes connect with mine, and God, it's tempting to lean in closer.

My heart twists in my chest as a wave of lust and nerves pulses through me. *Be cool, Larkin.*

"Well, I'm grateful you were open with me. I know it takes a lot to open up like that. You made it easy on me." I glance down at my watch. "I should probably get to bed if we have a big day ahead of us tomorrow."

"And what would that day be?" he asks as he follows me to his door. He opens it, and I step into the doorway while he grips the frame, his large body creating a domineering and nearly irresistible presence.

"Looking for an itinerary?"

"You know how much an itinerary pleases me." And finally, a little joke.

There's something to be said about making someone feel better when they're at an all-time low, and I can proudly say I helped Ford Chance feel better.

"Okay." I lean against the doorframe, our bodies only a foot apart. He doesn't move, though; instead he leans in closer—close enough for me to catch a whiff of his signature cologne that smells like sandalwood and bergamot. "An itinerary."

"Yeah, an itinerary," he chuckles.

Pull it together, Larkin. It's a simple whiff of cologne, not a love spell.

"Sure, how about this," I say, gathering myself. "We get in a good run tomorrow, clear our heads and start the day off right. Shower and then walk over to the juice bar and grab some kale smoothies."

"Yum." He laughs. "I love a juiced green."

"If I didn't know you, I'd think you were being sarcastic, but that's not the case here."

"Not even a little. What's after the smoothie?"

"We go to your parents' house and clear out your room. This is where we will collect evidence."

"You make it sound like we're solving a murder."

"Maybe we are." I chuckle. "The murder of your . . . uh . . . childhood?"

"If that helps, sure."

"Great, so we're solving the murder of your childhood, which makes things exponentially more depressing. Maybe we don't solve a murder, but instead, solve an awakening."

"An 'awakening'? Yeah, that doesn't sound right either."

I tap my chin. "Okay, let me think on it. But anyway, we'll clear out your room, reminisce, and look for incriminating items that I can use against you for years."

"Years." His brows raise. "Does this mean I didn't scare you off and I shouldn't expect a resignation letter anytime soon? Because you know that would be devastating."

I smile. Can't hear that enough.

Seriously, he's always made me feel needed, valued, and it's a big attribute when it comes to working with him.

"It'll take a lot more than a conversation by the fire to scare me off."

"It wasn't just a conversation," he says quietly. "It was beyond what you should have to talk to me about."

"And I told you, I'm your friend too. You've been there for me, many times. I'm just returning the favor." I poke his side. "It's not a one-way street. Helping each other emotionally can go both ways."

"I guess so," he says with a sigh. "Okay, so I guess I'll see you bright and early tomorrow morning for a run?"

"Yeah, seven work?"

"Sure does." He gives me a soft smile. "Thank you, Larkin."

"Of course. Have a good night." I turn away and feel his eyes stay on me while I make my way to my room. Something desperate inside me wants to turn back around and run into his arms, give him a hug, tell him everything is going to be okay. But I know that would be crossing the line. Even the little pokes and touches I can't help are crossing the line.

So instead, I keep my eyes forward and let myself into my room before I can do anything stupid. Once the door is shut, I lean against it and take out my phone. Pulling up the text thread with Beau, I shoot him a quick message.

Larkin: Shit went down with the Chance family. Be prepared.

CHAPTER NINETEEN
FORD

"Larkin!" Mom shouts, pulling her into a hug, bypassing me in the hallway of my childhood home. I bump into the wall as my mom gushes over my assistant.

Even though I want to be insulted, I get it. It's not the first time she's chosen to hug Larkin first, and I'm sure it won't be the last either.

"You've been here for a week, and we haven't seen you yet—do you not like us anymore?" Mom asks, still squeezing Larkin tightly.

"It's not by my doing," Larkin says, her voice muffled by my mom's shoulder. "Your son has been bogarting me. Take your complaints up with him."

My mom lets Larkin go from her bear hug but doesn't let her get far as she reaches down and holds her hand. Yeah, if Larkin was anybody else, they'd probably be reporting us to human resources in a second, but not Larkin. According to my parents, she's a part of this family, and it didn't take my parents very long to stake such a claim on her. Dad remembered her from visiting the store so much, and Mom was immediately charmed by Larkin's smile. It's pretty much impossible to keep it professional with Larkin where my family is concerned.

"Oh, I've been letting him know how unhappy I am that he's secluding you in the bed-and-breakfast. Did you know I told him you two should stay here? I even offered up his bed for you, but he denied that request faster than I could ask."

"What? He didn't tell me that," Larkin says, giving me a suspicious look. "You know the breakfast would be a thousand times better here." *Suck-up.* I hold back my smirk.

"That is precisely what I told him, but he decided to deny you my pancakes. The nerve."

"Larkin will survive," I say.

But, of course, Larkin plays along and drapes the back of her hand over her forehead. "I won't. He has me living on kale smoothies."

"Preposterous. Is that what you had this morning?"

She nods. "Forced it down my throat via straw."

"Way to be dramatic," I say, rolling my eyes and making my way to the kitchen.

"It was horrible. He said, 'Drink this or you're fired,'" Larkin drones on as they follow closely behind.

"You poor dear. Shall I make you some scones while you're here?"

"Oh, you don't have to, but if you do, you know I'll eat them."

As I enter the kitchen, I spot Palmer at the kitchen table hovering over a bowl of Froot Loops, head down and giving off a "stay the hell away" vibe. She glances in my direction, her face completely emotionless, and I realize our spat from yesterday has not simmered. It's still full-on boiling.

Why did I think she wasn't going to be here? From the look on her face, she wasn't expecting me to show up either. She drops her spoon in her bowl and pushes away from the table before standing and bringing her bowl to the sink. She sidesteps me and heads toward the hallway, where she runs into Mom and Larkin.

"Palmer, hi," Larkin says in a cheery tone. "How's your wrist?"

"Broken," Palmer answers flatly as she pushes past them and heads toward the stairs, her irritation in full bloom.

"Don't worry about her," Mom says. "She's been cranky lately. I think she's missing her friends in New York."

"Then why doesn't she go home?" I ask, casually.

"I think she's working on some sort of travel thing about Washington, but then again, she hasn't done much since she's been here." Yeah, the PNW thing she's mentioned, but not a single person has seen her work on it, which only helps confirm my suspicion that there's more to her story. "Can't be quite sure with that girl; just glad she's here." Mom clutches Larkin's hand to her chest. "Can I have a few minutes with Larkin before you make her do whatever she's here to do?"

"Clean my room," I answer.

Mom's brow pulls together in distaste. "Excuse me? She's here to clean your room? Oh no, sir, that will not be happening. Have you lost your mind? She's your assistant, not your maid."

"I offered to help," Larkin says kindly.

"I know he pays you a lot, dear, but he doesn't pay you *that* much."

Larkin laughs, and the smile that pulls at her lips makes her look so sweet that just one glance in her direction puts me at ease.

"It's really okay, Mrs. Chance. I have a mission to find some incriminating evidence to use to my advantage."

"Ahhh." Mom nods sagely. "Very smart lady, indeed. If that's the case, I'd start with his closet and the green boxes on the top shelf."

"What the hell's in the green boxes?" I say, not recalling any such things. Worry prickles at the back of my neck as my mind wanders to the kind of "incriminating evidence" Larkin could find. Maybe I didn't think this all the way through. The last thing I want right now, especially with all these confusing thoughts running around in my head about Larkin, is for her to find something embarrassing about me.

It's bad enough she had to see me question myself; she had to see me at an all-time low. It's bad enough she's seen my armor crack, my strong determination falter. And the things I value so much, like my family and the business, she's seen me question my knowledge of, my understanding. It's been humiliating, humbling. For my assistant, it's been enough for her to witness for a lifetime.

"Oh, you'll see." With a laugh, Mom lets go of Larkin's hand and heads over to her apron, which hangs on the pantry door by a Command strip hook. My parents are firm believers in Command strips. They've even gone as far as to claim they've changed the home-decor industry. "While you two are discovering little trinkets of damning knowledge about our dearest Ford, I'll be making some cherry-honey scones. I will call you down when they're ready."

"Sounds great, thank you, Mrs. Chance." Larkin takes off toward the stairs, and my anxiety kicks up. She's moving far too fast for my liking. I need to get ahead of her. "I am so excited to see your childhood room and find those green boxes." Shit, she's really fast.

As she "sprints," I try to take a mental inventory of what I could possibly have kept in my childhood room. What would be damning enough to make me want to act like an ostrich—stick my head in the ground and pray for tomorrow.

But as I rack my brain, I can't recall anything. But it has to be something, because Mom made a big deal of pointing it out.

"What could you be hiding in those green boxes?" Larkin's voice bounces with humor.

Sweat breaks out on the back of my neck. I don't fucking know. "There are no green boxes," I hiss. At least I hope there are no green boxes.

Are there green boxes?

No . . . there aren't. Are there? Fuck, I have no idea.

Her pace picks up; so does mine. And as if we're in a race, bumping against the walls and trying to pass one another, we head up the stairs. Panic sears through me, embarrassment clawing at my throat while Larkin brims with excitement.

She reaches the landing before me, and she looks around while asking, "You know, I don't even know which room is yours."

Oh . . . duh. I inwardly chuckle: here I am, trying to bulldoze my assistant up the stairs, when in reality, she's never been to my childhood home before.

I scratch the back of my neck. "You know what, I just remembered something: I already moved all my things out of my room a few years ago." I motion with my thumb toward the stairs. "Maybe we just head back to the hotel."

She slowly steels me with those eyes of hers. "Nice try, boss. If you're not going to tell me, then I'll just find out for myself."

She takes in both sides of the hallway and unfortunately is smart enough to turn right.

"Did you hear that? I think my mom just called your name. Maybe she wants help with the scones," I say as she opens the bathroom door and then closes it.

"She didn't call my name. She's singing along with the Rolling Stones currently." She opens Cooper's door, and I watch her take in the space. She shakes her head and shuts the door. "You would never have sheets that don't match the comforter."

In this very moment, I hate that she knows me so well. I could have passed Cooper's room off as mine. Then again, I have NO idea what kind of damning things Cooper might have in his room, and I'm not willing to take that kind of risk.

She gets closer to my room, and panic heightens, my brain working in overdrive as I do the first thing that comes to my mind.

Please know, I'm not proud of this, but I've embarrassed myself enough in front of this woman; whatever awaits in that room needs to go untouched.

Gripping onto the hallway wall, I clang my foot against the baseboard—loudly—and say, "Oh shit, my toe." She turns around just in time to see me fold like an accordion down to the floor.

"What on earth?" She steps away from my door and kneels down on the floor next to me. "What happened? Are you okay?"

Was I going for less embarrassing? Because as I pretend to grip my toe in pain and she hovers next to me, I'm quickly realizing that this was not a great choice to uphold my dignity.

"Uh . . . I, uh . . . I ran into the wall."

Yup, didn't want to humiliate myself in front of her anymore: doing that perfectly while curling up into a ball out of reaction to a "stubbed toe." Real smooth, Ford.

"You ran into the wall?" she asks, a smile on her lips. "You realize they're solid, right? If you want to get to the other room, you have to open a door."

"Yeah, thought I would try something different."

"Well, I see that's going well for you." She pats me on the shoulders, stands, and then walks toward my door again before I can make something else up, like a groin tear—because that's the only thing my mind can come up with. She opens the door and then sighs in contentment. "Found your room."

I hop up to my feet and say, "How do you know it's mine?"

"Easy." She glances down at my foot, and I pretend to limp. "Incredibly tidy, neat, and not a thing out of place. Forest-green walls, so you—one of your favorite colors. Navy-blue comforter with matching navy-blue sheets, just screams Ford Chance. This room looks like it was plucked from the army barracks. It's obvious."

She's right. Not a poster on the walls.

Not a knickknack or trophy on display.

Not a thing out of place.

It's just . . . boring.

Another wave of embarrassment hits me hard. What does she actually think of seeing such a lack of personalization from me? And why do I have this overwhelming need to earn her approval? It's like . . . I want her to like me. Not as a boss, but as a person, and the more I dive deep into the man outside the suit, I realize I'm less and less charming when removed further and further from the office. If I don't even really like myself, how could someone so positive, so . . . hell, so beautiful like Larkin find me likable?

As she walks deeper into the room, her eyes travel around and she asks, "If I open your dresser, is everything going to be organized in bins?"

"If you open the dresser drawer, you're going to find nothing, but I know the closet is organized." Shit, why did I just say that? "On second thought, I really think my mom is calling you . . ."

On a snort, she walks toward the closet, and panic swallows me whole. I can't remember what the hell is organized in there, nor can I recall any of these green boxes. I swear if Mom just said that to freak me out, I'm going to . . . hell, do nothing. But I need to save face, so I rush in front of her and stop her from opening it. "I can handle the closet. You know, I really think my mom needs help with the scones. Or you can search under the bed."

She folds her arms across her chest. "And I would do what? Take a magnifying glass to the floor, looking for a speck of dust that might bring back memories? Not sure if you've noticed, but there's nothing in this room."

I can't help chuckling. "You know, you've become awfully lippy in the last couple of days."

She smiles up at me. "Deal with it." Then she moves past me, her shoulder brushing mine, and goes to the closet. She flings the door open, revealing stacked box after stacked box, everything labeled, everything neatly placed. Oh okay . . . yeah, not so bad after all. I take in the labels—astronomy, writing, awards—nothing damning. "Ugh, this is infuriating."

"Why?" I ask with relief.

"Because I was kind of hoping for this to be a Monica Geller–type situation, where everything is clean besides this one closet and it's her dirty little secret."

"Sorry to disappoint."

And just as the tension in my shoulders leaves, Larkin scans up toward the top of the closet. "Aha, the good stuff. The green boxes." Shit, really? She reaches up on her tiptoes for them but barely makes it up to the top shelf. "Damn." She turns to me. "I'm going to need a boost so I can get these."

"And you think you're going to get that boost from me?"

"Uh, yeah. Be a good boss and lift me up."

"You've lost your mind." Knowing Larkin, she will find a way to reach these boxes with or without me, so I might as well be the one who touches them first so I can filter out anything she doesn't need to see. I move her to the side and easily reach up to grab one of the boxes. Larkin claps her hands enthusiastically and reaches for it, but I block her instead, allowing myself a peek inside.

"Hey, I need to know the contents of that box." She jumps behind me, attempting to look over my shoulder.

Ignoring her, I let my eyes adjust to what's inside, and that's when I spot a black spiral-bound notebook. That's it, just one notebook. Nothing else. That's odd. Why would I . . . *ohhhhh shit.*

And then it hits me like a freight train.

Oh hell no.

Nope.

No way is she going to see this.

I snap the box shut. "Nothing in here. Let's, uh . . . let's try another box."

Larkin's face lights up—she doesn't believe me for a second. "Oh, there's something good in there, isn't there. I can tell from the blush on your cheeks. Let me see." She reaches for the box, but I keep it out of reach. "Ford, stop, I want to see."

"This is none of your concern."

"With the way your upper lip is starting to perspire, this is most definitely my concern."

"No, I really think we're good leaving this one alone."

She lunges for the box, but I hold it above my head where she can't reach it.

She jumps.

She swats.

She even attempts to tickle me, but I hold strong.

"Give me that box!" Her voice is strained as she keeps jumping at my arm.

"Never."

"Give . . . it . . . here."

"Stop that." I push her little jumping body away. "This is none of your concern."

"Give it."

"No."

"Ford, hand it over, right this instant."

"It's cute that you think your barely authoritative voice is going to make me change my mind. Now, if you'll excuse me, I need to discuss something with my mom." Because why the *hell* would she keep something like this?

No one in their right mind should ever see this. Ever.

Especially Larkin.

Humiliation is already creeping up the back of my neck . . .

I take a step toward the door, but Larkin stands up on my bed and jumps midair onto my back, knocking me off balance. We both slam into the wall and slide down to the floor, the box flying out of my hands.

"What the actual hell," I say as she scrambles off my back and across the floor to the green box.

Thinking quickly, I grab her foot and stop her, inches from taking hold of it.

"Let go," she says, kicking her leg around.

"Jesus, you're strong."

"This is not boss-like behavior. I will take you to human resources," she pants, twisting and kicking her legs.

"And I will tell them how you pounced on me first."

"HR likes me better than you—they'll take my side." She scrambles, and she's gaining centimeters on me.

"I sign their paychecks—they'll always side with me."

"Ugh, not everyone is about money."

"Most people are." I yank on her foot, bringing her back a few inches.

"Let . . . me . . . go!" She kicks out, hitting me in the chest and sending me backward. Stunned, I drop her foot, releasing her just enough to scramble the rest of the way to the box. She scoops it up and, like a ninja, hops up on her feet, leaps over the bed, and opens the box—to my intense horror. "Oh, a notebook . . . oooh, what could be in here?"

"Don't open—"

Too late. She flips the cover open, and all the life in my body drains at what I know she's seeing right now.

Fuck . . .

"Oh . . . my . . . God!" Just as quickly as she opened the notebook, she shuts it, her face red, her smile impossibly big. "Ford Chance."

Groaning, I slide back on the floor and cover my eyes with my hands.

"You dirty, dirty boy." From the sound of pages crinkling, she obviously opened the notebook again, turning this embarrassing moment into a full-blown nightmare. "You have a notebook of just boobs. Cutout boobs. Boobs in lingerie, boobs in tight shirts, naked boobs. What on earth?"

Yup, this is my life now. My assistant knows I have a boob book.

"And I will never be able to look at you again," I say, wishing the floor would swallow me whole right about now.

She takes a seat on my bed, the squeak of it alerting me. "I mean, where did you get all of these pictures? Some of them are printed out,

I can see, but some of them are magazines . . . wait, are these from catalogues? Oh my God, this one is totally from the Watchful Wanderers magazine. She's wearing a shirt I recognize. Ford, you clipped out boobies from your family's store magazine."

"Can you not call them 'boobies'? Jesus." Humiliated, I stand and reach for the book, but she snatches it out of the way just in time. "Larkin, hand it over."

"Why? You going to take it back to the inn?" She wiggles her eyebrows. "Maybe set up a fire, pour some wine, have an evening to yourself with your . . . friends?"

"If you're trying to make me shrivel up and die from embarrassment, I'm seconds away."

She chuckles and continues to flip through the pages. "You know, I have noticed one commonality among all the breasts: you like them small."

"Good to know. Now can we get to work?"

"This is work." She flips through more. "This is so telling. Really getting down to the nitty-gritty of what makes Ford Chance tick." She snaps the book shut and meets my gaze, clutching the notebook to her chest. "Tell me, Ford, what makes you lean toward a smaller set of breasts?"

I drag my hand over my jaw. "You know, this was a bad idea. I think I can do this on my own. I will report back with my findings. You can go back to the inn."

"Oh no." She shakes her head. "I need to know what else is in those boxes." She gasps, hand to heart. "Dear Jesus, am I going to find another notebook, but this one is cut-up butts? And then cut-up—"

"There is one notebook," I say before she can go any further. "That's it."

"Uh-huh, well, we're just going to have to find that out for sure, aren't we?" She nods toward the closet. "Go on, pull down more. We have some things to pick through."

"I have never been more confused and fascinated at the same time," Larkin says, sitting in the middle of my room, my belongings surrounding her. She looks up at me with those bright, intriguing eyes. "Who knew you were so complex?"

I'm sitting on my bed, my back against the headboard, letting her paw through my childhood possessions. I gave up helping after she found the Nano Kitty I called Ralph stuffed away in a box. "Complex? I think I'm pretty simple."

She shakes her head. "No way. Look at all of this." She motions to the open boxes. "This does not read 'simple man.'" She lifts up an old diary. "Through this fantastic literature, we learned that you appreciate the smell of grape soda. And this"—she holds up a binder full of loose-leaf paper—"this let us know that you are positively irrational because you kept every piece of geometry homework you ever had after you decided it would be a 'nifty' goal for the year."

"Everyone has to have goals, no matter how big or small."

"And this." She lifts an old piece of fabric out of a box. "You kept this piece of plaid fabric because the colors reminded you of the summer day you had your first kiss."

"It was during a sunset—very romantic for a thirteen-year-old."

She laughs out loud and then leans back on her hands. "I wasn't aware you were so sentimental."

"It was a first kiss; weren't you sentimental about yours?"

She considers it. "Not really."

"Must not have been good, then."

"Was yours?"

Wistfully, I look up at the ceiling. "It was a beautiful day—"

"Okay, okay, I don't need to hear the story. Who was the poor girl who took your kissing flower?"

"Raina Mastiff. I believe she lives in Texas now and is married to a pro football player."

"Seriously?" Larkin asks.

"Yeah. She might have the life of luxury now, but nothing will ever beat that first kiss."

Larkin chuckles. "You know, I like it when you joke around. You should do it more often."

"I joke around with you."

"Not nearly enough." She picks up a notebook, which we established I kept but never wrote in because I liked the mountain on the cover too much. "How about we use this for your bucket list?"

"The untouched mountain notebook? I'm not sure I'm ready to make that kind of commitment."

"We have to start somewhere, and what better than with this cherished notebook you never wrote in but kept for years." She picks up a pen, flips the front page over, and then places the pen on the paper.

I jokingly gasp, which makes her laugh as she scrawls something across the top.

"What are you writing?"

"'Ford Chance's bucket list.'"

"You realize a bucket list is representative of things you want to do before you die."

She glances up at me. "Well aware, but we're still calling it that." Pen still poised, she says, "Okay, from what we've conjured up while looking through these boxes . . . you were incredibly anal retentive and never had any fun . . . besides cutting out boobs."

I point a finger at her. "What did we say? No more referencing the boob book."

She holds up her hands in defense, a smile passing over her lips. "That was the last one."

"Better be."

She chuckles. "So, tell me, Ford Chance, what are some things you always wanted to do as a kid?"

I shrug. "I don't know." I look out the window, where rain is starting to smear across the glass. Dark clouds loom all around the island, promising a storm is about to break open the sky. "Honestly, I have nothing to complain about. I've had a wonderful life. I was given what I consider a second chance when I was seven and my parents came along. I've never complained since then. I'm just grateful."

"Did you ever ask for anything?"

I shake my head. "No. I had everything I needed. A home, people who cared about me, food, clothes . . . I was set."

She pauses, and her head tilts while she studies me. "Because you didn't have those things when you were with your birth mom and grandma?"

I smooth my hand over my cheek. "You know, the foster care system will help you realize one thing—the safety of a home is more important than any other material item. Growing up, that's all I wanted for me and Cooper: to maintain that safety, to hold on to it." I take in the four walls surrounding us while thunder rumbles in the distance. "I think that's why I was hit pretty hard when my parents said they were going to move. Because this house brought me a level of comfort that's hard to explain." I blow out a heavy breath, a bittersweet sadness overtaking me. "Hell, I don't think I realized how much it mattered to me until just now. Losing this place."

Larkin glances down, growing serious. "I can't say that I fully understand the connection you have, but what you're saying makes so much sense."

"And the reason why these boxes seem so sad is because I didn't spend much time doing anything for myself. I helped around the house a lot. I did most of the chores. I wanted to do my part, because . . ." I bite down on my bottom lip and look up toward the ceiling. I hear Larkin move from the floor and make her way to the bed, where she sits down and places her hand on mine. "I know my parents adopted us, but I always had the fear in the back of my head—no matter how many times they reassured me—that we were going to have to leave, to give up this home and the love in it. I was worried Cooper and I were going to be split up, because that was a heavy concern while we were floating around in foster care. I was constantly trying to make sure that we were on our best behavior so we'd have a place to stay, a place where we could stay together."

"Oh, Ford." She places her hand in mine now. "I can't imagine what that must have felt like, carrying that worry on your shoulders. Did you ever talk to your parents about it?"

I nod. "I had a panic attack one night. It was right after I forgot to mow the lawn that day. I remembered and bolted out of bed, down to the garage, and tried to start the lawn mower in the middle of the night. Mom and Dad stopped me and asked me what I was doing. When I told them how sorry I was and begged them to keep me, they had a long conversation with me about how they would never get rid of me, ever. But by then, I was in high school."

"I can't believe you held that in for so long."

"I never wanted to worry Mom and Dad. And it's not to say we never did anything fun, because we did." Thunder cracks just outside, growing louder. "We went on vacation, but when I was home, I was keeping my room clean, taking care of chores, helping my siblings, anticipating their needs before Mom had to worry about it. I was doing the big brother stuff. And then in high school, I decided to hang out with Dad in the office and learn the business because I knew he'd put his life into the store, and I wanted to make sure that lived on." I love the store, I really do, but a small part of me knows that I'm running Watchful Wanderers to prove to my parents that they made the right decision in adopting me and Coop many years ago. There's a need to prove my worth, and I'm not sure that will ever fade away.

"So then, there seems to be a lot that you haven't done, that you missed out on because of your fear."

"Seems that way."

She twists her lips to the side as she thinks. "You know, I happen to know a lot about this island," she says. "And I happen to know a lot about the store." Her eyes meet mine, our hands still connected. "What would you say to letting me show you around *my* childhood? You could experience everything from the smallest of things, like eating ice cream on the perfect rock, to going to Watchful Wanderers with an adventure planned."

"It sounds like I'm in good hands."

"Yeah?" she asks, hope blooming across her face.

"Yeah. I think that's just what I need."

Chapter Twenty

DR. BEAU

Rain pelts my windshield as I navigate Marina Island's narrow back roads.

I hate house calls.

It's the one thing I can't stand about being a doctor on an island. And yeah, that might make me look like an ass, but there's something about not having all the things that I need when making a house call. This is my second time returning to town after having to drive back because I didn't have all the right tools; thankfully this return is bringing me back home rather than having to make another trip. And because of that, I'm now stuck driving five miles per hour in a torrential downpour.

Using the controls on my steering wheel, I turn down my music, because that always seems to help people drive better during stressful situations. I keep my hands firmly placed at ten and two as I lean toward the windshield, hoping for any sort of visibility.

I've reduced my speed to barely moving when I catch a flash of teal and red off to the side. I brake and spot a lone figure wandering along the side of the road.

"What the . . ." I pull forward some more until I'm right next to the person.

Palmer.

Why the hell is she out here in the storm?

I roll down my window and shout, "Palmer, what are you doing?"

Startled, she jumps to the side, trips, and falls flat on her butt in a puddle of mud.

Thankfully no one is attempting to travel these roads besides me . . . and Palmer, apparently, so I put my car in park, throw on my hazards, and hop out.

Drenched, she has her cast arm cuddled into her chest, her short ponytail is clinging to the back of her neck, and her T-shirt is practically see-through.

"What are you doing out here?" I shout over the pounding of the storm.

"What does it look like?" she yells back, still on the ground. "Enjoying a lovely walk in the rain."

"You're not supposed to get your cast wet."

"Well aware, Dr. Obvious."

I open up the passenger door of my car and hold out my hand. "Let me help you up and get in."

"I'm wet and muddy and you have a nice car."

"That's what car detailing is for!" I shout, yanking her up by her good arm.

Before she can protest, I guide her into my car, shut the door, and then quickly get in on the driver's side. The rain pelts the metal of my car as I take a deep breath. "Christ, you're really far from your parents' house."

"I know," she answers.

"Well, let me get you back there."

"No," she says quickly, placing her hand on my arm. When my eyes meet hers, a flash of vulnerability crosses her expression, and I'm reminded of the text conversation I had with Larkin. Something bad happened between the Chance siblings. "Please don't take me to my parents' house. Anywhere but there."

The pain in her voice. The sadness, desperation. It makes me say something I probably shouldn't, something I'll most likely regret, because I have feelings for this girl. I've always had feelings for her, and seeing her again has only made them resurface. And sure, she wanted to push my chin dimple and said I smelled good, but that doesn't mean anything. The girl never stays in one place; she's always moving around the world. Getting attached to her is a bad, bad idea, my logical brain reminds me, especially after the history we share. But that doesn't stop me from saying, "You can come back to my place. We should change out your cast anyway."

"You don't mind?"

"No, not at all." I swallow down the lie.

"I would be really grateful," she says, squeezing my arm.

Good job, Beau. Now your heart is going to be tripping in your chest all night as you navigate around this girl.

"Sure." I put the car in drive and turn off my hazards.

We drive in silence, winding our way slowly through the back roads. I have tons of questions on my mind, leading with *Why such a long walk?* followed by *Why don't you want to go back to your parents' house?* Ending with, *Do you ever think about me? Because I sure as hell think about you.* But I stay quiet and focus on the roads.

When we get to Marina Ave, I let out a low breath, grateful for the wider roads, and I drive toward my house.

"I don't know where you live; is that weird?" she asks, finally breaking the silence.

"I live in an apartment above the practice."

"Really?" she asks, surprise in her voice. "I guess I never thought what could be on the upper level, but that makes sense."

"It's easier that way—only have to pay one mortgage."

"Smart man." She shifts on her seat. "You know, I'm going to be honest with you: my mud ass is getting all over your nice leather seats. I'm nervous to see what kind of damage I've done."

I chuckle. "It's fine. Really. I'm not worried. I've had worse in my cars. I actually helped a lady deliver a baby in the back seat once. The detailers at the body shop know me well, and I was due for a clean. This just gives me an excuse." I drive up to the cream-colored Victorian house with sage-green and burnt-orange accents—the place I call home.

"I can, uh, give you money for it."

"Yeah, that's not going to happen." I pull into the driveway looping around the back of the practice, where I've grown a peaceful garden full of colorful peonies. Last summer I installed a stone walkway that leads to a small bistro set canopied by a grove of overhanging ponderosa pines. "Your money's no good here, but nice try." I put the car in park and let the rain fill the silence for a few breaths. "Are you going to want to shower?"

"Would you mind if I did?"

"Not at all. Your cast is already wet, and it would be good to get you warmed up and get the mud off your ass. I have some clothes you can borrow. Warning: they will be large on you."

"That means they'll be comfortable." She smiles softly.

"After that, we can reset your cast. We're going to have to be extremely careful because it's been a week, and resetting right now is not ideal."

"I'll be the best patient: still and a good listener."

"Good." I glance at the time on my watch. "Did you want me to take you back home after that . . . or did you want to stay longer?"

"Can I?" she asks, her perfectly moss-green eyes staring up at me, begging me.

"Of course. We can eat dinner or something . . . that's if you're hungry."

"Starving."

"Then it's a plan. Stay right there, and I'll help you out of the car."

◆ ◆ ◆

"You're super gentle," Palmer says as I carefully rewrap her wrist with cotton.

She took a quick shower, which was surprising. I somehow expected her to be in there longer, but she was in and out and popped out of my bathroom smelling like me and dressed in my clothes.

For a guy who has compared all girls to the one in front of him, it's hard to see her in my clothes, to see her in a position that a girlfriend would take. Especially since I know there's no way she'd ever look at me like that, regardless of my chin dimple. Not after everything we've been through.

"Are you saying I have good bedside manner?" I tease, focusing back on the present.

"I would say that you do. Your hands are even warm."

"Keep the compliments coming. I'm loving them."

She chuckles. "Your shampoo smells nice, and I'm shocked that your bathroom was spotless. I assumed a bachelor would have a nasty bathroom."

"You assumed wrong," I say, snipping the cotton. "What kind of guys have you been hanging out with?"

"All the wrong ones," she says while I prepare the fiberglass wrap.

"So, you're saying no one has tickled your fancy while traveling around the world?"

"Who our age says 'tickled your fancy'?"

"Apparently doctors with warm hands and good bedside manners." I wink, and she smiles.

"No, I haven't." She continues to hold still while I wrap her up. "I think everyone assumes I've had this glamorous life, traveling from country to country, eating delicious food, dining with celebrities, wearing designer brands. And yes, it's been a once-in-a-lifetime opportunity. I know I'm quite lucky with all the places I've seen and the people I've met, but I've also spent that time traveling alone. There are a lot of isolated nights, way more than the nights full of company."

"I can see how that would get tiresome after a while. Is that why you're back home? For some companionship?"

She shakes her head. "I'm back home because I can't afford to live in New York City anymore." Her voice goes quiet, and I glance up at her. Tears well in her eyes. "Shit, don't repeat that to anyone—no one knows."

"What do you mean? Did you lose your apartment?"

"I didn't lose it—I told the landlord I couldn't make rent and luckily found someone to take over my lease." She shrugs as I finish wrapping her cast. "Jobs dried up, passed on to celebrities and influencers with more status, and so did the money." A tear slips down her cheek, and she quickly wipes it away. "I came back here thinking I'd have time to gather myself, to figure out where to go from here, but as you know, my parents are selling the house and moving to some apartment in Seattle, which means I have no idea what I'm doing."

"Is that why you were walking in the rain?" I ask, my heart aching for her.

"Sort of. I just needed to get out of the house. I didn't want to face Ford or hear him joking around with Larkin, so I took off and just started walking. I lost track of time and where I was, and once it started raining, I just let it fall down on me. I didn't seek shelter, didn't attempt to call anyone. I wanted it to rain on me. I wanted that moment of sadness, the chance to reflect on where I've landed."

"Did you get it?" I finish up and throw away the packaging.

"No." She shakes her head. "But I did get a friend instead." She gives me a halfhearted smile. "I mean, I guess I forced myself upon you."

"You didn't." I take her hand and help her off the exam table. "I invited you."

"Because I begged you."

"Hey." I lift her chin, her sad eyes meeting mine. "How about we forget all that crap and enjoy the evening. You have a new cast, you're no longer Mud Butt, and you finally smell decent."

"Wow." She laughs. "What high standards you have for company."

"I think so." I lead her out of the doctor's office and up toward the private residence. "We can make the most of this night, turn that frown upside down."

"How did I not realize you're a bit of a goofball?"

"A goofball?" We make it up to the top of the steps, and I open my apartment door. "I'm not a goofball—I'm a strong alpha man that everyone fawns over."

"Is that where you were coming from when you found me on the side of the road? Nursing a fawning patient?"

"More like a warty patient."

I shut the door behind her and then make my way to the kitchen. I converted the upstairs to an open-concept floor plan, connecting the living room, kitchen, and dining room into one giant space and leaving the living quarters to the back with the bathroom. It's small, but it works perfectly for me.

"Wait, what?" she asks. "You did a house call for a wart?"

"It started off with a cough, ended with a wart. I had to come back to the office to get the proper tools to remove the wart, which is why I was driving in the rain."

She takes a seat at the kitchen island. "So, what you're telling me is that I owe a debt of gratitude to a wart?"

I chuckle and pull out some eggs and bread from my fridge, along with some milk. "A finger wart, to be exact."

"Which finger?"

I smirk. "Middle. French toast okay for dinner?"

"That's perfect. And so, does this mean your patient was flipping you off the entire time while the wart was being removed?"

I crack a few eggs into a bowl and toss the shells in the garbage. "Indeed, the entire time."

"And how did that make you feel?"

"Honestly . . . used and abused," I tease.

"Poor Dr. Beau, dragged around Marina Island for wart removals while being flipped the bird."

With a fork, I whisk the eggs together and add some milk, cinnamon, nutmeg, and a touch of vanilla. "You'd be surprised by the amount of warts on this island."

"Seriously?"

I nod. "Oh yeah, I've made many house calls for warts, which makes me wonder why I don't keep all the necessary tools in my bag. Maybe someday I'll learn."

"What's been the worst wart removal?"

I walk over to the pantry where I keep my griddle and pull it out. I set it up so it's facing Palmer and I can talk to her while dunking the bread slices and cooking them. "The worst wart removal? You really want to know?" I bring the egg mixture and bread to the island. Thankfully my griddle heats up fast.

"Oddly, even though this isn't predinner talk, it's keeping my mind busy, so yes, tell me your most horrifying wart removal."

I dip a slice of bread in the egg. "It wasn't a home visit, thankfully, but I was not expecting to walk into the exam room to an older gentleman with his pants off."

"Oh my God." Palmer covers her mouth. "Was it on his penis?" she whispers.

I shake my head and place the bread on the heated griddle. "No, thank God, but it was in the crack of his butt, and it was bothering him, so he had to spread for me, and I had to remove it."

Palmer cringes. "Oh God, I could not even imagine."

"Worst part about it? He said I was so gentle that, before he left, he scheduled a prostate exam for the next week."

Palmer lets out a cackle and covers her mouth. "Dr. Beau, your bedside manner really is impeccable."

"I enjoy pleasing my patients, in more ways than one."

"So disturbing." She shakes her head, grinning.

"You have to have some sort of horror story for traveling."

"Oh, I do for sure."

I place another slice of bread on the griddle. "Care to share?"

"I mean, it would only be fair, right? You talked about your butt warts—a wonderful dinner conversation—might as well delight you with something equally fascinating."

"I'm all ears," I say with a wink.

"Which means I need a good story." She sits back in her chair and gives it some thought. I keep my eyes on her and see it the moment she thinks of something that would evenly match a butt wart.

That smile, absolutely stunning. Equally devastating to my will.

"You have a story, don't you?"

She nods, her cheeks turning pink.

"I do, but oh God, it's embarrassing. At least your story was about someone else; this is about me."

"Would it help you if I said while removing the wart, I slipped and accidentally moved my fingers a little too far . . . if you know what I mean? Hence the scheduled prostate exam?"

Her smile lights up the kitchen as she leans forward. "Really . . . you slipped?"

"Unfortunately. Not my finest moment . . . nor was it his. But apparently we bonded, so there you have it. And don't forget how I passed out on a lady's butt while giving her a shot. Looks like I have a penchant for fascinating butt stories. I'm sure I have you beat on the embarrassment scale."

"Okay, that does make me feel better." She moves her hand through her wet hair, pushing the strands to one side. "I was in Santorini, doing a shoot at this quaint restaurant run by an older couple. It's been passed down from generation to generation. It overlooked the cliffs and was positively beautiful with the white walls and the blue ocean behind it. Lit only by candles—just so romantic. I dressed up for the occasion, really going for a fancy look in a bright-red silk dress that draped low in the back. I took some stunning photos that are some of my favorites to date."

"I think I saw those pictures," I say, glancing up to her surprised face.

"You follow me on Instagram?"

"Yeah." I shrug as if it's no big deal. "Good to keep up on people, you know. Maybe live vicariously through them on occasion."

"I didn't know that. I should follow you."

"Be prepared to be bored. It's mainly pictures of Marina Island and the hikes I go on. An occasional picture of my food because I heard that's what you're supposed to do. I don't dare use hashtags, though."

She laughs. "Too scary?"

"Just not clever enough. But I'm Dr. Beau Beau, if you want to follow me."

"Dr. Beau Beau is your IG name? Oh, that's great." She picks up her phone and quickly searches for me. "Found you." I watch her scroll through my feed. "You're right, lots of Marina—wait a second." Her mouth falls open as she looks up at me. "Uh, hello, thirst trap."

"What?" I ask.

She turns her phone toward me, showing the picture I took on a hiking trail. I'm shirtless, sweaty, and possibly flexing just a little.

"This is totally a thirst-trap picture."

"What's a thirst trap? And how would you know?"

"I'm the queen of thirst-trap pictures—well, respectable ones— because my parents do follow me after all. A thirst trap is supposed to entice people sexually . . . you know, a flash of a leg here and there or, in your case, a shirtless picture showing off your endless abs."

"They're not endless," I say, feeling myself blush.

"Well, you have shorts on, so I can't really see where they end." She gives me a coy grin, and I swear I can feel the back of my ears heat up. "But either way, this picture is a total thirst trap, and I'm here for it. And this looks way better than Watchful Wanderers' terrible Instagram." She rolls her eyes at that comment. "You should post more of them."

"For whom? My sister? Pretty sure I have five followers. Six if you just followed me."

"You have two hundred and seventy-four."

"What?" I ask, shocked. "That's . . . a lot. I don't even think I know that many people."

"That's what happens when you post a thirst trap."

"All right, all right, enough with the shirtless picture—I want to know what happened in Greece."

"Oh, right." She sets her phone down. "So, I took some scenic pictures with a wineglass, you know, the typical IG shots, and then I was preparing a video of me eating some of their most popular dishes. The owner was so horrified that I was going to eat in such a pretty dress that she begged me to wear a bib."

"A bib?" I say, my eyes widening. "Like . . . a baby's bib?"

"She had these fancy ones—it wasn't like a Mickey Mouse ABC bib. So I figured, why not—it would be a good way to show off my silly side—so I put the bib on. I did the entire video with it on, ate some of the most delicious food of my life, and drank the evening away."

"Sounds like the perfect night."

"It was, until I took the bib off."

"Uh-oh, did you stain your dress?" I flip the toast on the griddle.

"I wish," she scoffs. "I went to take off the bib, and when I was undoing it, I was unaware—thank you, wine—that I'd undone the top of my dress as well, and because the dress was low cut in the back, I was braless . . ."

"Oh shit," I say, putting down the last slice.

"Oh yes, the owners got more than a thank-you from me. They got an entire show, and the worst part? I was just drunk enough that I didn't notice until I went to shake the horrified owner's hand, and she told me that my breasts were pointing straight at her."

I laugh out loud, my chest rumbling with laughter. "That's freaking amazing. Did you cover up quickly?"

"You would think, but instead, because of wine—once again—I said in America, we thank each other with a tit to tit."

"Please . . . please tell me what that is." I can't hold back my smile. "And please tell me you did it with the owner."

"I attempted to. Like the wino that I am, I lifted my naked breast and tried to 'high five' it with the owner's. She was so shocked she shielded her breasts and told me to get out." She taps her chin. "Hmm, now that I think about it, I've gotten into a predicament or two thanks to wine." She lifts her cast up in the air. "This being one of them."

"Makes for a good story, though—which, by the way . . . did you come up with a good story to tell people about how you hurt your arm?"

"Well, since I don't ever talk to anyone, no, I haven't."

"You haven't met up with any of your old friends since being here?" I ask, flipping the french toast over. Golden brown, perfect.

"Don't have many friends here. Ever since the fire, I really haven't stayed connected with anyone."

"And here I thought it was just me that you weren't talking to," I tease, but the joke falls flat.

"It was too hard," she says quietly.

"I was kidding, Palmer. And you know . . . we really weren't that close."

"I guess we weren't." Her eyes meet mine. "I still don't understand what you were doing there that night."

"I guess right place at the right time," I say, trying not to remember that horrific night—Palmer in the midst of flames, searching for a way out as she crawled across the floor of Watchful Wanderers.

"You weren't there for the party," she says, shocking me, since we've never talked about what happened. "Were you?"

I shake my head. "No, I was going for a walk, trying to clear my head. I saw the party and, I don't know, I thought I would see what was going on. Like I said, right place, right time." I pause. "Do your parents know that the party was your plan?"

She shakes her head. "No one knows. They still think it was a bunch of rowdy teenagers, breaking in and causing trouble. They don't know it was all my doing, that I almost burned down their business." She looks off to the side. "I almost destroyed everything my dad worked for. It took Ford and my dad a long time to bounce back from what happened." Tears well up in her eyes. "I haven't talked about it with anyone . . . ever."

"It's not good to hold things like that in, Palmer."

She shakes her head. "There's no way I could tell them. Ford would never talk to me again. I think my dad would disown me. They don't know the truth, and I plan on keeping it that way."

"Is that why you fled? Why you left Marina Island?"

"Yes," she answers. "I never had any serious intention of traveling around the world, despite what I told my family. But I was too nervous to go back home, to face the reality of what I did. So, I put on a facade in front of them—I was just too horrified to let them know the truth."

"And what was the truth?" I ask.

"I almost took away their livelihood, Beau. I couldn't be around the store and look at what I'd jeopardized day in and day out. I needed to escape the guilt. And I wanted to punish myself in a way, pay a penance by distancing myself, but also be someone other than the family screwup. My parents always said to pave your own path. And that's what I set out to do, not just to prove to them that I could do it, but to prove it to myself."

"I can understand that."

"It's not like my choices affected anyone else, though. The store thrived, my family lived on, and I . . . well, I grew more and more lost."

She looks down, and I realize we've reached an incredibly heavy part of our conversation, so I decide not to dive too deep. It's obvious her mind is reeling, and the last thing I want to do is make her feel worse. She came here for solace, and that's what I'm going to give her.

"Well . . . we missed you around here," I say, taking the toast off the griddle and putting it on a plate for her. "Maple or regular syrup?"

CHAPTER TWENTY-ONE
PALMER

We missed you around here . . .

Those five little words pack such a punch that I feel like I can barely grasp enough air for my lungs.

And sitting across from Beau, wearing his clothes, smelling like his fresh soap, and staring into his brilliantly understanding eyes, makes it that much worse. I've never talked about what happened out of fear of judgment and hate. But Beau isn't looking at me like that; instead, he's offering me comfort, the same kind of comfort he offered me that night, all those years ago.

The night he saved me.

The night we almost kissed . . .

Those sirens screaming in the dark of night, breaking the lock of our eyes, the comfort of our embrace after he saved me—they still play in my head late at night, causing me to break out in a heavy sweat.

The guilt consuming me, eating away at my resolve until my lungs don't feel like they're filling up with enough air.

And yet, to this day, I still can't say anything. I can't fathom coming forward and telling them the truth. I would be isolated, more than I am now.

When I left Marina Island, I left with my tail tucked between my legs, fleeing the scene of a crime, not looking back out of fear that no one would ever welcome me with open arms. I kept my mouth shut, I forced Beau to lie, and in the end, I only hurt the people I loved, leaving them to clean up my mess.

It was supposed to be a secret party in the back of Watchful Wanderers. My parents were out of town, it was the end of my senior year, and we all wanted one last hurrah before we went off to college. I'd just finished a long shift of unpacking new products, taking pictures for the website, and enjoying every second of my job. I remember being in the best mood—the night was young, and my life felt so full of promise. I set up the party, with candles in the back of the store as our only source of light so we wouldn't attract any onlookers. The security cameras had recently been set up, but I knew they weren't on just yet, which gave us the chance to have a party without getting caught. It was the perfect plan, the perfect last moment before we all went our separate ways.

And that perfect moment turned into the worst night of my entire life. I was out back, saying goodbye to my friends, and from the corner of my eye I saw a flame in the store. A soft glow of terror. My stomach dropped as I realized I never blew out the candles. I burst through the back door and attempted to put out the flames using a bucket and water from the sink, but it didn't work: the flames grew to a powerful force, and I was caught in the middle of it, crawling on the ground, screaming for help.

That's when Beau showed up out of nowhere. He wasn't even in the same grade as me, but he happened to be back home from college for the weekend. He pulled me from the flames just as the firefighters arrived. He held on to me as I watched the back of the store go up in flames, crying hysterically. And when the police questioned me, he held me then too.

After the EMTs cleared me, he walked me back home, brought me up to my room, and told me everything was going to be okay. That's when I told him it wasn't. That's when I told him what had happened.

He's the only one who knows.

And he's kept that secret ever since.

"Palmer?"

"Huh?" I ask, my eyes snapping up to his.

"Maple syrup or regular?"

"Oh, sorry." I blink a few times. "Uh, maple, please."

"Is everything okay?" He's always been so perceptive, protective, and quick to lend a hand. That's evident by what happened tonight. And the night of the fire.

"Yeah, sorry. Just letting my thoughts get to me."

"I shouldn't have brought up the fire and all of that," he says, handing me a plate and placing his next to me on the island. "I'm sorry."

"Don't apologize. I know I'm probably long overdue to talk about it."

"Probably." He joins me at the table. "But it's not something we need to talk about now. We can talk about other things, like . . . that time I nailed you in the head while playing kickball back in high school."

I let out a light laugh. Even though Beau was two years older than me, we still ran into each other throughout school. Our grades collided, our extracurricular activities crisscrossed, and there were plenty of times when we were around each other. But we never spoke. Or it was rare when we did. The most I ever talked to Beau was probably when he was at the store with Larkin and their dad, searching for different goods for their next adventure. I would direct them to the aisle they needed or check the back for stock.

And oh my God was Beau the dreamy older senior when I was a sophomore. I think I was the only one in my grade who thought so, because he was shy, reserved, and spent more time with his glasses on, reading books on the bleachers, than participating, but when you got him to open up, to have a little fun, he would get into it, and that's when his smile would come out to play. But I was never the one who opened him up—I just observed from a distance. It was Larkin who could guarantee the best smile from him.

Talk about a massive crush, though. Gosh, I thought Beau Novak was everything.

So, the fact that I'm sitting in his apartment, in his clothes, smelling his soap all over my body, and sharing a meal with him—my little teenage heart is going pitter-patter.

And my grown-up heart, well . . . that's thumping hard as well.

"Sure, you want to talk about how you made my nose bleed in front of everyone?" I ask. "Let's talk about that." I cut a piece of french toast with my fork.

"It was a drip of blood, not a geyser," he retorts.

"Still, you made me bleed." I take a bite of the french toast and groan as I chew. "Dr. Beau Beau, this is delicious."

"Never thought how ridiculous that name was until you just said it out loud. And something tells me you'll continue to use it."

"Easily." I smirk. "Seriously, though, this is really good. So . . . you heal people, and you cook. How are you single?" And then it hits me—maybe he's not . . . "Wait, are you single?" I glance around his apartment as he casually eats his french toast.

"Yes, I'm single. Between all the wart removals and prostate exams, haven't had much time to meet anyone."

"And how can you be in the mood after all of that?"

"Compartmentalizing. It's my only savior. When I clock out, I'm done. I don't bring work home with me—well, unless I'm on call."

"Smart, but . . . your home is right above your work."

He lightly chuckles. "Yeah, there's that, but it's pretty easy to let go of what happened that day. I do a lot of hiking, as evident on my Instagram. It helps me escape."

"I can't remember the last time I went on a hike. Sort of traded in my hiking boots for a pair of heels."

"Do you miss it?" he asks before putting a large piece of french toast in his mouth. "Hiking, that is?"

"I don't really know. I think I've blocked that off. Anything to do with the store, I've kind of cut out of my life." Including my family . . .

"Do you miss traveling?" Beau asks. "All the fancy meals, the escapism—are you desperate to get back?"

I shrug and push a piece of french toast around on my plate. "I don't miss being alone. Honestly, I have no idea what I miss at this point. I know you're not here to be my psychologist or help me solve my problems—you just got caught up in giving me a roof and a clean pair of clothes—but if I were to lay it all out there, I'm not sure what I want, or what I'm supposed to do with my life. I'm at a loss."

"I can understand that. Larkin was the same way after our dad passed away. She was really lost, and the one thing that she clung to was the store. It wasn't our childhood home, it wasn't the lake, it was the store where she would go so often with Dad. If it wasn't for Ford giving her a chance, I'm not sure she'd be where she is today."

"But she knew what she wanted, right?"

"No, not what she wanted, but she knew what she loved." Beau turns toward me in his chair. "So, what do you love, Palmer?"

Good question.

Feeling ashamed, I say, "I don't really know."

"Then maybe you should figure that out, and then the rest will fall into place."

"How do I figure that out?" I ask.

He taps my plate with his fork. "Not sure, but I do know these won't taste good cold, so eat up."

"So, this is what single men do at night by themselves?"

Beau chuckles. "The *cool* single men."

I glance over all the puzzle pieces scattered across his dining room table. "They build gardenscape puzzles? I mean, it's not even something manly like . . . I don't know, Darth Vader or something like that."

"Gardenscapes are more challenging." He carefully shuffles through the pieces, looking for the edges. "I like a good challenge. Now, if you're going to stay here, then you're going to have to help out. No free rides, Palmer."

"I don't know if I've ever done a puzzle like this before."

"Then now is the perfect time to start, because I'm an expert." He adjusts his glasses on his nose, and I can't help but think how cute he is. Wearing a pair of sweatpants, some sort of doctors' kickball team shirt, with his feet bare of socks, he's casual but also incredibly sexy in a nerdy kind of way. The perfect kind of way.

I've seen my fair share of men around the world, and they're always trying to impress you with their fancy cars, their designer clothes, and their opulent dwellings. Not Dr. Beau. He's simple in the best way. A modest apartment above his private practice. Basic clothing that speaks nothing but comfort, and he couldn't have cared less that I sat in his passenger side with a muddy butt. He welcomed it, actually.

He's down to earth.

He's real.

He's just . . . wonderful.

He knocks my knee with his knuckle. "Come on, help me sort."

"I'm down a hand," I say, lifting my cast.

"Which means you still have one working one." He nudges me again. "I think you'll find joy in the simple pleasures." He turns to the side. "Alexa, play soft pop."

"Soft pop?" I snort.

"Playing soft pop based off your listening history," Alexa says just as "The One" by Taylor Swift starts to play.

"Soft pop is where it's at," Beau says. "Soothing, catchy, and puts you in the puzzling mood."

"I didn't know there was such a thing."

"There is. Now help me with the edges—if we're going to complete this by the end of the night, you need to get your hand dirty."

"You think we're going to complete this?" I ask.

"If you start actually working, we will."

Chuckling, I begin to sift through the pieces. "How long have you been puzzling?"

"Years."

"Years?" I ask, surprised.

"Ever since high school. My grandpa was a big puzzler, and when he was sick, I'd go spend time with him, and we would do puzzles together while listening to his favorite jazz music. It was relaxing, and I've carried on the tradition ever since. I have a whole closet full of puzzles that I'll rotate through, and most of them are from my grandpa's collection. He was the one who got me into gardenscapes as well."

"That's actually really charming."

He lifts a brow when he looks at me. "Why, Palmer Chance, are you calling me charming?"

I toss an edge piece into his pile. "I think I am."

"Nothing like the nerdy doctor charming the popular girl."

"Popular girl? No, that's not me."

He laughs. "You were easily the popular girl growing up. Even as a senior, I knew you were the popular girl. Everyone loved you, and there was a reason—you were so outgoing and fun. You made a bloody nose during kickball the new trend."

"Stop." I laugh. "That's not true."

"Seriously, though, you were the *it* girl." He connects two pieces together and pushes them to the side. "I honestly was surprised you even talked to me at times."

"Why would you say that?" I ask, confused. Did he not know who he was? Need I remind him . . . Beau Novak, the accomplished, handsome, and beautifully sweet boy.

"Because I was kind of on my own path. I didn't hang with the popular crowd. Kind of buried in my books."

"But that's what I thought was so great about you. You didn't care what others thought, while I was super concerned with what everyone thought of me. Seeing you during lunch, leaning up against a tree, your hair falling over your brow, a book in your hand . . ." I shrug. "Drove me crazy."

His hand pauses as he slowly turns toward me. I keep my eyes focused on the puzzle pieces as my confession rocks my nerves. I can't believe I just admitted that to him.

"Drove you crazy? As in . . . ?"

How could he not know? How can he really be this clueless?

Did he not notice all the times I looked at him longingly while he was at the store? How I fumbled my words when he was around?

Every instinct begs me to change the subject, but because I honestly think I've lost my mind, I clear my throat. "As in, you know, like, a crush."

Now he shifts on the couch and truly faces me. "You had a crush on me in high school? Like, an actual crush?" He shakes his head. "There's no way that's true."

I nod slowly. "Oh, it's true. I had the biggest crush on you." I finally look at him. "I thought you were so fascinating, so different from everyone else, and that captured me."

"You're not just saying that?" he asks.

I shake my head. He reaches out and touches my chin, bringing my eyes to his. I swallow hard when I see the way his irises grow darker from the connection of our gazes.

"I had a crush on you. A terrible one," he says, pulling all the air from my lungs. "Why do you think I was always in the store? Especially whenever I visited from college. Anything to catch a glimpse."

"Seriously?" I ask, my stomach now doing somersaults.

"Oh yeah. I had it bad." He wets his lips. "Really fucking bad."

"I . . . uh . . . I didn't realize."

He pulls on the back of his neck and glances over my shoulder. "That night, the night of the fire, I was actually walking over to the store because I heard you were going to be there. I was going to ask you out on a date."

My mouth falls open as I fully turn toward him. "You were?"

"Yeah. I was only there for a few days, but I couldn't go back to school without knowing what it was like to take you out. Never got the chance, and then by the time I was able to make it home again, you'd taken off."

Talk about completely shocked. I would never have thought that someone like Dr. Beau Novak would even look my way. He's so down to earth, so grounded, and I'm . . . well . . . I'm a train wreck. What does he even see in me?

"What are you thinking?" he asks. "I can see a shift in your body language. Did I say too much?"

I shake my head. "Not at all. I'm just . . . surprised is all. You're so great," I say, speaking the truth. "You have so much going for you. You're levelheaded, a good person, an intelligent man with drive and purpose. What could you have possibly seen in someone like me? Someone who's broke, homeless, and makes bad decisions involving wine?"

He smiles softly. "Your smile can brighten anyone's mood. And your spirit—it's vibrant, passionate, addictive. You're a ray of light on the darkest of days, and maybe you've made some decisions that didn't pan out in the past, but you're also so brave, so daring, that it makes me want to try new things, to put myself out there."

"Why don't I feel like any of those things?" I ask.

"Because you've cast a veil of doubt over yourself. It just needs to be lifted by the right person," he answers.

"And who would that person be?"

He shrugs. "That's for you to decide." His eyes fall to my mouth and then travel back up to my eyes.

I wet my lips, the thought of kissing Beau careening through my body like a semi bumping and tumbling my nerves with anticipation.

I've waited so long to know what his lips taste like. I've thought about it. Dreamed of it. Conjured up ideas of how he might've kissed me when I was in high school.

On a picnic table overlooking a lake.

On the top of a hiking trail while taking in the beautiful views.

In the back of a movie theater while holding hands.

On the hood of his car while we shared an ice cream.

All the images flash through my mind, images I thought of over and over, all those years ago.

But I never pictured this. As a grown-up, sitting on his couch, wearing his clothes, solving a puzzle with him as he confesses his attraction to me.

I take a deep breath. "What if I've known what I've wanted for a long time but have been too scared to take it?" He was older than me; he was Beau Novak, the beautiful bookworm who was out of everyone's league. I was so convinced he'd never even give me even one glance back then.

"Then I'd say you're not living your life the way you should. If I've learned anything from my parents, it's that life is too short to not take action." He says the words, and it's as if something crosses over in his thoughts, a realization. He chuckles. "I should probably take my own advice."

"What do you mean?" I ask.

He lets out a deep breath. "Palmer, I really want to fucking kiss you. I've wanted to kiss you for a long time, and I know that if I don't kiss you, right here, right now, I'm going to regret it. So, I'm asking you"—his eyes connect with mine—"can I kiss you?"

I look into his hazel eyes, the same hazel eyes that have tortured my dreams for years.

I want him too.

I want this kiss.

I want this more than anything.

I wet my lips. "I don't think I can leave your apartment without knowing what your lips taste like . . ."

CHAPTER TWENTY-TWO

NORA

The rain is like a constant sheet of water drenching the streets just outside my shop, pounding against the window and racing down the gutters. Thunder rattles the walls as flashes of lightning brighten the dark night sky.

Yeah, I won't be leaving anytime soon.

I take a seat behind the counter and pull out my iPad, where I open up my brick-breaking game. The cakes have been baked and stored, the buttercreams are prepared for tomorrow, and the kitchen has been cleaned. Since I have to walk home, I prefer not to endure a torrential downpour. I might as well wait for the storm to pass.

Lightning lights up the shop just as a boom of thunder shakes me to my core. I glance up toward the street, and another bolt of lightning strikes the sky, illuminating a dark figure at the door.

"Ahhh!" I scream as the figure walks into my shop, hood draped over its head, soaking wet. I pull a pen from my pen cup, click it, and point at the dark figure. "I don't carry cash—don't even ask for it."

The figure removes its hood, and I'm met with jet-black hair and silvery-gray eyes.

"Cooper." I exhale sharply. "Good God, you made me wet myself."

He moves his hand over his face, shedding water onto the floor. "Sorry. I texted you that I was coming over."

"My phone is in the back." I calm my racing heart. "I thought you were going to murder me."

"Why's your door unlocked?"

"Why are you walking around in the rain?"

He takes his jacket off and sets it by the door. His shirt underneath isn't wet, but it sure knows how to cling to his rock-hard chest.

Cooper is like fine wine: ages well. Especially since his divorce, he's turned into this ruggedly handsome, physically fit, and sarcastic man that I can't seem to stop thinking about.

"I got your text about the cake," Cooper says as my eyes wander over his chest and then back up to his piercing eyes.

"Oh, yeah, you mean the Sleeping Beauty cake?"

He walks over to the counter and takes a seat across from me, a confused look on his face. "Sleeping Beauty cake? What the hell is that?"

"You know . . . blue, pink, blue, pink, how her dress keeps changing color, just like this cake keeps changing flavor."

"I wish that wasn't the case, but my sister seems to have other ideas."

I lean across the counter. "Lavender is a romantic flavor."

"And my parents will hate it. Stick with the butterscotch."

"You know, that's something you could have just texted me. You didn't have to come all the way down here to say that."

"I wanted you to know how serious I was," he replies, turning toward me.

"Isn't that why GIFs were created, to express emotions through text better?"

"I'm not a fancy texter—you're lucky if you get an emoji out of me."

"I've noticed," I say as my eyes float down to his lips for a brief second and then back up to his eyes. *Get it together, Nora.* He's not here for a make-out session, even though the thought of that happening sends a thrill through me.

"What are you playing?" he asks, looking at my iPad.

"It's like Tetris, but not. You can't rotate the blocks, but you have to try to eliminate lines. It's mindless and keeps me busy when I'm waiting for things to bake or cool down or I just need a break. You should download it—clear your mind when you're not editing. How's that book coming along, by the way?"

"Fifty pages left. Fifty pages of pure torture."

I shake my head. "I don't get it—why are you an editor if you don't enjoy it?"

"I don't enjoy nonfiction. I like fiction, but I've been roped into the driest, most tedious nonfiction—despite hating it, I'm good at it."

"That's unfortunate."

"Very."

"So then . . . find something you do like."

"It's not that easy."

"Really? Seems easy to me," I say. "Figure out what you like and then go for it."

"Yeah, I tried that," he says softly, looking away.

"And what happened?"

"My brother told me no."

"You wanted to work with Ford?" I ask, confused.

"Yeah." He runs his hand through his hair. "He's rebranding the store, and I wanted to help. I had some good ideas, have been drawing things out."

"You draw?" I ask, shocked.

Dealia and Cooper were married for five years before they divorced, but despite being Dealia's best friend and maid of honor, I really didn't get to know Cooper well at all. I had a few beers with him and some friends in that time, but it didn't extend past that. We may have been intimate later on, but I still don't know much about him other than what Dealia has told me.

And from what she's told me, I know he can be closed off and unwilling to look outside his little radius. He turned down an opportunity to work abroad that Dealia was excited about, but he didn't want to leave Seattle. And that was the straw that broke the camel's back. It drove Dealia crazy that he wouldn't go anywhere, wouldn't do anything. She wanted more, and he *said* he wanted more, but when push came to shove, he never followed through.

But I don't see what Dealia was talking about when I look at Cooper.

I don't see someone with no follow-through—I see someone who is persistent about making things right.

I don't see someone who's afraid to move out of their radius—I see someone who is protective of his family.

I don't see someone stuck in their ways—I see someone wanting to break through his old patterns, but he just needs a helping hand to make that happen.

Makes me wonder if Dealia actually knew Cooper, or if there was a thin veil of denial she wore, preventing her from seeing the man I see. Dealia wanted more when it came to their marriage, and when those ideas and plans had to change, I wonder if her mindset ever changed as well.

Because Cooper is a good guy. A caring man. Dependable. Someone who goes the extra mile. I see it. I see him.

"Yeah, I've been taking some graphic design classes at night for a year now. I do everything on a digital drawing tablet, and it connects to my computer, bringing it to life."

"Seriously?" I ask. "Wow, Cooper, I had no idea."

"No one does . . . well, besides my dad. You're actually the only other person I've told."

"Wait, so you've been taking classes and learning a new skill, and you haven't told anyone? Why not?"

"Because of the image I seem to carry. The guy with no follow-through. It's the same reason Ford didn't hire me for the rebranding, because he believes there's a great chance I would fail. I didn't want to have to deal with any negative comments or thoughts when I was finally doing something positive in my life."

I frown. "Your brother thought you'd fail, and that's why he didn't hire you?" He nods. "Wow, that's really shitty. Did he even listen to what you had to say? Well, clearly not, if he doesn't know about your design abilities."

"I worked on a few mock-ups for the rebrand when my dad told me what Ford was up to. I used it as part of a class project, and I actually thought it was good, so I brought it to show Ford. His mind was set the minute I started talking to him. There was no way he wanted me involved, and instead of pushing him, showing him what I could come up with, I just backed away and let it be."

"Do you have them with you?" I ask. "On your phone?"

He shakes his head. "No, I deleted them after Ford wouldn't look at them."

"Deleted them from your computer?" I ask, stunned.

"No, just from my phone. They're still on my hard drive."

"Well, you need to show me sometime. I want to see your work. Do you have anything else finished that I can see?"

He scratches the back of his neck. "Nothing I want you to see."

"What do you mean by that? What could you possibly draw that you wouldn't want me to—ohhhhh." I smirk. "Are you one of *those* guys?"

"'One of those guys'? What the hell does that mean?"

"You know . . . draws himself . . . naked?" I'm teasing, but I have to admit, I'm not opposed to the idea.

"What?" he laughs and shakes his head. "No. I'm NOT one of those guys."

"Then let me see something." When he doesn't budge, I poke him in the chest. "Come on, let me see."

"You're not going to stop badgering me, are you?"

"No."

He sighs. "Fine. But don't say it's good just to say it's good. I hate that shit."

"If it's trash, I'll let you know. Don't worry."

"You don't have to be brutal either. I am a fragile man, after all." I laugh as he pulls his phone from his pocket and searches through it for a few seconds. He looks up at me again. "Also, no judging."

"Any more rules before the big reveal?"

"Don't ask to see any more. This is it. Onetime show. Got it?"

"Oooh, I love when you speak with authority." He rolls his eyes and then lays his phone flat on the counter in front of me. I focus in and find a drawing of my bakery front, with an illustration of myself holding a cake. And oh my God, it's good, it's adorable, and look at my boobs. I glance up at him, catching him gnawing on the corner of his lip. "Have me on your mind, did you?" I ask, trying to play it cool.

He just shrugs.

"You know, the coloring of my eyes is off."

"Nah, that's the color when you're annoyed, the color I seem to bring out in you."

My heart skips a beat.

"My hair is far too neat."

"Didn't think making you look like your usual hot mess was polite."

My heart tugs in my chest.

"My boobs are entirely too large."

His eyes scan to my breasts, study them, and then travel back up to my eyes. "They look pretty damn accurate to me."

My cheeks flush.

I clear my throat and try to hold it together, even though my entire body heats up from my toes all the way to my ears. "Besides those items, this is really good, Cooper."

"Yeah, it's my favorite so far that I've done. It's why I showed it to you."

"Oh, so you're not trying to impress me with your ability to accurately—according to you—draw my breasts?"

"Nah, if I wanted to impress you, I would have made them much bigger."

I chuckle and push his phone back to him. "You're good, Cooper, and you know I wouldn't just say that."

"Yeah, I know. And thank you." He stuffs his phone back in his pocket.

"So . . . are you going to send me that drawing?" I ask.

"What would you do with it?"

"Well, first I would print it, then I would have you sign it, then I would frame it, and then I would hang it right over there." I point to a blank spot on my wall. "It would be perfect there, don't you think?"

"You're not hanging it in here. It's not *that* good."

"Oh, it's good. I should have it printed on my cake boxes. How cute would that be. But we would have to reduce the boob size."

"The boobs are accurate."

I stand up straight and grip my boobs, staring down at them. "They're a decent size, but they are not accurately portrayed in that picture."

"I've held your boobs before and I've seen them naked—trust me, the drawing's accurate."

"Oooh, look at you, bringing up the past." My tone is light, but the mention of that night sparks a deluge of emotions: embarrassment, passion, excitement. I lean against the counter again, this time a little closer to him. "Does that mean you're finally relaxing around me?"

"When have I not relaxed around you?"

"Every time you've been here. Your shoulders are up around your ears, and you have a constant crease between your eyes. It's obvious you think about what happened between us but don't ever want to dive into it . . ."

He turns completely toward me now. "Yeah, because I fucked my ex-wife's best friend . . . thanks to two meddling parents and beer."

CHAPTER

TWENTY-THREE
COOPER

Nora was right: I didn't have to come here. I could have just called to change the order.

I could have probably even texted her to change it back, since we've been casually texting.

But I didn't want to do either of those things.

I wanted to talk to her in person.

I wanted to see her.

I wanted to hear her infectious laugh and have her tease me, just like she's doing now.

It's why I walked through the rain to her cake shop, and it's why I showed her my drawing—because I have this need to be near her, and it's stronger than ever.

Her finger reaches out and casually strokes the back of my hand. The small touch has an enormous impact. The last time I was touched like that, yeah . . . I was with her, and even though it was one night, it has stuck with me for a long time.

Now she's looking at me with wide, laughter-filled eyes. "Are you saying your parents are the reason you came back to my apartment that night?" she asks.

"Is it completely humiliating to say they were my wingmen? They were offering me beer and shots. They were the ones who turned on my favorite song. They were the ones who encouraged me to ask you to dance."

"Stop, really?" she chuckles. "Please delight me more with that story." She props her chin on her hand and flutters her lashes at me.

I'd rather not. It's humiliating enough to think about how I'd sunk to rock bottom and agreed to go out with my parents because they said I needed to get back into the game.

"Not something you should hear—you know, since I'm trying to save face around you."

"You're trying to save face? Why would that be?" she asks, her finger moving up to my wrist now. I attempt to hold back my gulp.

One little touch.

That's all it takes.

I'm fucking buzzing to do more with this girl. To take her back to my place, talk to her until the early-morning hours.

"You know, because I walked out of your apartment without a phone call or text back."

"And . . . if you ever want a chance with me again, you need to save face. Is that what you're saying?"

"You think I want another chance with you?" I ask, attempting to not show all my cards at once.

"Why else would you be here?"

"The smell of the shop?"

She laughs and shakes her head. "No, you want another wild night with me. I can see it in your eyes." She sits up and takes off her apron. "Too bad for you, though, Cooper. I'm not offering single nights anymore."

She hangs up her apron and goes to the back of the shop, then grabs her phone and coat and brings them to the front. She sets her phone on the counter while she puts her coat on.

"Leaving?" I ask.

"Yup, I feel like taking my chances in the storm."

"Am I really such bad company?"

She puts her phone in her coat pocket and rounds the counter. "No, you're coming with me."

Am I?

She tugs on my hand, making me stand.

Guess I am. And to be honest, I'm fucking ecstatic about it.

"You think you can just force me to go with you?"

"Yup." She smiles and hands me my soaking wet coat. I put it on, and we step out of her shop. She locks up and pulls her hood over her head. "I'm two blocks away, in case you forgot. Care to walk in the rain with me?"

"Walk or run?"

Lightning flashes and thunder rumbles.

Giving me a nervous look, she says, "Run." And then she takes off, still holding my hand, leading the way.

Together, we beat through the rain, our shoes soaking up every last drop, our laughter drowned out by the pounding of the sky above. Two blocks isn't far, but when you're trying to part the rain like it's a curtain, it feels like forever. We finally reach a glass-front apartment building and stumble into the vestibule between doors while she searches for her apartment key. Water rolls off us in droves, soaking the entryway rugs and dripping puddles on the tiled floors beneath us.

Finally locating her key, she lets us in and leads me to the elevator.

"Look familiar?" she asks as we step inside.

"Not really. The intricacies of your apartment building aren't really what I remember from that night."

"And what do you specifically remember, Cooper?"

Your purple lingerie.

The way your head fell back when I kissed your neck.

The sounds of your moans when I entered you . . .

"The dust on your mantel."

Her eyes widen, and she pushes at my shoulder. "There was no dust."

I shrug and stick my hands in my soggy pockets. "We'll just have to see about that."

"What are you? The clean police?"

"No, but I do hold people to certain standards. You're lucky I didn't leave when I saw how much dust had accumulated on your mantel."

"Stop it." She shoves me again, but this time I grab her and pull her into my chest, where her hands land.

Her eyes smile up at me. "If you think you're going over to my mantel when we get to my apartment, you're completely and utterly wrong."

The elevator dings, and the doors slide open. She releases herself from me and heads down the hallway to the right, where she stops at her apartment. I follow and wait for her to unlock her door. When she does, she turns toward me, face serious. "I didn't invite you up here to have sex."

"Okay." I chuckle. "I wasn't expecting to come up here and have sex."

"What were you expecting?" she asks.

"Someone to keep me company. Someone to make me laugh. Someone to possibly offer me some food and a drink."

"Demanding," she says, opening her door and letting me in. "Clothes off—I'll grab you a towel."

"You said no sex, and yet you're making me strip down?"

"I'm going to dry your clothes for you." She flips on a light and takes off her jacket and shoes before heading down her hallway, where I hear her open a closet. I take in her quaint apartment. Nothing looks different; then again, I'm not entirely sure I remember what everything looked like when I came here the first time—I was a little too concerned with taking Nora's bra off. A contrast to her bright-pink cake shop with yellow accents, her apartment is very subdued, monochromatic, with lots of plants lining the span of windows in the living room. "Here you go," she says, walking into the room and tossing me a white towel.

"What do you expect me to do with this?"

She waves her finger at me. "Strip down, wear it around your waist, stay covered up while your clothes dry."

"And what do you plan on wearing?"

"A turtleneck and extremely unattractive high-waisted sweatpants." She smirks and then takes off, back down the hallway. "I'll be quick, so unless you want me to see your manly bits, I would get undressed quickly."

"They're not bits," I grumble.

When she disappears down the hall, I contemplate the towel for a second and realize there's no way she's going to let me sit in her apartment soaking wet. So, towel it is.

I strip out of my coat, pull my shirt over my head, and then take my shoes and socks off, followed by my pants. Glancing down the hallway, I check for her and then quickly take off my briefs before wrapping the towel around my waist and securing it tightly at the side. Bending down, I pick up my wet clothes and walk down the hallway. "Where's your dryer?" I ask.

"Bathroom," she calls out. "First door on the right."

I open the door and stick my clothes in the dryer, grateful for her idea, even though it means I'm wearing a towel and just a towel. I turn on the dryer and turn around to find Nora standing behind me wearing a pair of light-pink silk pants and a matching silk sleeveless top.

I practically swallow my tongue, especially since it's blatantly obvious that she's not wearing a bra.

"Uh, that's not a turtleneck," I say, unable to stop myself from staring.

But I'm not the only one staring. When I finally look up at Nora, her eyes are eating me up, one inch at a time.

"Started working out, did you?" she asks, walking up to me.

"Yeah," I say as her hand reaches my chest. She caresses my skin, dragging her fingers over my pecs, and then down my stomach, running across my abs. "If you don't want to have sex tonight, then you're going to need to stop that immediately." My body starts to stir from her touch, and the last thing I want is to have a boner in front of her when there's nothing I can do about it.

"Am I getting you excited?" she asks, her fingers trailing back up to my pecs.

I reach out and place my hand on her hip, spinning her so she's pressed up against the bathroom counter. I slip my fingers under her shirt and move them up to her ribs. She sucks in a harsh breath, and I chuckle. "Are you getting excited?"

Eyes wide, she wets her lips. "Touché." She removes her hand and places it on the counter behind her.

"So, we agree that there will be no touching unless you want this towel ripped off."

She glances down at the towel and then back up at me. "I don't think I thought this through."

"You didn't."

"How was I supposed to know you were going to be walking in here like Thor?"

"Thor?" I raise a brow. "That's quite a comparison."

"Well . . ." She motions to my body. "Seriously, Cooper. When . . . how?"

I chuckle and release her from my grip. Taking her hand in mine, I lead her out of the bathroom and down the hall to her kitchen. "After our one-night stand, I felt a bit out of control. Like I had no grip on my life. I needed to focus on something, so I focused on my health. Simple as that."

"More like obsessed," she mutters. "You're like a Transformation Tuesday on steroids."

"Except this is a steroid-free body."

"Of course." She gives me another once-over. "I was going to make a frozen pizza, but now I'm afraid you only eat lettuce, and I don't have any of that."

"Pizza is fine." I smirk and walk over to her freezer, where I find four frozen pizzas. "Stock up?"

She reaches past me and grabs one. "Late nights lead to not being in the mood to cook for myself. And, you know, since I'm single and all, I have no one to welcome me home and cook dinner for me."

"Is that an invitation?" I ask, feeling more confident after her appreciation of my body.

"That's a statement—take it as you wish."

While she preheats the oven, I ask, "When do you usually get off work?"

"Depends on the day and how many orders we have. I usually stay later to clean up the kitchen so my employees can go home and have a normal life."

"That's nice of you."

She plops the pizza on a pan and puts it in the oven. "I remember when my parents used to call it a day and just leave all the dishes and pans for everyone else to clean. I'd get so mad. I know they owned the shop, but it wouldn't have killed them to stay back every once in a while." She walks over to me and takes my hand, guiding me over to the couch. "I told myself that when I took over the shop, things were going to be different, and guess what? I don't even have to ask for help now. The employees offer because they see that I'm putting in the work too. But I'll always be the one who stays late."

We take a seat on the couch, and I adjust my towel so I'm covered up while she sits down, putting a few inches between us. Her arm drapes behind me on the couch, and her finger starts to draw a small circle on the back of my neck.

"I thought we weren't touching," I say, even though what she's doing feels amazing.

Her finger stops. "This is getting you excited?"

"Nora, any part of you touching me is going to get me excited. Keep that in mind."

"Oh." Her cheeks flush as she removes her fingers. "My mistake. So maybe I'll just keep my hands to myself."

"Might be best," I say as I glance down to her chest and catch her hardened nipples pressing against her silk top.

Jesus.

This is going to be a long freaking night. I'm still a little confused as to why I'm here. As to why I can't seem to keep my distance ever since I walked into her shop to order a damn cake.

Something about Nora is more addictive than I thought. After our one-night stand—even though I hate calling it that—I didn't give myself a second to think about what we'd done. I just chastised myself for having sex with her, given who her best friend is, and tried to forget about it. But now that I've faced what we did—and even though there's still guilt, I realized that in the grand scheme of things, I didn't do anything wrong—I can't seem to stop myself from thinking about it, or from gravitating toward her.

"So, tell me how the party planning is going."

"Disastrous." I blow out a harsh breath. "The Chance siblings had a huge blowout yesterday in the midst of party planning."

"What do you mean by 'blowout'?"

"Oh, you know, pointing out what's wrong with each other, why we don't get along—classic sibling things."

She winces. "Sounds painful."

"It was." Even though I said no touching, I gently lift a lock of her wet hair and twist it around my finger. "It was less than ideal to hear about how my brother thinks I fail at everything and for my sister to tell me I don't care about anything but myself."

"She said that?"

"In a roundabout way. Honestly, it was as if we took each other's flaws, elevated them, and threw them in each other's faces."

"Why would you do that?"

"I don't know, honestly. I was really fucking angry because they assumed I don't care about the party, when I do—I just don't care about making it fancy. I care about honoring Mom and Dad. They're also mad at me because I helped our parents decide to move and sell the house. But Ford and Palmer aren't here day to day—they don't see how much Mom and Dad have been struggling with the house."

Nora places her hand on my thigh in a soothing way. I allow it.

"My mom told me you're over there all the time. Fixing things, watching YouTube videos to help you through the process." She chuckles. "I thought that was kind of cute, picturing you watching a video while attempting to put together a shelf or something."

I smirk. "Yeah, not quite the handyman you might think I am. And Dad's strength in his hands has faltered. Over the last few years, he's needed more and more help around the house. He claims he doesn't want to spend the money on hiring someone to help when he has me, but I know that's just a farce. He doesn't want people to know."

"Know what?" Nora asks softly.

I sigh. "We knew something was happening with Dad, but it wasn't until a few years ago that he was actually diagnosed with Parkinson's disease. I was there, at the appointment with Mom and Dad. I can still hear the almost silent cry from my mom and see the deflated bow to Dad's shoulders when the doctor told us the bad news. Mom and Dad held hands and stayed quiet while I asked questions. They pretty much did anything to ignore the fact that he was sick. He's a proud man, my dad, and he doesn't want people on the island to know, to see him weathered and worn. It's why he colors so much, because he wants to try to stay in tune with his fine motor skills as much as he can."

"I had no idea. Do Palmer and Ford know?"

I nod. "Yes, my parents told them over a phone conference, but Mom and Dad downplayed it. Of course, Palmer and Ford don't see the daily deterioration that I've seen. It's the main reason I want them out of that big house. Dad needs a simple place to live where everything is taken care of and he can just focus on enjoying his retirement, you know?"

"Makes sense. Having a huge house like that is probably hard to keep up."

"Especially since I'm the only one he'll call for help. But there's this YouTuber who's all about fixing things around the house—he and I have become well acquainted."

"Do you wear a tool belt when you're acting like Mr. Fix It?" she asks, her eyes turning dark.

"Nah, just a towel like this."

"Kinky, I like it. Bet your dad really likes it when your towel parts just right."

I quirk an eyebrow at her. "What is wrong with you?"

"Not sure." She chuckles. "But you were the one who brought up the towel. Maybe we're both deranged."

"Maybe we are." I look her in the eyes. "So are we not going to address the elephant in the room?"

"The fact that we've had sex? You already brought that up. I thought we were over it."

So not over that.

I would very much like to revisit that.

I would very much like to take Nora out on a date. To let her know this isn't just a one-night-stand thing to me; this is so much more.

But that's not what I was referencing.

"We already touched upon the sex thing—I'm talking about Dealia."

"What about her?" Nora asks casually.

"She was there at the shop the other day . . . it was awkward."

"That it was, wasn't it? Love invigorating moments like that, don't you? They get your blood pumping, remind you that you're alive."

"Moments like that also make your scrotum turn inside out in horror." Took me a few hours to beg the poor guy to come back down.

Her head falls back as she laughs. Hell, what I wouldn't give to move my lips along her neck right now, to taste her skin, to make my way to her lips.

"If I knew your balls shriveled up in my shop, I would have taken you to the back to blow them back up to the right size."

I play along. "And how exactly would you do that?"

"Blowing on your penis, of course."

Of course.

Just like that.

Jesus.

I swallow hard. "Now that wouldn't have made things extremely awkward."

"It would have been a conversational moment, for sure."

I raise an eyebrow at her casual response. "Aren't you worried about Dealia?"

"Are you?"

"She's my ex-wife. I worry a little. Even though things ended badly, I still wouldn't want her feelings to get hurt."

Nora smooths her hand over my chest. "I think she's fine."

"How can you be so sure?"

Nora sits up on her knees and then straddles my lap, her hands falling to my shoulders. "Because, I talked to her about it."

"You . . . you what?" I ask, my stomach bottoming out. "You told her we slept together?"

"Yup." She smirks.

"And what the hell did she say?"

CHAPTER

TWENTY-FOUR

FORD

"Are you sure?" I ask my mom over the phone. "I can come and get you."

"No, not necessary. We're having a lovely time with Tom and Linda. And we don't want you driving in this weather."

I glance toward Palmer's room, which is empty. The reason I know this is because I went to ask her if she wanted to eat dinner with Larkin and me, extending an olive branch, and after a while of knocking, I opened her room to see that she wasn't there.

"Have you heard from Palmer?" I ask.

"Yes, she's with Dr. Beau."

"Uhh . . . what?" I ask.

"Apparently he was driving back into town and spotted her on a hike. He had to redo her cast. She's fine, though."

"Oh, okay. And you're sure you're okay. Dad's okay? He has his medicine?"

"You know I always carry it with me. Now stop worrying and enjoy your night with Larkin."

"Don't say it like that," I say.

"Like what, dear?"

I lower my voice. "Like something is going to happen."

"I would never imply such a thing. She's your assistant, after all."

"Goodbye, Mom."

"Bye, sweetie."

I hang up and toss my phone on the bed. I borrowed a pair of sweatpants from my dad—crotch still intact—and I head down to the main level, where Larkin is currently making pasta and sauce because that was what was in the pantry.

When I reach the kitchen, I catch her swaying to the simple instrumental music playing in the old CD player attached to the bottom side of the cabinets. Her hair is pulled up into a bun, and she's still in her leggings, but she borrowed one of my old Watchful Wanderers sweatshirts that was hanging in my closet, which looks . . . hell, it looks damn good on her.

But the best part is that she's not actually cooking on the stove or with my parents' pots and pans.

Instead, she broke out the camping gear that was in the garage, set the cooking utensils up in the kitchen, and then, in the living room . . . you guessed it, she put up the two-person tent. To top off the night, she moved the couch cushions around the space to look like "boulders" and is using my parents' wood-burning fireplace as our "firepit." It's creative, cute, and is setting the tone for what's to come in this journey of "finding myself."

Once the storm intensified, we both thought it would be smart to stay in place until it was over. It hasn't let up yet, so Larkin chose to get started on sharing her childhood with me, which includes faux camping and all.

"Need any help?" I ask.

With a satisfied smile stretched across her lips, she looks over her shoulder. "I'm just about done. How are your parents?"

"Good. They're staying at their friends' house tonight."

A loud crack of thunder shakes the house, and Larkin scrunches her shoulders for a brief pause before relaxing. "Good, and how's the fire?"

Another rumble, a blast of light, and then . . . black.

The lights flicker off.

The clocks on the fridge and microwave go blank.

And the hum of the house settles to a peaceful quiet, allowing the bellowing beats of the storm to fill the silence.

"Did the power just go out?" she asks.

"I believe so."

"Well, it's a good thing we're camping, then, huh?" she says in a cheery voice. Nothing seems to get this girl down. Always positive. One of her finest qualities. One of the reasons I find myself drawn to her all the time. "So, is the fire started?"

"It is," I answer.

"Perfect, let me plate dinner and grab some utensils, and I'll meet you by the fire. Can you snag some drinks from the cooler for us?"

Yes, we even have a cooler.

When she was planning out tonight, she didn't want to miss one opportunity to bring camping full circle. And she was so excited that there was no way I could say no. So, I went with her plan, which seems to be turning into a perfect evening, even if the lights did go out.

"Sure." I head to the living room, which is lit up by the fire I started—I'm not completely incompetent; I do have survival skills—and open the cooler, where we have drinks shoved up against ice packs. I grab two Diet Mountain Dews and then shut the cooler just as Larkin walks toward me, the cooking pot in one hand, a towel protecting her hand from the heated bottom, and two forks. "No bowls?" I ask.

"Why dirty more things when you can eat straight from the pot?" She takes a seat on the blanket I laid out on the floor and pats the spot next to her. "Sit, enjoy the fire, have some cheesy pasta with sauce."

"Cheesy, huh?" I ask, taking a seat near her, but not too close.

"It's how my dad used to make it. He would boil the pasta, heat up the sauce, and then mix them together with a pack of mozzarella. It was a special addition to a simple meal that Beau and I loved as kids." She pats the spot right next to her again. "If you want to share this pot with me, you're going to have to sit closer. I'm ravenous and can't guarantee I'll share well if you're too far away."

I scoot closer so our shoulders are brushing. I'm not sure if I've ever been this close to her before. Her usual perfume has a soft floral scent to it, and it's that much stronger now without an inch of space between us. I like it.

"Thank you for making dinner." I take a fork from her and dip it in the pot, pulling out a very cheesy piece of rigatoni.

"It was my pleasure. It really made me think of my dad, which was exactly what I needed on this rainy day."

"Are you missing him?" I ask.

"I always miss him, but he used to love storms. He'd sit out on the deck and just watch the lightning and thunder roll through. Water would seep through the cracks of the covered porch, but he wouldn't care. He'd just rock in his chair and enjoy Mother Nature at her finest. I'd join him whenever Mom allowed it, and we'd spend hours just rocking back and forth, getting wet, and listening."

"Sounds peaceful."

"It was. One of the many things we would do together. But when we were camping, just like this, in a small tent, right next to a firepit, Dad would make this meal the first night, and he always dumped in a huge block of cheese. Beau, Dad, and I would hover over the pot and eat, knocking at each other's forks and trying to eat the most. Beau always won."

"Are you competing against me now?" I ask, playfully knocking her fork away. Her eyes light up, and she knocks back at mine.

"No, but I can compete if you want. You've never seen me shovel food in my mouth, but there's a first time for everything."

I chuckle. "As much fun as that seems, I'd rather enjoy this. It's really good."

"It's the cheese," she says on a sigh.

"Was your mom ever into camping?"

Larkin shakes her head. "Not really. She wasn't much of a nature person. She was also sick for most of my freshman year in high school, so she would stay home and encourage us to go camping. Beau would sometimes stay home with Mom, and it would just be me and Dad, but I remember Mom saying she didn't want us hanging around the house, worrying about her. Life is short: she wanted us to experience it, and that was the best gift we could give her."

"She sounds amazing."

"She was. Dad was too." She chuckles. "God, he would be so thrilled to know that I work with the Chance family. He really admired your store and your family. He always said he loved how you all worked together for the greater good of the store. He saw you and Palmer and Cooper always helping out. He'd tell me what great parents you had to instill that kind of comradery."

"Yeah." I sigh. "It seems as though we've kind of lost that along the way." I fork a piece of pasta. "I guess I don't remember Cooper and Palmer helping out as much because I was always in the back."

"Cooper was the folding king." Larkin plops some pasta in her mouth, her eyes focused on the fire. "He told me that once, when I was in the store. He was folding an endless pile of shirts and refused to use the folding board; said he was better than any board because he was the folding king. I remember that day specifically because my dad bought a shirt and knocked over a large pile that Cooper had just finished folding. His face turned bright red, but he reassured my dad it was okay because, like he said, he was the folding king."

"Really?"

"Oh yeah. I know our families never mingled, but I had small moments with your family as a customer. From behind, I always thought Cooper was you and that I was about to catch a glimpse of the elusive Ford Chance, but when he turned around and I saw his younger face, I knew it was Cooper."

That surprises me. "You were trying to catch a glimpse of me?" Kind of like how I try to catch glimpses of her at the office.

She opens her soda and takes a sip. After a roll of her eyes, she says, "Come on, every girl in town was trying to catch a glimpse of you. You were Ford Chance, with the devastatingly light eyes and contrasting black hair. Both you and Cooper were so different from anyone else on the island; everyone was hoping for a sighting."

"And if you had caught a glimpse, what would you have done?" I ask, my voice defying me when it cracks.

Her eyes bounce to mine, and I catch the flicker of the fire in her pupils. "Blushed, probably, and then told my friends about how I saw you. How you emerged from the back for a second and graced us with your presence."

I chuckle. "Are you saying that you might have had a thing for me back then?"

I don't know why I ask it.

But hell, now that it's out there, I really want to know. Did she have a thing for me?

And why the hell does it matter so much?

Why am I holding my breath?

Why am I leaning a little closer to her now?

Why the hell did I just wet my lips?

"Had a thing for you?" she asks, all of a sudden looking nervous, and I realize from the tic in her jaw that I'm her boss, she's my assistant, and I should never have asked her that. What the hell was I thinking?

"Sorry." I clear my throat and stab a piece of pasta. "I shouldn't have asked—"

"I wouldn't say a 'thing' necessarily," she starts. "More just fascinated. You might not know it, but the town was very enamored with the Chance family."

"Because of the store?"

"Because of the dynamic. You're a blended family, but you never would have known—it was beautiful to see. Beautiful to see all these personalities and circumstances come together to show that love really does win out . . . every single time."

"Yeah, I guess I never think of it that way."

"Because it's your family; why would you? And it's not different, by any means, just beautiful. Ugh, I don't know if I'm making sense or being offensive."

"Not offensive at all," I reassure her. "You're making perfect sense, and I'm sure my parents would really love to hear that. They always prided themselves on the family they raised, more than the store they built."

"It shows."

I sit back, my right hand propping me up. "If my parents heard the way my siblings and I spoke to each other yesterday . . . man, they would be upset."

"You know, the more I think about it, the more I wonder if maybe it was a good thing."

"What do you mean?" I ask as she motions for me to eat more. I take a big scoop and plop it in my mouth.

"Maybe you needed to get all of that out in the open, off your chests, you know? You're never going to move past something if you just let it fester."

"But none of us are talking to each other."

She shrugs. "Takes time. Which means you should take the time to loosen up as well." She grips my shoulder and shakes it. "Enough of this depressing talk. Tell me something exciting."

"Something exciting? I'm not sure if I have anything exciting to tell you."

"Okay, then just tell me something, anything. Something that makes you smile."

The first thing that comes to mind is her. She makes me smile. Seeing her cooking in the kitchen, swaying back and forth, looking completely comfortable in her surroundings. That makes me happy.

Seeing her wearing my sweatshirt, that also makes me happy.

Sitting here in front of a fire, the fire blazing while rain pelts the house outside, Larkin by my side—that makes me happy.

"I can see you're thinking of something," she says, gesturing to my eyes with her fork. "What is it?"

I look down, avoiding all eye contact. Hell, what would she say if I actually told her the truth? Probably run for the hills. And that's exactly why I'm not going to tell her. If I've realized anything over the time we've been here on Marina Island, it's that I need her. I need her professionally—she's like the glue that holds me together—but I also need her mentally and emotionally. She makes me tick, she helps propel me forward, she helps me relax.

Yeah . . . she's . . . she's everything I need.

"Uh . . . I like this blanket." I rub my hand over the blanket, knowing precisely how lame and unbelievable that statement is, but it's better than the truth.

And it doesn't slip by Larkin because she pokes me and frowns. "That is so not what you were thinking."

"Yes, it was."

She sets her fork in the nearly empty pot and then places it in front of us, out of the way. "So, you're telling me that this blanket, this run-of-the-mill flannel blanket purchased from Target, is what makes you smile?"

"Yeah," I say, sticking to my story. "It's soft."

"Ford."

"Hmm?" I look up at her, those fucking eyes boring into me.

"You're lying."

I set my fork down. "How can you accuse me of such a thing? How do you know this blanket doesn't mean a lot to me? That there isn't a story behind this wonderfully woven blanket?"

"Is there?" she asks, eyebrows raised.

"There is."

Facing me, she crosses her legs, her knee butting up against my thigh. "Okay, then please, delight me in the significance of this blanket."

"I will." I stretch my legs out and lean back on both hands. "It was a snowy, wintery day—"

"I bought this blanket for your parents when they were visiting you in Denver last winter. Your dad told me it kept his crotch warm. Your mom told me she likes how it felt against her unshaven legs."

I stare blankly at her.

Why the hell do my parents think it's okay to be that creepily open with my assistant?

Larkin smirks.

Larkin puffs her chest.

Larkin looks so goddamn breathtaking that the mere act of pulling her close feels inevitable, and it's terrifying. I'm not sure I've ever looked at her like that. I've never had the urge to pull her into my chest, to hold her hand, to find out what her lips taste like. Yes, I've always thought Larkin is beautiful, there's no denying that, but I've never let myself consider the romantic possibilities—until now.

Until we're sitting in the dark, the fire providing the only light, her kind yet brutally honest and welcoming heart on full display. It's as if a light bulb has been switched on in my head, and I now see her in a completely different light.

I see her as someone I could easily get lost in.

"Have anything to say about the blanket on your mom's unshaven legs?" she asks with a giggle.

I swallow, wet my lips. "Well, I knew about the warming of my father's crotch, and that frankly puts a smile on my face, because a father's warm crotch is a . . . uh . . . happy son?"

Larkin lets out a wail of a laugh. "Oh my God, I'm never going to be able to look at you the same."

I laugh as well, hating that I'm not as quick on my feet as Cooper. If he were in my place, he'd have no doubt made up a long-ass story about the warm blanket for crotches and unshaven legs, and he would make it believable.

"Don't worry, when I look at myself in the mirror tomorrow, I'll be ashamed."

"As you should be." She wipes under her eyes and then nudges me with her foot. "Now you have to tell me the truth—no lying. What were you thinking about when I asked you what puts a smile on your face?"

"I don't remember—"

"Yes, you do. Don't lie to me, Ford. I can read you like a book."

"Can you?" I ask. "So then why don't you tell me what makes me smile?"

"I want you to say it."

"But if you know me so well . . . ," I tease.

"Then I know this is hard for you, and I want you to be able to speak your mind, so speak up."

"But if you know me, then you already know," I challenge, trying to delay the inevitable while I attempt to think of something else. Definitely not the blanket.

"Ford."

"What?" I smile.

"Tell me."

"Why?"

"Because I want to know."

"Just because you want to know doesn't mean you *should* know."

Her brow creases. "You tell me everything."

A dry laugh pops out of me. "Not everything."

"Then share with me—come on."

I shake my head, my heart rate starting to pick up from her nagging. "No."

"Ford, I'm serious. Let's get it all out there. In the open."

"Not a good idea," I say, shaking my head as she scoots closer and puts her hand on my thigh.

"No, this is a great idea. This would be a great way to move forward. Get everything out there."

"Larkin." I shake my head. "No."

"Why? Are you scared? You don't need to be scared around me."

"I'm not scared around you—"

"Then what is it?"

"It was you!" I shout, unable to hold it back any longer.

"What?" she asks, looking stunned.

Knowing this is crossing the line in the worst way possible, but unable to take it any longer, I reach out, grip her cheek, and rub my thumb over her soft, rosy-colored skin. "It was you, Larkin, that made me smile. All fucking you . . ."

CHAPTER TWENTY-FIVE

PALMER

I hold my breath.

Thunder rumbles in the background.

The puzzle rests in front of us, untouched.

And my body itches with desire as Beau glances down at my mouth and then back up at my eyes.

I want him to kiss me.

I want this more than anything.

As he leans in, my breath catches in my chest, my pulse hammering impatiently, drowning out the commotion of the storm outside. I wet my lips one last time, and as he closes the space between us, I brace myself for—

Bang. Bang. Bang.

"Dr. Beau, are you home?"

Beau shoots back and stands from the couch.

"It's an emergency, Dr. Beau, please tell us you're home."

The affectionate, easygoing, sweet man who was just wooing me in all the right ways morphs into Mr. Emergency Room. He bolts over to the door, flinging it open to reveal a woman holding what looks to be a two-year-old in her arms.

"Margorie, what's wrong?"

"He did it again," she says.

The boy turns around, showing off some sort of action figure dog stuck in his nostril.

"Chase is on the case," the little boy says. "On the booger case." And then he laughs, his voice nasally.

"He won't let me pull it out. Please, can you help remove it?"

"Of course," Beau says with a reassuring touch to the mom's arm. "Meet me downstairs and I'll be right there."

"Thank you," she says and takes off, the kid giggling the entire time.

Beau shuts the door and goes straight to his bedroom. I'm about to ask him what he's doing, but when he comes back wearing a pair of jeans, his hair slightly styled to the side, I realize he's in doctor mode. As he puts on his shoes, he looks over at me, still sitting on the couch, our mood completely ruined by a plastic dog up the nose.

"Shit. I'm sorry, Palmer."

"It's okay." I smile at him. "Go have fun plucking that out."

"It'll take two seconds, I promise."

"Seriously, it's fine. Do what you need to do."

"Promise you're not going to leave?"

I glance out the window and then back at him. "It's still raining, I have no way of getting home, and I don't want to get another recast because I get this wet again," I say, holding up my arm. "I'm pretty sure I'm going to be staying put."

"Good." He walks up to me, places both hands on the back of the couch, and leans down, pressing a kiss on my forehead. "Be back." My stomach flutters.

"Okay." I wave. "Have fun."

"Yeah, so much fun." He chuckles before shutting the door behind him.

Sighing, I lean back on the couch and mentally curse the child who put Chase on the case, whatever the hell that means. So close.

So freaking close to finally finding out what it's like to have Beau Novak's lips on mine, and now I'm sitting here, feeling like I have a heavy case of . . . hell, of blue balls.

How is that even possible?

This morning, I woke up with the worst hangover, not from wine, but from my family. I decided to flee the nest, get some perspective, do some thinking, and next thing I know, I'm being saved by a knight in a white lab coat.

A knight I used to think about all the time.

A knight I chose not to think about after the fire.

A knight who has serendipitously come bounding back into my life.

I need to tell Laramie.

Reaching for my phone, I type out a quick text to him.

Palmer: I'm in Dr. Beau's apartment. He almost kissed me.

I spoke with Laramie the other night and told him how I keep running into Beau. Laramie insists I call him "Dr. Beau" because he thinks it has a better ring to it. He also insists on pictures. I've been able to sneak one, but that's about it.

My phone dings.

Laramie: Heaven help me, is he naked in the other room, wearing nothing but a stethoscope and ready to give you a physical examination?

I chuckle and text back.

Palmer: No. I WISH!

Laramie: Ugh, then what the hell are you doing? If he almost kissed you, why aren't you making it actually happen?

Palmer: A patient with something stuck up their nose came by.

Laramie: Medical emergency! What was stuck up the patient's nose?

Palmer: Does it matter?

Laramie: To me it does. You know how I watch the shit out of all of those medical shows. I need to know what it was.

Palmer: Uh it was some child with a dog named Chase up his nose.

Laramie: CHASE? From Paw Patrol! Oooo, what a twist. Did not see that coming. I would also like to know the diameter of that figurine. Either it was a small Chase or that kid has quite the set of nostrils.

Palmer: It looked pretty small, but it wasn't the kid's first offense according to the panicky mom.

Laramie: God, kids are the absolute tits. Look at this toy, I'm going to shove it up my nose, ruin everyone's night, and laugh it off later while I make plans to do it again.

Palmer: That is scarily accurate.

Laramie: Three vengeful nieces will prepare you for the way they think. Trust me, that kid thinks he's the king of Toyland right now.

Palmer: Well, he ruined my first kiss with Dr. Beau.

Laramie: The nerve. Paint the picture, let me see if we can get you back in the mood when he gets back. What were you doing?

Palmer: Building a puzzle.

Laramie: *Blinks* A . . . puzzle? Like a real jigsaw puzzle?

Palmer: Yes, of a gardenscape.

Laramie: Oh damn. Babe, you're going to have to take your shirt off and shimmy your titties at him to get him back in the mood. There is no way a gardenscape jigsaw puzzle is going to do it on its own. Especially after he has to dig for gold in a little punk's nostril.

Palmer: That's what I was afraid of. So, you think I should take my shirt off? That's pretty forward, I'm not sure I can do that.

Laramie: What are you wearing now?

Palmer: Long story, but his clothes. Mine were dirty.

Laramie: Dear Jesus, I just had an idea! Does he have any of his lab coats in his apartment?

My eyes land on the coatrack near his door, which does in fact have a few lab coats on it.

Palmer: Yes . . .

Laramie: Time to strip, babe. Wear nothing but the lab coat, and when he arrives, tell him the doctor is in the house.

Palmer: I think you fail to realize that is something I would SO not do.

Laramie: Fine, then let the puzzle carry the mood for you. Good luck getting your first kiss fifty years from now.

Palmer: Do you really think he's not going to be in the mood when he gets back?

Laramie: He just plucked a dog from a schnoz. There's no recovering after that unless you take it up a notch. You've wanted him for a while, so go get him.

I nibble on the corner of my lip and study the lab coats from the couch.

Palmer: I don't know . . .

Laramie: Do it. You know you want to.

Palmer: I can't believe I'm actually considering this.

Laramie: Do it. Do it. Do it ← then thank me later.

Palmer: Gahhhhh. I'm going to do it.

Laramie: That's my girl.

I think I've lost my freaking mind.

Setting my phone down, I stand from the couch before I lose my nerve and go over to the coatrack, where I pluck one of the lab coats down.

This might be taking a bold step, going from first kiss to naked in a lab coat, but I know that's where this was going. The look in his eyes, the little touches here and there. The compliments, the confessions. It's been a buildup. Add on the storm relentlessly setting the backdrop, and we're golden.

And I hate to admit it, but Laramie is right. A gardenscape puzzle isn't going to make things sizzle when he gets back. But this will.

Before I can change my mind, I quickly drop my pants and take off the sweatshirt Beau gave me. Heart pounding, I throw the lab coat over my shoulders. It's way too big, but I make the best of it by buttoning the bottom button so my southern area is covered, and then I roll the sleeves up to my elbows. I leave the rest of the coat untouched, letting it show off the middle of my body but not revealing too much, just enough to gather his attention.

I spot an extra stethoscope on his coatrack as well and grab that too. I drape it around my neck and then casually swing the end around.

I pick up my phone, angle high, and take a picture that I then send to Laramie.

His response is immediate.

Laramie: Look out for incoming erections. Dr. Beau is going to need some medical attention in his pants when he gets back.

I laugh out loud just as I hear the stairs to the front door creak. I drop my phone and get in position on the edge of the couch, lifting one leg to rest on the back while the other is on the floor, keeping me balanced. I adjust the coat so it covers everything up but also shows off enough, puff out my chest, and put on a smile just as the door opens, revealing Beau . . . and another man.

"Palmer, have you . . . oh my God . . ."

"Oh my God!" I shout, pulling a pillow from the couch and dragging it over my body.

"Oh my God," the other guy says, covering his eyes. "Jesus, I'm sorry."

"No, I'm sorry," I say quickly. "I was—I, uh . . . I didn't know . . . was there a doctor in the house? I mean, I'm the doctor. No, I'm not a doctor, just a doctor of boners." I cover my eyes. "No, not boners, this was a boner, I mean bonehead move. I'm not naked." I try to hide my face in the pillow. "I'm just . . . uh . . . I'm practicing for when I get my medical degree. Is this . . . is this not the proper attire?"

"Jesus, Beau. I didn't know you had company. I'll leave."

I pop my head up, pillow still covering me as I stand from the couch and slowly back away from the door. "No, don't leave. I was, uh . . . I was just getting ready to leave. You know, all those medical books I need to read."

"Palmer," Beau says, walking toward me.

"Dr. Beau, it was a pleasure getting to know you." My eyes widen as I look at the guy. "Not like that. Nothing happened. I don't mean getting to know him in a personal way, like naked, but you know, just intellectually. I'm not . . . I know how this looks, but I promise, it's not what it seems. My clothes are drying, actually, and this just happens to be something—" I sigh, giving up. "I'm not a naked lunatic."

"Palmer," Beau says again, this time closing the space between us, a grin pulling at the corner of his lips. "This is my cousin Roger. He missed the ferry because of the storm and was hoping to spend the night."

"Oh, sure, yup." I thumb behind me. "I was just heading out. All research here has been conducted. No need to worry—I'll be out of your hair in a few." Pillow in hand, stethoscope dangling from my neck, I take off toward Beau's bedroom, where I quickly close the door behind me and cover my eyes with my hand. Embarrassment swallows me whole.

I'm going to kill Laramie.

The doorknob turns behind me, and the door opens a crack. "Palmer, let me in."

"Um, no thank you," I say.

"Palmer."

"Really good. Just changing. Be out shortly."

He eases the door open carefully, letting his large frame in before he shuts it behind him. I lean against the wall, still clutching the pillow, completely and utterly humiliated as I stare up at him.

His eyes are full of humor, his grin has yet to be swiped off his face, and he leaves no space between us as he takes the pillow from me, tosses it on his bed, and gently caresses my cheek with the back of his fingers.

"What do you have going on here?"

"First-class embarrassment. What does it look like?"

"It looks like you were attempting to seduce me."

"What? *Pffft*, you got that from this?" I motion up and down my body. "Clearly you're not up to date on your seduction techniques. This is actually a new, modern way of greeting your host. A fun party trick, if you will."

"Is that right?" he asks, his fingers playing with the lapel of his lab coat.

"Yup. It's very popular in Europe, actually. Greet your host in a lab coat. Extremely normal, not at all odd or embarrassing, or utterly demeaning. Completely natural."

"Looks like it." His thumb swipes across my collarbone. "It suits you."

My breath catches in my chest at his touch and the sexy glint in his hazel eyes. "Well, glad you enjoyed my little party trick. But, since you have company, it's best I be going so you two cousins can catch up. And hey, you can work on that puzzle. What a delightful evening for you." I pat his chest. "I'll just get out of your way—"

Beau pins my hips still and gently pushes me against the wall, keeping me in place. "Are you listening, Palmer?"

"Huh?" I ask, confused.

"Are you listening to me? I'm about to tell you how this night is going to go, but I need to make sure you're actually listening."

I swallow hard from the authoritative tone in his voice. "Yes, I'm listening."

"Good." He tucks a loose strand of my hair behind my ear. "I'm going to go back out to the living room and grab your clothes. You're going to get changed so my cousin doesn't have the privilege of seeing you in this European tradition." He raises a brow at me. "And then we are going to all puzzle together. When it's time for bed, Roger is going to take the couch, and then you're going to sleep with me, in my bed. Okay?"

"In . . . your bed?" I ask, swallowing back my nerves that just spiked again.

"Yes, in my bed. Understood?"

"Yes." I nod. "But . . ." I wince. "What are we going to tell Roger?"

"What do you mean?"

"I mean, what's the reason I'm spending the night?"

He smirks at me and leans in, placing a soft kiss on my nose. "Not sure, but you seem to be pretty good at coming up with European traditions we Americans have never heard of before. Maybe try one of those?" He smirks and then tugs on the lab coat. "I'll get your clothes."

CHAPTER TWENTY-SIX

COOPER

Nora is sitting on my lap, wearing some sort of silky outfit that's doing far too many things for my imagination.

Her legs are straddling mine.

Her nipples are hard.

Her hands are gripping my shoulders.

And I'm reminded of just how fucking great our one night together was.

But my mind isn't focused on any of that. It's focused on what she said.

She told Dealia.

About what we did.

What the actual fuck?

"What the hell did she say?" I repeat.

Nora reaches up and smooths her hand through my hair. "She was pissed."

I take Nora's hands in mine and then force her to look at me. "Nora, this is serious—you told my ex-wife that I fucked her best friend."

Nora shakes her head. "No, I told my best friend that I had sex with her ex-husband."

"It's the same thing."

She shakes her head. "It's not, because your situation looks like a revenge fuck, whereas mine reads as betrayal, and that's the exact reason I told her the day after it happened."

"What?" I say, moving Nora off me and standing, making sure my towel is secure. "You told her the day after? So she's known this entire time?" I pull on the ends of my hair.

Nora grabs one of the throw pillows from the couch and holds it in front of her. "Of course she's known. There's no way I could do something like that and not tell her. She's my best friend, Cooper."

"I'm well aware of who she is. Fuck." I pace her living room. "And she was pissed?"

"Of course she was. She didn't talk to me for months."

Why is Nora so calm right now? How could she possibly be calm when Dealia knows that we had sex? I'm about to lose my goddamn mind.

"She never said anything to me."

"Probably because you're her ex-husband, and she has no control over what you do or where you choose to stick it," Nora says, an edge to her voice.

I pause and turn toward her. "Why are you getting mad at me?"

"Because you're getting mad at me. Instead of worrying and acting like you got caught, maybe you should sit down and talk this out like a normal adult. You know, maybe ask how I am? Not everything is about you, Cooper."

Shit, she's right.

Dealia is just my ex-wife—our ship has sailed. But Dealia and Nora are still friends. Nora risked so much more being with me that night than I did. She risked her friendship, one she's had for many years.

Taking a deep breath, I sit down next to her. "Shit, I'm sorry, Nora. How are you doing?"

"Right now? I kind of want to punch you."

"Punch me? Why?"

"Because why do you care so much what she thinks? You seriously look like you're about to throw up. You're not married to her anymore, Coop. It's not like you cheated. Maybe used me—"

"I didn't use you," I say, even though the words don't feel right coming off my tongue.

"You didn't? So you just fucked me and forgot my number or where I worked or where I lived? Or how about the texts I sent you—that went unanswered—to see if you were okay? If you're going to be open about this, let's be honest about everything."

"Why are we even being open about this?" I ask.

"Because it's the elephant in the room, and I don't know, it seems like when you keep coming to visit me at the shop, it's not really about changing the cake order and more about using that as an excuse to see me. Or am I wrong?" When I don't answer, she shakes her head and looks off to the side. "Just leave, Cooper. You're clearly not ready to be a man about this."

My initial instinct is to stand from the couch, grab my clothes from the dryer, and take off, but that's exactly what everyone would expect from me.

Crawling under a rock when I don't want to face the reality.

And the reality right now is that I like Nora. I like her a lot, but a black cloud is hanging over the beginning of something that I think can be great. But I'm terrified. I'm terrified of opening up, of what she might think when we do address the elephant in the room. I'm terrified of losing a second chance at being with this girl.

But if I want to move forward with Nora—which, with each passing moment, I realize that I desperately do—then I need to face the facts. We have to talk about this.

So instead of falling back into old habits, instead of running away from tough conversations like I did time after time with Dealia, I don't get up. Instead, I look Nora in the eyes and take a deep breath. "I'm worried if I address the elephant in the room, you might not like what unravels, and I don't want to lose out on a second shot with you."

"Instead of assuming the kind of reaction I might have, why don't you give me the opportunity to react in my own way?"

I nod. She's right. I'm not allowing her to react, and that's not fair. "Okay." On a deep breath, I continue: "Dealia didn't understand me. And I know I did my fair share to ruin our marriage, and even though we've been divorced for a while now, I still feel like I can't navigate through a healthy relationship properly . . . with anyone."

"What do you mean she didn't understand you?" Nora asks, the anger in her eyes turning to concern.

"Listen, she's your best friend, and I don't want anything to change that, but our relationship was never on the right wavelength, and we ignored it until we couldn't anymore. We had plans. We had these dreams of moving around every six months, exploring the world. But then my dad was diagnosed with Parkinson's, and that felt . . . life changing to me. It put my entire thought process into perspective, and I started canceling on all the trips she wanted to take. I stopped dreaming with her."

"But she knew about your dad's Parkinson's."

"She did, but she didn't understand when I told her I had to stay close. I hurt her by giving up on her dreams, on her ambitions—"

"You didn't give up."

I shake my head. "I did. At that moment, my wife took a back seat to my family. Then from there, it went downhill. Everything I did was wrong. Everything I said was offensive. I couldn't do right by her, no matter how hard I tried, but I knew the one thing she wanted, the one thing she asked me to do, I couldn't give her."

"What did she want?"

"For me to put her first." I pull on the back of my neck. "It shouldn't have been a choice. I realize now I should have been able to have both, but she wasn't happy with that idea. I said instead of moving, maybe we just visit these places she wanted to go to, but that wasn't good enough. That's all I could give her, though. And I even told her I didn't want to give up on our dream, but I couldn't give up on my dad either."

"I don't understand. If your dad was sick, then why couldn't she find it within her to help you?" Nora presses her hand to mine. "She never spoke about this, so I'm sorry if I'm prying."

"You're not." I look away. "I just don't want this to hurt your relationship with her."

"Why don't you let me decide how I handle my friendship."

I nod. "Fair." I let out a deep sigh. "The problem was, my dad didn't look any different. He was diagnosed, yes, but he wasn't showing any outward signs. My mom and I noticed changes, and so did my dad, in their everyday routine, but to anyone on the outside, he was the jolly man he's always been. So, Dealia didn't fully understand why I wanted to stay close, why I *had* to stay close."

"Because you wanted to take care of him," Nora says as more of a statement than a question.

I nod slowly and stare down at where her hand is entwined with mine. "Because Ford was in Denver and Palmer was living the life we thought we wanted, it fell to me to take care of our parents. And yes, am I bitter about it at times? Of course I am. I see my brother and sister dreaming big, taking charge, while I'm stuck here, taking the ferry back and forth to Marina Island to check on our parents."

"But you feel obligated," Nora says.

I shake my head. "I don't feel obligated—it's more than that. I feel as though it's my duty."

"You say that with such conviction. Is there a story behind that proclamation?"

I roll my teeth over my bottom lip as I squeeze my eyes shut for a breath. "It was right after we were adopted. I was still terrified that maybe we weren't going to stay with Mom and Dad forever. I know Ford had the same fear. It happens when so many people you've loved are taken away from you, one right after the other, and, of course, the foster care system is flawed in many ways. But there was a night when I woke up from a night terror. I screamed so loudly that I woke up my dad. He came barreling into my room and asked me what was going on. I told him I had a dream I was taken away." My lip quivers as I remember that moment in the dark. "He gripped my face with one hand and looked me dead in the eyes. He pressed his forehead against mine and said that, for as long as he breathes, he would never leave me. He told me I was his and he was mine, our souls were connected, and for as long as he was allowed, he would always take care of me."

I glance at Nora as tears well up in her eyes.

"Hey," I say, tugging on her hand.

She drops the pillow and straddles my lap again, but it doesn't have the same sexual connotation that it did last time. Instead, it feels like she just needs to be closer to me.

"You're a good man, Cooper Chance."

"I'm a confused man." I place my hands on her hips. "And then I freaked out about Dealia finding out because when it comes to her, I think I'm still stuck in the past." I suppress a shiver as the truth of this statement hits me. "I think I'm projecting all the angst of our failed relationship and assuming that you'll handle conversations the same way she might—since you're friends. Fuck, that sounds bad."

"I can understand that." Nora lifts my chin and forces me to look her in the eyes. "But you realize I'm not going to do that to you, right? You don't need to expect the same kind of behavior from me, and I hope you know I can also stand up for you when you need it."

"What do you mean?" I ask.

She presses her hands against my chest and slowly brings them up to my collarbone. "When I told Dealia about what happened between us, I told her I was sorry if I hurt her, but I wasn't sorry about what happened, because things had been over between you two for so long, way before they were actually over. She didn't talk to me for months, but she came around, and do you know what she said?"

I shake my head.

"That you and I were far more suited for each other than you two ever were."

"She . . . she said that?"

Nora nods. "And when she came to see me the other day at the bakery, she was stopping in from a long trip to Alaska, and after you left, she asked if you were there because we were seeing each other. I told her no, that we're just friends, and she actually encouraged me to take that next step, to make it more than just friends. Well, maybe not at that exact moment, because she was a little shocked, but she said that soon after."

"Seriously?" I ask, an odd mixture of disbelief and relief flooding through me.

"Yes. Seriously."

"And what, uh . . . what did you say to her?" I ask.

"I don't know: you're sitting here in my apartment, wearing just a towel while I straddle your lap. What do you think I said to her?"

Hell . . .

Chapter

Twenty-Seven

LARKIN

"It was you, Larkin, that made me smile. All fucking you . . ." His voice trails off as he looks to the side.

Me?

He was . . . he was thinking of me? That's what made him smile?

I don't know what to say.

What to do.

How to react.

For years I've dreamed of what would happen if I ever crossed that line with Ford, my boss, and for years, I've tamped down that feeling, knowing it would only end up in a complete disaster—because there was no way Ford would ever look at me like that.

I'm the twig of a girl who came storming into his office, half-ready to break down into an emotional mess and half-determined to make something of myself, begging for a job, any kind of job, just something to keep me connected to my father.

I never would have considered him thinking of me that way.

"Fuck," he mutters and pushes his hand through his hair. "I'm sorry, Larkin, I never should have—"

Before I can stop myself, I close the distance between us, grip the back of his neck, and pull him close as my mouth descends on his.

Together, we sit there, stunned.

Our mouths are touching, but that's about it.

We're not moving.

We're not wrapped up in each other's embrace.

We're not attempting more than two pairs of lips pressing together, and that's when I realize I've made a giant mistake.

I quickly release him and scoot back, putting a few feet between us as I cover my furiously blushing face with my hands. "Oh my God, Ford, I'm so sorry. I never should have done that. I don't know what I was thinking. I wasn't even thinking at all. It was stupid and careless, and I was caught up in the moment." I remove my hands to look into his stunned eyes. "I'm sorry."

He doesn't say anything, just clears his throat and pulls his legs into his chest.

Yup, I messed this up so bad.

So freaking bad.

Trying to hold back tears, I stand from the floor and pick up the pot. "I'll, uh . . . I'll take care of this."

Quickly, before he can see a tear fall, I walk into the kitchen, pot in hand, and set it in the sink before gripping the counter and taking a deep breath.

Don't cry, Larkin. That will only make matters worse.

It was a mistake; mistakes happen. This is something we can move past.

So, you kissed your boss. You're a smart girl; you can think of ways to get through this monumental moment that never should have happened.

I suck in a few sharp breaths, attempting to steel my emotions as they run rampant in my head.

Embarrassment.

Humiliation.

Fear.

Confusion.

They all hit me at the same time, consuming me, overwhelming me, and pulling tears from my eyes.

Stupid, stupid, stupid.

What on earth would possess you to kiss your boss?

Yes, the moment felt heavy, but that's how it can get with Ford. That doesn't mean you KISS HIM.

From the way he didn't move, just sat there stunned, as if he was counting the nanoseconds until I let go of him, it's clear I read the situation entirely wrong.

I make him smile . . . as a friend.

Not anything else.

As a friend, you naive, naive girl.

Gathering myself, I take a deep breath and wipe at my eyes. I need to go in there at some point or he's going to come out here to make sure I didn't fall in the sink or try to throw myself down the garbage disposal. Both viable options right now.

But if anything, I'm resilient. I've gotten over worse. Yes, nothing this embarrassing, but I can do this. *Just be confident.*

I let out another deep breath, set my shoulders back, and with a twisted stomach of nerves and embarrassment, I walk back into the living room, where Ford is sitting, staring at the fire.

This has got to be one of the first times since I started working with him that I can't read him. I have no idea what he's thinking or feeling, and that terrifies me.

And lucky for me, this is the first time I'm dealing with the "I kissed my boss" situation, so I'm navigating uncharted waters.

Desperately trying to act casual, I step over the "boulder" cushions and take a seat next to him while also giving us at least two feet of distance, in case he thinks I'm trying to make a move again. Learned my lesson; won't be doing that again.

I bring my legs into my chest, mirroring his position, and hug them close while I stare at the fire as well. The tension is so thick, so uncomfortable, that I'm not sure I'll be able to make it through the night unless we clear the air.

"Do you want to play cards or something?" I ask, noticing that the rain outside has eased up to a steady fall, something I wouldn't mind walking in just to escape this moment.

Running in the rain all the way to the inn feels more tempting by the second.

"No, I'm good," Ford says, his voice barely audible.

God, I totally ruined this entire night. Stomach positively aching, I say, "You know, I'm actually not feeling too great. It looks like the storm has let up a bit; might be a good idea for me to take off, give you some space."

I go to stand, but Ford places his hand on my knee, keeping me in place. With a sharp intake of breath, I look up at him, confused, as his eyes meet mine.

His hand reaches out, locks behind my neck, and he pulls me closer until his lips are pressed against mine, but this time, they're not stunned; they know exactly what they want. Tears fill my eyes as Ford kisses me.

Truly kisses me.

The distance between our bodies closes, and before I know what's happening, Ford is lowering me down to the ground, his strong, domineering body hovering over mine as his lips explore and take simultaneously.

The humiliation, the fear, the raw emotions of the moment before, they all fade to black as I move my hand to the back of his head so my fingers can sift through his hair.

And then his mouth parts and his tongue swipes against my lips, looking for entrance. I brace myself as I part my lips as well and our tongues clash. He groans against me, his body pressing into mine as his hand grips my jaw, his thumb pressing my chin up, giving him a better angle.

I let him take control, not just because it seems like he needs it, but because I need to feel it—I need to know that I didn't just mess everything up, that I'm not forcing him to do this, but in fact, he's taking me into his arms, that this moment in front of the fireplace is actually meant to be.

He presses a small kiss across my lips.

Then my nose.

Then he lifts up a few inches and stares down at me.

"Fuck," he whispers. "I never realized how much I've wanted to do that until just now."

"Kiss me?" I ask, breathless.

He nods. "So much." He leans down and presses another kiss to my lips. "It feels like I've wanted this, us, forever, but never truly understood that until you reached out and stunned me with your kiss. It was like you unlocked the door to feelings that I've kept hidden for, well, years."

"So you weren't disgusted that I just kissed you? I didn't ruin anything?"

"Disgusted?" His brows pull together. "Larkin, I was fucking bewildered. I didn't know you thought about me that way. I was reeling, trying to decide if that actually happened or if I dreamed it." He leans down and presses another kiss against my lips. "But it's real. So real. You want me, just like I want you."

"So much," I admit, my lungs working extra hard to catch up with my heart. "You saved me, Ford. You have been nothing but kind to me, and that kindness captured me. I've wanted you for a very long time, but I was afraid to cross that line, afraid to ruin what I have with you."

The light from the fire flickers off his strong jaw and distorts the silver of his eyes as he studies me. Then he lifts up onto his knees, reaches behind his back, and pulls his shirt off, tossing it to the side.

My pulse hammers through my veins as his hands go to the hem of my sweatshirt. Well, his sweatshirt, his sweatshirt that feels so perfect draped over me. Without even thinking about what could happen after this, I shift up and allow him to take it off, leaving me in nothing but a simple purple bra.

Gently, he lays me back down and dips his head to place a few kisses on my lips, then my jaw, and then down to my collarbone. I suck in a sharp breath when his teeth nip at the swell of my breast.

"Ford," I say softly when he pulls down on the cup of my bra, exposing me.

"You okay?" he asks as he kisses my breast.

"Yes," I answer breathlessly just as his mouth descends over my nipple and sucks it past his lips. I drive my hand through his hair and keep him in place as my chest arches against him. "God, yes, Ford."

His hand snakes under me, where he finds the clasp of my bra. With one flick of his fingers, he unlatches it and then tears it off me and tosses it to the side.

"You're so beautiful," he says, lifting up to look at me. He takes one of my breasts in his hand. "Are you sure you want this? You want me?" Vulnerability flashes through his eyes, and I almost laugh out of disbelief.

Instead, I lift up and smooth my hands up his chest until I'm gripping his cheeks. "I want you more than anything, Ford. I just don't want this to ruin anything."

He shakes his head. "It won't. It can't possibly ruin anything, not when I feel this strongly about you. It will only enhance what we have." He pushes a strand of hair behind my ear. "You make me happy, Larkin. I wouldn't want to do anything to lose that."

"You won't lose me," I say, moving my hands to the waistband of his sweatpants.

His eyes soften and he takes a deep breath as I slip one hand past the waistband, where I find his erection, already begging for release.

For a brief second, I allow my fingers to take in his length, and then I curl around him, feeling his girth. God, he's so perfect. I move my hand down lower, where my fingers caress his balls.

"Fu-uck," he says, his chest tensing, his muscles firing off.

I look up at him. "I want you, Ford. All of you."

He wets his lips and then pushes down his sweatpants and his briefs. With my hand in his, we both stand, and he pushes his pants to the side before reaching for mine and dragging them down my legs, leaving me in nothing but a thong. He spins me around and presses my ass up against his erection as both his hands smooth up my stomach to my breasts. His mouth finds my neck, where he rains tantalizing kisses, lighting up my skin with goose bumps.

"I feel like this is crossing a line, a big one, but fuck if I can't stop myself now."

"I don't want you to," I say as his hand glides down my stomach and under the waistband of my thong. "Feel that?" I ask when his finger dips inside of me. "Feel how wet I am."

"Fuck yes," he says, surprising me with how many swear words have come out of his mouth since I've kissed him. It's as if he's dropped the thin veil of being a boss and is letting his true colors show now.

"You make me feel like this, Ford. Turned on. Wanted. Needed."

He growls into my ear, spins me around, and then pushes my thong down to the ground, and I step out of it.

His hand goes between my legs, and I part them a little more for him as I hold on to him, my stance on the ground feeling wobbly. His finger glides over me, in and out, in and out.

Just the right amount of pressure.

Just the right pace to build me up.

To make me feel like I'm in a frenzy.

To make me feel crazy.

"I need you to be inside of me," I say, pulling his mouth to mine, frantically kissing him as his fingers continue to work in and out of me. "Please, Ford."

"I don't have protection," he says.

"I'm on birth control and I'm safe. Please, Ford."

He pulls away just enough to see my eyes. "Are you sure?"

"Positive. I need you."

"I need you too," he says as he gently pulls me down to the ground, into the tent, and onto the cushioned sleeping bags. He goes to lay me down, but instead, I place my hand on his chest.

"I want to ride you," I say, courage and lust swelling within me.

His gaze heats up, and without a word, he lies on his back and places one of his hands behind his head as I climb over him. On my knees, I hover above his erection. His hand smooths up my stomach, and he slowly grips my breast, allowing his thumb to pass over my nipple. Reaching between my legs, I bring the tip of his cock to my entrance, where I playfully smooth him over my arousal.

The most delicious smile spreads across his face. "Damn, Larkin. You're a goddamn tease."

I smile back at him. "Just enjoying every aspect of this."

"Me. Fucking. Too."

I position him right where I want him and then I slowly start to lower down on his length.

The first few inches, I lose my breath at the overwhelming sense of him stretching me wide.

The next two inches, my head falls back from how absolutely magnificent he feels.

And the last few inches cause me to brace myself on his chest as I allow myself to mold to him.

"God, Ford," I whisper. "I didn't know it could feel this good." I start to rock up and down, savoring his entire length.

"Neither did I," he says, now gripping my hips to help me. "Hell, Larkin, you're so hot."

I lean forward, still rocking my hips, and take his mouth with mine. His hand smooths up my back, to my hair, where his fingers dig into my scalp, and it's the most satisfying feeling as he possesses me. Controls me. Loves on me.

"I need more of you," I say.

"Take what you want, Larkin. I'm all yours."

I lift up again and place my hands on either side of his waist to give myself leverage as I rotate my hips over his length.

Pulsing.

Rocking.

Shifting.

"Fuck," Ford mutters quietly, his hands guiding me, helping me.

"It's so good," I say, "but I need more."

Just then, he lifts up and flips me on my back. Taking my hands in his, he pins them to either side of my head and then drives into me with such power that I feel all the air leap from my lungs.

"Yes," I cry out.

He brings his lips to my neck, kissing along the column, up to my jaw, and then to my mouth, where he demands more from me with his tongue.

I open for him to take what he wants.

I spread my legs even wider for him.

And I grip his hands even tighter, letting him know I'm all his.

His hips piston in and out of me.

Building.

Climbing.

A rumble of pleasure boils in the pit of my stomach.

"Jesus," he says, moving faster, harder. "So good, Larkin. So fucking . . . good." He groans and rotates his hips as he continues to pulse in and out.

A spike of pleasure shoots through me, up my spine, bringing me closer and closer to the edge as an intense sense of euphoria starts to take over all my senses.

"Ford, yes. I'm so close."

"Me too," he grunts.

"Right there," I say, bringing my knees up to my chest, giving him more access and putting just the right angle on his pulses to shoot me over the edge. "Oh God!" I cry out as white-hot pleasure bursts through me, up my veins, down my muscles.

I spasm around him, contracting, pulling, causing him to groan out the sexiest "Fuck" I've ever heard in my entire life as he stills and comes inside me.

Together we ride out our orgasms until there's nothing left, and he collapses on top of me.

He lets go of my hands, and we lie there lifeless as I slowly drag my fingers up and down his back and his lips press gentle kisses against my shoulder.

After a few moments of silence, Ford lifts up and caresses my jaw while looking me in the eyes. "Please don't report this to human resources." He gives me a sexy smirk.

A laugh pops past my lips as I reach up and push his hair to the side. "No chance in hell."

Growing serious, he leans down and kisses my lips. "This, what happened between us, I want to build on it, not shy away from it."

Butterflies erupt in my stomach. "Me too," I say. "But I want to keep my job, Ford."

His brow creases. "Why wouldn't you keep your job?"

"I don't know. I'm not sure how this is all going to work."

"One step at a time, that's how."

"I don't want this to distract us from what we're here for, though. For finding you, for finding the brand."

A smile tugs at his lips. "Got a little sidetracked, didn't we?"

"Just a little. But it's important to me that we figure this out for you, now more than ever."

"Why now more than ever?" he asks.

I drag my finger over his jaw. "Because now that I've had a piece of you, I'm not going to want to let go, and I know we can never have a healthy relationship unless you're mentally healthy too."

He nods, and I'm relieved to see he understands. "I want this. You and me. I want it more than anything."

"So then we can figure this out together, right?"

"Yes . . . while naked."

I laugh as he buries his face in my neck, kissing me all over, letting me know just how lucky I am.

CHAPTER TWENTY-EIGHT

DR. BEAU

"You have everything you need, Roger?"

"Yup, all good." He looks over my shoulder to where Palmer has retired in my bedroom. "Dude, I'm so sorry again."

I shake my head. "Don't be sorry, it's fine. I honestly had no idea she was going to be dressed like that—we were stunned together."

"I know, but I feel like I'm cockblocking you."

"Nah, I wouldn't have taken it that far anyway. She's emotionally raw right now, and I want to respect that."

"Okay, well, I'll be out of here early to catch the first ferry. Thanks again."

"Anytime." I give him a quick nod and then turn out the lights as I head back to my bedroom, part of me still in disbelief over who is waiting inside. As I step in and gently close the door behind me, I find Palmer sitting on the edge of my bed, wearing one of my button-up shirts now, nibbling on her lip. We already got ready for bed—she took the bathroom first while I situated Roger on the couch. "You okay?" I ask.

She stares at the bedroom door. "Are you sure you don't want to share the bed with Roger? I don't mind taking the couch."

I lightly chuckle and pull my shirt over my head. I fold it and drape it on my dresser. Her eyes take in every last inch of my chest before focusing back on my face. "Yeah, pretty sure I'm good with not sharing a bed with my cousin."

She looks away. "I'm really embarrassed. I know Roger was cool about everything, but I still feel foolish. I chastised Laramie for the ridiculous idea."

I walk up to her and tilt her chin up, meeting her eyes. "First of all, it wasn't foolish. If Roger wasn't with me, I would have had a really hard time keeping my hands to myself. Second of all, don't feel embarrassed and don't chastise Laramie. What you did was really sexy, and I'm just mad Roger missed his ferry."

"You're not just saying that?"

"No," I say, taking her hand in mine. I kiss the back of it. "Promise." I bring her to the side of the bed and lay her down. I pull the covers over her and then go to my side, where I crawl in and turn the light off. The rain outside isn't as heavy as it was before, but it's still steady, offering the perfect lullaby. I move in close to her and rest a tentative hand on her stomach as she stares up at the ceiling. "How's your wrist?"

"Sore."

"Did you take the pain medicine I left you on the bathroom counter?"

"Yeah," she whispers. "Thank you."

"Let me know if it hurts in the middle of the night, okay?" I say, my hand spanning her stomach, my heart pounding at her proximity. She shifts lightly beneath me, moving a little closer.

"Okay."

"Just wake me up."

"And how do you propose I wake you up?" she asks.

"A little tap will do," I say, tapping a finger on her stomach. "A whisper will work too," I say, lowering my voice, my breath tickling her ear.

She lets out a deep sigh and then pushes the blankets down to her waist.

"Everything okay?" I ask her.

"Yes." I hear her swallow. "Just hot."

I smile to myself. Hot or turned on? My guess is going to be the latter, given how I found her when I came back up to my apartment, Roger in tow. I still can't get over the fact that she was naked in one of my lab coats. I'm not ashamed to say I've had similar fantasies before. When I used to come home to visit and catch a glimpse of her, my crush still strong, and I always wondered what it would be like to find her waiting for me when I got home.

Can I just say it's better than I ever expected?

"Hot, huh?" I say, feeling brave. "Let me help you with that." I move my shaky hand to the top button of the shirt she borrowed and undo it. "Did that help?" I attempt to swallow back my nerves, but Jesus, I'm in bed with Palmer Chance and she wants me, just like I want her.

"No, still hot," she says, her chest rising higher than before.

"What about this?" I undo the next button.

"Worse," she says, squirming under me.

"Hmm, what about this?" I undo the next two buttons. Pause, and then the last few, leaving just the bottom one clasped together. Then, gently, I push the sides of the shirt open just enough to expose her skin but nothing else. "That better?"

She shakes her head. "No."

"Strange," I say playfully. "I'd have thought that would do the trick. At least it was a good attempt, right?"

"That's . . . that's all you're going to try?" she asks, the strain in her voice turning me on now. Hell, maybe I didn't think this all the way through.

"I'm not sure there's much more to try, other than cooling you down with my fingers."

"How . . . uh"—she swallows—"how would you do that?" Man, she's tempting me. Not sure how much I'm going to hold back, not when her voice sounds so desperate.

Moving my fingers to her exposed skin, I start at her sternum and very slowly drag them down past her cleavage, to her stomach, and to her belly button, then back up again.

"Oh . . . Jesus," she says as I feel her legs spread, one of them knocking into my leg.

"That helping?" I ask.

"Yes," she whispers.

"What about this?" I lazily draw circles all the way down the center of her body and then back up again.

"Mm-hmm," she says, her good hand fumbling under the bedcovers, bumping against my bulge.

She goes to grab it, but I stop her. "I don't need cooling down, just you." Then I move my fingers under the fabric of the shirt, growing closer to her nipples before pulling away and working my way back down to her belly button, this time passing by it to where the waistband of her underwear would be, but to my fucking surprise, she's not wearing any.

Hell.

"Beau," she whispers.

"Huh?" I ask, moving my fingers back up to her sternum.

"You're making me hotter."

"Oh . . . should I stop?" I go to remove my hand, but she clamps it back down to her chest.

"Jesus, don't stop." Her legs bend and tent the bottom half of the blankets as she wiggles underneath my touch.

"You want me to keep going?" I whisper into her ear.

"Yes, badly."

"But you're already a little too vocal. I'm afraid of what will happen if I keep going. Roger's trying to sleep."

"I'll be quiet," she whispers, moving my hand farther down her stomach, to the last button. "Please, Beau."

"Begging?" I ask, nibbling on her earlobe.

"Pleading."

I undo the last button and push the sides of the shirt open.

"Yes," she whispers.

Keeping my eyes on her face, I lift my hand back up to her chest, where I draw a small figure eight over her breasts, coming closer to her nipples but never touching them.

"You're going to make me touch myself," she says.

"I wouldn't be opposed to that." I move my nose over her jaw. "I'd love to see you come on your own fingers."

Her head turns so our noses touch, and we stay like that for a few seconds, the sexual tension building, the moment pulsing between us, the air so goddamn heavy that I feel the need to cut through it just to have access to her beautiful face.

We each take a breath.

She wets her lips.

I wet mine.

And then, she leans in ever so slightly and nips at my lips before pulling away. It's a cautionary kiss, and it ignites something inside me. I lean in closer and take her lips with mine as my hand moves across her chest and connects entirely with her breast and her pierced nipple.

Fuck, I forgot about that.

I groan into her lips, barely believing that after all these years, I'm actually touching her, kissing her.

Heady lust courses through me while I get lost in her mouth. My fingers play with her hardened nipple, moving the barbell back and forth ever so slightly. She moans quietly and turns to face me, but I stop her and push her back on the mattress.

"Stay where you are," I say, catching my breath.

I position myself so I'm hovered above her now. Looking her in the eyes, I move one side of the shirt all the way open, revealing one of her breasts. Glancing down, my mouth waters as I take her in. I play with her nipple piercing. "When did you get this done?"

"Italy," she says, her body lightly rocking beneath me. "Spur of the moment, loved it ever since."

"Does it feel good when I play with them?"

"More than you can imagine." Her legs part again, and she scoots up on the bed. "I'm going to need you to play a little farther south," she whispers.

"Is that so?" I smile. "Are you ready for me?"

"Very." She takes my hand in hers and pulls it down her body, placing it right between her legs before taking my fingers and running them along her slit.

"Shit, Palmer," I say as I move my fingers inside her. "You're so wet."

"You're killing me." She takes the back of my neck and pulls me down to her mouth again. I get lost in the way her tongue flicks against mine, in the way her mouth molds to mine, in the demanding way she asks for more while I slowly move my fingers in and out of her. I start with one finger but gradually move to two. She stiffens for a moment but then relaxes and lets me pulse in and out of her, her hips joining in on the movement.

My cock aches as it casually rubs against her leg, and I wonder if I'm going to be able to get through this, making it about her, though I know that's what she needs. This isn't about me and my needs—it's about Palmer and feeling worthy.

She's worthy of so much, and I'm not sure she sees that about herself.

At least I can help her a little.

I glide my mouth across her jaw and back to her lips while I move my thumb to her clit. Her mouth pops open, and I swallow her moan before she can make too much noise. "Quiet," I whisper with a grin. "You promised to be quiet."

"S-sorry," she stutters as she starts to shake beneath me. Her good arm wraps around my neck, holding me in place, her mouth unrelenting as it takes and takes.

And I let her.

I let her have control.

I let her twist and thrust under me.

I let her set the pace.

"Yes," she pants into my mouth, now riding my fingers as I keep them still. "Oh my God, yes, Beau." Her voice is a strangled whisper as she pumps harder and harder. I press harder on her clit, and her fingernails dig into my back. "Oh . . . fuck," she mumbles right before I feel her clamp around me, and she rides my fingers with abandon as she comes.

Her moans feel like shock waves down my spine.

Her grip spurs me on.

And the way she rubs against my erection makes it so goddamn difficult to stay focused on her.

When she slows down, I take a deep breath with her and then straighten her shirt and button it back up.

"Wh-what are you doing?" she asks.

"I'm making sure you're covered up."

"Why?"

"Because." I lean down and kiss her nose after finishing with the last button. "It's time to get some rest."

"But—"

"I said time for some rest."

"Beau, I can feel how hard you are."

"Perfect, so can I." She gives me a look, and I smooth her hair down while pressing another kiss to her lips. "That was just for you. What you can do for me is get some rest."

"But I don't understand."

"There's nothing to understand," I say. "I like taking care of you—let me do that." I took care of her after the fire, and I'm taking care of her now. It feels right, like this is what I'm supposed to do, protect this woman. Be the man she deserves.

"Okay." She looks unsure. "What happens tomorrow?"

"What do you mean what happens tomorrow?"

"In the morning." She turns toward me. "When it's time to leave. Do we shake hands and say thank you? Do we talk about maybe, I don't know . . . like a lunch date or something?"

As if I could shake hands and be on my merry way. Not with her. This moment, having her in my arms, it brings . . . relief. Like I've been holding my breath ever since I left high school, and now I finally get to exhale.

I inwardly smile. She wants to know about the "morning after." Well, it's an easy answer for me, but I'm not sure where her head is.

"What do you want to happen?" I ask.

She shakes her head. "I need to know what you want."

I drape my hand on her hip. "I think you know what I want, Palmer, but I happen to live here. This is my home, and it's where I'm going to be for a very long time. It's up to you to decide what you want."

She closes her eyes and snuggles in close to me, her cast moving over my stomach. "I don't know what I want, Beau. I have no idea what I'm doing with my life."

"Then take some time to sort it out. I'm not going anywhere."

"Are you going to go out with anyone? You know, while I'm here?" Her insecurity hurts me. I'm not sure what kind of man she thinks I am, but if she's basing this off the other men she's been with, they must have been assholes.

"I have no desire to see anyone else. I haven't for a long time. Does that answer your question?"

She nods and she looks up at me. "Will you go out to lunch with me tomorrow?"

Hell, she's cute.

I bring her in closer to my chest. "I'll have to check my appointments for tomorrow to see when I'm free, but I'm sure I can swing it in between wart removals."

She laughs and presses a kiss to my chest. "Thank you, Beau, for everything."

From the tone of her voice, I don't think she's thanking me just for tonight.

CHAPTER

TWENTY-NINE

NORA

The timer on the oven beeps, reminding me that I put a frozen pizza in there.

I get up from Cooper's lap and walk over to the kitchen, my body buzzing from being that close to him again. I can practically taste him already.

I feel like he needs me.

And oddly, a little piece of me needs him.

I slip an oven mitt on and open the oven. A wave of heat hits me as I bend down and pull out the pizza. When I lift up and set the pizza on the stove, Cooper is leaning against the counter, arms folded, a perplexed look on his face.

I toss the oven mitt to the side. "What's that look for?"

He glances at me. "Why does Dealia think you're good for me?"

Leaving the pizza to cool, I hop up on the counter opposite him, putting some much-needed distance between us. "I think she just noticed our chemistry. You know?"

"Do you think there's chemistry?" he asks.

"I do. And I believe I know enough about you to understand where your heart stands. I wouldn't say I'm an expert, but from what I know, I get your need to give back to your parents, even if you're sometimes irritated by the responsibility. I understand that you had plans and dreams that were taken away the minute your dad was diagnosed. I realize you want more for yourself, but you don't know how to make it happen. And I know you want a change and you're ready to make that change, but you need some outside encouragement to make that happen."

He grips the counter behind him and connects those gray eyes with mine. "I think you know more than you let on."

"Did I ace the quiz?" I ask with a smile.

He scratches his chest. "I'd say so. I'm not sure Dealia would ever be able to give me an answer like that, but not because she didn't care about me."

"She cared about you." This much I know is true. She did care. I'm just not sure she saw him, truly saw him for the man he is. "She just couldn't see the reasoning for your actions. It doesn't make her a bad person—it just shows she wasn't *your* person, and that's okay."

"How can you be so casual about all of this?" he asks.

"What's the point in worrying about it?" I ask. "Worrying has done nothing but stress people out and cause problems. I spent so many of my earlier years worrying about things that in the grand scheme of things didn't matter. I would stress myself out, stop eating, and I became extremely unhealthy."

"Really? What would you stress out about?"

"Mainly trying to prove to my parents that I could take over the store. With everything I baked, I tried to be perfect, and when I wasn't perfect, I would be so hard on myself. Berate myself for wasting the store's resources. It was incredibly unhealthy, and it wasn't until I looked at myself in the mirror and realized what I was doing to my body that I made a change. I was doing more harm than good, but it took a while to realize. So, when it comes to the little things, I try not to worry about them—they find a way of working themselves out."

"It's why you waited on Dealia to come around."

I nod. "Granted, I was a twisted ball of nerves at first, but I really, really hoped she would, and she did. She just needed time to process. Just like your siblings. They'll come around to selling the house; they just need time. They won't be mad forever."

He slowly nods. "Yeah, I've had time to realize that our parents aren't the same people we grew up with, physically, and I understand the need for the change. Now that they're here, maybe they'll see it too."

"Exactly. Until then, you should focus on the things you can control."

"And what would those things be?" he asks as he steps up to me and places his hands on my thighs.

"Well, for one, you need to get involved in the company branding. You're talented, Cooper, and you need to be confident in that talent."

"Ford doesn't want me—"

"Who's close to Ford?" When he gives me a questioning look, I continue: "Larkin. I'm not saying go behind his back, but maybe you need a little help. Meet with her, show her what you have, and maybe she can talk to Ford. It's worth a shot."

He gives it some thought. "Yeah, I never considered that."

"Sometimes you're so caught up in the initial no that you forget to look for the maybes. Larkin is a maybe, so approach her and see what she says."

"Okay, yeah, that's actually a really good idea."

"And then, while you're putting yourself out there, maybe ask me out on a date, because, you know, I'd have a really hard time saying no to that."

"And why would I ask you out?" he asks with a smirk.

I reach out and brush his hair to the side, heart thumping. "Because I think there's more to us than just a one-night stand, and I don't think

I could forgive myself if I didn't put myself out there and ask for more." Cooper comes with baggage—it's lurked in every moment of our conversation tonight. But he intrigues me, he makes me smile, and those are qualities that don't come around often. So even though he has baggage, I don't mind helping him carry it.

His smirk widens into a grin. "You just put it out there, what you want, don't you?"

I shrug. "Why not? What's the worst you can say? No? Well, at least I asked. It's better than sitting around, wondering if there was ever a chance." I move my hands to his waist, and relief wafts over me, knowing I've finally put it all out there. "Do you think there's a chance?"

Taking my chin in his thumb and index finger, he brings my mouth close to his. "There's a large chance." And then he presses a gentle kiss across my lips. It's like a whisper of lust—not enough pressure, and surely not the passion my body wants, but just enough to soothe me as he pulls away. "Nora, will you go out on a date with me?"

"Oh my gosh, I'm so surprised." I widen my eyes and fan my face, which makes him chuckle. "This is just so unexpected. I'm not sure what to say." He laughs some more and buries his head in my neck, where he presses a kiss.

"You know exactly what to say."

Chills run up my arms and legs. "When you say it like that . . ." I move my head to the side, giving him better access. "I guess I could go out with you."

He pulls away. "It's not a 'guess you can.' I'm going to need a solid yes from those beautiful lips."

I run my thumb over the rough scruff on his jaw. "I would love to go out with you, Cooper, under one condition."

"What's that?" he asks, his hands moving farther up my thighs.

"We focus on each other, not the sexual side of things."

He slightly pulls back to look me in the eyes. "Are you proposing we go celibate for a certain amount of time?"

"Would you be opposed to that?" I ask.

"I want to hear your reasoning first before I make a decision." His voice is teasing as he pokes my side.

"Well, we've already seen each other naked."

"That's accurate."

"And we've already been carnal with each other."

He chuckles. "Definitely carnal."

"We've had each other's private parts in each other's mouths."

He nods slowly. "Yup, that is carnal for sure."

"And we both know we can make each other orgasm . . . more than a few times."

"Another true statement. Statements that make me look incredibly good."

"And even though I'd like to take this new body for a run," I say, moving my fingers over his delicious abs and thick pecs, "I think it would be best that we move forward on an emotional level. You know, really get to know each other and let the carnal orgasms take a back seat for a second."

"I appreciate your description of the kind of sex we have—makes me feel like I made a lasting impression."

"You did. So much so that I haven't been with anyone since," I admit.

He grips my chin. "Me neither."

"Seriously?" I ask, surprised.

"Seriously. Haven't found anyone worthy enough, despite my parents' attempts to get me out there more." He strokes his thumb over my cheek. "Which tells me one thing—you're special, and I would do anything to keep that something special in my life."

"Even be celibate?" I wince.

"You know you're more to me than a carnal night, Nora. I didn't come to the bakery or text you because I was looking for another night. I came because I was looking for someone with a kind heart, someone who can make me laugh. Is the sex amazing with us? Fuck yes, but I think the emotional part of a relationship, the side I've been craving, can be so much more."

That makes me smile.

"Well, then, it's settled," I say, heart full. "I'll go out with you."

"One more quick question about this dating thing."

"What's that?" I ask, wrapping my legs around his waist and bringing him close.

"This celibacy pact, does it include kissing?"

I shake my head. "No, kissing is a must, but it doesn't go past that."

"Okay, so we are going to get more connected while attempting to give each other a furious case of blue balls."

"Accurate, yes."

"Perfect." He chuckles. "Get ready to be taunted and teased while I emotionally stimulate you."

"Oooh, give it to me hard with that emotional stimulation."

"I'm going to pound it into you, relentlessly, until you can't take it anymore."

Chuckling, I grip his cheeks and press a quick kiss to his lips. "God, I can't wait to get emotional with you. We're going to come so hard in each other's minds."

His brows rise.

"Too far?" I ask.

"Too far." He laughs and presses another kiss to my lips as I hold him, happy about what's to come.

CHAPTER THIRTY

FORD

"Good morning," says Larkin's sweet voice as she kisses my chest.

I rub my hand over her back. "Mmm, good morning."

Her hand floats over my stomach, stirring me awake . . . everywhere. "You are aware it's your assistant that you're lying naked on the floor with, in a tent, in your parents' living room, right?"

"Well aware."

"And you're okay with that?"

"Perfectly okay with that." I kiss the top of her head. "Why all the questions?"

"Just making sure. Normally in situations like this, I feel like people wake up and then all of a sudden they're, like, 'What the hell have I done?'"

"I *am* thinking what the hell have I done." Larkin stiffens next to me. "But not in the way you meant. More like . . . what the hell have I done? And why didn't I do it sooner?"

I can feel her smile against my chest. "Smooth talker, even in the morning."

"I try to—"

The garage door opens, and I hear Mom call out in a cheery voice, "Good morning!"

Oh.

Fuck.

I sit up straight, knocking Larkin off me with the sleeping bag. I glance down at my naked body and then look at hers. "My parents are home," I whisper.

Her eyes widen, and she scrambles for the pillow to cover up.

"Oh my God," she whispers back. "I'm naked in their living room."

"We're both naked in their living room. Shit."

"Are you awake?" Mom calls out from the kitchen.

I scramble around, looking for my clothes. "Where are my pants?"

"Outside of the tent, on the living room floor."

"Shit," I say again.

"I think they're still sleeping," I hear Mom say.

"Or they're out for one of their runs," Dad says. "Slick roads, though; might not be smart."

I turn to Larkin. "They can't see us naked."

"Obviously," she whispers. "God, and what would they think of you sleeping with your assistant?" She places her hand on her forehead in distress. "They're going to think I'm a harlot."

I glance toward the kitchen and then back at Larkin. "They won't." I pause. "Shit, I have no idea what they might think, but I have a feeling if they see us naked, they will have something to say about it."

"Anyone in their right mind would have something to say about finding two individuals naked in their living room," Larkin says, her panic rising.

I grip her hand for a brief moment. "It's okay. We can be really quiet and let them believe we're not here, and then we'll sneak out while they're taking showers."

"That's a great idea and all, but all of our clothes are outside this tent."

"Fuck," I mutter and then lean an ear toward the kitchen. Luckily, we didn't zip up the tent, so I can partially see the living room. "I think

I see my pants. Why don't I get dressed quick and distract them in the kitchen while you get dressed?"

She nods. "Okay, yeah, that's a great idea."

"Good." I ease out of the sleeping bag as quietly as I can and reach out for my sweatpants, which are about three feet away. I look over my shoulder to find Larkin staring at my bare ass. "Can you not look at me from that angle?" I ask. "It's not entirely flattering."

She clamps her hand over her mouth, suppressing a laugh. "It's flattering on this end."

"That's never a flattering angle."

She motions to the living room. "Just grab your pants; who cares what angle I'm seeing your ass at."

"I care. Because you're not just looking at ass . . ."

"Are you referring to your balls? Because those are nice too."

My cheeks flame. "We have severely crossed the line."

"We crossed it last night, when your face was between my legs the second go-around." She smirks, nibbling on her bottom lip.

"Don't get me—"

"Your coloring book is in here," Mom says, her voice drawing closer.

Fuck.

I quickly snag my pants and then pop back into the tent while Larkin dives under the sleeping bag.

I'm a sitting duck with two options.

Pray I can put my pants on faster than my mom can enter the living room, or I can duck under the sleeping bag as well.

Can you guess what I decided on?

Hint: it wasn't the right choice.

"Yes, I'll grab your colored—Ford," Mom says, her mouth falling open as she steps into the room. I'm inside the open tent, with one leg in my sweatpants, one out. She assesses the living room, and I hope to God she doesn't notice the discarded thong somewhere around here. "What are you doing?"

I blink.

I swallow.

I try to look like I don't have company.

"Uh . . . you know . . . camping."

"Camping? In the living room?"

"Did I hear camping?" Dad's voice booms down the hallway.

"Yes, Ford is camping."

"Outside?" Dad walks into the living room and assesses the mess. "What on God's green earth is happening in here?"

I clear my throat and wish that I wasn't half-naked—one leg still out of my sweatpants, completely bare. "Camping," I answer.

"In the living room?" Dad asks, confused. "Naked?"

"He's not naked," Mom says and then takes a closer look at me. "Are you naked? In my living room?"

"No, not naked. Why would I be naked in your living room?" I ask nervously as they stare me down.

I'm thirty-six years old, but in this moment, I feel like a teenager caught with his pants down. Half of that statement is true.

"I don't know, that's what we're asking—" Mom pauses and then glances up the stairs. "Dear Jesus, Ford. Is Larkin upstairs? And you're naked down here? What the hell do you think she'd do if she came down here to see you camping naked in the living room, for Christ's sake?"

"Larkin is here?" Dad whisper-shouts. A bead of sweat rolls down my back. If they only knew. "For the love of God, get your pants on. What are you . . . some kind of pervert?"

The sleeping bag shakes next to me, no doubt from Larkin barely holding in her laughter.

"No, Dad, I'm not—"

He points a finger at me. "I didn't raise a pervert."

"I'm not—"

Mom clutches her chest. "Oh no, is he a Peeping Tom? You weren't naked, looking in on her bedroom, were you? I don't think I could handle that."

"And what's with the tent? Is it a pervert tent?" Dad asks.

"I'm not a pervert, and I wasn't doing any Peeping Tom shit. Jesus, who do you think I am?"

"I don't know." Dad tosses his arms up in the air. "I didn't think I would come home to my adult son naked in our living room with his assistant upstairs, but here we are, so excuse us for questioning if you're a pervert."

Wow, are my parents taking this too far?

But I have no idea how to cover this up, how to explain why I'm half-naked in their living room. Think, Ford . . . think . . .

Decided to pitch my own tent? God no, that would be alluding to the pervert thing.

Loves to sleep naked, can't get enough of it? Uh, still slightly perverted, because who can't keep it together for one night in their parents' house with said assistant upstairs?

Hmm . . . spilled juice on my pants? Now this is a viable possibility, but I'm not sure if my parents have juice—

"Ahhhh-choo!"

Oh . . . fuck.

Mom and Dad's eyes widen as they glance toward the sleeping bag, where Larkin is lying as flat as can be.

Thinking quickly, I say, "Uh, pardon me." I laugh nervously. "Gassy in the morning."

Dad shakes his head. "Unless your asshole is a nose, that was not a fart." He scans the living room, and his eyes land on something. From the narrowing of his eyes, what he's staring at is most likely incriminating. "Peggy. A lady's garment."

Yup.

Mom gasps, and then her head whips toward me.

"You have a *woman* in that tent with you? While poor Larkin is upstairs? You . . . you miscreant."

"Mom, it's not what you think."

"Make yourself known, woman!" Dad's voice booms.

"Dad, that's not necess—"

The sleeping bag shuffles, and Larkin pops her head out, shocking the pants right off my parents. I bury my head in my hands as they both take a step back. Stunned. Shocked. Aghast.

"Larkin," Mom whispers in shock.

"I don't believe my eyes," Dad says in awe.

Oh God, here it comes.

My parents are good people, they really are. They took in Cooper and me when we were desperate for a family, for any kind of love. They have raised us to be the men we are today through creative parenting, thoughtful lessons, and many, many lectures.

The type of lectures that have been imprinted in my brain and are now used as guidelines as I walk through my life. Some end on a positive note, a pat on the back, a simple handshake. And the negative ones, the ones that carry the most impact, those are accompanied by disapproving eyes and obvious condemnation.

From the situation unfolding, I mentally steel myself for an onslaught of *What the hell were you thinking? Have you lost your damn minds?* and the classic *What could you possibly gain from a decision like this?*

I can feel it.

I can smell it, the scorning that's about to unfold.

I can taste it, the stony frowns ready to erupt on my parents' faces.

I brace myself.

Disappointment, coming my parents' way.

"Mr. and Mrs. Chance," Larkin says, "I'm so sorry about all of this."

"You don't need to apologize," I say to her. "What happened last night was totally on me."

"And what precisely happened last night?" Dad asks, hands on his hips, his gaze boring into me. "Blink twice if he's holding you against your will."

"Dad, it's not like that. It's . . ." I look over at Larkin, at her terrified face, and then back at my parents. Jesus Christ, I can't find my words. How do I explain this? How do I—

Out of the blue, Mom throws her head back and lets out a roar of a laugh while she clutches onto Dad. "Oh, Martin, I can't hold it in any longer."

Dad cracks a grin and then expels a nose-shaking snort that frankly is terrifying.

"What's happening?" I ask, feeling like my balls have shriveled up into nothing from the pure terror pulsing through me.

Mom wipes her eyes. "Here we thought you were playing around with your . . . ding-a-ling while Larkin was upstairs, but in fact, she was the one playing with it."

"Mom!" I say with a stern voice.

Ignoring me, Mom turns to Dad. "What a relief."

He nods his head and wipes under his nose. "Really thought we raised a pervert for a second."

"But it's only just him and Larkin."

"Only?" I ask. "What's that supposed to mean?"

Dad chuckles some more. "Surprised it took this long."

"I know. The sexual tension has been eating me alive." Mom clutches her heart.

Excuse me?

Dad grips Mom's shoulder and rubs it. "We can all let out a collective breath now."

Mom motions to my lower half and says, "Finish putting your pants on. We shall discuss this new development while enjoying some quality breakfast."

"I'll get started on the bacon," Dad says, a pep in his step.

Once they disappear, I let out a long breath as Larkin lies back on her pillow. "Oh my God, Ford. I'm so sorry."

"Why are you sorry? I'm the one who fucked up."

She sits up again, hugging the sleeping bag to her chest. "You think you fucked up? Like, that this was a mistake?" Her worried gaze meets mine, and I see what she's asking.

"No," I say, quickly, reaching out and cupping her cheek. "No, that's not what I meant. This was not a mistake. Maybe it was a mistake doing it in my parents' living room, where they could walk in at any point, but kissing you, pushing past that fine line, that's not a mistake." She nods. "I promise, Larkin," I continue, "I'm happy last night happened."

She smiles softly. "Me too. Really happy."

"Good." We stare at each other, and then together we let out a quiet laugh. "Fuck, I'm sorry about my parents."

She pinches my side, with humor. "Why? They're precious, utterly concerned with their son being a pervert. I find it charming."

"You find *that* charming?" I ask. "I think you need to get your priorities checked."

"Possibly." Her grin does all kinds of fluttery things to me.

"So, should we get dressed and go discuss with my parents?"

"Or"—she cringes—"I can go take a shower and you can do all the dirty work."

I laugh. "No fucking way am I going in there by myself. You made the first move, so you have to go in there with me."

"What? I did not make the first move."

"Uh, you kissed me first."

"Because you said I made you smile," she counters.

"That's just a compliment."

She shakes her head. "No way. Now get me my clothes so I can ask your parents who made the first move."

"You are not asking them that."

268

I finish putting on my pants and then snag her clothes. I watch as she drops the sleeping bag, revealing her perfect breasts before putting on my borrowed sweatshirt. She glances up at me with a sly smile. "None of that gawking."

I press my hand to my lower back. "Can't help it, barely got my fill last night."

She rolls her eyes, puts her pants on, and then climbs out of the tent. I take her hand and kiss her knuckles. "There's still a scenario where you can avoid this—pretend it never happened, and I'll convince my parents they're going senile and that they came up with the entire thing."

She chuckles. "But that would mean giving you up, right?"

"Unfortunately, that would be the trade-in."

She stands on her toes and presses a soft kiss to my jaw. "Then if that's the case, let's get this over with."

◆ ◆ ◆

My parents are sitting at the dining room table, two glasses of champagne and a cheese danish resting between them. Mom is in a jovial mood, Dad is happily coloring in his coloring book, and, to my surprise, there is something already baking in the oven. That was fast.

"We popped a quiche in; should be ready in about twenty minutes. Until then, have a danish," Mom says, gesturing toward the counter.

"I'm really okay," Larkin says while she plays nervously with the hem of her shirt.

"Take a seat," I say to her softly. "I'll grab some coffee for you and a danish, just in case you change your mind."

Her eyes have a hint of surprise in them before they turn to gratitude. Yeah, it's a different dynamic in this very moment. Not that I'm an asshole boss who demands she get me my coffee every day, but she is always the one taking the initiative to make sure I'm well fed and caffeinated. Now . . . it's different. Just like that, and I like it. From the look in her eyes, she does too.

Once I grab everything, I take a seat next to Larkin at the table and set the danish plate and cups of coffee down, only for Dad to jump in with the questions. The invasive questions. "So, let me get this straight," Dad says. "You both decided to just . . . have sex last night. Out of the blue? In our living room? In a tent?"

It's hard not to feel like a teenager in this moment, getting apparently grilled by my dad.

"I don't think it was out of the blue," I say. "It wasn't like we were bored and I turned to Larkin and asked her to have sex."

"So then how did it happen?" Dad asks.

"You really want the details?"

"Not *those* kinds of details," Dad says flippantly. "But, you know, how did this all come about?" He waves his hand in the air and then goes back to coloring.

I guess we're doing this, then. Clearing my throat, I say, "I've always found Larkin attractive—it's hard not to notice how beautiful she is, inside and out—but I never tapped into that thought. I pushed it to the back of my mind, because she's always been my assistant. But it wasn't until the past few weeks, which have had me spending so much time with her and assessing my present life, that I realized she makes me happy. Emotionally, mentally, she fills up my cup, and there's nothing I want more than to be the man that holds her hand. Simple as that." I steal a glance at Larkin, wishing I was saying this to her rather than my father.

"Why now, then? Office romances can be tricky and hard to navigate—I know from experience, especially when they're boss and assistant relationships." Dad motions to Larkin. "You can't lose her, son; she's a huge asset to the company." He's not mad, but I can see he's trying to cover all bases. Make sure we know what we're getting into. I guess after all the thoughtful and in-depth conversations I've had with him in the past, this doesn't surprise me.

"I know." I take Larkin's hand in mine and say, "I don't plan on losing her."

But Larkin fidgets next to me. I can practically feel her nerves spiking, and before I can calm her down, she says, "It was my fault."

"Larkin," I start, but she places her hand on my chest. She clearly isn't reading the room properly. My dad can be an intimidating man, even if his socks don't match.

"Please don't be mad at Ford." Yeah, she's not understanding my dad's questioning at all. "I made the first move. I kissed him. It was an intense moment—we were talking about feelings, and something came over me and I went for it."

Mom takes that moment to chime in. "You made the first move?" she asks.

"Yes, Mrs. Chance," Larkin answers. "And I know that's completely unprofessional, and I understand there might be consequences to my actions—"

"You're damn right there are consequences to your actions," Mom says, pushing away from the table and standing. Oh shit. Maybe *I* was reading everything wrong. Confused, I'm about to step in to defend Larkin when Mom scoops Larkin into a hug. "Oh, baby girl, welcome to the family. I just knew you two were supposed to get together. From the moment I met you, I knew you were the perfect match for my Ford, and the fact that you made the first move . . . well, that makes all the difference. You *like* him."

From over my mom's shoulder, Larkin looks at me with confused eyes but then hugs her back. Trust me, I'm just as confused. Maybe we should have waited to have some more coffee in our systems before having this conversation.

"I do like him," Larkin says, making my stomach do a somersault.

I glance over at Dad, who has a smirk on his face as he leans back in his chair. When he glances at me, he picks up a glass of champagne and lifts it in a mock toast. "So glad you're not a pervert, son." But then, turning serious, his eyes connect with mine and he says, "Woo her, son. She's the type of girl who deserves wooing."

I look back at Larkin and I realize that my dad could not be more right. She is a forever type of girl, and the only way to keep her is to make sure she knows I'm in this for the long haul.

TO: Palmer Chance, Cooper Chance
FROM: Ford Chance
SUBJECT: The Anniversary Party

Just checking in to see how everything is coming along. Larkin and I will be working on mapping out the store today and talking with the employees to see how we can make the most out of the space, especially the back.

Cooper: Have people been RSVPing? How's the list coming along? Rentals? The "fun" you promised.

Palmer: Cake and food set?

TO: Palmer Chance, Ford Chance
FROM: Cooper Chance
SUBJECT: Re: The Anniversary Party

Cake is fine. Palmer doesn't have to do anything with that.

Everything else is taken care of.

TO: Cooper Chance, Ford Chance
FROM: Palmer Chance
SUBJECT: Re: The Anniversary Party

What have you done to the cake? Did you change it back? I swear to God, Cooper, I'm going to murder you.

Also, you can respond to Ford in the body of the email, and not me?

TO: Palmer Chance, Ford Chance
FROM: Cooper Chance
SUBJECT: Yup. Also, murder is a sin.

TO: Cooper Chance, Ford Chance
FROM: Palmer Chance
SUBJECT: Why are you a dick?

TO: Palmer Chance, Ford Chance
FROM: Cooper Chance
SUBJECT: Why are you a hag?

◆ ◆ ◆

TO: Cooper Chance, Ford Chance
FROM: Palmer Chance
SUBJECT: STOP CHANGING THE CAKE

◆ ◆ ◆

TO: Palmer Chance, Ford Chance
FROM: Cooper Chance
SUBJECT: JUST BECAUSE YOU USED CAPS, DOESN'T MEAN I'll LISTEN

◆ ◆ ◆

TO: Cooper Chance, Palmer Chance
FROM: Ford Chance
SUBJECT: Re: JUST BECAUSE YOU USED CAPS, DOESN'T MEAN I'll LISTEN

Enough.

We have a week until the party. Get your shit together. Show up for Mom and Dad and then we can go our separate ways. Think you can handle that?

CHAPTER THIRTY-ONE
LARKIN

Cooper: Meet you there at noon.

I glance up from the text that Cooper sent me an hour ago, just to make sure I got the time right. It's two minutes past noon, and he's nowhere in sight. The island is pretty quiet today: not much traffic toward the store, which is the main draw, and the lunch crowd is fairly sparse as well. Surprising for a summer day. Maybe the locals are lucky for the reprieve, because I know tomorrow it will probably pick up. It always does. With some of the best hiking trails in the area and the popularity of the original Watchful Wanderers store, Marina Island is easily a top-five summer destination in the PNW.

It's been an eventful day, to say the least, but Cooper texting me still came close to being the biggest surprise. I was about to ask Ford about it, but Cooper told me not to tell Ford about us meeting.

Granted, this is not something I would normally keep a secret from Ford, especially now that we're . . . dating. Yeah, we're dating; I can't even fathom that change in events right now. But after Ford battled through emails with his siblings this morning, I thought that Cooper might be looking for some insight on how to mend things with his brother.

At least that's what I'm hoping.

If I can be a helping hand in the matter, then I will.

I glance at the time on my phone again and then look up toward the harbor, where I spot Cooper jogging toward me.

"Hey," I say when he gets closer.

"Sorry," he says, slightly breathless. "Someone's car stalled out on the ferry, which made for a backlog of cars trying to get off."

"Not a problem at all." I nod toward the sandwich shop. "Want to take a seat?"

"That would be great." We walk to one of the picnic tables behind the shop, next to the air conditioner. It will make for a noisier meeting, but it seems like Cooper wants some privacy. When we take a seat, he swings his backpack from his shoulders and pulls out his water bottle. He takes a sip while removing a tablet from his backpack, and my mind starts to reel with what he could possibly want from this meeting. "Thanks for meeting with me," he says.

"Of course. When I got your text, I was tempted to ask Ford what was going on." I wince. "He showed me your emails this morning."

Cooper rolls his eyes. "Of course he did. Palmer is such a pain in my ass. She has the baby-sister nagging down to a science. But that's not why I want to talk to you."

"It's not?" I ask, slightly confused.

"No. I want to talk to you about the rebranding for the store."

"Oh, Cooper. I don't think that's a good idea," I say, my thoughts immediately going to Ford and how angry he'd be about this.

"Hear me out."

"I don't know, Cooper. That's something I think you should talk to your brother about."

"I tried, but he won't listen to me."

"I know, he told me. Ford has his reasons, and I wouldn't feel right going behind—"

"Please, Larkin," he pleads. "I need someone to listen to me. He won't, and I don't want to get Dad involved, so you're my next-best option. Just hear me out, okay?"

"I don't know . . ."

"Larkin." His eyes, which perfectly match his brother's, bore into me, pleading, begging. The silver of those irises might belong to someone else, but they have the same effect on me as Ford's. "Please. Please be the one who listens to me. That's all you need to do—just listen."

Damn it.

I look off to the side and try to weigh out my options. I don't have to do anything. I can just listen like he says and then maybe bring it to Ford. Listening isn't going to really hurt anything. And from the way he's pleading so passionately, I know what he has to say must be important. And he's gone to such great lengths to talk to me, even taking the ferry out here.

"Okay," I say. "I'll listen."

"Really?" he asks, brightening up.

"Yes, but that's all. Just listening."

"That's all I'm asking." He opens his tablet, excitement in his face as he clicks through a few things. "When I met with Ford, I didn't get a chance to tell him that for the past year, I've been taking digital art classes online."

"Oh, really?" I ask, surprised.

"Yes. I haven't been happy at my normal job."

"So I've heard. That nonfiction really killing you?"

"Historical nonfiction. I think we should leave it to *Drunk History* on the comedy channel and call it a day."

I laugh. "You know, I did hear school districts are starting to drop history as a class and making kids watch that instead."

"Now that's proper education." We both laugh. "But yeah, the nonfiction editing game isn't for me. I want more. I've always doodled here and there, but one day, I decided to take those doodles to the next level and started taking classes. Come to find out I'm pretty good at it, especially graphic design and branding for companies."

He puts his tablet in front of me and swipes through his work.

It starts with a simple brand logo for a local beer company. Simple but eye catching, and they only get better. Seattle businesses—bookstores, florists, even an ax-throwing bar—are all represented with bold colors and clean lines.

"Wow," I say. "You created all of these?"

"Yup. This is a lot of the classwork we had to do. As you can see, there's some serious growth as the year went on."

"I love the colors you use and the shading." I flip through and come to a logo for Cake It Bakery, which I recognize from growing up on the island. "Oh my God, that's Nora's bakery. Have you showed her this? It's so perfect."

"Yeah, she wants it printed and hung in her bakery."

"It should be—it's so cute." I glance up at Cooper with a smirk. "The boobs are . . . perky."

He chuckles. "Trust me, they're accurate." That statement snags my attention, but I don't comment on it, opting to store it away for later. Nora and Cooper: I could *so* see that.

"Well, these are amazing. Which makes me think—did you make some for the rebrand?"

"I did." He takes the tablet from me and taps another folder. "Now, I have no idea what you guys are going for, but I do know the store, I do know our family, and I thought I might have some insight on what Ford might want. Would you like to see?"

"I'd love to see."

He sets the tablet in front of me and opens up a file, displaying a half-circle logo. Mountain in the background and then silhouettes of a family with walking sticks and hiking gear, the kids trailing the parents like goslings. It's modern but has a family feel to it.

"And you can give it a vintage feel too," Cooper says, flipping to another logo. This one features a new and improved font for the company, which consists of more rigid lines but still has a little bit of whimsy to it, along with the mountains in the background. The colors he chose are appealing, with a teal and light blue with accents of black and gray. It's everything I suspect Ford has been looking for. "The vintage can go on T-shirts for the younger crowd."

He flips to another file, showing off different variations, all centered around his family and his parents.

A wave of nostalgia breaks over me as the logo takes me back to the times in my life that brought me pure joy, the times I was with my brother and my dad, hiking through the island trails.

It speaks to the family brand.

I can see my family in this logo.

I can see the Chance family in it.

It's . . . perfect.

After taking them all in, I lean back in my chair. "Cooper, these are . . . wow, these are incredible."

"You're not just saying that?" he asks.

I shake my head, my heart heavy but also filling with excitement. "No. When it comes to the company, I would never lie about anything." I smile. "I could see my dad wearing a shirt with this logo on it. He would easily wear it with pride."

Cooper taps the screen, bringing a set of logos into view. "They're all the same but with slight variations for different generations. I think one of the greatest attributes the company has over the competition is that we started from a family-owned business. Watchful Wanderers isn't just a store; it's a brand itself. People love the feeling behind it. It's like North Face, and people would wear the logo just because it's well known in the outdoor community, and I do think that's something the company could do better with—merchandising its own brand. These logos could help jump-start that."

My mind starts turning and spinning. The possibilities are endless, especially if we have someone on hand who can create merchandise that represents the company so well.

"This is . . . wow, Cooper, this is huge."

"Yeah?" he asks, his eyes bright with hope.

"Yeah."

"So, can we show Ford?" His eyes plead with me. I can see how much he wants this. How much time and thought he's put into these logos—from the silhouettes that look like his family to the joyful colors and the endless blue sky, full of possibilities.

But . . .

I shake my head. "No. We can't bring them to him."

"What?" He leans back in his chair, deflated. "But you said—"

"I know what I said, but we can't talk to him just yet."

"What do you mean?"

I fold my hands and place them on the table in front of me before looking Cooper in the eyes. "I want to make sure when you present this to Ford, he's in a good headspace. The party, the fighting through emails, the tension between you and your siblings—it's pushing him away, and even though I know he's a fair, sensible man, I have a feeling he would not look at this in the right light, if that makes sense. So I think we should wait until after the party, after the tension eases between you three, and once that's all cleared out, we approach him. I think he will be in a better headspace, more open. Does that make sense?"

"Yeah, that's actually really perceptive. I wasn't in the best headspace at our so-called brunch, nor did I help the situation. I didn't make it easy on Ford. My irritation got the best of me, so I can imagine how he might be feeling. I can wait," Cooper says. "As long as you're not blowing smoke up my ass."

"I would never do that. Trust me: Ford needs to see these logos. He'll be floored with what you've come up with. But I think we need to pick our timing properly so he's more invested in actually hearing you out and not going on the defensive. He's insecure right now, especially where the company is concerned, so I think if we showed this to him right now, it would only make things worse. Give me a week, okay?"

"A week? Okay, yeah, sure." Cooper picks up his tablet and stuffs it in his backpack before looking back at me. "Thank you for meeting with me, Larkin. I really appreciate it."

"Of course. I should probably go order a sandwich and get back to the inn before Ford thinks something happened to me."

"I'm sure he'd send a search party." Together we stand, and I feel awkward, not sure if I should give him a hug or a handshake, but when he steps away and offers a wave, I realize that's probably where we're at. It's a little bit sad, actually.

A simple wave. Nothing more.

"I'll be in touch."

"Sure thing," Cooper says before taking off toward the harbor again.

Wow. That was the last thing I expected Cooper to talk to me about, but if I can time this right, I think it could be the solution Ford has been looking for—one that could help Cooper as well.

CHAPTER THIRTY-TWO

PALMER

"I have to get back," Beau says, leaning down and pressing a kiss to my lips as the perfect summer breeze picks up around us, cooling our heated skin from the blazing sun. It was the perfect day for an early lunch outside: not very busy and with beautiful blue skies after last night's downpour.

"Unfortunately, I know. And my mom texted me; she wants me to grab a bag of ice for her. I swear they're the only people who still buy ice instead of making it at their house."

"It's the old-school things that give them the nostalgic vibe." He presses another kiss to my lips. "Appreciate those little things—you never know when they might stop asking for that ice."

"You're right," I say, realizing I shouldn't complain about my parents to Beau, who's lost both of his.

"What do you have planned for the rest of the day? Maybe telling your parents about your apartment and job?"

"Yeah, not sure I'm ready for that. I think I need to figure out what I'm doing with my life first so when I break the news to them, I'll have a backup plan to show them that I'm not a complete failure."

"You know"—he grips my cheek—"sometimes it's in moments of failure that we lean on family the most. They might be able to help you out more than you think." He presses one more kiss to my lips, making me sigh. "Got to go. I'll call you later."

"Bye." I wave at him as he takes off down the sidewalk, looking all sexy doctor-ish in his formfitting khakis and tucked-in navy-blue polo.

Dr. Beau Novak. I still can't believe I can kiss him.

Giddy, I walk behind the sandwich shop to the ice chest. I used to come down here on my bike every Friday to get ice for the family. I'd put it in the strong wicker basket on the back of my bike and then make the trek back to my house like the little delivery girl I was. Sometimes, if my mom gave me a ten-dollar bill rather than a five, I would buy myself a Rice Krispies Treat from the sandwich shop. You know, as tax for my vigorous effort.

When I reach the chest, I'm pulling on the handle just as, out of the corner of my eye, I spot Cooper sitting at a picnic table just a few yards away. But he's not alone—he's sitting with Larkin. What the hell are they doing together?

Are they in cahoots?

I shut the ice chest and creep up behind a tall bush that hides me from their view but gives me the perfect vantage point to see what they're doing. Faintly, I can hear their voices, but I can't really make out anything.

Cooper opens up a tablet and starts showing Larkin something. From my angle, I only see the sides of their faces, so I can't get a good read on what they're saying or talking about, which is frustrating— clearly the plan here is to forget about the ice and snoop instead.

What could they possibly be doing together?

Are they working on the anniversary party together? Maybe Ford assigned the party to Larkin to take care of. I could see that happening. He's too busy, so he makes his assistant do it.

Rolling my eyes, I'm about to pull away when Larkin lifts up the tablet, revealing a teal and light-blue Watchful Wanderers logo.

I grip the bush leaves in front of me as I lean closer.

Caught, red handed. This isn't about the anniversary party. This is about the company.

And those are new logos.

Different logos.

Nice, actually.

Where did they come from?

And why is Cooper involved?

Wait . . . why *is* Cooper involved? Are they all working together? I thought Ford turned down Cooper? Was that all a lie to make me think Cooper isn't helping out with the business? Is that why Ford was weird about the rebranding? Because he was secretly working with Cooper and wanted to keep me out of it? Like he's kept me out of other areas of the business, despite his knowing I want to help?

Anxiety roars through me as a wave of momentary embarrassment strikes. They've never really wanted me to be a part of the store, and I've never known why.

Maybe if I can lean in a little more to hear what they're saying . . .

The air conditioner turns on next to me, drowning out their voices completely.

"Damn it," I mutter as I look around, seeing if there's a way I can get closer.

If it was about the anniversary party, whatever. They can talk all they want. It would annoy me that Ford wasn't actually doing his part, but nothing to get all tied up about. This clearly isn't about the anniversary party, though; this is about business. A business I'm not allowed to be involved in, however much I desperately want to be.

So, I need to know what they're talking about. If anything, just to have a taste of that insider knowledge.

And that starts with getting closer. I spot a trail through the bushes that abuts their table, and if I'm careful, I can stay undetected. Incognito. I'll need to move around these bushes while the air conditioner is still running to distract from any noise I might make. As the youngest of three, I know I can be a stealthy sleuth, but I'm weighed down by a cumbersome cast that could throw me off balance at any point. Got to be smart about these things.

Pushing past a few branches, I pause to see if they notice, but they're both transfixed by the tablet. I make a quick pass through the bushiest shrubs and then land lightly on my feet, arms spread for balance. They're still focused on the tablet, so I make another leap over a tree branch and then duck under one.

My foot gets caught on the root of a tree and I nearly face plant, but I quickly grab onto a branch with my good hand and hold in the squeal as a wave of "close encounter" heat erupts up my neck.

Ooof, steady, Palmer.

Taking a deep breath, I regain my composure and close in the last few feet, drawing even with their table just as the air conditioner shuts off. Could not have timed that more perfectly.

Quiet, they both study the tablet, and I stand on my toes to get a better look at it.

It's a new logo for sure.

And it's good.

But why the hell are Cooper and Larkin working together? And where is Ford? Especially if this has to do with the branding, shouldn't he be part of the conversation?

"They're all the same but with slight variations for different generations," Cooper points out with his finger. "I think one of the greatest attributes the company has over the competition is that we started from a family-owned business. Watchful Wanderers isn't just a store; it's a brand itself. People love the feeling behind it. It's like North Face, and people would wear the logo just because it's well known in the outdoor community, and I do think that's something the company could do better with—merchandising its own brand. These logos could help jump-start that."

Cooper is talking like he knows the business, like he cares.

"This is . . . wow, Cooper, this is huge," Larkin replies.

"Yeah?" Cooper asks.

"Yeah."

"So, should we show Ford?"

So Ford doesn't know? That doesn't seem right. Ford knows everything that's happening to the business. Are they—holy crap . . . are they going behind his back?

Just then, the air conditioner spikes on again, and I nearly swear out loud at the old janky thing. Even this close, I can't hear what they're saying. But I can read body language, and from what I'm seeing, it looks like they're definitely working together.

From the shifty looks on their faces to the over-the-shoulder glances . . . yeah, Ford is not aware of this meeting, which means . . . Larkin is working behind his back, and with Cooper of all people. The brother Ford didn't want involved at all.

But *why* is the question.

Why doesn't Ford want either of us working with him?

They stand together and awkwardly wave goodbye. Cooper walks toward the harbor while Larkin heads toward the shop's outdoor counter.

Suspicious behavior.

A nooner meeting behind the sandwich shop, where they probably didn't want to be seen.

And a quick parting with no handshake or hug.

There is something going on, something they shouldn't be—

"Ahh!" I scream as a spider crawls up my arm. "Get off me, you arachnid!"

I twist.

Swat.

Screech when it crawls up my arm some more.

Swat again.

Twist again.

Foot gets caught.

Balance is lost.

And . . . splat.

Whack.

Sitting in a pile of mud, cast covered in yesterday's rain puddle, I watch as the branch that just whacked me between the eyes bounces back and forth in front of me.

I lift up my cast and groan as I realize, once again, I got it wet. But not only wet: I got it caked in mud.

Sore from the fall, I lift myself up, my muddy butt practically suctioned to the ground, and stand, feeling every nick and scrape from the branches.

Really great.

Huffing, I pop through a gap in the bushes that leads to the back of the shop and make no attempt to brush myself off; there's no use.

Sighing in frustration, I'm heading toward the front of the shop just as I run into Larkin.

"Oh, Palmer. Hey." She glances at my cast and then back up. "Oh no, did you fall?"

"Unfortunately," I say, my voice bitter. Questions linger on the tip of my tongue. Questions like *What the hell are you doing talking to Cooper?* And *Why are you trying to create a brand without Ford?* And *OH GOD, can you see it on my face that I was with your little brother last night?* And *Why does your hair always look so damn perfect every second of every day? Is that a strong-hold hair spray, or more of a Spray & Play?*

But I hold everything back because anything I say is going to come out way angrier, thanks to my current predicament.

"Oh, I'm so sorry. Can I help you?"

"No, no, that's fine."

"Larkin," the person at the counter says, handing her a bag. Larkin quickly grabs it and holds it tightly in her hand.

"Grabbing lunch for Ford?"

"Uh, yeah. You know how he loves the roast beef."

Her eyes shift to the side, where Cooper just retreated.

Could she be any more obvious?

"Can't get enough of it, huh?"

"Yup." She pats the bag. "Well, I should get back to the inn. Lots of work to be done."

"Yes, and you wouldn't want to keep the boss waiting too long, right?"

"Right," she says hesitantly. "Well, then, if you don't need any help"—she gestures to my hand—"then I guess I'll get going."

"Have a good day." I wave to her as she takes off, glancing over her shoulder at me as if I've lost it.

And maybe I have.

Maybe I have completely lost it, but there is something afoot, and from the looks of it, Ford has no idea. And even though we've said some unsavory things to each other recently, there's one thing I know for sure: Ford *needs* to be aware of what's going on.

CHAPTER

THIRTY-THREE
DR. BEAU

"Dr. Beau, Cooper Chance is here," Tara, my receptionist, says. "He needs a refill for his dad."

"Oh, sure. Send him in," I say as a wave of anxiety shoots up my back.

I shouldn't be nervous, but for some reason, all I can think about is that I was with his sister last night. That I kissed her. Felt her. Touched her. Played with her.

Will he be able to see it on my face?

Would he care?

"Hey, Dr. Beau," Cooper says, crossing the threshold of my office.

"Hey, Cooper," I say. "What brings you to the island today?"

"Oh, you know, had a meeting and then was going to go check on my parents, but my mom called and asked if I could pick up the refill prescription you have for my dad's meds."

"Yeah, let me see if I have that."

I pull up Martin Chance's chart on my computer and go to his medications.

"I don't understand why the pharmacy won't just let you send it or call it in. This is such a pain in the ass for everyone."

I pull out a prescription pad from my desk and write out his medication and dosage with the pen my dad used to use when he'd write poems on his hikes. "It's really okay on our end. Not a big deal at all." Nervously, I reach for my water and take a drink, only to spill it over my shirt.

"Whoa, everything okay?" Cooper asks, looking around, probably for a napkin of some sort.

"Yeah." I laugh nervously while picking up a napkin from my desk. "Sorry. Long night."

"Storm was crazy, right?" Cooper asks just as there's another knock on my door.

Tara pops her head in. "Dr. Beau, Palmer Chance is here with an emergency."

Oh hell.

She joked at lunch how she was going to come to my office with an emergency, only to surprise me with her naked body in a trench coat, needing an "exam."

Please, Jesus, don't let her be in a trench coat. If she was embarrassed last night with the lab coat, she'd be horrified showing up in a trench coat, only to find her brother waiting for a prescription.

"Is she okay?" Cooper asks Tara, concern in his voice.

"She looks okay."

Oh shit.

Shit. Shit. Shit.

She's in the trench coat.

"Um, tell her I'll be right with—"

"Beau, I need your help," Palmer says, coming into my office but stopping short when she sees her brother.

Thank God there's no trench coat. I let out a sigh of relief. That could have been particularly awful for everyone involved.

I take that moment to look her up and down. That's when I notice a few scratches on her legs and arms and . . . oh hell, what did she do to her cast?

"Cooper, what are you doing here?"

"Picking up Dad's prescription." He stands. "Palmer, you can't just come barging in here when Dr. Beau is with other patients. That violates so many laws."

"It's fine," I say, trying to calm the tension that seems to be brewing between them. "Palmer, I'll be right with you. Wait for me in the exam room, okay?"

She eyes Cooper and then looks back at me. "What are you two talking about? Me?"

Jesus Christ.

"No—"

"Why would we talk about you?" Cooper asks. He looks back at me and then at Palmer.

Palmer folds her arms, her muddy cast highlighting her defiance. "Maybe because Beau and I slept together last night."

What in the living hell is she thinking?

"You what?" Cooper turns toward me, and I hold up my arms.

"We didn't *sleep* together, sleep together. Just shared a bed. Nothing like you're thinking," I say in panic. The number one thing I'm sure Cooper doesn't want to hear: how his sister spent her night.

"And we kissed and—"

"Palmer," I say, trying to send her a warning through my eyes.

"Do you have anything to admit, Cooper?" Palmer asks, her hip jutted out.

Why do I have a feeling that things are about to explode, and not in a good way at all? *Defuse, quickly.*

I pick up the script for Cooper, hand it to him, and then stride over to Palmer. Gently, I take her arm and guide her out the door. "Wait in the exam room. I'll be right there."

"I know what you're doing, Cooper. I'm onto you," Palmer says over her shoulder. "Watch your back, son." I shut the door and take a deep breath.

Jesus, what did I get myself into?

I glance up to see Cooper standing there, script in hand, brows narrowed, not looking happy at all.

"You and my sister?" he asks.

"I found her out in the rain last night. She needed a place to stay. We've both had feelings for each other for a while, and we kissed." The confession rushes out of me. I don't know why I'm so nervous. Cooper and I are about the same size, but there's just something about respecting the family of the person you're interested in. He doesn't need to know exactly what went on.

"Is that all you did?"

I clear my throat. "Um, there might have been some wandering hands, but that's neither here nor there. What really matters is that my intentions are pure."

Cooper steps up to me, inches away from my face, and I brace myself. "Good luck," he says simply. "You're going to need it." And then he takes off.

Uhh . . .

What?

Good luck? No older-brother lecture?

No "don't hurt my sister" threat?

That was not what I expected at all.

Leaning against my desk, I let out a deep, relieved sigh and wonder if that's it, if that's all the Chance-brother questioning I'm going to have to deal with. A part of me thinks I'm not that lucky, especially since the most protective brother still doesn't know.

I make my way to the exam room and shut the door. Palmer is sitting on the table, one leg crossed over the other, looking very angry.

"So, care to explain to me why your new cast is muddy and wet?"

She points toward the door. "He's up to something, Beau. I saw him with your sister." She's fidgety, excited, conspiratorial. Not the same girl from last night.

"With Larkin?" I ask, a stupid question since I only have one sister.

"Yes. At the sandwich shop. They were in there working together."

"How do you know this?" I ask. "Were you spying on them?"

"Of course," she answers, as if that was a dumb question.

"And this spying . . . did it lead to you needing another new cast?"

She glances down at her arm and then back up at me. "You know, a little support here."

"I'm trying," I answer. Because hell, I am trying. I'm trying to piece together what has gotten into her in the last half hour, since I left her with a parting kiss. "Just trying to get the whole story. So, you were spying . . . in the mud?"

"Of course not." She rolls her eyes. "I was spying in the bushes. It's why I have all these scratches, because I was battling relentless foliage. Actually, how is my forehead? One branch slapped me right between the eyes."

I examine her face, trying not to be distracted by how beautiful she is, scratches and all. "It's just a little red. Seems like a tough afternoon." I attempt to hold back my chuckle, and the thought of Palmer squatting and hiding behind bushes to get closer to Larkin and Cooper and whatever they have going on. Knowing my sister, probably nothing of importance, but it's cute seeing Palmer trying to "solve a crime."

"I'm glad to hear it. I don't need another bandage on my head." She sighs. "Anyway, I lost my balance and fell backward into a puddle. It's why I have a muddy ass again and why this cast is a mess."

"You realize your wrist is going to have serious issues healing if we have to keep changing the cast? It needs time to heal."

"It's not like I meant to fall into a puddle. Granted, I've done it twice in the past twenty-four hours, but despite the glaring evidence, it's not my favorite pastime. Just keep getting caught up in the wrong situation."

"Both seem a little like your fault," I say as I grab my cast saw.

"Excuse me?" she asks, her voice rising. "How are they my fault?"

I choose my words carefully. "Yesterday, you went for a walk, leaving you a victim to the inclement weather. And today, well, crawling around in bushes to spy on your brother doesn't necessarily scream 'taking care of my cast.'"

She props one hand on her hip. "You only said one correct thing. 'Victim.' Yes, I'm a victim. A victim of my brothers. Both have sent me careening into a puddle." She leans forward. "Do you understand the kind of humiliation that goes through a person when they have to deal with soggy-mud ass . . . twice . . . in front of the person they like?"

I smile. "The person you like, huh?"

"Naturally I like you." Her chin rises. "If I didn't, then I wouldn't have let you play with my nipple piercings last night."

I nearly choke on my own saliva. She gently pats my back.

"There, there," she says. "It's going to take some getting used to hanging out with me. Prepare yourself, Dr. Beau. I hold nothing back."

Evidently.

CHAPTER THIRTY-FOUR

NORA

"Please take a seat," Ford says, gesturing to a chair in front of me. I'm not sure I've ever been to the Marina Island Bed and Breakfast. It's . . . floral, but oddly, it also works.

I set down my pink bakery box and take a seat, completely entertained by this entire situation.

I forgot just how much Cooper looks like his brother. Practically identical, but whereas Cooper has a dimple in his chin, Ford does not. And Ford has a few more laugh lines around his eyes, which, unfortunately, just makes a man more distinguished and attractive. I've upped my nighttime care routine because of those same lines, which make me look haggard and worn.

"I like your vest," I say, nodding toward his ridiculous outfit.

I want to ask him if he went to Watchful Wanderers and got dressed in the fly-fishing department because . . . wow. He's wearing waders that are practically kissing his nipples, a camouflage shirt that does not scream "Ford Chance," a matching vest with lures dangling from the pockets, and, to top it off, a fisherman's hat. I secretly want to take a picture to show Cooper because I don't think he'd believe me if I told him his brother dropped the suit and put on some gear, but that would mean telling Cooper I met with Ford, and that's something I definitely don't want to divulge.

Ford pats down his vest. "Thank you. I just got it. Larkin and I went to the store this morning and bought a few things to test out." His eyes light up. "Did you know we sell underwear with fish on them at the store?"

"Are you wearing said underwear?" I ask.

"Well, that's a highly inappropriate question." He places both hands on the table, and he looks like a young child waiting for Santa. "But to answer, yes, and the quality is less than desired, but the knowledge that my willy is catching fish is enchanting."

Is he drunk?

I feel like he's drunk.

From what little interaction I've had with Ford over the years, and from the stories Cooper has told me, this is not typical Ford behavior—which means he has to be drunk. Really drunk, but I don't smell booze, so color me confused.

"Fishing with your willy—what an enjoyable feature you offer customers. But be careful." I wag my finger at him. "Make sure the tip doesn't get bitten off."

He winces and laughs. "Very true."

Things I never thought I would be talking to Ford Chance about . . . his penis getting bitten off by illustrated fish on a pair of briefs. But there's always time for new experiences in life. Chalk this up to one of those.

"So, I take it that you're going to go fly-fishing today?"

He nods. "Oh yes, with Larkin. She's going to show me the ropes. She would have preferred we fished at dawn, because that's when they're feeding the most, but she thinks dusk will hopefully be just as good."

"Have you ever been?"

He shakes his head, which surprises me, given that he's CEO of an outdoors company. "No. Larkin and I are going to test some activities out this week that I haven't done before. Should be fun."

"Well, that does sound like fun."

"Anyway, thank you for coming to the island—I know you're busy."

"I have a pretty great staff. They work hard, which gives me opportunities to do things like this."

"Seems so." He studies me for a second. "Can I ask you a question?"

"Of course."

"You own your own business, and it was a family business that you took over, correct?"

"Yes." I nod. "My parents started the business, and when I graduated from high school, they really started to get me involved. I mean, I would make cakes and decorate them, even when I was a kid, but after I graduated, they really brought me into the business side of things, which of course is never fun. I like the creative aspect better."

"Ah." He nods. "I enjoy the numbers, but it feels like being locked up on the business side has left me confused about the actual store, like I've lost touch with it."

"That happened to me a few years ago."

"Really?" he asks. "What happened?"

"I was approached by a franchising company. They were impressed with the business model and our product. They wanted to see how we could go from a small, independent shop to growing our company to something more. Like you did. So, I put down the spatula and took a seat behind the desk. I realized quickly I was not happy about that and would rather not franchise if it meant not liking what I was doing. But it doesn't seem like you hate the business side."

"I don't. I enjoy it. I like the challenge."

"Did you enjoy working at the store when you were younger?"

"I've always enjoyed working at the store. But when I was younger, it was different. Palmer and Cooper were always being idiots on the main floor, scaring each other, hiding, and now that I think of it, making it fun. Mom and Dad would get so irritated with us, but then I was separated from their shenanigans when Dad started teaching me how to run the business."

"Did he teach anyone else?"

Ford shakes his head.

"Huh, interesting."

"Why is that interesting?" he asks, and, honestly, I can't take him seriously in that getup.

"Because I have a sister, and my parents let us both learn about the business. Cheryl decided she wanted nothing to do with it and went off to do her own thing. Occasionally she'll come to the store and help me ice cakes because she needs the creative release, but she's a teacher, and it's a job she finds so much more joy doing. But she had the choice, the chance to test things out."

Cooper never got that chance.

Palmer didn't either.

But from the look on Ford's face, he's not making the connection.

"Anyway," I say, "I think you just need to find the passion for the company again."

"I think you're right." He pats his chest. "Working on that passion. No better way to start than fly-fishing. Right?"

"Totally." I chuckle. "Anyway, shall we get down to business? The real reason I sneaked onto the island with a bakery box?"

"Yes, of course. Please tell me: What's the cake scheduled to be right now?"

"Currently, it's lavender. I got a call from Palmer this morning." When she called me, I did everything I could not to laugh. I knew Cooper was going to lose it if he found out. And it's something I planned on telling him later—even though he said to keep the cake butterscotch, this is obviously more fun for me. The Chance siblings are a special kind of crazy.

But a crazy I enjoy.

"Does anyone know you're here?"

I shake my head. "I've come completely undetected. Even threw on a baseball cap on the ferry, just to make sure."

"Smart move," Ford says, looking all too serious now. I honestly can't take it. I tamp down the smirk that wants to make itself known from how ridiculous this entire situation is. "Okay, let's see what you have."

Opening the bakery box, I pick up the plate the inn provided for us and place five pieces of cake on it. A lavender, a butterscotch, a coffee, a chocolate, and, of course, a plain vanilla.

"Now, on the lavender and the vanilla, I had to use a plain buttercream, but those could always change. The chocolate has a raspberry buttercream, and then the coffee and butterscotch both have a fudge frosting."

I hand him the plate, and he picks up his fork, using it to poke each piece of cake.

Well, hello, is he inspecting the crumb? Am I under culinary examination over here?

"I'm so done with this battling over the cake," he says, still prodding away. "If I didn't know my parents wanted a cake from you, I would just buy a pie and call it a day."

"The pie, my nemesis."

He laughs. "Not a fan of the pie?" He takes a bite of the chocolate cake, and his face remains neutral as he chews.

"Well, clearly it's not a cake, so of course I'm not a fan. Pies try to take the glory on Thanksgiving, but let me ask you this, Ford—have you ever had a Thanksgiving cake?"

"Can't say that I have." He bites into the vanilla after taking a sip of water.

"Well, you are missing out. People like to boast about a pecan pie; well, try a pecan turtle cake on Thanksgiving. Life changing."

"I'm going to have to remember that this year." He bites into the butterscotch, and, once again, he remains neutral. I can just picture him doing the same thing when looking over merchandise, showing not an ounce of excitement while he takes everything in.

"You'll thank me." I wink as he finishes up the cakes and then sets down his fork. With a napkin, he dabs at his mouth.

Takes a sip of water.

Stares at the plate.

Then . . . "Let's go with the chocolate raspberry. That will be the clear crowd favorite. The lavender's a nice flavor, but I'm not sure everyone would appreciate it. The butterscotch . . . well, it's butterscotch. I think the general preference among all invitees would be the chocolate raspberry."

"It's a very popular flavor at the bakery."

"I can see why." He glances at his watch. "Well, I should be going. I have some fishing to attend to. Thank you again, Nora, for making the trek out here."

"Of course." We both stand from the table. "Anything for the Chance family."

We say some quick goodbyes, and I head toward the harbor, where I'll wait for the ferry to take me back.

Three siblings, three different cakes.

I'm pretty sure I know what I'm going to do now.

Isn't it obvious?

Butterscotch for Coop.

Lavender for Palmer.

And, of course, chocolate raspberry for Ford.

But naturally, I'll let them keep fighting over the flavor until the very last day because the ever-changing cake is quite entertaining.

CHAPTER

THIRTY-FIVE
COOPER

"You look good," I say, taking Nora's hand and pulling her into my embrace. "Who knew you owned a dress?"

She pokes my side, making me laugh. "You act as if I'm not a lady."

"Oh, I know you're a lady—remember the logo I drew of you?"

"Yes, everyone knows about the logo and the stacked bosom you gave me."

A date with Nora. An actual date.

Hate to admit it, but I fretted over what to wear tonight, what to say, and how many squirts of cologne I should spray. Three, if you were wondering.

To sum it up, slightly nervous, really fucking excited.

"Mr. Chance, your table is ready," the hostess says. I take Nora's hand in mine, and we follow her through the quaint restaurant to our intimately placed table, where we take our seats under a very large picture of a half-naked lady with a large rack.

When the hostess leaves, I open my menu and nod toward the picture. "The resemblance is uncanny."

Nora rolls her eyes. "My boobs are not *that* big."

I glance at her cleavage. "Once again, I beg to differ."

"It's the bra."

"Babe, a bra isn't that magical."

Her brow rises in question. "Are we at the 'babe' phase?"

"Why did I know you were going to call me out on that? Always a ballbuster."

"Someone has to keep you grounded." She opens her menu and glances over the options. "Oh, sausage. I love me some sausage, and since I won't be getting any tonight, maybe I'll indulge at dinner."

"Are you making it your mission to slowly drive me insane?"

"Yes, how am I doing?"

I smile. "Magnificently."

"Good." Her phone lights up on the table, and naturally, my eyes float to it—Ford's name crosses the screen.

My back straightens and my guard goes up as I set down my menu.

"Why is my brother texting you?"

"Huh?" she asks and then looks at her phone. "Oh, uh, he was, uh . . ."

"Don't lie to me, Nora."

Sighing, she lays her menu flat on the table and folds her arms over her chest. "If you must know, we're having a raging affair up at the inn. He calls me 'darling,' I call him 'daddy,' and we spend the afternoon pleasuring one another."

I lean forward. "He changed the goddamn cake, didn't he?"

"I find it odd that you're more upset about a cake flavor than my possible affair with your brother. Didn't you hear me? I call him 'daddy.'"

"You and Ford having an affair is one of the most absurd things I've ever heard."

"Why is that absurd?" she asks. "I might be a little loose on the mouth filter, but I can be dignified with him."

"It's not you; it's him. It's obvious he has something going on with Larkin, plus my mom told me she and Dad caught Ford and Larkin together, naked, in the living room." Something I never thought I would say out loud, especially since Ford is so stiff, so . . . professional all the time.

"Really?" Nora asks, eyes wide open. "Oooh, tell me more about that."

"Not until you tell me about the cake."

She rolls her eyes and reaches out to touch my hand. "I'm not sure you're ready to hear this kind of information. You seem fragile."

"Nora," I grit out.

"Fine, but I warned you." She takes a deep breath. "Your brother called and asked me to bring some sample cake slices to the island."

"You let him test your cake?" I nearly shout, attracting a few stares. Quieting down, I repeat, "You let him test your cake? I haven't even tested your cake."

"Technically, you have." She wiggles her eyebrows.

"I'm being serious, Nora. Please tell me you didn't let him test the butterscotch. Please."

She winces. "He wanted to know what it tasted like."

I slap the table. "God damn it." I point a finger at her. "You know how important that cake is to me. Let me guess: he didn't like it."

"It was not the one he chose." The corner of her lips pulls up, and I know she's getting too much joy out of this.

"If you tell me he chose lavender, I'm going to scream, right here in this restaurant. I'm going to scream like a goddamn girl."

"Is that supposed to be a threat? Because I feel like you should know by now that's something I would love to watch you do."

"Just tell me, is it lavender?"

She pauses and studies me for a few breaths before shaking her head. "He was a fan of the chocolate raspberry."

"Ugh, of course he was." I give her a stern look. "Were you even going to tell me about this meetup?"

"Wasn't planning on it."

I grip the edge of the table. "So, you're telling me that you weren't going to clue me in to your secret meeting with my brother, where you talked about changing the cake that I specifically told you not to change?"

"Correct. I was not going to tell you."

"And what were you going to write on the order form?"

She smirks. "What do you think?"

"If you want a good night kiss, it better be butterscotch."

She chuckles and brings her water glass to her lips. "Well, pucker up, handsome."

"Damn right," I say, satisfied.

She shakes her head, an amused glint in her eyes. "There is something wrong with the three of you."

"Possibly," I answer, picking up my menu again. "But at least we're going to have butterscotch cake."

CHAPTER THIRTY-SIX
FORD

TO: Ford Chance, Palmer Chance
FROM: Cooper Chance
SUBJECT: STOP CHANGING THE DAMN CAKE

^^^^ Read that, multiple times. Just STOP!

TO: Cooper Chance, Ford Chance
FROM: Palmer Chance
SUBJECT: Re: STOP CHANGING THE DAMN CAKE

Did you change it back to butterscotch? Cooper, do you even have tastebuds at all? Frankly, I'm concerned that you're in charge of decorations. All I can envision is the birthday party Dwight and Jim from *The Office* put together with half blown up balloons and a printed-out birthday sign.

TO: Palmer Chance, Ford Chance
FROM: Cooper Chance
SUBJECT: Re: STOP CHANGING THE DAMN CAKE

Ford was the one who changed the cake this time. Bro doesn't know how to stay in his own lane apparently. And no need to worry about the decorations. There won't be any.

TO: Cooper Chance, Ford Chance
FROM: Palmer Chance
SUBJECT: Re: STOP CHANGING THE DAMN CAKE

WHAT DO YOU MEAN THERE WILL BE NO DECORATIONS?? Are you insane? There have to be decorations. How else will people know it's a party? Honestly, why did we think you could be in charge of this? Clearly you don't care.

TO: Palmer Chance, Ford Chance
FROM: Cooper Chance
SUBJECT: Re: STOP CHANGING THE DAMN CAKE

Decorations are a detriment to the earth and a waste of resources. They're used for a few hours and then discarded where they rot in a landfill for years.

And people will know it's a party because there will be food there, unless . . . have you dropped the ball on that?

Mom and Dad said they would like sandwiches from the deli. I was thinking about picking up some of those chips they like too.

TO: Cooper Chance, Ford Chance
FROM: Palmer Chance
SUBJECT: Re: STOP CHANGING THE DAMN CAKE

Over my DEAD body will be serving GD sand-wiches. I have a conversation with a local caterer today. Do not touch the food. Talk about staying in your lane . . . *bro*. And what about the gift? Have we figured that out yet? I was thinking a commem-orative vase. But we only have a few days left, so not sure.

TO: Palmer Chance, Ford Chance
FROM: Cooper Chance
SUBJECT: Isn't the party the gift?

TO: Cooper Chance, Ford Chance
FROM: Palmer Chance
SUBJECT: Re: Isn't the party the gift?

I would suggest pulling back on your attempts to annoy me. I know things about you, Cooper, things you don't think I know. But I do know. I know . . . *things*.

TO: Palmer Chance, Ford Chance
FROM: Cooper Chance
SUBJECT: Sure you do

TO: Palmer Chance, Cooper Chance
FROM: Ford Chance
Subject: Re: Sure you do

Can we not argue? We have a few days left of planning this thing. How about this, everyone show up with their assigned tasks and be done with it. No talking, no discussing.

Palmer, get whatever gift you want, we will give you money.

I have more important things to do than read your bickering emails.

Show up at the party with a smile on your face, and then we can all part.

TO: Palmer Chance, Ford Chance
FROM: Cooper Chance
SUBJECT: Re: Sure you do

Finally, someone speaking some sense.

And stop changing the goddamn cake.

CHAPTER THIRTY-SEVEN
FORD

"We're almost there. How are your heels holding out?" Larkin asks, pushing a branch to the side as we finish the "short" hike she planned for us.

"Pretty sure there are pools of blood in my brand-new hiking boots."

"But your whistle's still intact," Larkin teases.

I toot on my whistle, which is supposed to scare away wildlife. "So, when I'm bloody carnage, unable to move, thanks to these shoes, at least I'll have my whistle to ward off predators. Told you it wasn't a stupid purchase."

"You're right—thank God for the whistle." She looks back at me and chuckles. "You've never looked more attractive in my eyes."

I pause and stand up straight. "What did I tell you? No making fun of me."

"You borrowed your assistant's pink hat because the sun was too bright on your eyes."

"And it's rather fetching; at least that's what the birds have been chirping as we've walked by."

"Aww, and here I thought you were a novice when it came to outdoor adventure, but you're already picking up on the language of the birds."

I tap the side of my head. "Quick learner."

We're met with one more four-foot rock before we reach the top of our hike. With ease, Larkin uses a smaller rock to propel herself on top and then turns around, hand outstretched.

"I think I can handle it," I scoff.

"Oh, I was just offering to hold your whistle."

"As if I would trust you with such a brilliant outdoor tool." I stuff it in my pocket. "No, thank you—I will be handling my own whistle."

I step up on the small rock and launch my body over the tall boulder, rolling across the rock and then standing on my feet.

I brush myself off as Larkin starts to slow clap. "That was the most graceful thing I think I've ever seen."

"No doubt in my mind," I say, knowing damn well I just looked like an idiot. After brushing myself off, I take in the views of the harbor. "Wow," I say as I reach for Larkin's hand. "It's beautiful up here." Stretched in front of us is endless ocean. Standing on the west side of the island, we aren't graced with the Seattle skyline, but rather are offered the perfect escape from the bustle of the harbor around us. The sky mirrors the ocean, a magnificent blue with minimal clouds in the far distance. Breathtaking.

"It's one of my favorite places to hike because you get a beautiful panoramic view of the channels, and if you're lucky, you can catch whales breaching out in the distance."

"You know, I don't take enough time to do things like this."

"I know," she says. "You're always working, and when you're always working, you tend to lose who you are. You don't take a moment to actually live in your own head. Getting lost in work is easy; stepping outside of that work and exploring yourself, that's hard."

"And I work too hard, which has left me ignorant to what I'm missing out on." I open my arms up. "To all of this—nature, what the company was built around. That and bloody feet." I glance down at the death-trap boots. "There is no possible way we can carry this company anymore in the stores, especially if this is what happens to our consumers. Blood feet."

Larkin laughs. "You do not have blood feet, and you're probably dying because you're not wearing the proper socks. I told you to buy—"

"I know what you said, but who thought buying a certain kind of sock would help?"

"I did. I knew," Larkin says, pointing to herself.

"I thought you were just trying to make me look like an idiot, like you did yesterday."

She feigns shock. "How on earth did I make you look like an idiot yesterday?"

"I did not have to wear the waders around everywhere. I could have put them on when we got to the stream."

She laughs out loud. "But where's the fun in that? Seriously, though, seeing you in that getup, eating dainty slices of cake with Nora—best thing I've seen in years."

I pull her in close and kiss the top of her head. "Glad I could amuse you."

"I don't think you're just amusing me—I think you're amusing yourself."

I pull her toward a rock that overlooks the majestically blue views of the channels. "I think I'm starting to amuse myself."

"You're more relaxed," Larkin points out. "Normally, when you get an email thread from your siblings, you're irritated all day, but it's like you let this last one roll off you."

"There's no point," I say. "I can tell them to back off until I'm blue in the face, but they're not going to listen. It is what it is."

"Why do you think they don't listen?" Larkin asks.

"If I knew that, I'd fix it."

"There has to be something that is causing all of this tension. I've seen those emails—they're a powder keg, ready to explode. And do you think it would help if you solved things with your siblings?"

"I honestly don't know. I think there might be too much history, too many disagreements to actually fix anything. And the weirdest thing is I can't really say how it all began—and I think we're all the same in that, but no one will address it." I sigh. "But I don't want to talk about that right now. Not when we're here, in this beautiful place. Not when we're together, alone, enjoying nature like you used to with your brother and dad."

She leans into my shoulder. "What do you want to talk about, then?"

"Us."

"Us?" she asks, a quirk to her brow.

"Yes. Us. I know you want to focus on me, but I can't just sit around, focusing on me, when you're a part of me as well. I want to treat you like you deserve. Can I take you to dinner tonight?"

"You want to take me to dinner?" She draws back, slightly shocked. "Like, on a date?"

"Yes, on a date." Looking out toward the water, I reflect on the last few days. The tumultuous conversations with my siblings, the slow understanding of what I've been lacking as a leader, the need for Larkin on a whole new level. "If there's one thing I've noticed since our camping foray in the living room, it's that I feel lighter when I'm around you, Larkin. And with all of these adventures, I feel like a new person, in a good way—and I know a lot of it has to do with you. Your encouragement, your help . . . your teasing."

"The teasing is the best part," she says with a smile, bumping my shoulder.

"I'm sure it is, but I think a big part of finding myself is not just going on these treks together but also making sure I keep you too." I lift her knuckles up to my lips. "I'm not sure how to navigate this whole dating-my-assistant thing, but what I do know is that we need to figure it out, because I've realized I want to take you out, show you off, be the man you deserve."

"Well, I didn't expect you to say that on the top of this rock." She turns toward me and cups my cheek. "I want the same thing, but I also want you mentally healthy, and I think a part of that has to do with solving things with your siblings."

My jaw grows tight as I stare down at my hand, linking with Larkin's. "You're not going to make this easy and let me sweep everything under the rug, are you?"

"No. I'm not. Do you know why?"

"Because you care about me?"

She nods and presses a kiss to my cheek. "I care about you a lot, Ford. Which means we're going to work through this, and who knows, maybe something will come along for the rebranding that will change your way of thinking."

"That would be the hope." I lean back on one hand. "But as for the new adventure man, what do you think of him so far?"

"I think he's rough around the edges, a tad rusty, but I really like his spirit."

"Are you holding it against me that I got caught up in my fly-fishing rod?"

She laughs. "Only a little. It's when you tripped and fell into the water that you lost your man card for a brief moment."

"The rocks were slippery—how many times do I have to say that?"

She laughs some more, and I pull her into my embrace as we both take in the horizon. It might have only been a few days so far, but I already feel different. Energized. Ready to leap forward. But I know Larkin is right: the only way to truly feel free is to deal with my siblings.

"How about that date?" I ask her. "Tomorrow night?"

"What about your siblings?"

"After the anniversary party. I want to get through that first, and then I'll hash it out with them. Let's just make it through the party without killing each other."

"I can wait for a date."

I shake my head. "I can't. Please, let me take you out. I know the perfect place. My parents used to go there all the time." I tug on her hand. "You know you want to say yes."

"Fine," she drags out. "But one date, and then you're right back to focusing on your siblings and fixing those relationships so you can move on."

"Deal."

CHAPTER THIRTY-EIGHT
COOPER

Cooper: What are you doing?

Nora: Lying in a tub of frosting . . . naked.

Cooper: That was going to be my guess, that or posing with cherries over your nipples for your Instagram feed.

Nora: You know me, always trying to capitalize on followers.

Cooper: And cherries on the nipples is the way to do it. How about taking those cherries for a test run with me?

Nora: What do you have planned?

Cooper: Date. Tomorrow night. You and me. Cherries for dessert.

Nora: Oooh, how romantic. I'll be there. Send details please.

Cooper: I will. Also . . . wear another dress.

Nora: Your wish is my command.

Cooper: Remember that for when we're playing around with the . . . cherries.

CHAPTER

THIRTY-NINE
PALMER

"Dr. Beau, how can I help you?"

"Is that how you always answer the phone?" I ask. I've been tasked by my mom with cleaning out my room today, and yet I can't seem to get my body to move, despite the boxes she placed near the door as a "hint." Instead I've been watching Dude Perfect videos on YouTube because it's not procrastination unless you're bingeing something completely out of your normal.

"Always answer the phone like that. How are you, Palmer?"

"Ahh, you know it's me." I lean back on my bed and kick my feet up in the air.

"Of course I know it's you. How's the cast?"

"Dry."

"Perfect answer," he says, chuckling into the phone. "So, I take it if your cast is dry, you haven't sat in any puddles lately?"

"Nope. Aren't you proud?"

"So proud. But why aren't you over here, hanging out with me? I thought that was the plan."

"I know, that's why I'm calling. I had some last-minute planning to do for the anniversary party." Procrastinated on that as well. "It's in two days, and after hearing from my brothers, I'm really worried nothing is getting done. I decided to spend the day making some calls to see if I can get any catering and whatnot." I feel a twinge of guilt—when I say "spend the day," I really mean an hour.

"Did you?"

"No," I sigh into the phone. "Seems like everything needs to be booked weeks in advance. Painful. I've come to the realization that the sandwiches Cooper ordered are what we're going to have to deal with."

"Everyone likes sandwiches."

"But they're so not fancy."

"Maybe not fancy is okay."

"But my parents deserve fancy. Don't worry, though—the cake will be good. I called Nora this morning and changed it back to lavender and made her swear not to say anything. She has to start baking it today. Caught her at the last minute."

"A battle well fought and won."

"Thank you, dear sir. So, anyway, I want to make it up to you, for not hanging out tonight. I know you were interested in some fondling."

He lets out a belly laugh. "Jesus, where's your filter, girl?"

"Lost it a long time ago. But I was hoping you'd go out to dinner with me tomorrow. I know the perfect little place."

"Would this be a date?"

"Yes, which means I'll wear uncomfortable underwear in the hope of you taking it off."

"Is that how all your dates work?" he asks.

"No, never, actually, but a date with you is different."

"Another good answer. You're two for two, Palmer. Want to see if you can go three for three?"

"Try me."

"Tonight, when you go to bed, are you going to think about me?"

If only he knew . . .

"What kind of question is that? Of course. You're what I've thought about for a long time."

CHAPTER FORTY

LARKIN

"Wow, I have never been here before," I say, taking in the small yet endlessly romantic hole-in-the-wall restaurant. If I were by myself, I never would have noticed this place. Sandwiched between two large brick buildings, it's covered in ivy and offers a dim dining mood with intimate lighting.

Earlier today, we rode the ferry into Seattle and did some paddling on the bay, which was hilariously horrible to watch.

Poor Ford. I think he was in the water more than he was on the paddleboard. Even when he went down to his knees, he struggled. At one point, he was on his back, looking up at the sky, and he still fell off. That time I almost wet myself laughing.

We accepted the fact that he was not a paddleboarder, which would be crossed off the list of activities he'd continue to participate in. But he has expressed interest in fishing again, camping, and hiking. He also wants to take a survival course at one of the stores, which would be a lot of fun, and also add some classes to the schedule, like camp cooking and the basics of fly-fishing so that beginners—like him—don't fall in the water. He also is very much interested in bringing back Snake Week, the idea I was telling him about. He's so engaged and excited—it's like his mind is exploding with ideas, and that's exactly what we were looking for. When I asked him if he thought of any branding yet, he was still blank, but I know if I can open him up to his siblings, he'd be more than willing to see what Cooper has to propose. A dark cloud is hanging over his family right now, and we need to brighten that up before we move forward. Easier said than done, though, and I'm treading carefully. The last thing I want is for Ford to think I've gone behind his back.

"See that booth back there?" Ford leans in, his breath tickling my ear as he points to a booth set back against the wall, beside a small fireplace.

"Yes, the one that lines up with the brick wall?"

"Yup, my dad proposed to my mom in that booth."

"Really?" I ask, a smile stretching over my face. "That's so special."

"Yeah, we've had many special family dinners at this restaurant. We always commemorated major moments here, like our adoption days and graduations. Things that mattered." Ford lifts my hand and lightly kisses my knuckles. "And since today marks our first official date, I figured we could—"

"Larkin?" I turn around and spot my brother, wearing a sport coat, khakis, and a confused expression on his face. "What's going on?"

Oh crap.

Oh God, it's my brother.

My brother is here, watching my boss kiss my knuckles.

"Hey, Beau," I say with a wave, trying to act as casual as possible. *This is all normal. Ford kissing my hand, totally normal.* "Uh, just having dinner. You?"

He takes a step forward. "Obviously you're having dinner. But what are you two doing?" He motions between Ford and me.

"Oh." I laugh nervously. With everything that's been going on, I forgot to tell Beau about Ford and me. From his narrowed eyes and furrowed brow, he's not liking the fact that he found out like this. "Well, you know, we're, uh . . . we're kind of dating."

"Dating?" Beau asks, his expression turning into worry. "Larkin, what about your job? What you've worked so hard for."

Ford steps in. "I assure you, nothing—"

"There you are, you hunk of meat . . . Ford, Larkin?" Palmer says as she appears at Beau's side and loops her hand through his arm. And, oh my God, does she look gorgeous tonight. Wearing a skintight navy-blue dress and nude heels, she is turning all the heads in the room . . . including my brother's. "What are you two doing here?"

"They're on a date," Beau says, eyes still on me. I can feel his worry, which translates into guilt for me.

"What?" Palmer says, louder than I think she expected. "You're on a date with your assistant? Ford, what the hell are you thinking?"

"I'm thinking I'm a grown-ass man and I can do what I want." He motions to Beau and Palmer. "And what's this?"

"This is exactly what it seems like. Beau and I are an item." Palmer cuddles in closer to my brother. Look at them, so cute. And the smile on Beau's face, well, that makes me—

"Since when?" Ford asks.

"Why does it matter?" Palmer shoots back.

"Yes, how long?" I ask Beau.

"Not that long," Beau answers, all of a sudden squirming, but then he turns it back on me. "Why didn't you tell me about you and Ford?"

"Why didn't you tell me?" I ask, gesturing to Palmer.

"Because I wasn't sure . . . if, you know, this was something to talk about."

"What do you mean 'if this was something to talk about'?" Palmer asks, pulling away and looking up at him. "Of course it's something to talk about, unless you're ashamed of me."

"I'm not ashamed of you, not even in the slightest. I just wasn't sure if—"

"Ford? Palmer?" The door that was just swung open shuts behind Cooper and Nora, who's also dressed in a tight, formfitting dress, but hers is yellow, and she paired it with navy shoes. "What are you doing here?"

Palmer's eyes narrow as she points. "Are you bribing the baker with your manly ways?"

"Oh good," the hostess says, cutting in. "You all know each other. The only seating we have left is a continuous booth, so we'll have to place you side by side. Right this way."

No one moves.

Instead, the siblings all just stare at each other. You can see their minds working, trying to process the whole situation.

Nora and Cooper are on a date.

Palmer and Beau clearly have something going on.

And then there's Ford and me . . .

Why does this seem like a recipe for disaster?

"Maybe we find somewhere else to eat?" I suggest. Calmly, I add, "There's a lot of tension between you three at the moment; I'd hate for that to ruin any of our nights."

I can see where this is headed. I've seen it in the emails. I've witnessed some showdowns in my time. They're all geared up; they're all on the defensive. If we eat together, this will not end well, especially if just seeing each other already has them nitpicking.

Ford is the first to acknowledge me. Quietly he says, "It will be okay. I promise. I'm not going to let anything ruin this first date for us. We had plans; we're sticking to them." He takes my hand and starts to follow the hostess.

"Well, I promised Nora lobster potato nuggets, and hell if I'm going to back down on the promise." Cooper falls in behind.

"I've been boasting about the bread-and-butter platter all day. Beau and I aren't going anywhere."

And then there were six . . .

Chapter
Forty-One

DR. BEAU

I don't think I've ever been this physically uncomfortable in my entire life.

If this were a movie and I was watching these poor souls try to navigate through a dinner with the siblings they can't currently stand, I'd be cringing behind my hand the entire time.

That's actually what I want to do, but behind my menu instead.

Oh man is the air thick.

The tension has forced me to take off my jacket and continually wipe my hands on my pants.

There's no denying there are unresolved issues between the Chance siblings; it's evident in how they all eyed each other in the lobby of the restaurant. The issues with the party, the instigating emails, the confessions they've admitted to since being here—I can feel it's all on the tip of their tongues. The kindling is there; it's as if they're just waiting for someone to light the match.

But besides the Chance sibling drama, I can't believe my sister didn't tell me she was dating Ford. We tell each other everything—we made that promise once our dad died. To always stay close, to be a constant presence in each other's lives, and to never hold anything back.

And here we are, both holding back information.

Every time I glance at her, her eyes turn down, almost as if she's ashamed.

"Hey, I'm over here," Palmer says, tapping my hand, which is resting on the table.

"What? Oh yeah, sorry. This evening caught me by surprise."

"Me too," Palmer says, her eyes looking worried. "But let's make the most of it, okay?"

"I would like that."

Awkwardly, we're all lined up together in one of those long booths that stretch across the wall, with a table and a single chair on the other side. And these tables are close, so I can hear Ford breathing and Cooper talking about the cake.

Oh no, not the cake . . .

"Did you say butterscotch?" Palmer asks, head whipping to the side.

"Can you not listen to our conversation?" Cooper says. "You have your own date. Focus on your doctor."

I see the irritation, the insecurity in Palmer's eyes, and I know Palmer well enough to understand that when there's insecurity, she goes on the defensive. "I'll focus on him when Nora confirms there will be a lavender cake."

I glance at Nora, who looks entirely too unperturbed. Can she not read the room? The tension is maddening. The glances are terrifying. And the unknown is slowly making me sweat out of my shirt.

Then again, I've always gotten along with my sister, so the Chance siblings' dynamic is untouched territory for me.

"Do not answer that," Cooper says, speaking with enough venom that Nora crosses her arms over her chest. From the look she gives him, Cooper is going to have to climb back from that little mistake. "Drop the cake shit, Palmer. It's been settled. This is my date with Nora—focus on yourself."

"Are you going out with her just to get your way?"

"Are you serious with that?" Cooper fumes.

"Can you two stop?" Ford leans in, startling me with his commanding voice.

"Ford, don't," Larkin says. "Let them do their thing."

"They're being obnoxious." Ford glares at his siblings. "You two are ruining everyone's evening."

"Everyone's or yours?" Palmer asks. "No one else in the restaurant seems to care what's going on over here in this small circle of hell."

I pick up my water glass and take a sip. Circle of hell indeed.

I need to help turn this around, bring it back to us, settle Palmer, who seems to be rattled and ready to dig her claws in.

Everyone just needs to take a big, deep breath together.

Reaching out, I grab Palmer's hand. "Hey, why don't you tell me what's good here. What should I order?"

She glances at both of her brothers and then back at me. Her expression softens, and she nods. "Sorry," she whispers and takes a deep breath. "Okay, you're going to want to try the roasted brussels sprouts with bacon; they are—"

"Smelly," Cooper says. "Unless you want everyone, yourself included, to smell like dirty socks when you leave here, don't get them."

"That's not true at all. They don't smell like a dirty sock, and it's one of their best dishes. They wouldn't still have it on the menu if it made people smell," Palmer retorts.

"I've smelled like a sock before," Ford says quietly, surprising me.

I glance over at Larkin, who has a furious look on her face. "Ford, stop."

"Sorry," he says.

Palmer chuckles. "Already have the upper hand—nice, Larkin."

"Hey," I say to Palmer. "Focus here."

"Right. Sorry."

"And look who has the upper hand over there," Cooper says. "At least I know Nora owns me."

Nora lifts her glass to the group. "Cheers."

How on earth can she be so calm right now? At this point, I want to crawl into my own scrotum from the tension bouncing around among everyone.

"Do Mom and Dad know you're seeing Dr. Beau?" Cooper asks Palmer.

Palmer keeps her eyes on her menu. "Haven't had the chance to tell them."

"Really?" I ask, a little surprised.

"You haven't told your parents about Beau?" Larkin asks.

"I'd be interested to hear what they have to say," Cooper says, and his tone makes me incredibly uneasy.

"Why do you say it like that?" Palmer asks.

"Cooper," Ford says from across the way. He shakes his head in warning. "Drop it."

"Drop what?" Palmer asks, looking between her brothers.

"Is there something your parents don't like about my brother?" Larkin asks. Ford attempts to take Larkin's hand, but she pulls away. "There's nothing wrong with Beau. He'd be a great catch for your sister."

"I'm aware. He's great for her. Let's go back to our dinner."

Larkin crosses her arms over her chest. "No, I would like to hear Cooper explain what's wrong with my brother."

"Nothing's wrong with him," Cooper says. "Dr. Beau is a great guy."

Thanks for that. Doesn't help the massive pools of sweat gathering under my arms.

"So why would you be interested to hear what your parents have to say about them dating?" Larkin asks.

Cooper picks up his water glass and looks Larkin in the eyes. "You know, because of the fire."

My stomach plummets, and the fear on Palmer's face matches the fear that's coursing through my body.

CHAPTER
FORTY-TWO
NORA

Talk about an absolute dumpster fire.

I've known the Chance family for a while, since our parents are friends, so I've seen my fair share of their fights. I'm willing to bet most of the island has heard the hushed bickering in the back of their store or seen the uncomfortable glares the siblings give each other around town.

But this night . . .

Man, oh man, it is next level.

Larkin fluctuates between anger and the desperate attempt to get Ford to ignore what's going on between his brother and sister.

Ford's eyebrows are doing the cancan over there. Angry, then date mode. Angry, date mode. Up, down. Up, down.

Palmer started out with a vengeful confidence that screamed "insecurity" the minute we showed up, but now she's wilting like a flower in the heat.

Beau . . . well, Beau looks like he wants to pull his scrotum over his head and hide.

Cooper is swirling the ice in his water glass like an evil mastermind, lost in his defense of pulling the attention away from him, which makes me slightly sad. He's made such progress in growing into a new man and being able to communicate effectively. What is it about his siblings that makes him take two steps backward in his progress?

And me. Well, I'm trying not to outwardly show how my nipples have inverted from the awkwardness that has descended over the three cramped tables.

From an outsider's perspective, I might look cool and calm, as if this isn't bothering me, but that's not the case. I'm trying to discern where this is all going so I can mentally prepare for what's to come.

"What, uh . . . what about the fire?" Palmer asks.

"Good evening," the waitress says, stepping up to us. "How are we doing?"

"Vodka and tonic, please," I say, not even waiting for her spiel. Mama needs something to ease the discomfort settling over her shoulders. Alcohol, I need all of the alcohol.

Cooper glances at me and then at the waitress. "IPA. Could you bring those out first and then we'll work on the menu?"

"Sure thing." She moves over to Palmer and Beau. "Good evening—"

"A bottle of wine. I don't care what kind, just bring me a bottle," Palmer says.

"And an extra wineglass," Beau adds.

"Sure, and for food . . ."

"We'll get back to that."

"Very well," the waitress answers nervously and then moves over to Ford and Larkin.

"Water is fine for me," Larkin says.

"Me too," Ford says.

Ooof, talk about a stiff table. *Yikes.*

"And are you going to wait on the food?" the waitress asks.

"Unfortunately, we haven't had a chance to look at the menu thoroughly," Ford answers.

"I'll give you more time."

Once the waitress is out of earshot, Cooper says, "The Goody Two-Shoes down there, able to handle the night without alcohol. Congratulations."

Something has snapped in Cooper. This isn't the man I know; this is another version of him. An old version.

"I didn't want to drink if Larkin wasn't drinking," Ford says. Boy sure looks like he needs one, though.

"If you want to get a drink, by all means get a drink. I didn't get one because I'm afraid if I have one, I'll have twenty, based on how this night is going." She folds her arms and leans back in the booth.

Double yikes. Ford has an unhappy date on his hands.

"What about the fire?" Palmer asks, bringing us full circle once again. You can see the insecurity in her facial features. It's clear as day. Something happened with the fire that she doesn't want people knowing about.

"Palmer, just drop it," Beau says with a shake of his head. The way he said that makes me believe he knows as well.

Huh, now I'm curious about the fire conversation.

"Do you really want to know?" Cooper says, a gleam in his eyes that makes Palmer sit tall. She glances over at Ford and then back at him.

"You know what? I think we should just drop it and focus on our own dates. Clearly, talking isn't getting us anywhere." Palmer picks up her menu again. Okay, something is up for sure.

"Or maybe we push our tables together and really talk," Cooper says, a crazed look in his eyes. And I realize he may have asked me out, but we're not really on a date. We're just watching a burning sideshow. I need to help him snap out of it. I need to help ground him. He might have made a lot of progress, but being around his siblings is triggering, that much is evident, and it's throwing him back into old patterns. I need to help break that pattern.

"Cooper."

His eyes flash toward me. "Yeah?"

"Maybe we just have our date."

"Listen to your girlfriend," Palmer says.

Ugh, Palmer, you're not making this any easier.

"She's not my girlfriend," Cooper says.

Not his girlfriend? That's a blow to the gut. I know we haven't had that conversation yet, but for him to react so harshly, so quickly, it hurts. His eyes flash toward mine, and he realizes his mistake.

"What I meant to say is we haven't made things official."

He might have recovered, but the damage has been done.

"Well, if I were Nora, I'd run for the hills."

The waitress drops off our drinks, and as a group, we all take a sip. Some of us longer than others.

And then silence falls over the three tables.

No one is looking each other in the eyes.

No one is attempting to carry on a real date.

"You know, I think it's best that I just go," Larkin says, breaking the silence. "This isn't the night I envisioned."

"What? No," Ford says in a panic. "We can ask for a different table."

"Ford, look around; these are the only tables available. And we clearly can't have a peaceful evening with your siblings."

"Do you need a ride back to the island?" Beau asks.

"Beau," Palmer says in shock. "We're on a date."

"And my sister is in distress—caused by your family. I want to make sure she's okay."

"I can make sure she's okay," Ford says. "That's my job."

"If you took your job seriously, then you would have shielded her from your siblings," Beau says, which doesn't seem to go over well with Palmer.

"Why are you taking her side?"

"Probably wants to distance himself because of the fire . . . ," Cooper says.

"Coop, don't fan the flames," I say, realizing that's exactly what he's doing.

Palmer's head snaps to the side. "Unless you want me to break the news to Ford about what I saw the other day, I'd suggest you keep your mouth shut." Cooper gives her a blank look, and she adds, "Your little afternoon date. Your secret one."

"Date?" I ask, confused.

"What date—?" Cooper's eyes narrow. "Palmer, you have no idea what you're talking about."

"I have eyes. I know what I saw."

"What date?" I ask. "Cooper, are you seeing someone else?"

"Of course not."

"Why would I want to know about his date?" Ford asks.

"I'm shocked Larkin hasn't told you," Palmer says, looking pleased to be in control of the conversation.

Larkin tosses her napkin on the table. "That's it, I'm done. This is not the evening I wanted." She turns to Palmer. "I've spent enough time with you to know you're not a mean girl, but you're being one right now. I don't know what's going on in your life that's making you act like this, but this is *not* the kind of person Beau is going to go for." She stands from the table and addresses Cooper. "You have potential, Cooper, but not if you keep spurring on this bickering." She turns to Ford. "I like you so much, Ford. But I can't deal with this." She motions to the tables. "It's not worth it." To Beau she says, "Please, take me to your place."

"Of course."

"Beau," Palmer says, looking confused. "You're going to leave me here?"

"Larkin needs me," he says, though by his large puppy dog eyes, it's obvious how sorry he is.

"And I need you," Palmer shoots back.

Beau glances between his sister and Palmer. Oooh, the battle between sibling and romantic love. Tough choice. Beau squares his shoulders. "I'm sorry, Palmer." And just like that, he stands from his chair.

I glance at Cooper to gauge his reaction. I can see there's something on the tip of his tongue, but he keeps his mouth shut and leans back in his chair instead.

"So, you're not dating anyone else?" I ask.

His eyes snap to mine. "I barely have time to spend with you—you think I'd date someone else?"

"Hey, you don't need to be mean about it," I say.

"Well, don't question me, Nora."

I press back, stunned.

"Cooper, you're clearly feeling out of control right now and need a second to gather yourself. Reset."

"Don't overanalyze me, Nora."

"I'm not. I'm trying to help."

His eyes flash to mine. "I don't need your help."

It feels like a slap to the face. His words sting, with his harsh tone and detached glare. I believe I'm a patient person, an understanding one, but I don't deserve this.

I think Larkin and Beau had the right idea. Gathering my purse, I stand from the booth, my glance sweeping over the fuming siblings. "Well, I was going to stick this out, but I don't need to be treated like that. Good night, Cooper."

"Shit." He scrambles. "Nora, I'm sorry. Please." But I take off before he can say anything else.

I'm done for the evening.

Chapter

Forty-Three

FORD

Beep.

Damn it. I should have known she wasn't going to answer.

"Larkin, it's me." I push my hand through my hair as I walk the length of my room at the inn. "I know you're not answering me right now, but I want to make sure you got to Beau's okay. I also want to apologize. I don't want to do this over the phone. I want to do this in person. I want to be able to hold your hand and look you in the eyes and tell you how sorry I am. That was not how I wanted the evening to go, and I know I deserve a lot of the blame. Please call me. Please come to the inn; please tell me how I can fix this. Okay, have a good night. Bye."

I hang up and toss my phone at my bed before sinking down against the wall and onto the floor, my hands tightly gripping my hair.

Chapter Forty-Four

PALMER

Knock. Knock.

I bounce back and forth on my feet, nervous, ashamed, fearful of what's going to happen.

The door cracks open, and Beau stands on the other side, barely opening it.

"Palmer, what are you doing here?"

"I came to talk to you."

He glances behind him. "Now's not a good time."

"You left me," I say, not caring if this is a good time or not. "I really needed you back there."

"And Larkin needed me," he counters. "She's my sister."

"So, if we were in a serious relationship, would you choose your sister over me as well?"

"It's not choosing one or the other."

"Yes, it is," I say, my voice rising. "I was having a hard time too."

"You were instigating the entire thing," Beau snaps, his anger flaring. "You were a different person tonight, Palmer. You gave no thought to the fact that you were ruining everyone's night, ruining our night. It was a side of you I didn't care for. You might not agree with your brothers, but they're family and you should treat them better than you did tonight. Frankly, it's not something I wanted to be a part of."

"What?" I ask, surprised. "What are you saying?"

"I'm saying . . ." He pauses and glances down at his bare feet. "I'm saying that this isn't going to work out between us. I thought I knew what I wanted, and there were moments when you were the amazing person I knew many years ago, but you also . . . hell, Palmer, you don't know what you're doing with your life."

"And you're going to punish me for that?"

"No. I was more than happy to help you find your next chapter, but you haven't done anything to move toward that next chapter. Instead, you've gone around terrorizing your brothers. I don't want to be a part of that."

"I see." I take a step back, feeling nauseated. "Well, I'm sorry that I don't have my shit together." My eyes well up and a tear rolls down my cheek. "And I'm sorry that I made you feel like any less than you deserve." I wipe at my eye and take a step back. "And I'm sorry that I dragged you into the mess that is my life. Every part of my life, including the past."

He sighs in frustration and opens the door a little wider. "Palmer—"

"No." I shake my head and take another step back. "You're right. I don't have my shit together, and why would someone like you, who knows exactly what they want, want anything to do with me?"

"It's not that I don't want you, because I do." He slips through the door and quietly shuts it behind him. "You know I want something special with you, but Jesus Christ, tonight was frustrating. That was not how I expected the evening to go, and the way you were acting . . . it felt vengeful and wrong. You're better than that, Palmer."

"Maybe I'm not," I say, the truth of the sentence hitting me harder than expected. "Maybe this is who I am." Maybe, I realize with a sick pang, this is the level I need to get comfortable with now. Rock bottom.

"You and I both know that's not the case. You're just lost."

"I am lost." I wipe at a tear. "I'm lost with no direction. And I know it's not your responsibility, but I was hoping you were going to help me. You were the only bright thing in my life. I thought you were my port in the storm, but now you're abandoning me to drown without a life preserver."

He grips the back of his neck tightly in frustration. "I don't think I can do anything to help you, Palmer. This is on you. You're the only one who can find the solution."

"You don't think you can do anything, or you don't *want* to?"

He lets out a deep breath and closes the space between us, cupping my cheek. "When you came back to Marina Island and looked at me with these jade-green eyes, you know I was sold. You know I wanted nothing more than to have you, like I've wanted for as long as I can remember. But I don't think we can take this any further until you're ready. As much as it pains me, you're not ready."

"You don't know that."

"I do," he answers. "If you don't figure out what you want, who you are, then you're going to get lost in me, and that's not the kind of relationship I want with you. You're bright, Palmer. You're a shining light—you're just dimmed right now. You need to figure out how to turn up your light again." Leaning in, he presses a kiss to my forehead before disappearing inside his apartment.

More tears stream down my face as I stand there, staring at his closed door.

How am I supposed to find myself . . . when I loathe myself?

Chapter

Forty-Five
COOPER

Cooper: Did you make it home okay?

Nora: What do you think?

Cooper: I'm going to guess yes.

Nora: You guessed right.

Cooper: Can I call you?

Nora: I'd suggest not doing that right now. ,

Cooper: I want to apologize about tonight.

Nora: I figured as much, but I'm exhausted and I'm not in the mood, Cooper.

Cooper: I understand. But I am sorry.

Nora: I'm sure you are. I'm currently draped across my couch in my lingerie I wore for you, eating some ice cream.

Cooper: Fuck. I hate myself.

Nora: Once again, as you should.

Cooper: Are you going to let me take you out again?

Nora: Honestly, I don't know. Tonight was an absolute disaster. I'm not sure I'm ready to be a part of that.

Cooper: They're only here temporarily.

Nora: But they aren't temporarily in your life. You've worked so hard at learning how to communicate your feelings, but they are a big trigger for you, a trigger that makes you revert to your old ways. They're your brother and sister, and at some point you're going to have to figure out how to effectively communicate with them.

Cooper: There's too much history.

Nora: That's what families are . . . history. They're not perfect. They're twisted and ugly at times, but it's how you navigate through those twisted and ugly times that strengthens the bonds you have with them. Your bonds are threadbare at this point.

Cooper: They don't understand me.

Nora: Bet they feel the same way. You never know until you talk to them. Call me once you do that.

Cooper: Are you coming to the anniversary party?

Nora: To drop off the cake.

Cooper: Can I talk to you then?

Nora: Probably not a good idea. Have a good night, Cooper.

TO: Ford Chance, Cooper Chance, Palmer Chance
FROM: Peggy Chance
SUBJECT: Your rooms

My dearest seedlings,

This is a reminder that you still need to clean out your rooms. Ford, you started to clean it out but then left everything on the floor. Palmer, I can't even walk through your room—there are clothes everywhere. And Cooper, your boxes are still stacked in the corner of your room. Didn't you say you were going to sell your bed as well?

We really need you kids to follow through on this. Your dad and I can't do it ourselves. Thank you.

Also, we are so excited about the anniversary party. We love you all for taking the time to plan this party out for us. We could not be more grateful for our three children.

I picked out a dusty rose dress that looks rather fetching on me, and I bought your dad a new pair of pants, no holes in the crotch. We might be old, but we know how to class it up when the opportunity presents itself.

Love you all,

Mom

CHAPTER FORTY-SIX

FORD

My feet pound against the pavement.

The dew from the night before glistens on every blade of grass.

And the sounds of Marina Island waking up fill the peaceful silence surrounding me.

But I feel anything but peaceful.

I feel a war raging inside me. A war I can't seem to get a handle on.

After leaving countless messages on Larkin's voice mail, I gave up calling her and went to bed, only to lie there, staring up at the ceiling, sleep eluding me.

And this morning, I woke up feeling empty.

Last night was not how I planned on things going. I planned on staying in Seattle for the night—I even booked us a hotel room so we wouldn't have to rush to catch the last ferry to Marina Island. I planned on sharing a wonderful dinner with Larkin, maybe stopping somewhere to get ice cream, and then heading back to our hotel room, where I would show Larkin just how much she means to me, how much these last few days have meant to me.

But that was not the case. Instead, I went to bed alone, woke up alone, and now I'm jogging alone.

I turn the corner onto Marina Ave and head straight to the inn with a very simple to-do list: take a shower, get dressed, and find Larkin.

Legs worn out from a seven-mile jog, I make my way up the steps of the inn and take a deep breath. A few diners are in the breakfast area, eating the dry muffins. I move past them and head right up the stairs toward my room—and stop dead in the hallway, my breath catching in my throat. Larkin is sitting next to my door.

When she spots me, she stands and brushes off her backside.

"Larkin," I say, approaching cautiously. "Have you been waiting long?"

"About ten minutes," she answers quietly.

"Hell, I'm sorry. If I knew you were coming by, I wouldn't have left."

"It's fine." I move in even closer, reaching for her, but she takes a step back, sending a wave of fear up my spine.

"I just came here to grab some work. I left my computer in your room."

"Oh, yeah, of course." I reach into my pocket and pull out my key. I unlock my room door and let Larkin in first. I follow close behind her and shut the door, tossing my key on the table next to the door.

Larkin goes straight to the table where we've been working, grabs her computer and charging cord, and then turns toward me, clutching both items to her chest. "If there's anything you'd like me to work on today specifically, just let me know. You can shoot me an email or text."

I nod, and she starts to walk toward the door. "Is this how it's going to be now?" I ask.

She pauses and glances up at me. "What do you mean?"

"Between you and me. That's it? Last night was all it took to lose you?"

"You didn't lose me, Ford. I'm just not sure you're ready for me."

"I am."

She shakes her head. "You're not. That was evident last night. You couldn't set everything to the side to just spend the night with me."

"You were getting in on the conversation too," I say.

"I know. I take the blame for last night as well, but I tried more than a few times to get you back to the date. And it didn't happen."

"It was impossible," I say, growing agitated. "You were there. You saw what it was like. A goddamn circus."

"But you could have risen above it all."

"I don't have the power to do that. I don't have it in me." I push my hand through my hair in frustration. "I'm exhausted, Larkin. Not only do I have the business to worry about, but I have my parents too. Just from being here a few weeks, I've seen a difference in my dad. I'm killing myself trying to navigate my siblings' needs—and then I have you to worry about."

"You don't need to add me to your burden, Ford."

"I didn't mean it like that. Jesus." I let out a low, frustrated breath. "You know what, maybe you're right: maybe I do need to get it together before we even consider an 'us.'" I straighten up and push past her. "I'll email you a list of tasks that need to be taken care of today. I have some things that have been piling up. Just email if you have questions."

I feel myself close up, shut down.

It's my only defense mechanism at this point.

I turn to my computer, wake it up, and hunker down in my chair, the comforting black hole of work taking over.

"Ford, don't get lost in your work; you've made so much progress."

I glance up at Larkin. There's a softness to her voice, encouragement, but I ignore it. I've had enough. I've had enough of everything.

"I need to take a shower, and I have a lot of work to do, Larkin. Please excuse yourself."

Her chin rises, and as she sets her shoulders back, I feel the intimacy between us snap. And in its place, a wall of professionalism separates us. "Sure. Let me know if you need anything from me."

I don't answer; instead, I turn to the hundreds of emails I've ignored over the last few days while I was trying to "find" myself. Yeah, lot of good that did.

CHAPTER

FORTY-SEVEN
COOPER

Palmer: Where are you?

I glance at my phone as the ferry docks.

Cooper: About to get off the ferry. I'm not late.

Palmer: You're not early. Ford isn't here either. The store looks normal.

Cooper: What do you mean normal?

Palmer: Like nothing is pushed out of the way.

Cooper: I'll be right there.

I set my phone down and drive off the ferry. I give the workers a quick wave and then take off toward Watchful Wanderers, which is only a minute away.

I'm in no fucking mood to be on Marina Island today, let alone dressed in a button-up and tie, but here I am, uncomfortable, pissed, and worried that I totally fucked up everything with Nora last night.

Thank you, Palmer and Ford.

The last two people I want to see.

But the two people I have to work with tonight.

I drive up to Watchful Wanderers and pull into the parking lot, parking in the far back to give room to the guests. We have an hour until the anniversary party, which should give us plenty of time to set up. At least that's what I hope. I didn't want to come any earlier.

I put my car in park but don't move. Instead, I stare out the windshield and try to pump myself up for this.

It's for our parents.

We love them.

It's only a few hours. Put on a smile and make them happy. Then it's over.

I grab my phone and keys and get out of the car before going to the trunk and pulling out a box of potted flowers. I'm not much of a decoration guy, but the potted flowers are a nice touch, and guests can take home the pots as souvenirs. Mom and Dad will like them.

I lock up and walk to the front door, where Palmer is waiting impatiently, arms folded.

"What took you so long?"

"Literally, it's been a minute," I snap at her. "Hold the door open for me."

She opens it, and I walk inside—only to make an abrupt stop.

I take in the store I grew up in. The racks of clothing, the rows of outdoor gadgets, the oak-log walls, and the kayaks hanging from the ceiling. And not a single table, chair, or any hint of a party.

Fuck.

"What the hell?" I set the box down by the door. "I thought Ford was in charge of the store. Didn't he say he was going to make space in here?"

"That's what I thought," Palmer says. "And because we shut the store down today for the party, there are no employees around to fix this."

"Shit," I mutter. "What about the back?"

"Full of merchandise."

Palmer leans against the wall, arms crossed, in a sleeveless black dress. Both of us are dressed up, and she has a cast on one arm. There's no way we'll be able to make the kind of room we need.

"And the rental company didn't drop off any chairs or tables. Nothing was dropped off, actually."

"What did you order?"

"I didn't order anything. I thought you were ordering chairs and tables."

I shake my head. "That wasn't my job. Maybe it was Ford's. Where is he?"

"Beats me." Palmer shrugs her shoulders. "He didn't answer his phone when I called."

I take a look at my watch and then glance at the store. "Fuck," I mutter. "We need to make some sort of space. Think we can at least push these clothing racks to the side? We can clear that shirt table and use it for the cake."

"There are some blankets we can unfold and put on top of the clothes so they don't get messy."

"It's the best we can do," I say as I start moving racks to the side, trying to play Tetris with the space.

We spend the next half hour attempting to clear the floor and draping blankets over the merchandise so people don't get handsy with it—not that they would, but just in case—and so nothing spills on it either.

Once the final rack is pushed out of the way, I check my watch again and pull out my phone. No missed calls or texts.

"Where the fuck is Ford?" I dial him, and it goes straight to voice mail. "What the actual fuck." I glance out the windows. "The inn is just up the street. I'm going to jog up there and see what's happening. You wait here for the food." I go to the door and kick the box of plants. "And do something with these."

I take off down the street at a brisk jog, cross the street, wave to someone who waves to me—not sure who that was—and make my way up the inn steps. I glance around the dining room and don't see him, so I go to the front desk.

"Cooper Chance, how are you? Come to visit your brother?" Harold asks, at the front desk.

"Yes," I answer breathlessly. "What room is he in?"

"Top floor, attic."

"Thanks." I take off up the stairs and realize . . . what if something happened to him? Larkin left last night, and he was not in a good mood, more distraught than anything. What if something happened?

No. I'm not going to think like that.

I make it to the top floor and don't even attempt to knock. I hope the door is unlocked as I turn the knob and let myself in to find . . .

Holy fuck.

"What the hell are you doing?" I ask as I see Ford hovered over his computer, wearing running clothes, in no way ready for the party.

When he glances up at me, his eyes are bloodshot, his expression blank.

"I'm working, Cooper. Please leave."

"You fuck," I say. "Mom and Dad's anniversary party is in twenty minutes."

His head snaps up. "What?" He looks at the time and then out the window. "Holy shit." He stands from the chair and glances down. "Shit, I never took a shower after my morning run."

"What the hell have you been doing all day?"

"Working." He runs around his room, shucking his shirt and putting on a button-up. He tosses on a few good swipes of deodorant and then puts on pants, followed by shoes and socks. He runs to the bathroom, where he wets his hair and quickly styles it. From the back of one of his chairs, he snags a tie and attempts to knot it while grabbing his phone and keys.

"You were supposed to set up the store. Palmer and I did the best we could, but we couldn't move everything."

"What do you mean? It wasn't cleared out?"

"No." Ford locks up, and together we rush down the stairs of the inn and out to the street, where we jog to the store, Ford tying his tie the entire time.

When we reach the store, we barge through the door to find Palmer helping Nora set up three cakes.

Jesus.

Her eyes land on mine, and I have a sudden urge to go up to her and plant a kiss on her beautiful face—not only for delivering, but for putting up with all three of us.

"There you are. Good God, Ford, what were you doing?" Palmer asks.

"He forgot," I answer for him.

"You *forgot*?" Palmer chokes out. "How on earth could you forget about the anniversary party that brought you here in the first place?"

"I've been going through some things." He takes in the space. "This is not nearly enough room for everyone."

"Well, it's the best we could do, given you didn't hold up your end of the bargain," Palmer says.

"Do you need serving ware and plates?" Nora asks, continuing to set up the cakes.

"I don't think so," I answer while Ford attempts to make more room. He clumsily shoves at a rack of clothes, pushing it nowhere. That one's nailed to the ground . . . idiot. "Palmer, you got all of that, right?"

"What? No. Why would I have ordered that?"

"Because you're in charge of food. Which, by the way, where is the food?"

"Uh . . ." Palmer blinks a few times. "You said you were getting sandwiches."

Sweat breaks out over my skin. "You have got to be fucking kidding me. You said sandwiches weren't fancy enough and you were talking to a caterer."

"Yeah, *talking* to a caterer. I didn't book them—they were already taken. Are you saying you didn't order sandwiches?"

"Of course I didn't order fucking sandwiches, Palmer," I yell. "Because you said you were getting a caterer, because you were in charge of food."

"We don't have food?" Ford asks.

"I highly doubt you have any room to judge," Palmer shoots back. "You forgot the party was even happening and completely neglected your responsibilities." Palmer looks at me, panic in her eyes. "What should we do?"

"Do we even have drinks?"

The doors whip open, and we all turn around to find Mom and Dad standing in the entry, their expressions of excitement quickly falling when they take in the empty, undecorated, and poorly set up space.

Fuck.

CHAPTER

FORTY-EIGHT
PALMER

"Mom, Dad," Cooper says, his voice shaky. "You're, uh, early."

"Just a few minutes," Mom says, holding her clutch tightly to her side while Dad presses his hand to her back.

Mom is wearing a beautiful dress that highlights her hourglass figure, and Dad is wearing a suit and tie that looks brand new for the occasion. Like a tidal wave, guilt and embarrassment wash over me as they take in the store, not an ounce of excitement in their expressions, just . . . disappointment.

"We're still sort of setting up," Cooper says, reaching for one of the potted plants in the box he brought in and setting it down on the cake table.

"I can see that," Dad says.

Ford strides up to us. "It's a rustic sort of event." Here comes the business spin he's so good at. "Wanted to represent the store, since it's a big part of our lives."

"That it is," Dad says, the strain in his voice making me start to sweat. "Is there food coming?"

"We have cake," I say, motioning to the table behind me. "Three kinds."

"Is there a place for people to sit?" Mom asks. "You know your father will have to sit at some point."

Shit, she's right, and all of us realize that at the same time.

"We, uh . . . we can bring an office chair up front," Cooper says.

"An office chair?" Mom folds her hands together, and I know that body language. She's not happy. Not even a little.

Oh God, we've fucked up so bad.

"Can you . . . give us a second?" I say, holding up my finger, just as a few early guests start to filter in the doors.

"People are here," Mom says, looking panicked.

"It will be a quick second." I look at my brothers. "Ford, Cooper. The back. Now."

"Palmer, this is hardly the time for a conversation with your brothers," Dad says. "What are we supposed to do with the guests?"

"Say hi to your friends. Mingle. It will be fine." I shoo them with my hand and then grab my brothers by the arms and march us to the back of the store, to the coffee alcove just out of view from the main floor. When we're out of earshot, I turn toward them. "What the hell are we going to do? Did you see the looks on their faces?"

Ford pulls on the back of his neck with both hands as he looks up toward the ceiling. "Fuck, this is bad."

"Really fucking bad," Cooper adds and then looks out toward the party. "Shit, more people have arrived, and I have no idea how to salvage this."

"What the hell were you doing, Ford, that prevented you from being here earlier?"

"I was lost in work," he says, distress in his voice.

"Shocking," I mutter.

"What's that supposed to mean?" Ford asks.

"You're always lost in work. You think you're doing this magnificent thing in 'taking care' of the family name by running Watchful Wanderers. But you're so disconnected from the family name you have no idea what's going on."

"This coming from the girl who thought Mom and Dad would want a lavender cake," Cooper says.

"I'm sorry I don't spend my Friday nights sitting on the couch between Mom and Dad because I don't have a life. We can't all be like you, Cooper."

"Don't fucking start," Ford says, stepping in. "We need solutions, not fighting."

"I don't know if there's a solution to this nightmare," Cooper says. "We don't have food; the store is a goddamn sardine can with everything just pushed to the side. There's nowhere to sit. There are no drinks. Basically, we're holding people captive with three choices of cake. And everything is closing on the island, so we don't have many options."

"Can we move it to Mom and Dad's?" Ford asks.

I shake my head. "They just had a bunch of boxes delivered for packing." That small detail pains me more than I care to understand right now.

"Fuck," Ford says again. He turns around, anger rolling off his shoulders. "This wouldn't be an issue if you two were able to keep your shit together."

"Excuse me?" I say. "I'm pretty sure you're the one who fucked up big time, Ford."

"More than not ordering food?" Cooper asks.

"I thought you were getting sandwiches!" I yell.

"Check the email, sis—you claimed food; this is on you. At least I delivered with centerpieces."

"And guess who was in charge of rentals?" Ford says, holding up his phone to Cooper. "You were."

Cooper's eyes focus on the screen, and his eyebrows shoot up as he realizes he messed up too.

"Don't forget the fun," I add. "Pretty sure you said there'd be fun, and if 'fun' meant dry and dull like your personality, then you nailed it."

"We all fucked up," Ford says. "At least I have a solid reason for dropping the ball."

I cross my arms over my chest. "Oh yeah, and what would that solid reason be for forgetting about your parents' anniversary party?"

"I broke things off with Larkin, so I'm a little messed up at the moment."

"This is why you don't fuck your assistant," I say, and Ford whips toward me, pausing inches from my face.

"Your incessant chatter and pestering made the fuel that lit the flame last night. But you don't realize that, do you? You don't see how your actions affect others."

"She never has," Cooper adds.

Both my brothers stare me down, and I take a step back, my mind whirling. "I take responsibility for my actions."

"Is that so?" Cooper asks, looking so sure of himself that I'm afraid of what might come out of his mouth. "Just like you're taking responsibility for the food, the food that you know you were supposed to order?"

"That was a miscommunication."

"Or how about blaming Mom and Dad for moving, when really you just don't have a place to live?"

How on earth . . .

"Remember I cosigned on your lease with you?" Cooper says. "Yeah, Palmer, your landlord called and said he couldn't get in touch with you, since you cut him short one hundred dollars of rent before giving up your lease."

My heart hammers in my chest, the thump so loud I can barely hear him.

"Or what about the fire." My lip trembles. My hands shake. "We all know you started it, Palmer; we've just been waiting for you to actually take responsibility for it. But it's been what, almost ten years? And you can't."

My stomach hits the floor as tears well up in my eyes.

How do they know?

I thought . . . I thought they assumed it was an accident. The cameras were destroyed in the fire, and they weren't even supposed to be running that night. There was no evidence it was me.

"Didn't think we knew, did you? Well, we do. Even Mom and Dad know. And they've never once addressed it with you, because they were so shocked they thought you would come forward. You never did. Instead, we've just picked up your pieces. Ever wonder why Ford never talks to you about the business? Because you nearly destroyed it."

I glance over at Ford. He's standing there with his hands in his pockets, head bent forward, but I can see the truth in his eyes. Cooper is right.

A tear falls down my cheek, and I quickly wipe it away. They've known all along. It's the reason they never talk to me about the store. They don't think I deserve to know. And even though I've spent so many years feeling unworthy, forcing myself to stay away—despite desperately wanting to play a part in the business—I didn't think they knew the truth, or saw what a screwup I actually am.

All those conversations about how proud they were of me for going off and making something of myself—was it all fake? Did they mean it? Or were they just glad I wasn't around to destroy the business all over again?

So many emotions—shock, guilt, panic—tumble through my brain, and it's too much. So instead of accepting what they're saying to me and being the bigger person, I shoot low. I turn on Cooper. "Yeah, well, does Ford know that you've been working with Larkin behind his back with rebranding?"

"What?" Ford asks, looking shocked.

Cooper's eyes bore into me. "You ass."

"You're working behind my back? When I clearly said no?" Ford asks.

Cooper adjusts the sleeves of his pressed shirt "Yeah, I brought her the designs I've been working on, and guess what? She fucking loves them. She believes they're better than anything you've come up with . . . you narcissistic asshole. You're not the only one who knows the business, but that would mean admitting you're not perfect, and that's just too goddamn hard for you, isn't it? The perfect older brother who does everything right. Who pleases his parents—"

"I had to please them," Ford yells. "We were foster kids, Cooper. If I didn't, then we were going to be shipped off to another house. Of course I've spent my goddamn life pleasing them so they always know they chose right."

"That's *enough*." Dad's voice booms from behind me, and I jump to the side in fright. "That is . . . enough." Gripping the edge of the wall, he glares at all of us, his domineering presence filling the space. "You are done, do you hear me? This night . . . is done."

"Dad—" Ford says, but Dad raises a strong hand, silencing him.

"Your mother has sent everyone home, and she's waiting in the car for me. I expect you three to clean up this sorry excuse for a party, make the store look exactly how you found it, and then report back to our house immediately. We have something to say to you three."

With that, he turns around and heads out the door.

"Fuck," Cooper mutters, leaning against the wall.

Yup . . . fuck is right.

CHAPTER

FORTY-NINE

FORD

I've never felt so sick in my entire life.

Seeing the disappointment in my dad's face, hearing the authority in his voice . . . it brought me back to the first time he ever yelled at me. I can't even remember what I'd done, but I was in trouble and I knew it, but I had no idea what was going to happen. That's how it feels right now: the unknown is lurking over us as we drive over to our childhood home in Cooper's car.

We haven't said a word to each other.

We haven't even bothered to look at one another.

What's the point?

All we do is argue, fight, blame one another.

No wonder Mom and Dad sent everyone home from the party—they weren't only embarrassed; they were ashamed.

Of us.

Cooper pulls into the driveway and puts the car in park. Together, we get out of the car and head to the front door, which Dad is holding open for all of us. Heads bent, we make our way into the house and into the living room, where we all take seats on the couch. Mom is pacing the living room, wearing a pair of jeans and a sweatshirt, uncommon for this time of the night. Normally she'd be in her pajamas and a robe.

When Dad enters, it feels like the room shrinks to one-tenth its size.

I want to speak up. I want to apologize. I want to try to make this all better, but that's what I always do—and I have a feeling that isn't going to work this time.

With his bushy eyebrows arched at a menacing angle, Dad stares us all down, pressing his hands into his hips. "This family was built on love, acceptance, and supporting one another . . . no matter what. Your mother and I have strived to instill those values in you. We have spent countless hours of our lives providing for you, giving you opportunities to not only succeed but to learn. We've clothed you, fed you, given you a roof over your head, and you have been the lucky few whose parents were able to bring a family business into the mix that doesn't just succeed but thrives. But the reason that business has been so successful is that it capitalizes on family values, creating adventures with the ones we love. How the hell do you think the public would feel, our customers, our investors, if they knew the family who built Watchful Wanderers is a complete joke?"

Mom sniffs and dabs at her eyes with a tissue.

Fuck.

FUCK!

I hate seeing Mom cry.

"Do you know why we wanted this anniversary party?" When no one answers, Dad continues: "It wasn't just to celebrate the love and life your mom and I have shared over the past few decades, but it was to bring you all together again. Over time, we've seen the way you've detached from each other. The jealousies that have festered, the insecurities that have only worsened. It's disgusting, and it's not the way we raised you. We thought it was a phase, that you three would come back together at some point, but apparently we were wrong."

Dad takes a deep breath, and Mom comes up to him, putting a hand on his back as encouragement.

"I'm not getting any younger, nor am I getting better," Dad says, his voice rough. "We decided to move, not because of Cooper's encouragement, but because we had to face the truth. I'm sick, and simple tasks are becoming harder and harder for me to handle. And even though it pains me to admit that I'm not the man I used to be, I know it's time to really seek help if I want to keep up with this disease. The Parkinson's Fitness Project is based in Seattle, and I've already signed myself up for classes. Living in Seattle will limit the ferry rides, since being on a boat isn't easy for me, and I'll be able to make some progress in managing this."

"Why didn't you say that before?" I ask. I knew he was sick, but I never knew he was having *this* much trouble. Then again, my head has been buried in the sand the past few years, and I've been constantly on the go, never really looking up to see what's happening. A fresh wave of guilt rushes up to meet me.

"Because I was hoping I wouldn't have to. I don't enjoy showing weakness or how this disease is affecting me. I was also hoping my children would be able to act like adults, come together for a family reunion, and enjoy each other's company. I had no idea that inviting you all back to the island was going to cause such a tumultuous string of events, ending in an embarrassing display of our family." He takes a deep breath. "I don't care about the party. Were we excited about it? Of course. Any chance to celebrate the love I share with this woman is a chance I want to take, but that's not what this is about. There's been a disconnect in this family, and your mother and I are done."

Mom steps away from Dad and goes behind a chair, where she pulls out two suitcases, which she sets down in front of them. She then picks up a canvas bag and walks over to us, holding it open.

"Your mother is collecting your phones, wallets, and keys."

We sit there stunned, unsure of what to do.

"Now," Dad's voice booms.

We all scramble and drop everything we have in the canvas bag. She closes it and drapes it over her shoulder.

"Food and drinks are in the kitchen, and Bart next door has a working phone in case of an emergency. You have twenty-four hours to fix this. Fix your relationship with each other, and I mean *fix* it, or your mother and I will be done with you three."

"Done?" I ask, my body responding with an all-out sweat.

"Yes." Dad's chin rises. "Done. We have given you our lives, our love, our strength, our courage. We deserve to see the children we raised, not mere shadows. We want to be proud of you three, and not because of your accomplishments or where you've gone or what you've done for us, but because of the kind of humans you are, the bonds you share with each other. That's what will make us proud." Taking a deep breath, he grabs Mom's hand. "I don't know how much time I have left in this world. It could be years, could be shorter, but I will be damned if I leave you three like this. Despondent. Jealous. Angry. Unloving. Uncaring. Discouraged. Belligerent. Your mother and I deserve more from you. From all of you."

With that, he turns and heads toward the entryway. Mom follows, popping out the handles of the suitcases and rolling them behind her.

We don't move.

We don't say anything.

Instead, we let them take off with our keys, phones, and wallets, leaving us in the house we grew up in. But we're not surrounded by love like we normally are—we're sitting in disdain.

The front door clicks shut, and silence falls over the room.

Cooper leans back on the couch and blows out a heavy breath. I lean forward, pressing my hands together. Palmer stands from the couch and mutters, "I need to get out of this dress."

"But you're coming back down here, right?" I ask.

She twists toward me. "As if I have an option."

And then she heads upstairs.

Next to me, Cooper undoes his tie and takes off his shoes. "I'm going to grab some spare clothes from upstairs. I suggest you do the same. Meet back down here in five. Hide the wine—you know Palmer will try to drink some."

And then he takes off too.

My initial reaction is to text Larkin. To look for some advice. To use her as a sounding board. I need her more than ever in this moment. I need her kindness, her intelligence. My dad is slowly dying; my siblings hate me; my parents are disappointed in us.

In me.

I've spent my entire life trying to make them happy, and yet here I am, knee deep in disappointment.

I would be lying if I said I wasn't disappointed in myself. I lift off the couch and head upstairs to get changed for the night.

It's going to be a long one.

Chapter Fifty

COOPER

"Where should we start?" Ford asks as we sit around the dining room table.

We took some time to get changed, gather ourselves, and then grab something to eat. We put some cheese and crackers on a plate, along with some fruit and iced molasses cookies, and we grabbed drinks, but no one has touched anything since we sat down.

Probably because we're all in shock.

I know I am.

Shock.

Embarrassment.

Hurt.

The emotions keep rolling around in my head, heating me up and then shaking my core to the point of nausea. And Nora was there. I can't imagine what she must think of us, of the shit show we put together. After all the fighting and bickering over the cake, that's the only thing that showed up. I almost smile as I think about the three cakes she baked, thoughtful and wonderful just like her—and then I remember they've gone to waste.

"We're going to need to talk," Ford pushes.

Palmer picks up a piece of cheese and eats it. I sip my water, unsure of what to do other than point fingers, and I know that's not going to help the cause.

"Fine, I'll start," Ford says. "I'm sorry for dropping the ball earlier—"

"I don't think that's what Mom and Dad want us talking about," I interrupt.

"Okay. Since you're the expert on Mom and Dad, then why don't you lead the conversation?" Palmer says as she pulls her leg close to her chest, her oversize sweatshirt drowning her.

"Fine, I'll lead the conversation." I adjust myself in my seat. "Let's talk about the source of the disconnect between the three of us."

"You really think you can pinpoint that?" Palmer asks.

I nod slowly. "Yes, I can."

Ford faces me. "What do you mean?"

"Palmer's senior year of high school." Palmer's eyes fall to mine.

"Why do you say that?" she asks nervously.

"Do you remember when you were in second grade and you came home in tears because some dipshit kid told you we weren't really your brothers?"

"Yes," Palmer says, looking confused.

"Do you remember the conversation we had?"

Palmer gives it some thought. "Not word for word, but I remember you telling me it didn't matter that we weren't blood—we were connected by our souls, and nothing could break that."

I nod and play with the napkin in front of me. "And I said that no matter what, we were never going to leave you. That night and for an entire week, Ford and I slept on the floor of your room to show you we weren't going anywhere."

"I remember that," Palmer says, a small smile pulling at her lips. "That's when Mom's cat Otis was stuck in the room and freaked out so bad that he ended up puking on Ford."

365

"I can still smell the puke," Ford says absentmindedly.

"We made it a tradition, that we spent the night in your room every year for the first week of school. Do you remember that?"

"I do."

"And then Ford went off to college, but it was okay, because I was still there with you. And when it was time for me to go to college, I stayed at home and commuted, so I was always there." Palmer nods. "But your senior year, I moved in with Dealia because we were getting married."

She looks away as she props her chin up on her good hand. I pause, waiting for her to say something as a tear streams down her face.

Finally, she takes a deep, shaky breath. "You were always so afraid Mom and Dad were going to leave you, but I was just as terrified I was going to lose my brothers—and I did."

"But you didn't lose us," Ford says.

"Dude, you have to listen," I say. "You have to listen to her feelings. Not to start a fight, but that's one of the biggest issues you have. You scratch the surface with us; you don't dive deep. So listen to Palmer."

Understanding crosses his face as he nods. "Sorry. Why, uh . . . why did you feel like you were losing us?"

Palmer looks grateful for the moment to speak candidly. She takes her time, though.

"I always . . . well, I always had you two by my side, loving on me, playing with me. I know you worshipped me more than you should have—I was definitely spoiled—but you two were amazing brothers growing up. Always dealing with my annoying little-sister tendencies. But because of the age gap, you left before I was ready to say goodbye, before I was ready to give up those everyday interactions. And I know it's not your fault, but it still gutted me. Ford, you took off, and it felt like you didn't look back. You came home for holidays and summers, but you were different. Serious. Didn't want to goof around, and it felt like you didn't have time for me anymore. And Cooper, you stayed at home, and I cherished those moments with you, but they also started to dwindle, especially when you met Dealia. I felt abandoned, and it's stupid because I know we're all supposed to move on, but . . ."

"You weren't ready."

She shakes her head. "No. I wasn't. And there was no proper good-bye, you know? You both just floated away."

"Is that why you didn't have a good senior year?" Ford asks.

Palmer nods. "I struggled. Honestly, I was lucky I got into NYU early after the grades I pulled."

"And the fire," I press, though gently this time.

Another tear streams down her face, but she doesn't wipe this one away. "But . . . the cameras weren't even running at that point, *and* they were destroyed in the fire. How do you know?"

"We love you, Palmer, but Mom and Dad had those security cameras, which you thought made the store look so hideous, installed that year *because* things were starting to be stolen. Some of your friends were a bit too friendly with the merchandise, apparently. And this is a small island—word spreads quickly, especially secrets. Between the rumors and the thefts, Mom and Dad realized their daughter was having parties in the store. Sure, they didn't have footage of what happened the night of the fire, but they knew it was you."

Guilt is written all over her face. "Why didn't they say anything?"

"They wanted you to learn the hard way. They thought if the cops were called or something bad enough happened to scare you, that would teach you a better lesson than any lecture they might give you. But then the fire started. And they were in shock; we all were. We thought that was it—you were going to finally tell us—but you never did."

"I was too ashamed," she says. "I thought that Mom and Dad bought the story that I didn't start the fire but was just trying to put it out, save the store. I thought it would all be okay, but that was the beginning of the end, wasn't it?"

I nod. "It was for me. That's where I felt the disconnect between us start to happen."

"I encouraged Cooper to say something to you," Ford says, "since you two were closer at the time. But he wouldn't."

"I didn't have it in me," I admit. "I couldn't look you in the eye, knowing you didn't claim one ounce of responsibility, especially after seeing how distraught Mom and Dad were. So, Ford and I got into a huge fight over it. We blamed each other for not saying something to you sooner." I sigh, remembering all the useless anger, the hurtful words we threw at each other. "Nothing came of the fight besides resentment—neither of us could take the blame, could solve the problem—and as a result, we ended up going months without talking. After that, it felt like our relationship was never really the same."

Ford nods. "Yeah. And you know Mom and Dad; they were never ones to truly punish us but to wait for us to learn from our mistakes. Since you never confessed, I decided to take matters into my own hands. I told them that since you didn't show any responsibility or regret for what happened, I didn't want you working with the business."

"That's why you've never offered me a job or included me in developments."

Ford nods. "I didn't want someone who didn't care about the store to be a part of it."

"But I do care." Palmer faces us now and wipes at her eyes. "I care so much. I have some of my best memories at the store, especially—" She chokes up as a sob escapes her. "Especially with you two. I couldn't face your anger, your disappointment in me. It was cowardly of me not to say anything, not to own up to what I did. And not a day goes by that I don't regret it. You two are my heroes, my . . . my everything. Being connected to the store meant I was connected to you. And then I lost it—by my own doing, but it was still a loss. So I did everything I could to flee, to build my own life, to prove to you that I didn't need my heroes in my life, that I could do it on my own . . . but I can't." She sucks in a sharp breath, and I feel the sudden, surprising urge to hug her. "I can't do any of this on my own."

"You've done a lot on your own," Ford says. "Give yourself credit."

"But it's landed me with no money, no actual job, and no home. I've failed. And I came back here, trying to show you just how great my life is, when it's really not great at all." She presses her shirtsleeve to her eyes, so I get up and grab a box of tissues off the counter. I hand them to her, but instead of taking them, she takes my hand, tugging it so I sit down next to her. She looks me in the eyes. "I'm so sorry, Cooper." She reaches her hand out to Ford, and he scoots closer as well. "I'm so sorry, Ford. I hurt you both, lost your trust, and I've fucked up this family."

"We all did," Ford says. "You were right: I haven't taken the time to listen to you two. I've just pretended like everything is okay so that I can keep moving forward with the business. But I think I'm struggling so much because the core of the business is this family. I don't really know it anymore."

"And I should have spoken up," I say, realizing this isn't all Palmer's fault. It's all of ours. We all failed each other at one point or another. Even our parents, although that's hard to admit because I hold them on a pedestal. I know they always let us solve our problems with each other, among siblings, but I think they approached this wrong. They should have stepped in. "Not just about the fire, but about everything. I've been harboring all these feelings, especially about Mom and Dad. I've been clinging to my resentment, my inadequacies, and I've taken them out on you two. My failure to go for the things that would make me happy has a lot to do with my fear of losing Mom and Dad, something I've been discovering in therapy."

"You go to therapy?" Ford asks, looking surprised.

"Yeah, ever since Dealia left. I needed help processing the failure of the marriage. Which I've come to realize wasn't the match I needed. It's still raw, talking about her, because we never really got closure, but I think a lot of that is because she's ashamed of how it all went down.

She actually encouraged Nora to go out with me, which I think is her peace offering."

"You two seem like a great couple," Palmer says, picking up a tissue and wiping her eyes. "I think you balance each other out nicely. Nora's always been a sweetheart and so understanding—hence the cake situation—but she also doesn't take shit from anyone. I have a feeling she'd call you out when you need it."

"She does." I nod, my heart aching. "She does call me out."

Palmer turns to Ford. "And Larkin, I think we've all thought you two would hook up at some point. It was just a matter of when."

"Yeah, I think that's always been the case with her, but I finally let myself have feelings for her. She kept telling me over and over how important family is, and I know it's because only half her family is still with her." Ford looks between us. "I've felt like I've had half my family too, but by choice."

"Me too," Palmer says.

"Same," I answer.

"So how do we fix it?" Ford asks.

"Talking about it works," I say. "Even though it's painful. It works. And this is a great start, but I think we need to keep going."

CHAPTER

FIFTY-ONE
FORD

"I can't believe you've been taking classes," I say, shaking my head in amazement. "Was this because you went to therapy?"

Cooper nods. "Yes. Fear was controlling my life—subconsciously, I was holding on to Mom and Dad, not wanting to let them go. You were always trying to make them happy, Ford. I was always trying to hold on to them. When Dad was diagnosed, those fears of losing him skyrocketed. It hurt my marriage, and it basically put me into a hole where I did nothing but attempt to be there every second of every day for them. I might have complained about it to you two, but I needed it. I needed them to need me. After talking through some of those emotions, I realized I was hindering my life with fear. So, I decided to do something about it and took a design class, just to try something new that had always interested me. One class turned into multiple classes, which then turned into this talent I didn't know I had."

"None of us knew you had it," Palmer says, taking a look at Cooper's sketch of the mock-up logo he'd shown to Larkin. "You should see it on his iPad—it's really freaking good."

Yeah, it is. I'm ashamed I didn't give him the time to actually show me, because he nailed it. This is exactly what I've been looking for. It represents the company, our family, and everything we believe in, but with a fresh take. And the branding ideas . . . hell, I'm a moron.

If only I'd listened. I would have saved myself a lot of time. And been a better brother.

"So, let me get this straight," Cooper says with a smirk. "You were spying on us? Where?"

"In the bushes, naturally." Cooper and I laugh. "But it cost me my third cast, because I fell into a puddle."

"Serves you right." Cooper nudges Palmer, eyes crinkling with humor.

"Worth it," she replies.

"So, you like it?" Cooper asks me, his eyes full of hope.

"I fucking love it, and before you ask, no, I'm not just saying that. I would obviously like to see the mock-ups you showed Larkin, but hell, man, this is exactly what we need." I glance up at my siblings, heart full. "It represents us. As a family."

"It does," Palmer says, grabbing our hands and holding them tight.

CHAPTER
FIFTY-TWO
PALMER

"You see how this is a stupid post?" I say. "What is the point of it? There's no engagement, no thrill behind the picture. It's just a pair of hiking boots against a backdrop. There's no feeling behind it."

"Yeah, I guess so," Ford says, looking at the computer. Mom and Dad thought they took all the electronics, but they forgot about my computer upstairs.

I go back to the Instagram feed for Watchful Wanderers. "When you look at your profile page, you don't really feel the brand; you just see things trying to be sold to you, sometimes with horrendous lighting. Everything bounces around—there's no commonality."

"She's right," Cooper says. "Your Instagram is atrocious. Who does it?"

Ford scratches the side of his face. "Our social media team."

"They need to be fired," I say, not even feeling sorry about it. "Look at your engagement—it's not even close to where it should be for the number of followers you have. Especially with the new stores coming out. You should be boosting excitement. Look at REI's Instagram." I type it in and show him. "It's customers enjoying the products; it's setting a mood. You come to REI, you have fun, you have adventure. Compared to them, you're like a Sears Roebuck catalogue."

"Ouch, that hurts," Cooper says.

"Tell me how you really feel," Ford says with a chuckle. "Hell, how did it get this bad? How did I become so disconnected?"

"It happens when you bury your head in the sand and don't address the real issue," Cooper says. He motions among the three of us. "*We're* the real issue. Mom and Dad built the foundation, but we burned the house down." He elbows me. "No offense intended."

I hold up my hand. "None taken."

"Build on us, build on the business. We all were at our best when we were together."

Ford looks between us. "Want to have a bonfire and s'mores by the water like we used to?"

"I'll grab the supplies; you two start the fire."

Together, we get up, and the boys head out back while I search Mom and Dad's pantry. Like always, there's a special s'mores basket full of the supplies and skewers we need. I quickly check on the date of all the food items—because you never know—and everything is good. I toss a few sodas and napkins in the basket and head out back, where Ford and Cooper already have a small fire going. Cooper moves some chairs around the pit, and I hand him the basket. We all take seats, and like the good brother he is, Cooper sets me up with a marshmallow.

This is exactly what I've missed. Hanging with my heroes, my brothers. Being present with them, nothing between us, nothing distracting us.

I'm the first to place my marshmallow over the fire, carefully roasting it with my good hand. Ford is next, putting his a little closer to the flames, but not enough to roast it. Then Cooper sticks his skewer in the flames, sets his marshmallow on fire, and lets it burn.

"Oh my God, I forgot you were a deviant."

Cooper blows out his marshmallow and smiles at me. "The best way to eat s'mores is with a burnt marshmallow."

Ford and I glance at each other before I say, "We do not agree."

Cooper makes his s'more while Ford glances up at the house. "I'm going to miss this place. It was our first real home. Our first safe place. It holds so many memories—I can't imagine saying goodbye to it."

"It was one of the reasons Mom and Dad didn't want to sell initially, because they knew what it meant to you and me, Ford. This house, this safe haven," Cooper says. "But they can't keep up with it."

Ford nods. "I can understand their decision. If Dad can get more help in the city, then I want him to move. A house is a house; we can replace that. We can't replace Dad."

"Hey, remember the time you decided to go skinny-dipping with Mallory Henderson when you thought Mom and Dad were sleeping?" I ask Ford.

He throws his head back and laughs. "I can still feel Dad's fingers pulling me by the ear while I tried to cover up my junk, soaking wet. I think he lectured me for two straight hours."

"It was a long time. I remember sitting at the top of the stairs while you sat on the couch naked, only a washcloth to your name, because that's how brutal Mom and Dad were," I say.

"It was the one and only time I did something I shouldn't have. And it was all because of Mallory."

"I would say Mallory and hormones," Cooper says, taking a bite of his s'more. "Those hormones will get you every time."

"Speak for yourself," Ford says. "I recall you getting yourself into a few predicaments."

"Tell me about it," I say, butting in. "I'd always hear Mom muttering in the kitchen about how Cooper was going to get some girl pregnant because he used his eyes to his advantage."

Cooper lets out a belly laugh. "Mom always complained about our eyes. Loved them but said they would be the death of her as well."

"Well, congrats on not getting anyone pregnant," I say as I lift my perfectly toasted marshmallow out of the fire. Cooper helps me with my s'more, and Ford makes one as well.

"For the amount of fear Mom and Dad had of us growing up, I think we all did pretty damn well," Cooper says.

"We did," Ford adds.

CHAPTER FIFTY-THREE

COOPER

"Dude, the boob book—I remember stealing this on occasion."

"I've never been more fascinated and disgusted at the same time," Palmer says, lying on Ford's bed and flipping through the pages for me while Ford buries his head in his hands. "I can't believe you let Larkin see this."

"Not like I wanted her to see it."

"Man, if she saw this and still kissed you after, you found a good one."

"Yeah, I did, but once again, I fucked it up like everything in my life."

I sit up. "It's nothing we can't fix."

"We?" Ford asks.

"Yeah, we. I mean, I'm guessing after the other night we're all suffering in our relationships?"

"You could say that," Palmer says, sitting up as well.

"Nora's the same. Wants nothing to do with me. Which means we're all in the same boat, and we all need to show them that we're mature enough to be with them. You know, since maturity was seriously lacking during that dinner."

Ford chuckles. "That was one of those nightmare dinners you see on a TV show that makes you so incredibly uncomfortable, but you can't look away because you want to see if it gets any worse."

"Oh, it got worse," Palmer says. "I think Beau was mortified to be sitting across from me, and I don't blame him. I don't blame any of them."

"So, what are we going to do about it?" Ford asks.

"I have an idea," I say, my mind whirring through possibilities and plans. "Palmer, do you still have Mom and Dad's wedding book in your room?"

She thinks about it. "Maybe. Let's go see."

Together we file out of Ford's room and head down the hallway. Ford and I stop at the door when Palmer walks into her room. Her disaster of a room.

"Jesus, Palmer," Ford says. "Even as an adult you can't keep your room clean?"

She glances around. "It's not that bad."

"I can't see the floor," I say.

"You are so dramatic." She steps over clothes, pushes past some papers strewn across the floor, and then opens her closet by yanking on the doorknob and pushing some blankets out of the way. "You two are welcome to come in."

I shake my head. "I'd rather not be swallowed whole by your clothes. I have a long life I want to live."

She rolls her eyes and looks through her closet, pulling a few boxes down until—

"Found it. Want to look at it on my bed?"

"No," Ford and I say together.

She chuckles and makes her way to the door. I take the book from her, and together we go down to the living room, where I spread it out on the coffee table. Back in middle school, Palmer went through a serious scrapbooking phase. She'd spend hours at the kitchen table putting together memories for the family. One of the first albums she did was Mom and

Dad's wedding album. Mom helped her, of course, and as she started to get better, Mom and Dad invested in more scrapbooking materials for her. But with the wedding album, we're at the bare minimum of supplies and skills.

"Why did I like scalloped scissors so much?" Palmer asks, wincing at the pictures she cut up.

"I think it looks classy," I say as Ford and Palmer both give me their snooty looks. I chuckle. "I guess some things will never change." I flip through the pages until I get to the reception. "This is what's going to happen. We're going to re-create Mom and Dad's wedding. Redo the party. Give them the recognition they deserve."

"That's a great idea," Palmer says. "And we can obviously use this for reference. But how can we pull it off on such short notice?"

Ford smiles. "Well, we have money, after all."

"You do," Palmer says.

"You have money too," I say. "You just haven't gotten it yet."

"What?" she says, looking confused.

"When you turn thirty, there's a trust fund waiting for you. Did you really forget about that?"

Palmer looks between the two of us. "I thought . . . I thought that was lost with the fire. Like, they had to use it to recover."

"Who did you hear that from?" Ford asks.

"I don't know; I thought Mom said it, or—"

"I said it," I say. "I was pissed at you; I offhandedly said it while talking to Dealia, knowing full well you could hear me." I shake my head. "Fuck, I'm sorry, Palmer."

"But . . ." She looks so confused. "You mean there's still money there for me to invest?"

"It's still there," I say.

"I don't deserve that money."

Ford lifts her chin. "Before the fire, you worked your ass off in the store, and if I have it my way, you're going to continue to work your ass off."

"What do you mean?" she asks.

Ford takes a deep breath, clear eyed, focused. It's two in the morning, and we haven't slept a wink, haven't even considered it. We've bounced from room to room, sharing memories. Reconnecting. Talking about life. "I need your help," Ford says. "I thought I could do this on my own, but with Dad retiring, I've felt lost. I've had Larkin, but there's only so much I can burden her with. I need you both to carry on the legacy. I can't do it without you. I don't want to do it without you."

"What are you saying?" Palmer asks as hope springs in my chest.

"What would you think about . . . I don't know, working for the company?"

"In what capacity?" I ask.

Ford drags his hand over his face. "I don't know. I would love to hear what your thoughts would be, what you would want to do." He glances down at his hands and says, "All I've ever done with you two is dictate, tell you what to do. Being the older brother, I thought that was my job, but now, I want to hear what you two think, what you believe would help the company, help me."

I glance at Palmer, whose lips are turning up in a smile.

"Didn't think I would ever hear him say that."

I laugh. "You and me both."

"Hey now," Ford says. "Take it easy on me, okay? This is all new to me, but after coming to Marina Island, there is one thing I know to be certain: I can't do this on my own, and not only do I need your help, but I want it. I want both of you by my side. So let me hear it—what do you want to do?"

I rub my hands together. "I would love to have a creative role in the company. Help with branding and work with merchandizing the store brand. And honestly, after speaking with Larkin and seeing the kind of knowledge she has, I think you should have her in a different position. She's too advanced to be your assistant."

Ford scrapes the side of his cheek. "You're right. On both accounts. You would be wonderful in branding and merchandizing, from the brief glimpse of what you've shown me. And Larkin needs to spread her wings, do more."

"She should do something with purchasing," Palmer says. "She's always had a keen eye for the latest and greatest equipment and apparel."

Ford nods. "You're right, Palmer." He then tilts his head and studies her. "What about you?"

Shyly, she says, "Well, you know, your social media presence could have a lot more appeal, and I happen to have a lot of experience in that department."

"That you do," Ford says. "That would be an ideal position for you. And that would make you happy?"

"I think so." I bite down on my bottom lip as Beau crosses my mind.

Ford seems to read me well because he says, "You could work remotely, from Marina Island." When I give him a confused look, he says, "Tell me if I'm wrong, but I think you need roots. You need your family, and your family is here, in the PNW. What better way to highlight the store and the brand, the experience, than where it first started? Plus, it might give you the chance to patch things up with Beau . . . that's if it's something you're interested in."

She sheepishly smiles. "I do. I like him a lot."

"Well, the job is yours if you want it."

"Seriously?"

Ford nods his head. "Seriously."

Palmer throws her arms around him while I give him a pat on the back. "You might regret this later, when we're constantly up your ass," I say.

He shakes his head. "Nah, this is exactly what I need." And then he pulls me into a hug as well. We stay like that for a few seconds before he releases us, his eyes misty. "Okay, we have a party to plan, money to spend, and people to win back. Think we can do it in the next . . . twelve hours?"

We all exchange glances and nod.

We got this.

Chapter Fifty-Four

LARKIN

Pound. Pound. Pound.

Bleary eyed, I sit up in bed, rub my eyes, and try to comprehend what that sound is.

Pound. Pound. Pound.

The door.

Someone is pounding on the door. What the hell time is it? Getting out of bed, I check my phone and see that it's six in the morning. What is going on?

I switch on a light and open my door, where I find Cooper jogging in place on the other side. He's holding a stack of envelopes and is a sweaty mess.

Very sweaty.

"Cooper," I say. "Is everything okay?"

"Great," he says with such liveliness in his voice that I'm worried he might actually have had eighteen cups of coffee in an hour. "Feeling great. How are you?"

"Uh, tired," I answer, hugging my arms around my waist. "You realize it's six in the morning, right?"

"Very much aware. Have a busy day ahead of me—it's why I can't stay and chitchat." He hands me an envelope. "Your presence is requested. Well, not just requested, more like kindly demanded."

"Where?" I ask, flipping over the envelope.

"It's all in there." He holds up the stack of envelopes. "I've got a lot more to run around the town. Don't have a car, so I'm getting in the exercise this morning. See you tonight." And then he takes off down the stairs without another word.

I shut my door and walk over to my bed, where I open the envelope. I pull out a homemade, scrapbooked card. It's cream and a mossy green color with a *C* on the front. When I flip it open, a handwritten note invites me to a wedding anniversary party tonight at the Chances' home. Below that is an arrow that points to the back. I flip it over to find Ford's familiar handwriting.

> Larkin,
> I know I'm the last person you probably want to hear from, or do a favor for, but I would be forever in your debt if you attended my parents' anniversary party tonight. I have something I desperately want to say to you, and I know my parents would be grateful to have you at the party, especially since they know how much you mean to me. How much you're my future . . .
> Please attend. Hopefully I'll see you tonight.
> Ford

Twisting my lips to the side, I read his note a few more times and then lie back on my bed, staring up at the canopy of flowers. What are those Chance kids up to?

Guess there's only one way to find out.

CHAPTER

FIFTY-FIVE

DR. BEAU

"Good morning, Doc."

"Jesus Christ." I jerk back against my door, the coffee in my mug sloshing around. "Ford," I say after taking a deep breath. "How long have you been waiting there?"

His eyes are bright, his smile a little creepy, and his energy more than what a man should have at this hour. I'm about to head down to the office early to get some precharting done before appointments start. I definitely wasn't expecting anyone to be in the stairway of my apartment.

"Not long. Was about to knock on your door. You saved me from pounding with my fist."

Composing myself, I give him a polite smile. "Well, glad to oblige." I walk down the stairs, Ford on my heels, and then open the office for the both of us. "Is everything okay? You seem very . . . sweaty."

"Been running around town." He holds up an envelope. "This is for you."

"You're giving me a card?" I laugh, taking it and then setting my coffee down on a side table in the lobby.

"It's not personally from me—unless you want me to write you a love letter, then maybe that's something I can arrange."

"You do have handsome features, but the wrong body parts."

Ford throws his head back and laughs, the jovial body language seriously throwing me for a loop.

"Are you sure everything is okay?" I ask.

"Everything's great. But we do hope to see you tonight."

"We?" I ask.

"Yup. We're throwing my parents an anniversary party—a redo, actually—and it would mean the world to us if you came . . . and, uh, if you could convince your sister to come too. She got an invite as well."

"I see."

"It would mean the most to Palmer if you were there."

I clutch the envelope, my pulse picking up. "How is she? Cast still dry?" I try to joke, but it feels flat coming off my tongue.

"She's doing better, and yes, the cast is dry. But I have a few more things I have to do, and I have to make the run back to the house."

"Sure, yeah. Okay."

Ford points at the envelope. "Read it. You won't regret it." And then he takes off.

When the door shuts, I carry my coffee and the envelope to my office, where I take a seat and open the envelope. I open the handmade card and read the handwritten invitation. Party tonight, at the Chance residence. An arrow points to the back, so I turn it over to find Palmer's handwriting.

Dearest Beau,

I know we left things in an awkward state and I don't blame you. I've been nothing like myself these last few weeks, let alone months, but one thing that I did realize while being here is how much I like you, how much I want to spend my time with you, how much our history means to me. So, I know you probably have better things to do, but it would be such an honor if you'd please come to my parents' anniversary party tonight. I really need to talk to you.

Hope to see you there.

Yours,

Palmer

I grip my jaw as I stare at her neat handwriting. She really needs to talk to me. What does that mean? If Ford delivered this, does that mean they worked things out? Is everything okay with her?

I know I broke things off, but I miss her, the real Palmer, the one who wrote this note.

I pull out my phone and send a text.

Beau: Did you get the invite?

Larkin responds right away.

Larkin: I did.

Beau: Are you going?

Larkin: I can't stay away, even if I tried. You?

Beau: I think I'm in the same boat, sis.

Larkin: Then will you pick me up and we can ride together?

Beau: Deal.

CHAPTER FIFTY-SIX
NORA

"I'm going to murder you," I say, swinging the door open to find Palmer on the other side, looking . . . nervous. I can't say I blame her—I can be a terror at this early hour.

She holds up one good hand, one cast hand. "Please don't murder me. I borrowed cash from my parents' secret coffeepot, rode a bike to catch the ferry, navigated the streets of Seattle without a phone—using printed-out Google Map directions instead—and a homeless person threw a bottle of Sprite at me on my way here. It's been a morning."

"It looks like it." I lean against my doorframe. "Did you come here for another cake?"

She winces. "Well, sort of, but also for another reason," she says quickly. "Can I please come in? I could really use a glass of water."

"Since you've traveled across land and sea, it seems like the least I can do." I let her in and move to the kitchen, where I pour her a glass of water. When I hand it to her, she nearly sucks the entire thing down.

She catches her breath. "Like I said, long morning. Actually, didn't go to sleep last night. Long story short: we are throwing a redo tonight of the anniversary, and we're doing it a thousand times better. But we need a cake, and I know it's your day off, but we'll pay triple whatever you charge. It doesn't have to be big; just needs to resemble this." She pulls a photo out of her purse and hands it to me. It's a picture of her parents on their wedding day, cutting a classic tiered cake with pillars, basket-weave frosting, and tiny daisies decorating the sides. "It's a vanilla bean sponge with fudge middle and buttercream on the outside."

I study the image. It wouldn't take me long, but it's the baking and cooling of the cakes that would be a small problem.

"I won't be able to make this size. Probably will only have time for two tiers, and I don't carry these pillars in stock anymore. I'd have to run to the cake-supply store and purchase them."

"I can do that for you, if you want. You could start baking and not worry about it."

She's very agreeable, very flexible right now, and it makes me wonder what happened in the last forty-eight hours to change her attitude.

I study her carefully and lean against my kitchen counter. "It seems like you have enough on your plate. I'll have one of my assistants help me."

"Are you sure?"

"Positive."

"You really don't mind doing this for us?"

"Not doing it for you guys. I'm doing it for your mom and dad. They've been great friends to my parents, so it's the least I can do."

"Well, either way. Thank you." She reaches into her purse. "I also have this for you."

"What is it?" I ask, turning the envelope over.

"It's an invitation to the party tonight. It's at our house. We'd love it if you attended as well."

"We?"

She nods and sets the glass of water down. "Yes, we, as in Cooper too. You'll see—just read the card. But I should get going. Thank you so much again. I can't tell you how grateful we are. I'll see you at the party tonight." She takes off, and when the door clicks shut, I open the envelope and take out a handmade card with a well-penned gold *C* on the front.

I open it up and read the inscription: PARTY TONIGHT AT THE CHANCE RESIDENCE. An arrow directs me to the back. I flip it over and see Cooper's name at the bottom. Like a little schoolgirl, I can't help but sigh as I read.

> Hey, you old bag of bones,
> ^^Not sure why I'm starting it off like that, especially since I'm trying to win you back, but it felt . . . right. Not that you're old or a bag of bones. God, this seemed easier when we came up with the idea. Anyway, I would love for you to come to the party tonight. I know things are shaky at best between us, but hell, Nora, I fucking like you and I want to make things right.
>
> I need your ELYSIAN heart.
> Forever thinking of you,
> Cooper

"Damn it," I whisper as I go to my phone in my bedroom and look up what "elysian" means.

Heavenly.

"Damn it," I say again, dropping my phone and flopping down on my bed so I'm staring up at the ceiling.

Dealia was right.

We do have amazing chemistry.

CHAPTER FIFTY-SEVEN

LARKIN

"Are you nervous?" Beau asks as he parks his car on the side of the street next to the Chance residence.

"A little. Are you?"

"Yeah." He stares out at the house. "I like her, Larkin. Always have."

"I like him too, more than I probably should."

"So, you think you'll take him back?" Beau asks.

"Honestly, the last two days have been positively wretched. I miss him. I miss talking to him. His smile. His concentrating face, the way his brows pinch together when he's deep in thought. I miss the way he laughs with everything in him when he thinks something's funny, and I miss how I always felt safe around him. But I'm nervous. He struggles with some things."

"Don't we all, though?" He shifts in his seat to face me. "We all have baggage, you and I included. We aren't angels when it comes to relationships, but we've also done the work, going to therapy together to help each other through the loss of our parents. Ford and Cooper most likely have some scars from their experience being in the foster care system. I don't know what it was like for them, but I know it probably wasn't easy. I think patience and understanding as a partner can go a long way. Some of us need it more than others."

"True. I just worry. Dinner was just a disaster. We saw a side of all of the Chance siblings that was less than flattering, and that startled me. They have a lot to work through."

"Agreed." Beau takes a pause and then says, "But if you think about it, these invitations were clearly made by Palmer, just looking at the handwriting alone. They were delivered by both brothers. Together they're throwing a party for their parents, who they love dearly. After such a huge blowout, they were able to pull it together, and from what they said on the back of the invitations, they have something to prove to us. Don't you think we should give them the benefit of the doubt, that they were able to work through some of their difficulties? That maybe they're all starting a new chapter?"

I tilt my head to the side, giving his response some serious thought. After being privy to the Chance siblings' bantering emails, I know their baseline of cooperation. Joining forces like this is leaps and bounds from what I've seen. Maybe Beau is right. Guess there's only one way to find out. "When did you become so wise?"

"I've always been wise—you've just been too stubborn to acknowledge it."

"So, you're going to jump right back into things with Palmer, then?"

"I mean . . ." He smooths his hand over his cheek. "I'm going to see what she has to say first. I want to see growth. But if she wants something with me, hell yeah. I fucking love her spirit. It's thrilling. I like her sass and her passion for all things. She excites me, but she also has a gentle, shy soul that is a huge turn-on."

"Ew, don't say 'turn-on' to me."

Beau laughs. "Either way. Yes, I want to date her, see where things take us."

"What if she's not staying on Marina Island?"

He shrugs. "That's something I'll have to accept, but I won't know until I hear her out." He nods toward the house. "Come on, let's see what the Chance siblings have to say for themselves."

We get out of the car and follow behind a small group of people. The door to the house is open, and soft music plays in the background as we approach. When we reach the front door, a sign points us through the house to the back door. We head out onto the deck, where the backyard has been transformed entirely.

Holy shit, how did they do this?

A white tent spans the length of the yard, with the lake beyond as a beautiful backdrop. Bulb lights are strung along the ceiling of the tent, softly illuminating the high tops and tables scattered around the open space. A food table sits off to the right, decorated with light-green linens and daisies. A DJ is in the far corner next to a dance floor, and to the left is a beautiful two-tiered wedding cake surrounded by daisies. Throughout the tent are scrapbook cutouts and triangular garlands strewn in yellows and greens, adding to the whimsical feel of the space.

It's positively breathtaking.

"Wow," I say as Beau gapes at everything as well.

"Wow is right. And it smells like heaven in here."

"I can't imagine how all this was done," I say, thinking about what it must have taken to pull this off.

"Hey." We turn to the side, where Nora is standing in a pretty pink sundress. Her hair is curled in soft waves and pinned behind her ear. She looks beautiful. "I'm assuming you two got a personal invite as well?"

I nod. "We did. Yours have a note on the back?"

"Oh yeah. It was a doozy too. That middle Chance child sure has a way with words."

"Looks like we're all suckers where they're concerned." I point to the cake. "Did you make that?"

"Yup. Got a beautiful wake-up call from Palmer this morning. Apparently, she rode a bike to the ferry and then struggled through public transportation to find me and ask for help."

"Really?" Beau asks, sounding surprised and proud at the same time.

"Yup. It was hard to say no, especially for Peggy and Martin. She gave me a picture of their parents' original wedding cake and asked to replicate it. I didn't have enough time for three tiers, so two had to do."

"Well, it's beautiful," I say as we all move farther into the tent.

"They're here!" Palmer says, appearing out of nowhere, addressing the crowd, which quiets along with the music. She's wearing a teal dress that matches her cast, and her hair is pinned up with daisies in the back. "When they come out here, yell 'Happy anniversary!'"

I glance at Beau, whose eyes are glued to her. He shifts in place, and I know just from that little moment that he's going to work out whatever he can to be with Palmer.

The tent quiets down, and we wait only a few seconds before Peggy and Martin step through the back. Both of them gasp as we all cry, "Happy anniversary!" They clutch each other's hands and take in their backyard—and within the span of one breath, they're both crying. Cooper follows behind them and then Ford. My pulse immediately quickens. He's wearing a simple pair of gray pants and a white polo. His hair is a little messier than usual, and even though he has a smile on his face, his eyes are tired.

Peggy and Martin turn toward their kids and give them loving hugs. After their embrace, the kids walk their parents down to the tent, where they hand them each a glass of champagne. Champagne is handed out to everyone by the waitstaff, and the DJ passes Ford a microphone.

He clears his throat and smiles at the crowd. "Thank you, everyone, for coming on such short notice to help celebrate the wedding anniversary of our parents, Peggy and Martin." He clears his throat and quickly glances around the tent. When he spots me, he smiles, and I catch my breath. "In a grand fashion, we messed up yesterday. It's as simple as that—no excuses.

And we wanted to make it up to our parents and show them that no matter what happens in our lives"—the Chance siblings all link hands—"we will weather the storm together because we're a family, and despite our differences, we will always love each other. No matter what."

Peggy lets out a sob as she kisses each of her kids, and Martin follows closely behind her. When they're done, Ford holds up his glass. "Now, I want to thank you again for coming out, for supporting our parents, and for being such big parts of our lives. Something Cooper, Palmer, and I realized over the last twenty-four hours is how much stronger we are when we're a team, and we wouldn't be a team without the tough love from our parents and the people they surround themselves with. So please raise a glass with us as we toast Peggy and Martin."

"To Peggy and Martin," everyone says.

We all take a sip, and Cooper grabs the mic from Ford. "As promised in my initial email invite"—a few people jokingly groan—"I know, I know, not my finest moment. But there are some yard games down by the dock, which will be the *fun*. There's music, so don't be afraid to bust a move, and there's plenty of food. Also, shout-out to Nora at Cake It Bakery for making a replica of our parents' wedding cake on such short notice." Cooper looks Nora in the eyes. "I get kilig every time I see you, babe." Then he hands the mic back to the DJ and winks.

Oh my . . . Cooper Chance.

I turn to Nora as the music starts up again. "What does 'kilig' mean?"

She pulls up her phone, does some typing, and then smiles to herself. "Butterflies in one's stomach."

"Oh man, you stand no chance."

Nora shakes her head. "Nope."

"Larkin, can I speak with you?" Ford says, appearing at my side and startling me.

"Oh, sure, yeah." I stumble over my words. He takes my hand in his, and we walk over to an outdoor seating area that surrounds an already-lit firepit. He guides us to a small love seat and sits us down.

He doesn't let go of my hand, and he's not shy about sitting close to me either. I can feel myself trembling, and he must notice, because he holds me even tighter.

"How are you doing?" he asks.

"Okay," I say, my voice a little shaky. "Nervous for some reason."

"Don't be nervous." He tucks a strand of my hair behind my ear. "But I do have some bad news."

"What kind of bad news?"

"I'm going to have to replace you as my assistant."

"What?" I say, panicking and trying to pull away, but he doesn't let me. "Why? Because of what happened between us?"

"No, of course not. I'm promoting you." When I give him a confused look, he continues: "If I've learned anything over the last twenty-four hours, it's that my siblings know a hell of a lot more than I gave them credit for. Because of you, I stepped back from dictating and instead I listened. Palmer said you've outgrown your position and you could be more valuable elsewhere. She couldn't have been more right."

I swallow hard. "She said that?"

He nods. "What I also learned is that my knowledge of the industry is vastly outdated. I've been stuck behind the desk for far too long, which means I know business. I know it inside and out. That's where you come in. I really want to focus on products that we endorse. I don't want to carry just anything in the store; I want to carry things we approve of as a company, products we would use. Which means I need someone to lead that research team. I think you'd be the perfect fit. You would report directly to me, you would have a team to work with, and you would be more involved with what your dad loved—the adventure of the outdoors."

"Are you . . . serious?" I ask, tears springing to my eyes.

"Very serious. You mean so much to me, Larkin, which brings me to the second part of this. I want to date you. I don't want you to be my therapist, and I sure as hell don't want you to make it your mission to help me find myself. That's not your job—"

"It is," I say, gripping his leg. "That's what it means to have a partner, to share those vulnerable moments."

"Yes, but that's not how I want to start this relationship. It's why Cooper gave me the name of his therapist, who is going to refer me to someone they trust so I can be healthy for you and put time into us—not have you put time into me."

I nod, understanding what he's saying, and even though I want to help him, I love that he's creating this boundary, making space to work himself out.

"I like you a lot, Larkin, and I'm confident that we'll grow and flourish, just like what my parents have. But I want to start it out right, which means you're not going to be my assistant. You're not going to get me coffee, and you're not going to be my pseudotherapist. And you're sure as hell not going to be the referee between me and my siblings. You're my girl. You're the one I want, and hopefully you still want me."

I smile and reach up to his cheek. "I don't think I could ever *not* want you, Ford." Bringing him close, I place a small kiss on his lips and then pull away with a sigh. "I missed you."

"I missed you too."

"I'm sorry I went behind your back with Cooper."

He shakes his head. "You were right to do it. I didn't give him the chance he deserved. He actually showed me the logo, drew it out for me. I hired him on the spot. Him and Palmer."

"Stop. Seriously?"

He nods. "I wasn't bullshitting when I said we're stronger as a team. It's true. I need them, but I need you more."

"You have me," I say, letting him pull me into a hug. "You have me for as long as you want me."

"That's forever. I hope you're ready."

"I've never been more ready in my life." I press my lips to his again and revel in his embrace.

Everything I want, right here. I couldn't ask for more.

Chapter Fifty-Eight

NORA

"You have a way with words," I say as Cooper walks up to me, an undeniable swagger in his step.

He looks so good: a heavy five-o'clock shadow graces his handsome face, and he's wearing a button-up shirt with the sleeves pushed up to his elbows. He definitely makes my heart trip in my chest.

"Yeah?" He takes my hand in his. "Does this mean you'll come sit down by the dock with me?"

"Are you going to show me your romantic prowess and whisper sweet nothings into my ear, promising a future with you in it?"

"Nah, was going to pay you for the cake, push you in the water, and then walk away."

"Well, sign me up for that," I joke as he laughs and tugs me toward the dock. When we reach the end, we take a seat and stare out at the setting sun. "You know, you three really outdid yourselves. Did you even sleep last night?"

"Nope." He sips from his champagne flute. "We had a lot of shit to work out, and we're all still raw, but we've promised to keep working on our relationships with each other."

"That's a vast difference from dinner the other night, which was a pleasure to be at, by the way, in case you didn't know," I deadpan.

"Yeah, and the way it ended was great too."

"Yeah, about that."

He looks away. "I sure know how to be an ass, don't I?"

"You've really fine-tuned that quality. It's impressive."

"Hey, and here I thought I didn't accomplish anything these past few years."

Laughing, I bump him in the shoulder. "Your card was sweet, your short speech even sweeter. Did you mean it?"

"You know I fucking meant it." He turns to look me in the eyes. "Listen, I know things have been up and down with me, but I've realized over the past few weeks that I like you . . . a lot. You're a fucking smart-ass and sexy, but you get me like no one else has, and you make me happy." He presses his hand to my cheek. "I like the man I am when I'm around you. Confident, content . . . courageous. You make me better in every way, and even though I'm an ass of a man, I'm also a smart man and I know when I've got a good thing in my life. You're a good thing, Nora, and I'll do pretty much anything to keep you around."

Talk about kilig . . .

But I've never made it easy on him, so why would I start now? "Anything?"

"Anything."

Smiling, I say, "Backflip into the lake and I'm yours."

Before I can take my next breath, he's standing and backflipping into the lake, shoes and all. Water splashes up at my legs as he surfaces with a giant smile on his face.

"I can't believe you did that."

"Believe it, babe. You're mine now." And then he reaches out and grabs me, pulling me into the lake with him. I go under, a yelp escaping my lips as I resurface and cling onto him.

"You are so dead," I sputter, completely drenched. "I spent far too long on my hair today, and you just ruined it."

"Nah, you're always sexy to me." He cups my cheek and grows serious. "You're mine, right, Nora?"

I lean my forehead against his and nod. "Yours, Coop."

And then, in dramatic fashion, he lifts my chin and presses a kiss to my lips.

And like in all the movies, I envision cameras swirling around us as I kiss him back.

Because he's mine . . . all mine.

CHAPTER FIFTY-NINE

PALMER

"Can I speak with you?" I ask nervously.

"Of course, honey," Mom says as she grabs Dad's hand. "Where would you like to talk?"

"We can go inside. I'd rather not do it out here."

"Very well."

Together, we go inside the house and step into the living room. They take a seat on the couch, and I sit across from them on the coffee table.

"Are you enjoying the party?"

They both nod. "I can't believe you three pulled this off," Dad says, admiration in his voice.

"Ford was right: we're stronger together, as a team. Just took a kick in the ass to realize it." I look at Dad. "Thank you. We aren't fully fixed, but we promised to make sure our relationships never get to where they were before. We actually missed each other."

"That's so wonderful to hear, and it's obvious you were able to put your frustrations behind you and band together to pull this night off.

It's . . . it's everything we could have dreamed of," Mom says, her voice growing tight.

"It's the perfect send-off for the house," Dad adds.

I nod and take a deep breath. "I need to talk to you guys about something, and I need to preface it by saying, if I get emotional, I'm sorry in advance." They sit there, intently listening, so I continue. "I'm sorry about the fire." Their expressions soften as they realize what I'm about to talk about. "I know you know, and I know it's the reason for the big disconnect between Cooper and Ford." Mom opens her mouth to say something, but I stop her. "We already talked about it. Talked through it. Everything we were feeling, the anger, the resentment, it stemmed back to that. It's okay. I accept it, but I owe you two an apology. A long-overdue apology. You deserved more from your daughter, much more. I not only allowed misconduct in your store, but I also lied to you about it and tried to make you believe that I was the one in danger, when really, I was the one who caused it all."

"You should not shoulder the blame," Dad says. He reaches over and takes Mom's hand. "We spoke last night too, and we realized our hands-off approach, letting you three solve things on your own when you were younger, might not have been the best approach, especially with the fire." Dad gets choked up, and Mom places her hand on top to show their connection.

"Your father and I feel as though we failed you three last night."

"What? No." I shake my head. "You didn't fail us."

"Let me explain," Mom says. "We should have recognized the fear you three harbored. We should have paid attention during those last few years when you were still living with us. We should have seen the signs of how you were feeling with your brothers leaving. We should have recognized the slightly reckless behavior with the parties at the store. But instead of addressing the root of the problem, we were trying to teach you a lesson, and it was an example of misplaced parenting.

After the fire, we should have said something to you. We should have addressed it."

"But we were in shock," Dad says. "We honestly at that point didn't know how to handle the situation. Instead of stepping up into the parenting role we should have taken, we backed away and waited . . . and waited for you to say something. But resentment from your brothers built, anger grew, and then we lost control. We should have done something."

Tears stream down my face. "I'm sorry I put you in that position. But you must know you two gave us the world: you gave us strength, and independence. I just wish I'd mirrored your strength more at the time."

Dad nods. "Thank you, Palmer. But your strength to become something of your own is exactly what we would have dreamed for you."

"But that's not what I wanted." I shake my head. "I wanted to be here, with you, help with the store. Stay where I grew up, where I've been comfortable. But instead, I ran. And I'm not going to line my apology with excuses, reasons why it happened. I'm just going to take the blame because the blame lies fully on me." I take a deep breath. "I haven't been honest with you for a while, and it's because I've been trying to prove that I didn't need this family to make it on my own. But really, I'm lost without this family. I didn't come here for a blog piece—I came here because I have no place else to go. I don't have any money, I'm out of a job, and I don't have an apartment anymore because I couldn't afford rent. You shouldn't be proud of the person I became, because I'm at rock bottom."

"Palmer—"

"No, Dad." I shake my head. "Coming back here was my last resort. I freaked out about the house because yes, it means the world to me; the prospect of it being sold also scared me to death. I had no place to go, and my pride got in the way of telling the truth, so I went on a rampage to make everyone's life hell instead."

"Palmer, you know you can always ask for help," Dad says.

"I know, but I didn't want to at the time. I saw that as a weakness, but I'm realizing pretty fast that's not the case. After last night, I was reminded family is pretty much the only thing you can count on to be tried and true in this world. Family is what I need." I twist my hands together. "And that was evident last night because come to find out, Ford needs some help with social media and the store. He offered me a job."

Both their eyes widen in surprise.

"Really?" Mom asks.

I nod, unable to hold back the smile. "He hired both me and Cooper. Ford said he can't run the business without us, but he wants me to stay here, on Marina Island, and really focus on using the original store to market the brand."

"Very smart," Dad says, a large smile on his face. Pride beams from his eyes, and I can tell he could not be happier with his decision to lay down the law last night. It worked, and it worked well.

"Which leads me to this." I close my eyes, take another deep breath, and then look at my parents. "I don't want you to sell the house."

"Sweetie, we can't stay here," Mom says.

"I know." I grab both their hands. "But this house means so much to me and the boys. There's history here, there's safety, and there's room for future generations to grow. It might take me some time, but if you can trust me—which I know might be hard, given my record—I want to buy it from you."

"You want to live here?" Dad asks.

I nod. "I do. You see, there's this boy I like. I can see myself starting a life with him, and I think I can make it work if I stay here, on the island. And what better place to start a relationship than in the very place my parents fell in love?"

Mom's eyes fill up with tears as Dad leans forward and grabs my hand. "Is this a boy who keeps changing your cast for you?"

I laugh and nod. "Yes. Dr. Beau—I seem to be infatuated with him."

"I called it." Mom waves her hand in front of her face. "I just knew you two would end up together. I didn't think it would take this long, but I knew it. You always had a thing for him."

"I did. And I'd love to see if we have a future together, which I think we do, and if all goes as planned, I'd love to start a family, right here in this house, where you raised us all so well. Where you blessed us all with a roof over our heads and love in our hearts."

"We'd be honored to pass the house over to you," Dad says.

"It would be an actual dream," Mom says before they both pull me into a hug. "You're not just doing this so you don't have to clean out your room, are you?"

I laugh into her embrace. "I love you," I tell them as tears fill my eyes. "I love you so much."

Chapter Sixty

DR. BEAU

"Where's Palmer?" Larkin asks, walking up to me, Ford in tow. He has his arm around her, and she's snuggled into his embrace. I smile to myself. We really can't resist the Chance siblings, can we?

"No idea." I glance around the tent. Nora and Cooper are in the lake, fully clothed, making out. I guess that's part of the "fun" Cooper boasted about as well. "Looks like you two were able to get it together."

Larkin smiles up at Ford. "We were."

Looking Ford in the eyes, I say, "I don't think I need to give you the brother speech, right?"

Ford shakes his head. "Don't worry—there's no way in hell I'm letting this girl get away, nor do I plan on breaking her heart."

"Good answer."

"Hey," Palmer says, coming up to us. Her eyes are watery, but she has a giant smile on her face. "Can I talk to you, Beau?"

My stomach lurches. Guess it's my turn.

I nod and follow her around the house to a giant oak tree that's far enough from the party to give us some privacy.

"How's your cast?" I ask, breaking the ice. "I don't need to change it, do I?"

She shakes her head and lifts it up. "All dry."

"See, you're getting the hang of it now."

"Only took three casts."

I chuckle. "I've seen other patients take longer to get the hang of it."

"I bet you a five-year-old is better at it than me."

"I wasn't going to mention it . . . but . . ."

She laughs and leans against the tree. "Beau?"

"Yeah?" I ask.

"I like you."

My heart hammers in my chest.

"I like you too."

"I want to be with you."

"I want to be with you too," I say back.

"I'm going to live here, permanently."

I scratch the back of my head, trying to play it cool. "Yeah?"

"Yup. Got a job doing social media for Watchful Wanderers. Ford thinks I can grow the brand, and I think he's right, especially if I post some thirst-trap pics of the local hunky doctor going on a hike."

A laugh pops out of me. "Nah, I think those pics are going to be saved for my girl only."

She pulls me in by the belt loop. "And who would that girl be?"

I tug on a strand of her hair. "I think you know who it is."

Her eyes search mine, and in them I see the girl I first fell for so many years ago. "I'm sorry for everything."

I shake my head. "No need to apologize. I'm grateful you took a second to figure it all out, because I really do want to be with you, Palmer. I want to see where this takes us."

"Me too."

"Because I have a feeling about you. A good one."

She smiles. "I was just telling my parents the same thing about you."

"So does that mean, after all these years, I can finally say Palmer Chance is my girlfriend?"

"I think you can, Dr. Beau." She lifts up onto her toes and pulls me down to her mouth.

Without hesitation, I press my lips to hers and loop my arm around her waist. The feeling of being weightless takes over as her mouth molds with mine.

This is what I want—her, in my arms, with nothing between us.

When she pulls away, she says, "I'm going to move into my parents' house. They're signing it over to me, but until they move out, we'll be staying at your place. I don't need the doctor examining me with my parents two rooms down."

I chuckle. "I can't disagree with that." I bend down and press another kiss to her lips before I take her hand in mine and walk back to the party, where we join Larkin, Ford, and her parents on the dance floor. "Unchained Melody" plays in the background, and as the sun finally sets, I can see it.

The wife.

The family.

The life.

Right here, with Palmer at my side the entire time.

EPILOGUE

FORD

"I now pronounce you husband and wife," Dad says. "You may kiss the bride."

Cooper cups Nora's face, and their mouths lock as the intimate ceremony erupts in cheers.

The sun sets behind their kiss, the lake stretching out behind them acting as a backdrop.

After traveling around the world for two years on and off—Cooper still working for Watchful Wanderers and Nora still baking—they finally decided to settle down and get married. They didn't want anything big, just a small wedding at the house that Palmer and Beau have been renovating over the last year. Something about the ancient tile not being up to code for their baby, who's supposed to be born any day now.

"May I introduce to you Mr. and Mrs. Cooper Chance," Dad says.

They raise their hands, and we offer them one more cheer before they head down the aisle.

I take Larkin's hand in mine and hold our sleeping baby close to my chest as we make our way down the aisle, right behind an extremely pregnant Palmer, who's been dealing with her extremely overprotective doctor husband. Ever hear of a helicopter mom? Well, Palmer has a helicopter husband. I think she'll be grateful when the baby is finally out, so she won't have to deal with Beau checking her vitals and watching over her every second of every day.

Dad and Mom follow close behind us, slower than normal, but Dad is still thriving at the fitness center. He's made great progress in staying strong and taking care of his diagnosis. The high-rise they're living in is only a few blocks from Cooper and Nora, and they've become the official grandparents of the building. Not only do they have Nora and Cooper checking in on them, but they have the entire floor helping them out as well. And because their building is amazing, the management planted a garden on the roof just for Mom. They've been thriving, and whenever they're tired of the city, they take the ferry to Marina Island and stay with Palmer and Beau for a few days.

As for Larkin and me, well, we have a baby boy, and we're currently in the process of receiving our foster parent certification. We want a big family and are hoping to move to Seattle in the coming months to be closer to the family. We're actually moving the entire headquarters to Seattle, which has been a task on its own, but well worth it, since our branding seems to match better with the area. Branding that Cooper has been smashing with his team. With the new stores and our new "experience" with the live snakes, and more hands-on classes, we've really taken the market by storm, and let's just say . . . we're all sitting pretty right now.

"Beautiful job, Dad," I say as we make it to the tent.

"Thank you. Took quite an effort to not cry. Marrying all three of my kids has been the honor of a lifetime."

"Something we'll never forget," I say, bringing Larkin's knuckles to my lips.

"How's our baby boy?" Mom says, cooing at Jacob.

"He's good. Passed out after a long battle before the ceremony."

"We couldn't have timed that better," Larkin adds.

"Beau, I love you so much, but I swear to Christ, if you touch me one more time, I'm going to punch you in your baby maker," Palmer says, waddling up to us, hand on her enormous belly.

"Listen to her." Larkin points at her brother. "I know how she feels."

Beau holds up his hands. "I'm just trying to be helpful."

I grip Beau by the shoulder. "You may be a doctor, but nothing is helpful at this stage. They'd prefer if you don't even breathe near them."

"Breathing," Palmer says, exasperated, holding on to her back. "I swear to God I can hear everyone's breath at decibels no one should ever hear."

"Isn't she so pleasant?" Mom says, leaning over and pressing a kiss to Palmer's belly. "You've created such a great home that your baby girl doesn't want to come out."

"Well, guess what, the eviction notice has been submitted—I'm pushing tonight."

Dad looks Beau in the eyes. "I fear for you, son."

Beau winces. "I fear for myself."

"Palmer complaining about being pregnant again?" Cooper says, coming up to the family circle.

"Wow, you sure know how to make a pregnant lady sprout devil horns," Nora says, looking so damn pretty in her flowy lace wedding dress and flower crown. "I suggest when we have babies, you don't say the same things."

"So, there are babies in your future?" Dad asks, looking all too excited.

"Adopted babies," Nora says. "Sorry, ladies, but I don't have it in me to push anything out of my vagina."

Dad snorts.

Mom claps her hands.

And Palmer and Larkin both nod, understanding her completely.

The photographer rounds us up for pictures, and I can't help but savor how our family has grown so much in the past few years. We went from barely talking to each other to moving close so we can raise our families together and continue to build on the foundation Mom and Dad have laid out for us.

Together we're stronger, and we're only building in numbers now.

Acknowledgments

When I was in fourth grade, I had a best friend I would spend every waking hour with. We were either at my house or her house. In my young eyes, she had this perfect family. Her mom would have fresh, homemade cookies for whenever we got home from school. Her parents never swore, they didn't have TV because they would always spend their time playing games with each other, and they constantly preached to me about what's right and wrong. I'm ashamed to admit it, but I remember being embarrassed by my family at times. We burped, my parents swore, we would watch TV while eating dinner sometimes; we did all these things that my friend's family looked down upon. There were times when I was nervous to ask my friend to come over because I knew my family was so much different.

What I didn't realize at the time is that every family is different. That just because one family might seem perfect doesn't mean that my family is any less. I learned it's okay to fight. It's okay to have miscommunications. It's okay to have falling-outs, because personalities will change, they will morph, they will grow. And as long as you're adjusting, accepting, and always there for each other, it doesn't matter if you have disagreements, because there will always be love.

My friend's parents . . . they divorced when we were in high school. Her mom was cheating on her dad with his best friend. ←I can't make that up. Just goes to show that sometimes what you think might be "perfect" is not perfect at all.

The Chance family is very much a depiction of not just my family but also my extended family. The ups and downs of aging parents, the siblings who are able to assist, the siblings who are trying to make something of themselves, and the siblings who very well might have been holding guilt for many years. What I wanted to show is that no matter what might happen to a relationship in your life, when family's involved, it's never too late to fix things if you have it in your heart to offer acceptance.

So this book is dedicated to my not-so-perfect family. To my dad's not-so-perfect siblings. To my mom's not-so-perfect brother and sister. To my two older brothers, who push me to try harder, to work smarter. To my parents, for keeping me honest, for showing me what true love really is. We might not have had a perfect childhood by any means, but one thing I know for sure is that it was full of love.

Aimee Ashcraft, my agent, thank you for testing my creative process, pushing me to dive deeper into each character arc, and for always believing in my ability to get the job done.

Lauren Plude, I still can't believe you said, "Sure, six POVs? Let's do it." I still can't believe I DID IT. But thank you for taking a chance on this story. It's unconventional romance at its best.

Lindsey Faber, your patience and guidance were exemplary. I'm not sure I would have been able to get through three rounds of edits without your well thought out critique.

To all the bloggers and readers out there, I don't even know how to express my deepest love for you. You take a chance on my books every time I release one, which is something I can never show enough gratitude for. Thank you for being the best fans a girl could ask for. You make this job so much fun!

Thank you to Jenny, for being my number one cheerleader. Couldn't get through these crazy, chaotic days without you.

And lastly, thank you to my wife, Steph. You believe in me—that is the biggest gift you could ever give me. Thank you for holding down the fort when deadlines persist, for taking care of the business, and the family, and for always being my sounding board. I love you.

Turn the page for a
sneak peek from
The Secret to Dating
Your Best Friend's Sister

Prologue

BRAM

I have a stupid-as-shit crush on my best friend's sister.

I know the exact moment it happened too.

It wasn't when I first met her, no, that was when I first found out she liked to wear tube socks with shorts. Nor was it the second time I ran into her, because she was a sour, bitter girl with an attitude that struck me dead in the nut sac. But even in her scary rampage, I thought she was pretty and interesting, but a crush? Not so much.

No, it happened many times after the first. I was a senior, and she was a sophomore in college. A nervous sophomore, who forcibly ventured out to yet another frat party, captured by her friends, and held hostage to have a good time.

She was a fish out of water, and I couldn't help but keep my eyes fixed on her as she awkwardly bumped into drunk assholes and tripped over empty beer cans, fixing her glasses that kept getting displaced from their perfect perch on her nose.

She was unlike any girl I had ever met. Strong-willed, obnoxious at times with her intelligence, cunning, and never too scared to back down. She intrigued me, held my attention, made me want to know what was spinning around in that beautiful head of hers.

I had to find out.

That night changed everything. Maybe it was the beer coursing through me, or the sheer curiosity in the girl who looked completely and utterly out of place, but I was drawn to her. I knew, in that moment, that I had a choice to make: either continue to sit with Lauren Connor and listen to her boring-as-shit stories, or remove my ass from the leather couch and say hi to Julia Westin.

Can you guess what I did?

ABOUT THE AUTHOR

Photo © 2019 Milana Schaffer

USA Today bestselling author, wife, adoptive mother, peanut butter lover, and author of romantic comedies and contemporary romance Meghan Quinn brings readers the perfect combination of heart, humor, and heat in every book.

Text "READ" to 474747 to never miss another one of Meghan Quinn's releases.

Made in the USA
Middletown, DE
14 July 2022